PROPHECY
the FULFILLMENT

PROPHECY
the FULFILLMENT

Deborah A Jaeger

Hampton House
Publishing

Prophecy ~ The Fulfillment

This is a work of fiction. All of the characters, names, places, events and dialogue contained within this novel are the products of the author's imagination, or are used fictitiously in this work. If there is any resemblance to actual people, places, or institutions, it is entirely coincidental.

Disclaimer: Any medical reference included in this entire body of work is the authors liberal interpretation of information and should not be quoted or relied upon as fact.

The Scripture quotations in this book were taken from
The King James Version. Copyright ©1996
By Broadman & Holman Publishers
Used by permission. All rights reserved.

Library of Congress Control Number: 2010914266

Interior Design: BelieversPress

ISBN 978-0-9828891-0-7

Printed in the United States of America

Published by

Hampton House Publishing LLC
6688 Nolensville Road Ste. 111
Brentwood, Tennessee 37027

10 9 8 7 6 5 4 3 2 1

For Saint Joseph… my heavenly protector
and
Lloyd… my earthly one.

"In the beginning, God created the heaven and the earth.
And the earth was without form, and void; and
darkness *was* upon the face of the deep. And
the Spirit of God moved upon the face of the waters.
And God said, Let there be light: and there was light.
And God saw the light, that *it was* good:
and God divided the light from the darkness."

Genesis 1:1-5

Prologue
December 2018

From the moment they entered the woods, the dense forest swallowed them as if they had never walked the earth. Trees closed thick around them, and the floor of the timberland was covered in layers of pine needles and fallen leaves.

"Ouch… Stephen. *For God's sake.* Slow down!" she pleaded.

Stumbling on the undergrowth, Jillian could feel the hysteria bubbling up the back of her throat. Stephen stopped only long enough to take her trembling chin in his hand and look into her eyes.

"It's not far now, but we have to keep going, Jillian. You can rest soon. I promise. We're almost there. Come on…we don't have much time." Stephen spoke in an urgent whisper, the sound of his voice doing little to calm her heightened nerves.

"I can't. I need to sit down… just for a few minutes. Please, Stephen. I'm begging you, please. I have to stop."

She wanted nothing more than to retrace her steps and go home. Her chest ached, her hands were numb and cold, and droplets of blood had dried on her cheek from the underbrush that had managed to escape the restraints of Stephen's outstretched arms.

Jillian could feel an undercurrent, as though the forest had its own secret language to announce their arrival. She had never in her life felt so small and alone. She was exhausted, bone tired and thirsty, and all at once hungry and sick. She was sure that one more step would send her hurtling face down in the path.

"Stephen, please. They won't find us." She tried to be brave, but found herself floundering.

He continued without slowing, propelling her forward, until the tears that had threatened all day and into the night finally escaped and rolled down her cheeks.

The moon cast a surreal glow on the scene before them. Their labored breathing and the occasional snap of dried twigs as they made their way through the thick walls of the forest, resounded loudly against the silent backdrop of the dark night. As they rounded yet another bend in the seemingly endless path and hurried through a stand of pine trees, she found the smell of fresh cedar an odd contrast to the deep musty pungency of the woods they had left behind.

When they finally came upon the cabin, it seemed a mirage, almost a miracle of its own. Stumbling, forcing themselves to move forward those last few steps, they were overcome with relief and exhaustion, and literally fell through the front door. As soon as they were safe within the cabin walls, Jillian's tired body slumped to the floor in surrender. Stephen rummaged in the dark and found matches and candles, the flames softly illuminating the interior of their hide-away.

Beyond exhausted, they barely spoke. That first night in the dark, even as her body ached from cold and fatigue, the adrenaline from all that led up to that moment was still running rampant through her veins. Stephen pulled her close to him on the pallet, the unfamiliar strength and warmth from his body seeping into hers. She was able to let go of the day, finally still and protected and free to sleep. Maybe that was when she first loved him.

"Shhhhh… it's okay." He whispered into the soft crevice of her neck, his breath warm and comforting, filling her with the hope that it was over for awhile, both of them in desperate need of rest.

"Stephen, I'm going to be sick."

He held a basin under her chin and when she was finished, he wiped her mouth and gave her water. She was not yet accustomed to the many changes that were taking place within her body.

Later, lying cradled in their makeshift bed, she noticed a small opening in the roof above her head. A sliver of night sky peeked through, and while she absorbed the vastness of that star-filled night, she felt her resolve slowly return. God created the heavens and the earth after all. Surely he would not have brought them this far only to have them fail.

* * *

It had been almost five months since it all started, and yet it seemed like yesterday. Jillian shivered as she stood in front of the window, shaking off the memories of the night they arrived. The night sounds usually pacified her, calming her frayed nerves and filling her with a sense of peace. Tonight though, the moon did little to soothe her and she was edgy and afraid. She had grown used to the seclusion and false security of their hiding place.

In the months since they had escaped to the cabin, Jillian had time to come to terms with all that would be expected of her in days ahead. But tonight she felt captured in a time warp, and she braced herself for the future and everything that had been set into motion. One thing she was sure of… it would not be easy. How was she supposed to prepare herself for the most important role of all time? She was only seventeen and she was homesick. And she was tired of waiting. Always waiting.

She placed her palm against the cool glass of the window and closed her eyes, forcefully willing herself to calm down, to breathe deeply. She could hear Stephen in the background, rummaging through their meager belongings. The dreams had started again.

Tonight, as she stared into the same woods that had offered them a safe haven these last months, she knew with every fiber of her being, that there was no turning back from the course they were to follow. The fantasy had become reality and there was no mistaking the power of the dreams, nor the compulsion to follow them.

The dim light in the cabin threw her reflection against the glass of the window as if she were looking into a mirror. She touched her hair, finally growing back and so badly needing pampering. She smiled when she remembered how important that had once been. Watching her reflection, she absentmindedly followed her hand as it trailed slowly, from her hair, to her neck, across her breast and finally came to rest, gently caressing her belly…swollen with child. The baby moved, pushing and straining against the confines of her body.

She instinctively knew her time was near. And she was afraid.

Chapter One
May 2018

Stephen Daniel Jacobs stood in the driveway of his home in St. Thomas, Ontario, and waved as his sisters drove down the street. Hands in his pockets, he stood for a minute looking up and down the familiar road, as if trying to memorize every last front porch and mailbox. He knew that the next time he came home, he would be a visitor. Tomorrow, he would be leaving the last remnants of his childhood behind.

The evening was still warm and he lingered as he made his way to the front porch. Looking up at the brightly lit house, he watched the lamps go out one by one, and knew his mother, Margaret Mary, was waiting to settle in and have a heart to heart conversation with him before he said goodbye.

It had only been a little over year ago that their father, Michael, died without warning while he slept. Losing his father when Steven was only twenty-four had been a devastating loss for their family, and as the Jacobs' only son, he had not been sure that he would be able to muster the courage to leave his family behind and go to the States to study.

He had been ready to quit graduate school and had tried in every way he could think of to fill his father's shoes. He had dropped out of college mid-semester, and began driving his mother around in his beat up Chevy Impala like an old man. However, Margaret Mary refused to let the death of her young husband be used as an excuse for any of her children to flounder. So, she kicked Stephen out of the house and back to school as soon as the next semester started.

He sat on the porch swing for a minute before he went inside, smiling as he remembered his family gathered around the table tonight for his goodbye dinner. Sandwiched between his sisters, the middle child, he never ceased to be amused by their antics.

"I am stuffed." Dropping a wadded napkin onto her plate, twenty-two year old Camellia pushed her chair back from the table and loosened her belt. "I don't think I can move."

Stephen watched his baby sister as she balanced on the two rear legs of her chair.

"Cami, I saw your byline in the Herald this morning. Way to go. How did you talk old man Phillips into giving you the lead story?" he asked her.

"I told him that if I had to write one more description of a Chantilly lace veil for wedding features, I would send copies of the pictures I took last week at the dog show and run them in place of the bride and groom."

His mother rolled her eyes. "Camellia, it amazes me that Mr. Phillips doesn't throw you out with last week's sale papers."

"Aw, come on. He wouldn't find anyone else to do the grunt work, Mom." Camellia shook her pony tailed head and laughed out loud.

"Besides, his daughter is getting married next month, for the fourth time, and he is counting on me to put a new spin on things." Cami righted her chair and turned the conversation to her sister.

"Hey, Mandy, what happened at the hospital yesterday? Marty Roberts said there was some kind of commotion in front of the emergency room." Always on the lookout for the next story, nothing slid by Camellia unnoticed.

"Put your pencil away, Sherlock. The laundry truck was late again and the hospital ran out of gowns. No big story, unless you want to count Nurse Halstead dressing down the truck driver, who, if the truth be told, did smell like he just left Jasper's Pub down by the pier."

As a nurse at the regional hospital, Amanda probably knew more about the secret comings and goings in St. Thomas than any one of the reporters at The Herald. Amanda had caused Cami to bolt from the dinner table in frustration on more than one occasion, unable to wheedle the slightest bit of confidential information from her older sister.

Amanda, the oldest, was quiet and much like their father in temperament. As a child, she rescued every stray and wounded animal in the Provence, bringing them home to be cared for. No surprise that she worked at the hospital during her senior year and went on to nursing school after graduation. She and Rob had married right before Michael died. Stephen could still picture his father and big sister, swirling together on the dance floor on that fairy tale night.

Stephen stretched as he rose from the swing, and went back inside, closing the door behind him.

"Come sit with me, honey." His mom was in her bathrobe, settled in the family room, newspapers on the floor at her side.

"Stephen, I am so excited for you. I won't get all sappy, but I am going to miss you something fierce. I just have to say it. If it doesn't feel right, or work out for you in Nashville, there is no shame in it. You come home. This is always home."

"I know. I know where I come from. I won't forget."

He still found it hard to believe that he had been accepted into the fellowship program at Bradford University in Nashville. He would finally be working toward his PhD in Theology. His interest in the history of early Christianity was more complicated than a mere thirst for knowledge. It had become his own secret quest for the truth. He had doubts, which did not bode well for someone who had chosen theology as a profession.

He was on his way to Nashville to study with Dr. Marc Macomb, at one of the most prestigious universities in America. His self imposed mission to untangle the mysteries of faith for himself, was closer than ever to becoming a reality.

An hour later, after reliving the evening and his sister's antics with his mother, he watched as she nodded off in her chair. Stephen stood quietly and gathered their dirty plates and glasses. He bent over her and whispered, not wanting to frighten her.

"It's time for me to turn in, Mom. I'm bushed."

Margaret Mary stirred and then opened her eyes. "You go on to bed, son. I'm just going to straighten up a bit and check on the animals, and then I'm heading up, too." She folded the afghan and turned to her son.

"Goodnight, Mom." Stephen hugged her and, groaning, she hugged him back.

"Dear Lord, child, you're stronger than you realize. You about squeezed the breath out of me! Now, get yourself up there and go to bed. I'll set my alarm early so I can make sure you're awake." She called after him, "And leave yourself enough time to shave."

Stephen climbed the stairs, instinctively skipping the step that always creaked. He could hear the sound of the teapot being filled and put on the back burner of the stove. He heard the clink of china as she got her favorite cup from the cabinet. And he swore he could hear his mother whispering just like long ago, when her children were finally tucked in their beds for the night... and she and her husband were in the kitchen alone, her feet propped in his lap, listening as he shared his day with her, while she had her last cup of tea before bed.

* * *

Stephen smacked the side of the dresser, forcing the sticky drawer to open stubbornly on its track. Taking out the last of his paperwork, he tossed the file onto the teetering mountain of clothes and other necessities waiting to be stuffed haphazardly into one of the two brand new duffel bags sitting at the foot of his childhood bed. His passport was new and seemed foreign and official to him.

Bare-chested, he caught sight of himself in the mirror over the dresser. Smiling at his reflection, he thought he probably *should* have shaved before dinner. He was tall, six feet and some change. The well defined muscles in his chest and arms defied the hundreds of hours spent hunched over books during the last six years of college. Whenever he felt the need to clear the cobwebs and unwind, or find the answer to a question that seemed just out of reach, he worked himself to the brink of exhaustion physically, as if that were the only way to open his mind and think clearly. The side effect of challenging himself by constantly pushing himself to the limit, was an amazing strength of body and mind.

Running a hand through his hair, he bent to empty the last drawer. He threw his leather sandals into the duffel bag and zipped it shut, finally finished with his packing.

The breeze from the open window blew the curtains softly into the room, along with sounds of the late spring evening. Moving the last few articles of clothing from his bed, he turned back the covers, got into bed and turned off the lamp. He felt himself relax, letting go of the day, anxious to start the next chapter of his life.

He could feel himself drifting off to sleep, pleasant and calm, until he plunged without warning…into the dream.

Chapter Two

The girl was huddled in a corner, trying desperately to protect herself from the brutal attack. Trembling, she lay curled in a fetal position as men and women surrounded her, taunting her loudly with promises of what was to come. Hot dry wind swirled around her, covering her in a fine layer of sand.

"Bitch." They spat at her.

"Whore."

"Let's see how freely you give yourself now."

"Go ahead. Remove her robes, Mica. See how she tries to protect the bastard she's carrying."

Stephen couldn't see the girl's face. He tried to push his way through the tightly packed crowd, tried to force his way to the front of the swelling sea of people. Dressed in ancient garb, they carried stones and pieces of food and waste. It was hard to breathe. He strained to be heard above the mob. He opened his mouth, but no sound escaped. He was sweating profusely, trying to shove his way through the solid throng, but he couldn't move forward. He saw what they planned, the sheer horror of what was happening just beginning to penetrate his consciousness.

"Stop. No!" Stephen shouted, but his voice was lost in the rising crescendo. The veins in his neck were bulging, his eyes wide with terror. He felt helpless as they threw the first stone, then the next. A hail of ammunition rained down on their tiny victim, landing with dull thuds. He heard, rather than saw. It was over quickly. Within minutes. They laughed as they dispersed, ambling off, going about their business as if it were any other market day. They were finally gone, leaving Stephen standing alone, paralyzed in his anguish.

She lay in the corner, unmoving, small and bloodied. In shock, he forced himself to walk slowly toward her, not caring if any of them remained to see his response, and then removed his cloak to cover her.

He tenderly brushed the fair hair from her face and with shaking fingers closed her eyes. She was so young. Her fingers curled tightly around something in her right hand, and Stephen gently pried it from her grasp. As his arm grazed her pregnant belly, he felt the babe kick sharply one last time. Startled, he jumped back, falling to the ground next to her, as the life-sustaining waters gushed bloodily from her womb.

Fierce hot tears flowed as he raised his eyes to heaven.

"Why, God?" His body racked with sobs, he stayed next to her for almost an hour.

"She is yours, then?" The old man stood next to him and Stephen jumped, startled by his sudden appearance. He looked up, shading his eyes from the sun with his cupped hand.

"No, man. Not mine." Stephen rose quickly, too angry to be afraid of what the stranger might conclude from his reaction to the stoning.

The old man put his hand on Stephen's shoulder to calm him.

"What you have just witnessed is the power Satan holds over the weak. She could have been saved, you know. She was turned away in her hour of helplessness. You, my son, are about to bear witness to the power of God. Believe in the dreams, Stephen, and take heed. You have been chosen. Do not doubt."

"Who are you? Rubbish. What the hell are you talking about? Look at her. How could anyone have saved her from this mob?" Stephen shook the old man's hand from his shoulder, not questioning how the old man knew his name.

"I am Gabriel, a messenger. Believe in the dreams, Stephen. You have been chosen."

Gabriel pointed to Stephen's fist, still curled around the piece of parchment he had taken from the girl's hand. Stephen turned back toward the

girl and held the scrap to the light, streaks of the girl's blood already drying, stiff and brown.

Only two words were written there. Words she protected with her life.

"What the hell is this? Who are you, man?" Stephen swung around to
face him, but the old man was gone.

Curious, the crowd had once again gathered, gauging his reaction to
the girl's death with renewed interest. Some of the men carried sticks and
were tapping them against the side of their legs.

"Mad as hell this one is, muttering to himself," they whispered among
themselves.

They approached him cautiously, spreading out to surround him
with their vile unrelenting judgment. Stephen raised his eyes once more
to the sky and bellowed.

"*Not. This. Time.*"

As he ran headlong into the crowd, his last lucid thought was that she
never cried. Even as they killed her, she never made a sound. The piece of
parchment fell from his hand and swirled high into the dusty air, carried
away, until snatched by the wind, it fell trapped against a stone wall.

Fat drops of rain fell suddenly from the sky, washing the dust from
the tiny scrap of paper, mingling with the blood and ink until the message disappeared.

Carried away in a swirling living sea of mud, it vanished, leaving in
its wake the carnage of the prophecy it foretold.

It begins.

Chapter Three

At daybreak, Margaret Mary stood on a stool in the kitchen, putting away the extra serving dishes from last night's dinner. She looked forward to every other Saturday night when the family gathered. It would be different now with Stephen gone, but she knew in her heart it had been the right decision for her only son. She hoped that whatever unanswered questions still lingered in his mind would at last be put to rest.

The kids said their goodbyes soon after dinner, leaving Stephen and her up well past midnight talking and reminiscing.

"Mom, are you sure you'll be alright?" Stephen had asked. He knew she would be fine, but wanted to hear her say it again. She knew he needed her permission to leave.

"Stephen, Dad's been gone for almost two years now, and I have the girls and Rob right here if I need anything. You won't be gone forever, and Nashville is not the end of the world. Stop worrying!"

"Okay…okay."

She knew he was relieved. They were all ready to take the next step, finally coming to terms with this new life without Michael.

She was putting the stool back into the closet when she heard him scream. She froze for only a second, and before she had time to react, she heard it again. Dropping the stool, she ran for the stairs, not able to move fast enough before the agonizing sound once again echoed down the hallway.

* * *

Pounding. He could hear pounding. Someone was calling his name, pounding on the door. Trying to open the door.

"Stephen! Stephen... open the door! You are dreaming, Stephen. Wake up. You're scaring me. Are you okay? Stephen!"

Margaret Mary stood in the hallway and pounded so hard she feared the door might splinter from its hinges.

"Stephen, wake up!"

She reached above the door frame, searching frantically for the little key that was hidden there. Her hands shook as she tried to force the door key into the small opening to pop the inside lock. She finally felt it give and, as the door sprung open, she saw Stephen sit straight up in bed, a look of murderous rage on his face. The sheets were a tangled mess around his legs and feet, pillows on the floor, and even from the doorway she could see the sheen of sweat and the evidence of tears on her son's face.

"Stephen. Oh my God, Stephen. What the...?" She ran over to him and as he slowly became aware, the look of raw terror and rage was replaced with one of confusion, and then slowly, finally, recognition.

He threw himself back against the pillows and put his arm over his eyes. "Awe, Mom, I'm sorry. I had the worst nightmare. I couldn't wake up. Damn, it was so real."

"Stephen Daniel, you scared the crap out of me."

"Did you say crap? It must have really been bad if you said crap." She watched as he struggled to compose himself, then went into his bathroom and returned with a cool washcloth.

"Are you okay? Do you want to talk about it? It's been a long time since you've had a dream." Margaret Mary pulled a chair over to his bed.

"No. I want to forget it. It was agonizing. It was so real, Mom. I was in ancient Jerusalem. It was horrible."

"Stephen, you've had your head buried in history books for the last seven years. It doesn't surprise me at all that you take it to sleep with you."

"I guess. But, Mom, it was as if...I could feel the sun and taste the dust. I heard...never mind."

"Honey, do you think it's because you're leaving? Dear Lord, I hate to think the dreams are starting up again and you so far away."

"Mom, no. It's nothing like that."

This was different. It wasn't like the night terrors that plagued him when he was younger. This was clear, more like a vision. But there was no way to explain the difference to her.

Stephen sat up straight. "You're right. It was only a dream. I am awake. I am starving and I desperately need a shower."

"Okay, if you're sure you're alright, I'll go down and start breakfast. Coffee will be ready when you finish your shower. If you still want to be on the road by ten though, you'd better hurry, Stephen." Handing him the key, she motioned to the spot above the door. She walked out of the room shaking her head, and shut the door behind her.

Stephen sat on the edge of the bed for a minute more, trying to shake the heaviness that still lingered from the dream. He decided he would try to put it behind him. He stood, and reaching over, grabbed the pillow from the floor and tossed it back on top of the snarled bedding. Walking over to the window, he kicked something across the room with his foot. As he bent to retrieve the object, he was overcome with another wave of desolation. He knew without looking what he held in his hand. The black stone was heavy and smooth. Stephen shuddered as he tossed it into the duffel lying open by the door, then went in and turned on the shower.

As he stood under the spray of hot water, he thought once again about the dream and tried to fathom what had caused such a vision to come to him in the first place. Introspective, but not one to dwell on the morose, he lathered once again and rinsed the remnants of the dream from his mind as surely as he did the suds from his shower, watching as both swirled slowly down the drain.

Chapter Four

Jillian Macomb raced up the front walk and into the house, depositing the contents of her locker unceremoniously onto the bench in the front hallway.

"Mom, I'm home." She yelled over her shoulder, never breaking stride, as she ran up the steps to her bedroom, two at a time.

"Hi, Jill. I thought you and your friends were going to Radnor Lake to celebrate the last day of school." Sara Macomb came in from the sunroom, newspaper in hand and glasses perched on the top of her head.

"Just came home to get my iPod speakers." Jillian kissed her mom on the cheek and ran back out the door. "I'll be home around six, in time for Dad's birthday dinner. Promise."

Sara stood at the door and watched her daughter hop into her boyfriend's black jeep that stood idling at the bottom of the driveway.

"Hi, Jamie. You two be careful, now. And wear your seatbelts."

Sara waved as he backed down the drive, and then closed the front door, side-stepping the pile of discarded notebooks and folders that were now sliding from the bench to the floor.

Seventeen year old Jillian Grace was their only child. Marc and Sara Macomb had been married for seven years before she got pregnant. They never really tried to have a child, nor did they try not to, so when Sara found out she was pregnant, they embraced the unexpected news with excitement and a sense of adventure and Jillian was a welcome surprise.

Marc and Sara had been drawn to each other the moment their eyes met on the campus in Nashville. They often compared notes on their similar Midwestern upbringings…both raised in strict Catholic families, dinner on the table every night by five o'clock, their moms taking care of hearth and home, while their dads went to work as the sole breadwinners.

Short of entering the priesthood, Marc joked that his D.P.T. in Early Christian History was a natural choice of majors. The timeline of his mother's pride in him began when he served mass as an altar boy in the sixties.

They had fallen in love with Nashville, so when Marc was offered the position at the Bradford University's School of Divinity, they leapt at the chance to stay. Sara's work as a clinical psychologist at the University Medical Center was flexible enough for her to be the primary caregiver for their young daughter, and still practice her profession.

Living in the Nashville suburbs was a tranquil and somewhat idyllic existence. Nestled in the hills, the tree-lined streets and cape-cod homes that had been built in the fifties, conjured up images of bygone eras, while at the same time, provided the perfect backdrop in which to raise a child. The sidewalks teemed with life in the evenings, the neighborhood friendly and welcoming. The city was only minutes away and offered an array of opportunities, from museums and beautiful parks, to the Country Music Hall of Fame and honky-tonk bars. And right in the middle of it all, the major university that had claimed her husband's heart and soul. They lived in Pleasantville and they knew it.

Sara walked into the kitchen and stood at the window over the sink. Looking into the backyard, she let her mind wander. They had been in the same house for nearly 20 years. The yard was cool with shade trees, some of which she remembered planting as seedlings. The recent rains of late spring had created a lush green landscape that served as a backdrop for the colorful annuals she had more recently put into the ground. Flowering trees, especially the dogwoods, had been breathtaking this year. When the brutal heat of summer descended, they would spend many afternoons sitting on the swing in the screened porch, ceiling fans whirring overhead, enjoying the view. They had a wonderful life here. Their neighbors and colleagues filled the spaces left by the absence of their families. They wanted for nothing and the community was as much a part of them as they were of it.

It was hard to believe that Marc turned sixty today. Her easy going husband was quiet and thoughtful. She had learned to read him over the years and found his contemplative nature easily the most calming influence in their marriage. He supplied the steady balm in their relationship, while she most often provided the drama. Perfectly complimenting each other in every way, Sara realized that in all their married life, she had never been bored.

Capturing her dark brown hair into a clip, she reached into the refrigerator for the vegetables. A glance at the clock confirmed that her husband would be walking in the door any minute. She was anxious to get the prep work for dinner out of the way so they could relax on the porch with a celebratory glass of wine before Jillian came home.

The phone rang as she rummaged through the cutlery drawer for the only sharp knife in the whole kitchen. Glancing at the caller ID, she grabbed the phone and propped it on her shoulder as she began cutting asparagus.

"Susie, you picked a perfect time to call. Wait a second… let me pour myself a glass of wine."

Her sister lived in Rochester, Michigan and Sara was happy to be able to catch up on all of the family news before Marc got home. At fifty-five, Susie was the older of the two sisters.

"What's going on?" Sara asked.

"I wanted to give the birthday boy a good razzing. Finally hitting sixty. Lord, I thought this day would never come."

"You two crack me up. He isn't home yet. He probably got waylaid at the school by the dean again. They are planning a reception next weekend for the new fellows. All Marc talks about is this new graduate from Canada, and what a catch he is. Hey, by the way, Jillian's last day of school was today. I am trying to pin her down so we can plan a college visit to Chicago. I thought we might head over to Rochester to see Mom and Dad after we tour the campus. If I can pry her away from Jamie, we will probably stay a week." Sara rinsed the vegetables and poured a marinade on the steaks.

"Why on earth would she want to winter in Chicago when she has one of the most beautiful campuses in the country right outside her own back door? Oh, never mind. I just answered my own question. Independence. She is so funny!" Susie laughed.

She was enamored of her only niece. She and her husband, Tom, were childless and had desperately tried every means known to man and medicine to conceive, spending thousands of dollars and bucking religious tradition in the process. When Susie turned forty-seven, she and Tom, by unspoken agreement, sadly resigned themselves to being childless and concentrated instead on being doting god-parents to her sister's daughter. At first heartbroken, Susie turned her energies to volunteering in the court system as an advocate for abused children, which fulfilled a primal need in her to nurture.

"And yes, please stay with us while you are here. Mom will be thrilled to see both of you. Daddy is driving her crazy. And she is doing the same to Tommy and me."

"My poor big sister!" Sara laughed as she heard the garage door open.

"Hey, the man of the hour is pulling into the garage. Listen, I'll say goodbye and give you a call next week when Jill and I firm up the dates. Love to all."

The back door opened and Marc came into the kitchen. Handing him the phone, Sara kissed his cheek and grabbed the jacket draped over his arm.

"Birthday wishes from Rochester." she said.

Sara overheard her husband's banter with her sister and smiled at the two of them. His quiet demeanor did nothing to sway her sister's good natured ribbing. He was still chuckling as he hung up the phone.

"That woman is certifiably crazy."

Sara poured him a glass of wine, and taking his hand, drew him out to the porch swing.

"Let's just sit for a minute and enjoy the quiet."

Sara never understood how her husband seemed to grow more handsome as he aged. Blond hair, with a touch of grey at the temple, and blue eyes just as clear as the day they met. He still had the power to capture her attention across a crowded room with a glance that let her know he had eyes only for her. At forty-six she was tiny, and had thick dark hair and a few errant freckles that ran across the bridge of her nose. Their teenage daughter had inherited her mother's features and her father's coloring and grew more beautiful with each passing day.

Marc rubbed the back of Sara's neck with strong practiced hands.

"Where is our daughter? Do you suppose we have time for a little celebrating of our own?"

The question lingered in the air for five seconds before the front door burst open with the passion and intensity of a small tornado.

"Daddy?" Jillian ran through the house to find her father and hopped into his lap, wrapping her thin teenage arms around him in a hug.

"Happy Birthday to you, Happy Birthday to you!" she sang.

Marc looked at Sara over his daughter's head.

"Hold that thought until later." she said.

The setting sun cast long shadows in the yard, and the warm breeze felt heavenly as they relaxed and enjoyed what was left of the evening.

Marc and Sara laughed as Jillian recounted her afternoon at the lake, spent with her friends in celebration of the long awaited end of her junior year.

"Jillian, Aunt Susie called and I told her we would drive to Rochester to see the family after we visited Champaign-Urbana."

"Are we staying with her and Uncle Tommy, or Grammy and Grumps?"

"Jillian Grace, we are staying with her, and it is Grandpa, young lady."

"Just kidding, Mom. You know I love Grandpa. He's just ornery, that's all. Anyway, Daddy, I want to get your present, so wait here and close your eyes."

Jillian ran from the back porch and came back momentarily with a package wrapped in black and blue paper.

"Varsity colors, in case you didn't notice" she said.

"Oh, I noticed." Marc slowly removed the wrapping from the small box. He noticed with amusement that his daughter was trying her best not to intervene, wanting desperately to speed the process along. He chuckled at her impatience, but as he opened the box, the bronze frame captured his attention and he was immediately mesmerized.

"Jillian, it's beautiful." Unable to think of anything more to say, the gift touched him deeply. The photo of Sara and Jillian had been taken in their yard a few weeks ago. They sat together on the hammock, appearing to float amid the flowering trees, and the photo had captured them in a moment of secret conversation, heads bent together, their attention totally absorbed in each other and the moment.

"Open the card, read it, Dad."

Marc opened the card and on the inside cover was his favorite bible verse.

"To everything there is a season, and a time for every purpose under the heaven." Ecclesiastes 3:1

On the back: To Dad on his Sixtieth Birthday. Love, Jillian

"Jillian, I don't know what to say. I am speechless. Thank you with all my heart. This is such a thoughtful gift. It's perfect."

Spreading his arms across the back of the swing, Marc pulled both girls close.

"Happy Birthday, sweetheart." Sara threw her head back and laughed at the three of them, such simple things to be grateful for.

Marc stood up and looked at his family. "Sixty has been great so far. My two favorite girls. What more could anyone ask?"

Jillian yawned and curled up on the swing.

"I am so tired. I can't stop yawning. I am sleeping in tomorrow morning. The first day of summer vacation. I can't wait." she said.

"Okay, child. I am going in to set the table. Dad will light the grill. Dinner will be ready in thirty minutes."

Marc went into the kitchen to grab the matches and Sara glanced back at her daughter, curled in the corner of the swing.

"Jillian, that was a special gift you gave your dad. He will always remember it. I am proud of you, honey."

But her daughter was already sleeping.

Chapter Five

Jillian reached out for the small clock on her nightstand. Bringing her knees to her chest, she turned toward the wall and pulled the covers over her head. Two weeks into the summer and she wakes up at six every morning, her body still in rhythm with the school schedule. No surprise to her that she is exhausted half the time. Her boyfriend Jamie calls her 'the old woman,' and she can't really blame him. Her curfew is eleven on weekends, but she is so tired she can barely stay awake until ten. She is beginning to wonder if she has some dreadful disease. Stretching slowly, she can hear her dad downstairs in the kitchen grinding coffee beans.

Groaning inwardly, she remembers that tonight is the reception for the new fellows at the university. The whole family has to go, but thank God, her parents said she could take Jamie. An evening with the professors will be excruciatingly painful as it is, so at least she will have someone to commiserate with when it's over. Jamie has been acting weird lately anyway.

Maybe this way they can have a few laughs, like old times. Jillian wondered at the change in him. They have been going together for six months and have known each other since third grade. All of a sudden it feels like she is looking at a stranger.

He is expecting things from her that she isn't ready to give. Sexual things. He tried to touch her breast last night when they kissed good night, and although she had to admit to herself that it felt nice when he pulled her close to him, it was obvious he was aroused and that scared her more than a little because she was, too. He started to sulk when they parted, as if she had let him down, and she didn't know what else she could have said to him. Last night had been the worst ever. He actually reached down to her waistband at one point before she shoved him away. She couldn't believe how he was acting and she blushed even now as she replayed their argument in her mind.

"Jamie, I have to go home."

"Oh, for Pete's sake, Jillian, it isn't even ten yet. Come on. Let's walk down to the park."

"Jamie, I can't. You're creeping me out. You know I made a vow."

"That was then, Jillian. You were only fourteen and still a kid. This is now and you are driving me crazy. I thought we loved each other. We've been going out for six months, girl. Damn, you'll be a senior next year and I'm off to college."

"I am not having sex until I'm married, Jamie, and that's that. I can't believe it's so hard for you to get it through your head, but when I made the promise it wasn't just to God, it was to me. *N.O.* Jamie. You knew this when we started dating. I never kept it a secret and I am not going to change my mind. Do you think I'm not tempted sometimes? It's not easy for me, either." She turned away from him and walked back toward the car.

"Jillian, there are other things we can do that aren't technically having sex."

"That's your opinion, and I happen to think those *other things* are still too close for comfort. Let's go, Romeo. Take me home before we both say things we'll regret."

When they pulled into her driveway he stared straight ahead, pouting when he said goodnight.

"What time tomorrow?" he asked.

"My dad says we have to leave by 6:30, so can you be here by quarter after?"

Jamie nodded and reached across her body, opening the door to the jeep. His arm brushed her breast, sending a shockwave through her body.

Inhaling sharply, she hopped down from the passenger seat and looked back into the truck in time to see him smile.

"You're a jerk. See you tomorrow."

They seemed to follow the same pattern whenever they were together. There were no rule books on the subject that she knew of, and the only way she felt in control was to stop things cold. She was almost glad she was going to Chicago with her mom to look at colleges. Even seeing Grammy and Gramps would be a welcome relief from the nagging guilt she was starting to feel about saying no to Jamie all the time.

She thought she loved him, but if he loved her, wouldn't he wait for her? In the grand scheme of things, college didn't last forever and if things worked out for them, they would have something momentous to look forward to. And if things didn't work out, she still had her virginity and her pride. If only it were that crystal clear when they were alone together.

Jillian stretched and realized she had to pee. She resigned herself to the fact that sleep was over for now and pushed back the covers. Forcing herself out of the bed, she walked over to the window and opened the shutters. It looked like a great day for the lake, but then she remembered she had promised her mother she would help run errands for the reception tonight. Heading into the bathroom, Jillian grabbed her blue shorts off the back of the chair. Oh, well. At least by this time tomorrow, her social obligation to her parents would be over.

*   *   *

Jillian and her mother spent the afternoon arranging the seating at the university ballroom, placing name cards at each numbered table. Sara positioned a few floral arrangements at the podium, while Jillian did a final table check to make sure every name on her mother's list was accounted for. The hospitality staff was setting china, and the smell of something chicken was starting to waft in from the kitchen area. They worked without stopping for lunch and when they finished, drove through town, stopping only to grab a burger to eat in the car on the ride home. By the time they got back to the house, it was already close to three o'clock.

Walking into the kitchen, Jillian dropped her purse on the counter-top and saw the message light flashing on the house phone. As she picked up the receiver, she punched in the password.

"Jill, it's me. Hey, I can't go to the reception with you tonight. Something came up this afternoon and I can't get out of it, but I'll call you in the morning." Jamie's voice came through loud and clear...and unapologetic.

Sara watched the expression on her daughter's face darken. "What's wrong, honey?"

Throwing the rest of her take-out meal into the trash can, she looked at her mother.

"He is such a creep." Without another word, Jillian stormed out of the kitchen, stomped up the stairs and slammed her bedroom door.

Chapter Six

Hey, girls, we have to leave in five minutes."

Marc stood at the mirror in the front hallway and loosened his tie just enough so he could swallow comfortably. They really had fifteen minutes and then some, but he learned from experience that it was better to give his two ladies the benefit of a little imaginary urgency.

He was looking forward to this reception, and even more so, to the introduction of the faculty to the new fellowship recipients. He still could not comprehend the full impact of these appointments to his program at the School of Divinity. Stephen Jacobs was an especially rare candidate, a true scholar at a young age, and he already had the makings of a historian.

During intense interviews for the position, the method of debate and the evident research that prefaced Stephen's answers and opinions on the most complex theological subjects, had astounded even the Dean of Religious Studies. Marc rarely anticipated the start of another semester as much as he did this one. His initial perception of Stephen suggested he would one day be a great scholar, and Marc looked forward to watching him grow to his potential.

Marc turned and watched as Jillian and Sara walked down the stairs at the same time. Sara looked beautiful, as usual. The blue sleeveless dress made her sapphire eyes shine. She carried a sweater over her arm and was putting her lipstick in her purse as she walked toward him, Jillian lagging one step behind.

"Mom, are you sure this skirt looks okay? It's so long. I feel like I'm a hundred." Jillian pouted as she followed her mother into the foyer.

Her afternoon nap had done little to improve her cranky disposition, and she was still furious at Jamie for backing out of the dreaded evening ahead. Marc opened the door for them and turned on the porch light, grabbing his keys off the table.

"You both look beautiful, and Jillian, even if you were a hundred, you'd look fantastic in that outfit. Now let's go or we won't be there in time to meet everyone before dinner."

"Dad, I can only hope."

Chapter Seven

The Divinity School at Bradford University held two receptions each year for the faculty, but tonight's was the most anticipated. The professors and alumni gathered to celebrate the end of the spring semester and to welcome the five new fellowship recipients with open arms. The diversity of the school was well represented by professors of every religious and cultural background. The evening usually proved lively and interesting, with animated discussions about the curriculum of the past year, and much anticipation for the year that lay ahead.

Most of the faculty came accompanied by their spouses, and a few, like Marc, brought their older teenagers to represent the future student population. There were close to one hundred and fifty people in attendance, but the room was arranged to encourage conversation, and it was a relaxed crowd, encouraging the newcomers to join in the casual festive atmosphere.

Round tables draped in white cloth were arranged so that each department head was seated directly adjacent to the next. The lights were dimmed during dinner and the background music was muted. Introductions were scheduled throughout the evening, so the only time people actually sat at the tables was during the meal. Much of the night was spent in amiable conversation and light-hearted banter.

"Dr. Macomb." Dean Albert Smyth balanced a program and a glass of wine and moved through the crowded room as gingerly as his ample girth would allow. Patting Marc's shoulder and bowing slightly at the waist, Albert Smyth acknowledged Sara and Jillian at the same time.

"Hello, dear Sara. Jillian, I do believe you look more like your lovely mother every time I see you. Sara, have you met Stephen Jacobs yet?" The Dean turned around, looking for his protégé.

Stephen followed Dean Smyth closely, absorbing the atmosphere in the room and quickly becoming accustomed to making the rounds. He had been looking forward all evening to reconnecting with Dr. Macomb. Moving out from behind Dr. Smyth, he acknowledged the introduction to Dr. Macomb's family, smiling at Sara as she extended her hand in greeting.

"Hello, Stephen. Marc has been singing your praises for weeks now. I feel as if I already know so much about you," Sara said.

Marc glanced over his shoulder, subtly motioning Jillian to come front and center to meet his new associate. She rolled her eyes for her father's benefit only, and then quickly replaced her bored expression with a polite smile, as she tried to squeeze herself into the tight circle.

"Stephen Jacobs, this is my daughter, Jillian."

Jillian looked up at Stephen, raising her hand in greeting.

"Hi," she said.

At least he was cute, unlike most of her father's nerdy students. She wondered though, at the way Stephen seemed to go pale at the sight of her. No one else noticed, but she did. He actually sucked in his breath. She felt him tremble slightly as he shook her hand, but everyone was talking at once and no one seemed to pay attention. Maybe she was being melodramatic. After all, she was beyond bored and so ready to go home. Her dad's students tended to be quirky, anyway. Not that she cared. If he was unnerved, he sure regained his composure in a hurry.

"I am so glad to finally meet the rest of your family." She liked it when he smiled.

Stephen looked handsome in his dark suit. Jillian forced herself to stop daydreaming and acknowledged his greeting.

"It's nice to meet you, Mr. Jacobs. My dad says you are moving here from Ontario."

Stephen watched her, forcing himself to concentrate. He ignored the quickened pulse in his neck, and prayed no one would notice his distraction.

"Please, call me Stephen. And yes, St. Thomas seems a long way away right now, but what I have seen of Nashville, I already enjoy. I'm looking forward to exploring some of the local points of historical interest before the semester starts."

"*Nerd Alert,*" Jillian couldn't help thinking to herself.

Sara liked this young man immediately. She remembered how it had been for them, so many years ago, when she and Marc were first learning their way around a strange new city.

"Stephen, you must come to the house next week for dinner. We can spend time getting to know you and I would love to hear about Ontario. I understand the countryside is beautiful. Anything you need, please let Marc know and we'll do our best to help you get settled."

"You are very kind, and yes, I accept. My mother will be extremely happy to know I am not wasting away, alone in my apartment."

Stephen spoke briefly to Marc before he was captured by Professor Ranchalamun to meet the members of the Ethics and Society group. As he walked away from his surreal encounter with the Macomb family, he excused himself politely from the newest wave of introductions and walked quickly down the hall to the men's room.

He studied his reflection in the mirror above the sink, then turned on the cold water and splashed his face. Outwardly, the eyes that stared back at him looked much the same as when he arrived this evening. He dried his face with a paper towel and leaned back against the cool surface of the wall tile. Closing his eyes, he tried to clear his head and calm his racing heart.

Dear Lord, he thought. *What was happening to him?*

I must be crazy. Looking into the mirror once more, he shook his head at his reflection.

The vision played over and over again in his mind, an endless loop. He saw the ancient city of Jerusalem and felt the oppressive heat, the stinging sand. He remembered every detail of the angry mob. He could still see the girl, bloody and lifeless on the ground. He watched himself gently move her hair from her face. He saw the old man, Gabriel, as if he materialized from nowhere.

He could not stop the images as they assaulted his memory, coming fast and furious. Stephen tried to remember if he had ever seen her before tonight. He knew he had literature, brochures and correspondence from Dr. Macomb. He had flown in to meet with him during his first interview with all the professors.

But, he had never met the professor's family at any of those initial meetings with the school. He felt dizzy and nauseous, trying to piece together the remnants of the vision, his mind reeling with unanswered questions. He'd never met Marc Macomb's daughter. Tonight was the first time he laid eyes on her. He was sure of it.

But that was not entirely true. Not so long ago in his dream world, he reached out in agonizing grief to close the unseeing eyes of a young girl, killed while trying to protect her unborn child. Jillian.

He noticed his hand, closed into a tight fist, and remembered how he had held the small remnant of parchment to the light, exposing two words that seemed prophetic to him now.

It begins.

The door to the bathroom opened and two men walked in, talking to each other about something that had taken place last semester. They barely acknowledged Stephen, and he took advantage of that brief moment to regain his composure. Slightly calmer, he forced himself to walk back to the reception. He was determined to put the dream behind him until he was back in his apartment, where he could privately analyze his thoughts.

* * *

At ten thirty, the lights brightened slightly in the banquet room, a subtle signal that the evening's reception was coming to a close. Sara found Jillian in a corner with her feet propped on another chair.

"Hi, Jill. Was it so unbearable?"

Jillian yawned and stretched her arms above her head.

"It wasn't so bad, actually. Tamara West and Bobby Tinian were here, so we snuck outside and smoked a joint."

"Jillian!" Sara pulled her daughter off the makeshift recliner and shook her head in exasperation.

"One of these days, someone is going to think you're serious and you'll be in a whale of trouble. Remember where you are, young lady. D-i-v-i-n-i-t-y."

"I know… I know. Please, can we finally leave and go home. I am so tired, I just want to crawl into bed."

"Here comes Dad. Come on. We'll go outside and wait for the car to come around."

Cupping Jillian's chin gently in her hand, Sara looked closely at her daughter.

"What's going on, Bean? You've been so droopy lately. Is everything okay with you?"

"I'm just tired, Mom. And mad as hell at Jamie."

"Jillian!"

"I know. I know. D-i-v-i-n-i-t-y."

"Come on, girlfriend. Let's get you home to bed." Sara took her daughter's hand and they headed for the car.

Chapter Eight

The Chevy Malibu wound through the narrow streets of the campus on the short ride home and Marc reflected on the evening. The reception for the chosen fellowship candidates was his favorite gathering of the year. Filled with promise, they added much anticipated excitement to the divinity curriculum. The lectures and discussions that followed their acceptance were the fuel that kept the program from becoming stagnant. Marc was always caught off guard by the clarity of mind that these young scholars possessed. He secretly thought many of the faculty members were too uptight and unyielding in their belief systems, so anything to shake up the status quo was a welcome diversion.

He had to laugh when he remembered Dr. Ranchalamum's reaction to the fellow who showed up with his iPod headphones plugged into his ears during the program. Having a teenager under his own roof did much to anesthetize Marc to the blatant indiscretions of the latest generation of students. Yes, indeed, the coming year was going to be interesting.

It had started to rain and Marc glanced into the backseat as he repositioned the rearview mirror. Preoccupied with her cell phone, Jillian seemed, for the moment, to be oblivious to anyone or anything but the task at hand. It always surprised him to realize that she was almost a woman now, and so beautiful. One moment a rough and tumble tomboy, and the next, she was agonizing over which outfit to wear to school. He gave a quick thought to the poor husband in her future and the hoops he would have to jump through. Jillian was sure to expect great things from her life partner.

Marc maneuvered the new car around the empty garbage can that stood forgotten at the end of the driveway. Damn. The intensity of the rain had increased, blowing the lid into the middle of the lawn. As he drove up the long driveway leading to the garage, he made a mental note to bring the can up to the house in the morning before he left for work.

The garage door rose slowly and Marc expertly pulled into the space beside Sara's SUV.

"Home sweet home, ladies," Marc said as he opened the passenger door. "Where's the umbrella?"

"On the hook inside the back door," Sara laughed, as she threw her sweater over her head and they ran in a huddled pack to the back porch.

Jillian squealed. "Open the door. Hurry. It's freezing out here."

Marc dropped the house key, and as Sara bent to retrieve it, the wind grabbed the storm door from her grasp and flung it back, hitting the wall of the house. Finally, the key found its way into the lock and the door swung open, as all three fell into the hallway, drenched, dripping and thankful to be standing in the warm kitchen at last.

Hair hanging in her eyes and water forming a puddle at her feet, Jillian looked at her parents and shook her head.

"I'm going to bed. This night has lasted long enough and you two are crazy."

"Good night, Jillian." Marc blew her a kiss as she ran toward the stairs.

Marc and Sara turned out the lights and walked down the hallway and into their room.

"Honey, you were magnificent tonight," Marc said as he hung his suit coat in the bedroom closet and made his way into the bathroom.

Sara sat at the dressing table and unclasping her necklace, placed it in the jewelry box in front of her. Marc stood in the doorway, his toothbrush in hand.

"The evening went off without a hitch and the new fellows seemed energized. Did you ever have the opportunity to have a full conversation with Stephen Jacobs?"

"I invited him to dinner next week, Marc. God, do you remember when we were that young? It seems like only yesterday, until I look in the mirror," Sara sighed, as she got up and followed him into the bathroom.

"He seems like a great addition to the mix. Doesn't come off like a know-it-all, either. And our daughter thought he was "cute" for an old college guy, so I guess he passed muster." Marc rinsed his toothbrush, putting it in the holder.

Sara sat on the edge of the tub and watched her husband as he unbuttoned his shirt. A bolt of lightning arced across the sky, followed closely by deep rumble of thunder that seemed to vibrate through the walls of the house.

"Boy, it's really coming down." Marc glanced out the small window into the yard as he swiped the hand towel across his face and through his hair.

He caught Sara's eye in the bathroom mirror.

"Hey, are you okay? I get the feeling that you are miles away at the moment. Really, the evening was a huge success. Even Smythie's wife was complimentary. And that is saying a lot. Come here." Marc pulled her to him and leaned back against the bathroom cabinet.

"Talk to me." he said.

"Okay, I think the dinner was great. It's not about that. I'm concerned about Jillian." Sara shot Marc a worried glance.

"Our Jillian? Is there something going on that I don't know about?"

"Nothing dramatic, but haven't you noticed that she seems tired all the time? And at night I hear her moaning and groaning in her sleep, like she's having horrible dreams. Remember when she was three and went through that horrible period when she had night terrors." Sara shuddered to remember her precious three year old running blindly down the hallway, screaming and pushing them away, not seeing them even as they held her, trying to wake her from whatever demons terrorized her sleep.

"It's not quite that bad, but when I question her in the morning, she doesn't remember anything. Sometimes I catch her staring off into space, as if she doesn't even know I'm there. She just isn't herself. I don't know how to describe it. There is nothing specific I can put my finger on, really."

"Well, she seems fine to me. A little moody lately, but after all, she is a teenage girl. I thought you females were supposed to be moody at that age."

"Glad you specified age, mister, and you're probably right. All the same, I may call Julie Richards and get her in for a checkup a few months ahead of schedule. Maybe some blood work. Make sure she's not anemic. I don't know. I can't pin it down or give it a name. Just mother's intuition, I guess."

"Listen, you're usually right when it comes to Jillian. I can't say I would have noticed anything unusual anyway, these last few months, as busy as things have been on campus. Our daughter has a big year ahead of her. High school senior, college visits. There's nothing wrong with scheduling a quick check-up for her. She probably just needs a good vitamin and she'll be back to her old self in no time. No worries."

"I'm sure you're right, Dr. Macomb, as usual. Now let's go back over the evening. I noticed another old college guy there tonight who was pretty cute." Sara finished unbuttoning Marc's shirt, resting her head against his chest. The combination of soap mingled with the musky scent of his cologne sparked something inside of her and she slowly peeled her camisole over her head, running her hands up and over his shoulders."

Marc leaned his head back.

"I like where this part of the conversation is heading. Shall we?"

The rain continued its brutal lashing, another streak of lightning slicing through the black sky. The last lamp in the Macomb house was finally extinguished, the house closed tight, safe and warm against the storm that continued to rage outside.

Chapter Nine

I t was the noise that woke him up. Stephen could hear the fury of the storm, but it was the drooping skeletal branches of the ageless oak tree as it raked across the bedroom window that pulled him from his sleep. The room flashed daylight as lightning arced across the midnight sky. He pushed back the covers, rolled out of bed and walked over to the window. Thunder rumbled in the distance, but was still close enough to cause the earth to vibrate under the old building.

Stephen grabbed the remote from the table and turned on the weather channel. Nashville weather was known to turn fierce at the drop of a hat, but the frequency of tornado and severe thunder storm warnings was a source of amazement to him. St. Thomas had storms, impressive displays over the waters of Lake Erie, but even these paled in comparison to the frequency and severity of the weather he had experienced during his few short weeks in the states. It hadn't been that many years ago that a tornado cut a swath right through the heart of downtown Nashville during rush hour. Even now, the plywood-covered windows of some of the high rise office buildings offered unmistakable evidence of the power these storms could unleash.

Good old dependable weather channel. No urgency this time. This was an innocuous summer storm, racing through the city and heading northeast at thirty miles an hour. The announcer was predicting hot and humid weather tomorrow, just like yesterday and the day before. Stephen turned off the television and went into the tiny kitchen to get a drink of water.

The dreams continued to haunt him and as the days progressed, they grew even more intense and mystifying. Stephen thought at times he must be going insane. He rubbed his hand over the stubble on his chin. It crossed his mind that he should talk to someone. He was getting ready to start his fellowship in a few weeks. The last thing he needed was this cloud of anxiety, and the sleeplessness that accompanied it, hanging over his head. He had trouble concentrating, and hanging on to the simplest train of thought was becoming an effort.

Since the reception last night and the shock of actually seeing the face of the girl in his dream come to life in the flesh and blood of Jillian Macomb, his mind had been working overtime.

"Get a grip, man," Stephen said out loud. Turning the ceiling fan on low, he walked back into the bedroom and sat on the edge of the bed, resting elbows on knees, running his hands through his thick dark hair.

"I have got to get a hold of myself. Okay, old man, one more week, and if you don't knock off the night time theatrics, you are going to see a shrink and that's it."

The problem was he half believed the dreams meant something. He was just too tired and rattled to figure out what the meaning was.

Throwing himself back against the mattress, Stephen mentally ran over the list of things he had to finish before his classes started in earnest. Trying to divert himself from this bizarre preoccupation with the dreams, he started planning the days ahead and all he hoped to accomplish.

The storm was fading now, drifting further away, and he could hear, but no longer feel, thunder in the distance. Next week he was having dinner at Dr. Macomb's house. He had to remember to pick up a bottle of wine. Tomorrow was his sister Cami's birthday. It was time to call home. He talked to his mom every couple of days and they emailed in-between, but the gang would all be there to celebrate with the required cake and ice cream and he hoped to talk to everyone. He missed the predictable silliness of it, everyone sitting together around the table.

He thought back to his last conversation with Mandy and wondered if she was past the morning sickness phase of her pregnancy. His family seemed so far away.

The digital display on the nightstand clock was flashing two thirty. He let himself drift off, vaguely aware that he should reset the clock, as the power must have gone off at some point during the storm. He felt himself falling, spiraling headlong into the dream world that was becoming as familiar to him as the world he inhabited by day. There seemed to be nothing he could do to stop it.

*　*　*

This time she stood in the corner with her back to him. She tried to hide herself from him and pulled her cloak tight against her tiny frame, as if to ward off the dampness of the cave. Darkness engulfed them, save for a candle that threw long wavering shadows against the stone wall.

"Turn around so I can look at you." He reached out to her, trying not to frighten her with his impatience. He dropped his hand in amazement as she started to speak. Her voice was familiar to him and although laced with an ancient dialect, a voice he easily recognized from earlier this evening, none the less.

"I cannot face you, as my heart is filled with confusion and shame. You ask me to show my face, my pain. How can I explain so that you will believe? I have been with no one, yet I am with child. I have no explanation, but for a vision that came to me while I slept, foretelling all that would come to pass. Can you believe me, Stephen? Are you willing to help me? I am a virgin and shall bear a son. Who will protect me? If I come to you, will you turn away? You shall see what you will see. But it has been written since the beginning of time and we are powerless to change the course."

She slowly turned to face him, removing the hood as she did, allowing a tangled mass of blond hair to escape. He found himself staring into the eyes of a perfect likeness of Jillian Macomb.

"I don't understand. Who are you and why do you come to me in my dreams? How can I help you? What is the message you bring?" Stephen crossed the cave and lifted her chin to better see her face.

As he touched her, the delicate features melted into his hand and he jumped back, amazed at what he had witnessed with his own eyes.

Standing in her place was Gabriel, the messenger from his first haunting dream.

"Stephen, the hour grows near. The girl speaks the truth and you must believe. Things will happen that make no sense to you. Trust your faith, Stephen. You must obey the will of God. There is no other truth. You will be called upon one day soon to take her away to your special place. You have been chosen to protect her, Stephen, and the child she carries. These are not random acts. Do not doubt the magnitude or the power of the dreams."

"What the hell is going on? Who are you, and why Jillian? Am I supposed to know her? I don't know her. I haven't even spoken to her. She's just a kid. Can't you just speak in plain English? I need some answers, Gabriel."

Stephen backed toward the opening of the cave, yearning for the escape offered in the darkness beyond. He knew he was dreaming, that none of this was real, yet it felt real. He stopped as he approached the mouth of the cave, the messenger Gabriel watching his every move.

"How do you know about the special place?" Stephen asked.

He covered his face with his hands.

"What am I saying? This is a dream and I have created all of you. How am I supposed to understand all of this cryptic nonsense? None of this is really happening. None of this would make sense to a sane man. I must be losing my mind."

Stephen rushed toward the old man, but once again, Gabriel disappeared as if he had never been. All that was left in the suddenly hot and oppressive cave was the smoldering light of the flickering candle.

He folded to his knees in frustration, pounding the earthen floor with his fists until the pain in his hands was unbearable and he had no strength left.

Somewhere in the distance he heard the rumbled beginnings of a new storm. In which world the new tempest brewed, he did not know or even care. But he could feel it. It trembled deep within the earth below him, and he felt it to his core.

Chapter Ten

I saw you kissing her on the tennis court, Jamie." Jillian slid from the hood of the jeep and marched to the side of the car where Jamie slumped against its dull black exterior.

The day started out badly. Jillian overslept and had almost missed her tennis lesson. She barely made it out the front door before her best friend, Evie, rounded the corner in her mom's van to pick her up. They made it to the tennis court with only seconds to spare…and that's when their light hearted laughter came to an abrupt halt. Jillian watched with a mixture of shock and humiliation as her boyfriend of six months casually planted a kiss on the lips of one of the most popular girls at school. A cheerleader no less. So cliché. And his hand was on the small of her back. Familiar, like it wasn't the first time. *And in front of everyone.*

Now, standing in her driveway with hands on her hips, she refused to give in to tears of anger and humiliation. Jillian steeled herself for the confrontation that was about to place.

"You can't just say nothing happened when I saw you with my own eyes. First, you skip out on the reception at the last minute, which, by the way, was really a creepy thing to do, and then you don't call until today. Wednesday. Almost a week. I don't get it, Jamie."

"What don't you get? Listen, this goody two shoes act is driving me crazy, Jillian," Jamie glared at her.

"That's one thing we both agree on. Listen, I don't know what's gotten into you, but maybe it's time for us to cool it. You leave for college in a few months. I can't figure out this whole Sherry Edwards thing and, frankly, I am tired of it all. It's obvious to me you want to test the waters, Jamie, so have at it. You are officially a free agent."

"Six months, Jillian. Six months is a long time to wait for you to come around. I wasted my whole senior year waiting. I'm not some kind of supernatural freaking hero. There's only so much a guy can take." Jamie pushed himself up from the side of the car and faced her, hands on his hips.

"You think *you're* tired of it all? How about just tired? You're like a freaking old woman sometimes," he said.

"And this is supposed to change my mind about anything?" Running to the opposite side of the car and yanking open the passenger door, Jillian reached in and grabbed her sweater from the seat.

Face burning with anger and embarrassment, she said between clenched teeth, "I never lied to you, Jamie. I never led you on. As for the rest of it, it doesn't matter anymore, does it? We are past tense, Jamie. Finished. Over. I feel so sorry for you. You poor thing. You can have the rest of the summer to find whatever it is you think you've missed out on with me. That's my parting gift to you."

Jillian slammed the door of the jeep and turned away from him without saying another word. She heard the engine start as she walked quickly toward the house. Don't look back, don't look back, *Do. Not. Look. Back.* She willed herself not to cry until he was safely out of sight.

Jamie leaned his head out the window and called to her as he backed down the driveway.

"You're living in a fantasy world, Jillian. It just doesn't happen the way you have it all worked out in your pretty little head. Six months, Jill. It's a long time for anyone to wait. I'm not gonna come around begging anymore. You want over, you got over. We're done." He punched the accelerator and was gone. Just like that.

Finally through the front door, Jillian threw her keys on the hall table and peeked out the window. Jamie was really gone. Even though she knew this was coming, she hadn't planned on feeling like her insides just got ripped out. She felt heavy, like the air was soup and she couldn't breathe enough in. Why was everything so complicated? Maybe she was a freak. It wasn't like she didn't want to let go. She watched other girls at school. She saw how they treated sex like it was no big deal. She just couldn't bring herself to give in, and it wasn't just because her dad's job was studying religion. To her, sex wasn't like polishing your nails, or getting a new haircut, or trying on clothes. It had to mean more than that. How long was long enough to know someone? At seventeen, she was only just learning about her body and figuring out about love, or at least what she thought it was supposed to be.

She walked down the hallway to the kitchen, flipping up light switches on her way. The trees threw long afternoon shadows across the yard. Grateful that her mom and dad were still at work, she opened the pantry and grabbed a box of Co-Co Pops. Big fat tears rolled silently down her cheeks as she looked in the fridge for something cold to drink. Settling on bottled water, she tucked the box of cereal under her arm, and wanting to shut out the world, went up to her room. Sitting on the edge of the bed, she peeled off her tennis clothes and put on an old t-shirt. Digging her hand into the cereal box, she grabbed a handful of the sweet crunchy chocolate and stuffed it in her mouth. What a difference one horrible day could make.

They were history. It was over. Finding refuge in her room, Jillian allowed her emotions to erupt just seconds before she heard her mother open the front door and call up the stairs to her.

"Jillian, I'm home. Dinner in an hour. How was tennis?" Thank God the phone rang and Jillian was spared from responding.

Throwing herself into the cocoon of her bed, she didn't even notice when the box of cereal overturned and hundreds of little puffs rolled across the floor like the open floodgate of her breaking heart.

Chapter Eleven

Marc drove cautiously down the tree-lined street, pulling up to the house and stopping outside the back door to unload the groceries. With his academic mindset, nothing could possibly be worse than a Saturday morning spent at the grocery store. He and Sara avoided these weekend outings like the plague. She met his eyes over the trunk of the car and mouthed a silent thanks. The past several days had been an emotional rollercoaster, with Jillian suffering full blown teen angst over her break-up with Jamie Tyler.

Marc couldn't say he was surprised. He liked the kid, but he was furious when he heard the whole story about the public humiliation of his daughter. The truth was, Jamie was leaving for college in the fall, and in his heart of hearts, Marc was relieved that Jillian would be free of a serious relationship while she tackled her senior year. Seventeen was hard enough without the exquisite pain of teen love gone wrong. Jillian's emotions had run the gamut the past few days and ranged between tears, anger, hilarity and a quiet resignation that had quite frankly been beyond the scope of his meager experience with teenage girls. He never knew which daughter was going to greet him when he got home from the campus and could only hope this first love gone wrong phase was over quickly.

"What time is Stephen coming for dinner tonight?" Marc pecked Sara on the cheek as he set the last of the grocery bags on the kitchen counter.

"Okay, Marc, let's try this one more time. Your protégé is coming at 6:30 and dinner is going to be at 7:30. His name is Stephen Jacobs, 26 years of age and he hails from St. Thomas, Ontario. He has two sisters and a brother-in-law. Sadly, his father died almost two years ago in his sleep, his mother's name is Margaret Mary, who, by the way, has never been out of Ontario… and he is your most promising fellow to date. Anything else you may have forgotten?"

"Ha. Ha. You are very funny, Mrs. Macomb, but also accurate. I've been slightly pre-occupied this week as you well know. Actually, I'm glad he's coming over tonight. I haven't really had any one-on-one time with him since February, when he was here interviewing for the fellowship."

Marc unloaded the bags and lined the groceries on the countertop for Sara to put away in her own meticulous manner. Marc had learned long ago that he was no match for her organization skills and he always inadvertently put everything in illogical places, then immediately forgot where they landed.

"I know. I only wonder which of our beautiful daughter's personalities will join us for dinner this evening. What a week." Sara shuddered as she carried the mushrooms to the sink.

"Why is it, that all my years in behavioral research have not prepared me to handle my own daughter's romantic breakdown?" she added.

"I guess some things are just meant to be experienced by trial and error, my dear wife. Speaking of behavior, did you set up the appointment with Julie Richards for Jill's check up?" Rinsing an apple under the running water, Marc leaned back against the sink.

"Well, yes and no. I set up an appointment, but when the sky opened up with this whole Jamie thing, I changed it to next week. I decided to give her a week to calm down. Did you hear her last night? She was tossing and turning. I went in to check on her and she was sitting straight up in bed, like she was wide awake. She wasn't, though. I called out to her and I swear she didn't hear me. She just kept saying yes, over and over again, as if she was answering someone. It was the strangest thing."

"Did you ask her about it this morning?"

"Of course I did. She just looked at me like I was crazy and said she had everything under control. She said she didn't remember having any dreams, but I don't know if I believe her. I guess it doesn't matter anyway. Her appointment is Monday at 9:30. I made it under the guise of a senior physical."

"Good. It's probably like you said. Anemic, whatever. I just want her back to normal. I am thankful this whole Jamie catastrophe will be behind us before school starts. Her senior year should be full of fun and excitement. Maybe having a dinner guest will help take her mind off everything. As long as she doesn't go all possessed on us!"

"Marc Macomb! You should be ashamed." Sarah playfully scolded her husband. "Anyway, we'll see. Speaking of dinner guests, either hand me the asparagus or grab a paring knife. It's prep time."

Chapter Twelve

S tephen stood outside the Macomb's front door and hesitated briefly, his finger poised over the door bell. He braced himself for the inevitable confrontation with the subject of his night-time apparitions, Jillian. He decided he would approach this evening the same way he approached every topic of research…with curiosity and open mindedness. He was not prone to hallucinations after all, and these unsettling apparitions might just be the combination of his father's death and leaving St. Thomas and his family behind, not to mention the pressure he felt to perform well at Bradford. Maybe the anxiety had manifested itself in his subconscious.

He knew Marc Macomb expected great things from him and from the moment he found out he was a finalist in the fellowship program, he had been more than anxious to prove himself. Tonight would be a test of sorts for him. Lifting his finger to the illuminated button, he pushed.

Marc threw open the door.

"Stephen, come in. Sara and I have been looking forward to this evening. Here, let me take that." Taking the bottle of Merlot from Stephen's hand, Marc enthusiastically led him through the foyer into a cozy den.

"Make yourself at home," Marc said.

He couldn't help but notice the similarities between his home in St. Thomas and the Macomb's home in Nashville. Family photos lined the shelves on either side of the fireplace. Sara's taste in décor was less floral than his mother's, actually quite sophisticated, but cozy none the less.

"Hello, Stephen. It is so good to see you." Sara came out of the kitchen wiping her hands on a towel.

"Why don't you gentlemen come into the kitchen and chat with me while I put the finishing touches on the salads. Marc can light the grill, and we'll start with a glass of this wonderful wine."

Stephen liked Sara and she immediately made him feel at home. She reminded him of his mother and oldest sister all rolled into one.

"Thank you so much for the invitation. I have to admit my culinary skills are more suited to the Canadian wilderness than to an apartment. My mother was ecstatic when I told her I was going to enjoy a home-cooked meal with you. I'm afraid the contents of my refrigerator are pathetic and I'll have to reciprocate one day soon at the restaurant of your choice."

Stephen picked up the corkscrew and began to open the bottle of wine, while Marc brought the wineglasses in from the dining room table. Sara was busy pouring dressing on the most fabulous looking salad that Stephen had ever laid eyes on.

"Our daughter will be joining us for dinner, but I must warn you in advance, she's had a horrible week." Stephen felt a jolt of adrenaline at the mention of Jillian, hoping he was able to outwardly keep his composure.

"Nothing serious, I hope."

Research, Stephen, research. He repeated the word in his mind while he waited for a response.

"Well, I am sure it's very serious to her. She has gone through a break-up with her first boyfriend and is dealing with all the emotional baggage that goes along with that. As are we. The truth is, it was very traumatic and the guy didn't handle the situation with much finesse. Poor girl. And poor parents! It has been an interesting week." Marc said.

"To say the least, Daddy." Jillian walked into the kitchen and over to the counter where Stephen had pulled up a stool.

"I have decided to survive after all, and to forgive and forget. Mostly forget. I'm sure my humiliation will go down in the yearbook as *The Girl with The Most Public Breakup* or something like that. Anyway, you will all be happy to know that I am fine. Or, I think I am. At least, through this dinner." As Jillian caught Stephen's eye, her expression darkened for a split second before she turned away to put ice in her glass.

"Well, then, we shall toast to bygones and all that. To a successful year ahead for all of us."

Marc raised his glass and they all followed suit. No one but Stephen noticed the look of confusion that had briefly crossed Jillian's brow. And no one but Stephen noticed that her hand shook slightly as she poured water into her glass. *Research.*

*   *   *

Jillian excused herself immediately after dinner, before her mother even had a chance to bring out dessert. She had made it through the whole evening without once humiliating herself. She told the truth. She was determined to be over Jamie, whether she was over him or not. The only way she could face her friends and the people at school this fall was to act as though she didn't care. She was almost glad they had company tonight. That way, at least her parents weren't watching her every move at the dinner table, waiting to see if she was going to flip out again.

She thought Stephen was kind of funny. And he was really handsome. Part of the night was boring when they talked about dissertations and lectures, but thank God she had been able to get away before they went into her dad's study to really talk. She had been around these dinners long enough to know that it was going to be a long night.

She liked hearing about his big family and Canada. The Macomb's had gone to the Canadian side of Niagara Falls on vacation once. They had pictures around here someplace. She was only five or something, so she really couldn't remember that much about it besides the waterfall. And the tunnel to Canada. She loved the way the green tiles on the walls went on for miles. She could still remember the echo of the horns and the cars that swooshed past. Her dad had patiently tried to explain to her that they were driving under the water, but she didn't get it.

When she first saw Stephen tonight, she was a little freaked out. He reminded her of someone she thought she knew. But the first time they met was for five minutes last weekend at the reception. It was strange, like walking into a room and knowing you were there before. It just seemed weird, that's all. It was the same feeling she got when she woke up from one of her dreams. It was scary, like something was going to happen and she had no way to stop it. She recognized his voice from somewhere. It made her feel safe. That was weird, too. Her mom would have a field day if she knew what she was thinking. No way was she going to spill those beans. They were watching her close enough as it was.

Jillian stretched and went into her bathroom to get ready for bed. She was supposed to call Evie, but she really didn't feel like talking to her now. Her head hurt and she had to pee. She was glad this week was over. She knew she had to go see Dr. Richards on Monday for a physical. Maybe she would ask her about being so tired and having to pee all the time, and the dreams.

Well, maybe not the dreams. She wasn't sure about that. But she just wanted to know she didn't have some killer disease that was affecting her brain. Pushing the power button on her iPod, she pulled back the covers and crawled into bed. She heard them talking downstairs and then her dad laughed out loud. It was a good sound. She closed her eyes and let the sound of her father's happiness carry her off to sleep.

Chapter Thirteen

Hi, Jillian. How are you? We are running a little behind schedule this morning, so have a seat and we'll be out to get you as soon as we can." Dr. Richard's nurse smiled at her when she signed in and Jillian tried to smile back, but her mouth felt numb, like she just had a shot of Novocain at the dentist's office.

Sara had dropped her off in front of the medical building because they were running late for the appointment. Her mom wanted to run up to her own office on the fourth floor for an hour to deal with messages and to grab some files to work on at home, so Jillian went alone to Dr. Richard's office to sign in. Thank God for that. At least her mom agreed she could have her physical in private. She was supposed to let the front desk know that Sara would be there shortly and would be in the waiting room when they were finished.

Jillian picked up a magazine and started thumbing through it. She glanced up when the outer door opened and watched idly as an old woman came hobbling into the office, bent double over her cane. Boy, was she ever old. She didn't sign in at the reception desk...she just slowly shuffled over to the empty waiting area and sat right next to Jillian.

Dear Lord, Jillian thought.

A whole empty waiting room and she sits next to me. Right next to me.

Jillian tried not to appear rude as she once again picked up the magazine and turned slightly away from the woman to read.

"You're worried about it." The old woman leaned over to Jillian and spoke in a whisper. She had a tissue in her hand and wiped the corners of her mouth after she spoke.

"Excuse me, ma'am?" Jillian could not believe her luck. The lady wanted to talk. And she didn't appear to have teeth. She tossed her magazine back on the table and turned to face the elderly woman.

"I'm sorry, ma'am, I didn't hear you."

"You don't have to worry about any of this. Everything is as it should be. It is written, you know. You can't keep pushing it away. Don't fight destiny, dear. You are the chosen one. You have been blessed by God."

The woman put her bony hand on Jillian's arm and leaned even closer.

"I'm sorry, ma'am?" Jillian tried to lean away, but the woman's bony hand tightened on her arm, her frail appearance belied her strength.

"I think you have me mixed up with someone else. I mean, are you supposed to meet someone here? Do you want me to ask the receptionist?" Jillian said.

She tried to move her arm from the woman's talon-like grip and was trying hard not to freak out. She thought the woman might have escaped from the nursing home across the street. She was old enough, that was for sure. Jillian looked over toward the reception desk, but there was no one there. Of course, that was her luck, as usual.

Jillian didn't think it was possible, but the woman leaned even closer.

"Do not be afraid of the child. You have been chosen. Believe with all your heart that this is right and meant to be. Trust your protector. Open your mind and the prophecy will be fulfilled." The old woman spoke with urgency.

"Let me just get you some help, okay?" Jillian tried to get up, but she couldn't move. The woman's hand was on her shoulder now, bearing down.

"Okay, now, ma'am, you're scaring me a little bit. You don't know me. You think I'm someone else. I promise I don't know you. I can get help for you, but you have to let me get up."

"It was written in the beginning and will soon come to pass." The old woman was shaking her, scaring her. Jillian desperately tried to pull away, tried to stand up.

"Someone, please. Help over here!" Jillian tried to yell.

*   *   *

"Jillian. Jillian. Wake up." Dr. Richard's nurse, Linda, stood over her, gently trying to wake her up.

"NO!" Jillian fought against the hand that was shaking her.

"Where is she, where is that old woman?" She was groggy and struggling to wake up. She tried hard to remember everything the woman said. But none of it made any sense.

"Jill, honey, there is no one here. You must have been dreaming. Wake up, sweetie. That was some dream you were having. Come on. Let's get you into the room." The nurse offered her a hand, but Jillian waved her off.

"No, I'm okay. You're right. I must have been dreaming." Jillian got up slowly.

She didn't want to argue with Dr. Richard's nurse, but knew she hadn't been asleep and it was no dream. Following Linda toward the exam area, she glanced back toward the empty chairs. On the floor, under the chair where the old woman had been sitting, was the tissue she'd used to wipe her mouth.

"I swear she was really here."

Chapter Fourteen

Okay, girl, hop up on the scale and let's get your weight." Jillian kicked off her sandals and watched as Linda adjusted the counter weight on the arm of the scale.

"Good girl. Come on into the room and we'll get your blood pressure and temp." Linda said.

Jillian sat patiently on the edge of the paper covered exam table and felt the Velcro band around her arm tighten and release. She watched the nurse pick up a clear plastic cup from the counter and write her name and the date across the top in blue marker.

"Jillian, I want you to go into the bathroom and pee in this little cup. As soon as you're finished, open the silver door next to the toilet and set the cup inside. Then come on back to the room and get undressed. You can leave your bra and panties on. Here is a beautiful designer gown and some footies for you if your feet are cold. As soon as you're ready, push the green button and Dr. Richards will be in to check you out." Linda finished entering information into the laptop and turned to leave the room.

"I thought this was just a school physical?" Jillian reached for the gown. "You want me to pee in this? You're kidding, right," she asked, as she took the cup from Linda.

"Jill, you're seventeen now and Dr. Richards ordered a full blown checkup for you. It won't be so bad. She'll be here in a few minutes, so hop to it."

Sitting on the edge of the exam table, Jillian pulled the gown back over her shoulder after it slid down for the tenth time. She couldn't remember what nurse Linda told her. Open in front, or open in back? She settled for front because it was easier to manage. The paper on the table crinkled every time she moved and she was moving a lot. She had to remember to thank her mom for making this humiliating appointment for her. When she told her it was a complete check-up, she didn't know it was going to be this complete. She heard her chart pulled from the plastic file pocket mounted on the wall outside the room. A soft knock and the door slowly opened.

"Are you ready? Hey, Jillian. How is one of my favorite patients?" Julie Richards was always cheerful, generally putting people at ease within five minutes of meeting them. She had been the attending physician on call the night Jillian was born and had been their family doctor from that day forward. Jillian had grown up with her and really liked her, but that did little to ease her embarrassment now.

Standing at the small stainless sink, Dr. Richards lathered her hands and rinsed them before grabbing a paper towel and turning toward Jillian.

"You know I talked to your mom? She's worried about you. Do you want me to pretend she didn't tell me her concerns, or do you want me to share them with you before you tell me what's really going on?"

How could anyone not like such a straight shooter? Dr. Richards always laid it out there, straight up. That's why it was so easy to trust her.

"Okay, for one thing, I am sitting here almost naked under this gown. I'm embarrassed and grossed out because I had to pee in this tiny little cup, or at least I tried to, which, by the way, was a total disaster. And there was this little old woman in the waiting room who totally creeped me out. But, of course, no one else saw her and that creeps me out even more."

Julie Richards smiled as she sat on a little stool with wheels and pulled herself over to the laptop. She looked at the chart and compared notes with the computer.

"I'm sorry about that, Jill. I would say it was probably one of Dr. Mitchell's patients, but he isn't here today. It could be someone who just wandered into the wrong office. It happens a lot in this building."

"Well, she thought she knew me and she grabbed my arm. I was really nervous"

"I'm sorry, Jillian. I'll talk to MaryAnn up front about it when we finish up. Okay?"

Jillian nodded.

"Fair enough. Listen, you are seventeen now. It is always a good idea to start with a baseline exam when you are this age, so we have something to use as a comparison when you start coming every year for a gynecological exam, which is only another year away. Your mom says you're tired a lot. She also said you're restless at night. Bad dreams? You just had a major breakup with your first boyfriend, but the tiredness and dreams started well before that. How am I doing so far?"

"Fine. My mom doesn't miss anything. But listen, I want to know if we can talk just between you and me. I mean, if I tell you some things that I'm worried about, do you have to tell my mom? I don't want her to go all psychologist on me"

"Jillian, listen. I will not tell your mom anything you tell me here, but if it is a matter that concerns your health, we will need to talk about that and decide together if it's something we need to discuss with your parents. I know you think your mom and dad are overprotective, but as parents go, they don't seem too bad. Are your mom's concern's justified?"

"Sort of. I mean yes. I am tired a lot and I do have dreams. But sometimes I think they are more than that. I think I might be crazy, or have a brain tumor or something. I mean, I dream the same things over and over. Sometimes, even when I'm awake, I'll be doing something or meet someone, and feel like I have been through the same thing before in my dreams. No wonder Jamie dumped me. I think he thought I was crazy, too." Jillian was agitated and wrapped her arms around her waist, rocking as she talked to the doctor.

"And, I have to pee all the time. All the time. It's so annoying."

"First of all, I doubt you are crazy. A lot of people dream. It is your mind's way of releasing energy and stress when something is bothering you during your waking hours. You may not even realize something is bothering you. Listen, your grades were good last semester, but you had a rough spot with your boyfriend. High school is hard, Jillian. Let's take a look and see what we come up with medically, before you check yourself into the psychiatric ward."

Dr. Richards pushed a buzzer and Linda came back into the room.

"Linda, I am going to need a draw. Let's get a full blood screen so we can send this girl on to her senior year with a clean bill of health. I'll do the exam first, and then you can go and get the draw kit."

Linda stood in the corner of the exam room with the chart.

"Okay, Jill, let's take a listen to the heart and lungs. Sorry, I know it's cold. I'll try to warm it up."

Dr. Richards held the stethoscope in her clasped hand for a minute, before moving it over her young patient's body to listen to the very normal rhythm of her heart and lungs.

"Everything sounds great in there. Okay, now I need you to lay down and put your arms over your head. I am going to do a breast exam. I will be palpating the tissue to see if I feel any lumps or bumps that are out of the ordinary." Julie Richards gently pressed her fingertips into the teen's flesh.

"Ouch. That hurts." Jillian squirmed and shrunk back, the tissue of her breasts painful to the touch.

"Sorry. Are your breasts always that sensitive, Jillian?" Julie made a mental note to document the tenderness in the chart.

"I don't know. I guess so. At least before my period."

"Everything feels normal. Okay, now I am going to do the same thing to your abdomen. This helps me make sure there are no obvious abnormalities in your reproductive system. And it's also one of the reasons we have you give us a urine sample before the exam. Your bladder is down here with your uterus and your ovaries. If a bladder infection is causing the frequent urination, we'll find out from the sample you gave us. This may be a little uncomfortable, so bear with me."

Dr. Richards frowned as she palpated Jillian's abdomen. She could feel the hard smooth outline of the uterine fundus above Jill's pubic bone, and closing her eyes, she paused for a moment before she moved on.

"What's wrong? Is something wrong?" Jillian propped herself up on her elbows.

"Nothing is wrong, Jillian. Listen, I want you to scoot down here so your bum is at the edge of the table. Let's put your feet in the stirrups here." Dr. Richards helped guide her young patient.

"Okay, Jill, I'm going to do an internal exam. I know you weren't expecting this, but I feel it's necessary. Do you want to talk to your mom first, or wait until she gets here? She can certainly be here with you if that would make you more at ease."

"No. I'm okay. Do you think there is something wrong with me?"

"No, I really don't. But I want to be thorough, and this is the only way I can make sure I have examined you completely. This may be just a little uncomfortable, but I promise I'm almost finished. How about if Linda holds your hand? Ready?" Jill nodded and squeezed her eyes shut as Dr. Richards completed the exam.

"How are you doing?"

"Is everything okay? Do I have a bladder infection?" Jillian asked.

"Done." Peeling off the exam gloves and moving the light away from the exam table, Dr. Richards turned to the nurse.

"Linda, I'm going to talk to Jill for a few minutes and when I'm finished I am going to want you to draw her blood. And check with the girls over in ultrasound to see if they have a room available in about fifteen minutes."

"You got it." Linda turned and left the room, closing the door behind her.

Turning back to Jillian, Dr. Richards reached for her hand to help her sit up. "Let's talk."

Chapter Fifteen

Jillian, let's chat about your symptoms. Besides being tired, you said you're urinating frequently. Anything else? Is your period regular? Are you nauseous?"

Jillian pulled the gown around her shoulders and looked Dr. Richards in the eye. "I guess it is. I know I'm supposed to keep track, but I forget. I never have been really regular so it doesn't always come around when I think it should. I can mostly tell I'm going to start by how I feel. That's all, really. Except for the dreams. Did you find something wrong with me?"

"I don't think you have a strange illness. In fact, I think you are normal in every way. We'll get the results of the blood tests in a few days, but the urinalysis results should be ready in a few minutes. That will give us more information, but I need to ask you a few more questions."

Julie Richards pulled the stool over closer to the exam table and sat down near Jillian.

"Jillian, everything we talk about here is confidential so you don't have to worry that I am going to report back to your mom and dad. How long has this been going on? I mean the tiredness and the dreams."

"A couple of months. I think maybe March, because it was right before Easter when I noticed I was tired after school and couldn't wait to get home and lay down. I didn't even care too much about spring break."

"Okay. Are you on any kind of birth control?"

"NO!" Jillian turned bright red and instinctively lowered her head and averted her eyes in embarrassment. "I never had... I mean, I never did... what I mean is...I don't... I never had sex."

Jillian fingered her necklace and looked directly at Dr. Richards, trying to keep unshed tears from rolling down her cheeks.

"I think that's why Jamie broke up with me. I promised myself I would wait until I got married and he didn't understand that. He hated it."

"Jillian, have you maybe experimented with anything sexually besides intercourse? Some teenagers think that other forms of sexual play are not technically having sex. It is important that I know the truth, Jill, so I can better understand what is going on with you."

"I know what the other kids do. Just because I said I was waiting doesn't mean I don't know about those things. I mean, I just don't get it. What's the point? Some of the girls talk about the things they do, and say how much they love their boyfriends, but then it's over before you know it. They break up and they move on to the next guy and the next. I just think there has to be more to it than that. I mean, don't get me wrong, Dr. Richards, I am not a goody two shoes. I am not saying that I don't want to do things, because sometimes I do. I just haven't yet. Am I behind schedule or something?"

Julie Richards smiled and studied her young patient.

"No, Jillian. You are not behind schedule. What about drugs and alcohol? Have you tried any drugs or have you ever been to a party where you can't remember everything that happened during the evening...or even afterwards?"

"Dr. Richards. Remember my dad? He's a professor at the Divinity School. I would never do that. And not just because of him. I don't want to take drugs or smoke, and I am not having sex before I get married. I am not the only girl who wants to wait for sex. I made these choices for myself and I knew what I was choosing. I thought about it. I believe in waiting. Here...I wear the purity ring on my necklace." Jillian pulled the chain up to eye level so Julie could see it clearly.

"I know you have to ask people this stuff all the time, but I'm really pretty boring. Well, maybe only a little bit boring. At least about all this stuff."

"Jill, I think... "

Both looked up at the sound of knocking, and the exam room door opened a crack. Linda poked her head into the room.

"I have the girls setting up for you in ultrasound. Are you ready for me to draw blood?"

Dr. Richards stood. "Yes, I think we are ready. Okay, girl. Linda will draw your blood and then she will walk you down the hallway to the ultrasound lab. Ultrasound will let us take a peek at what's going on inside of you. You've seen an x-ray before. It's sort of like that, but we can see the results while we are doing the exam. It's really kind of neat! We can see your organs and make sure everything is where it's supposed to be. It doesn't hurt a bit and I will be right there with you. See you in a minute."

Julie Richards walked into the hallway and made her way through the nurse's station and over to the lab. Jillian Macomb seemed sincere, and every professional instinct she possessed told her that the girl believed every single thing she said. Still, she worried that possibly Jillian didn't know enough about what she didn't know, to know she didn't know it.

"MaryAnn, did Mrs. Macomb say when she would be here to meet Jill?" Dr. Richards asked the receptionist as she was filing charts from a rack in the hallway.

"She called a little while ago to let Jillian know she would be here in about thirty minutes. That was at least a half hour ago. She should be here any minute, now."

"Okay. When she gets here, have her wait in my office. We're almost finished, and then I am going to want to talk to her." Dr. Richards picked up the results of Jill's urinalysis and walked down the hall toward the ultrasound room.

* * *

The ultrasound room itself was small and subtly lit, in stark contrast to the rest of the office, and looked almost like a bedroom, except for the equipment next to the exam table. There was a linen sheet on the exam table and a real pillowcase on the pillow. No noisy paper covers here.

Dr. Richards touched Jillian's shoulder lightly.

"Okay, Jillian, let's get started. Lay on your back. This is Tracy. She's our ultrasound tech. She is going to squirt some of this gel on your belly. Don't worry. It's nice and warm. Kind of squishy, but warm," said Dr. Richards.

"Gross. It feels gooey." Jillian watched with interest as the girl pulled the monitor over and turned it toward the bed. It was dark in the room, but she noticed that Tracy was pretty. She winked at Jillian as she helped her get settled in.

"Yes, it is kind of gooey, but it will help us get a good picture of what is going on inside your body right now. This is called a probe. It takes a picture through your skin and will send it up to the monitor here so we can see it. We can also print pictures of what we see." Tracy explained everything to Jillian as she was going through the set-up procedures.

Jillian just wanted to get all this over with so she could go home and forget about everything for a while. That old woman had freaked her out and she couldn't forget the gibberish she mumbled to her. She was still spooked, but no one else seemed to be the least bit concerned that a crazy woman was out in the waiting room, spouting nonsense and scaring their patients half to death.

But this part was okay, she guessed. At least it didn't hurt, not like the blood work. Her arm was still stinging where Linda had poked her. And she had to poke twice. She said she couldn't find a vein the first time. But then she finally did find one and Jill watched as her own dark red blood bubbled up inside three tubes.

"Okay, here we go." Tracy said.

She started to move the probe around on her belly. Jillian frowned as she watched the screen. She expected it to be a clear picture, like turning on the television. It looked more like the television set at Grammy and Gramps' house before they got cable and they used to put tinfoil on top of the antennae. They called them rabbit ears. Jillian thought that was so funny when she was little. Rabbit ears.

She was feeling a little nervous anyway, even if it didn't hurt. She was afraid Dr. Richards thought there was something terribly wrong.

She could tell by the way she checked her. All the pushing and poking. What was that all about? And all the questions she asked. Jillian guessed that when you were seventeen, they almost expected you to be having sex. You couldn't get a disease from just wanting to have sex, could you? Really, how ridiculous was that? Well, she supposed they would find out soon enough.

"Tracy, focus on the bladder and the uterus, please." Dr. Richards hovered close to the monitor.

Jillian kept her eyes on the screen as Tracy maneuvered the wand through the warm gel. "What is all that stuff? How can you tell what anything is? What is that black space? Do I have a tumor?" Jillian asked.

Now she was getting worried. It was hard to look at all those shadows and not think that something dangerous was lurking inside her belly.

Tracy poised the probe above Jillian's uterus and glanced quickly at Dr. Richards.

"Tracy, would you excuse us for a moment? I'll call you back to finish up in a minute. Thanks."

Julie Richards walked to the door as Tracy left the room and pushed it closed. Pausing for a moment, she leaned her forehead against the door, and then turned slowly, taking time to think carefully before she spoke.

"Okay, Jill, first of all, you are perfectly fine. There is nothing wrong with you. No disease. We are going to talk about what I see on the ultrasound for a minute, and then I'll answer your questions."

Walking over to the monitor's screen, she pointed to the images.

"I am going to point some things out to you. See this dark shadow here? That is your bladder. Looks like a normal everyday bladder. Nothing out of the ordinary that I can see, and I suspect your urine has come back clear. I have the results in your chart and I'll check them out later. Now, see this larger black space as you called it. That is your uterus. See how it is pushing against the smaller dark space of your bladder? That is why you have to go to the bathroom so often."

"So, why is it there and what do we have to do to get if off my bladder?"

Julie picked up a pen that Tracy left behind on the cart.

"See this little white shadow, Jillian, inside the larger black space? That is called a fetus. A baby. This is the baby's head. See the arms and the legs? That little flicker is the heartbeat. And when Tracy comes back in and turns the probe back on, you will be able to see it move. Judging by its size and developmental stage right now, I would guess you are thirteen to fourteen weeks pregnant."

Jillian scrambled to sit up, pushing the sheet to the floor. She couldn't breathe. Why couldn't she breathe? She tried to speak, but no words would come. She heard herself moaning, keening. This was a horrible mistake. This was a dream, a nightmare. Another nightmare. Like the old woman, and the dream before that and the dream before that.

Looking at the screen, she saw nothing but shapes and blobs that were black and grey and white. There was no baby there. There couldn't be a baby there. You had to have sex to make a baby. You had to at least see a penis, or touch a penis, to make a baby.

"*No- no- no- no- no- no- NO!* It's not possible. You are wrong. Do your test again. That is not a baby. I can't be pregnant. You have to have sex to be pregnant. I AM NOT LYING TO YOU. A baby can't just show up inside of you for no reason at all. *MOM.* I want my mom."

Jillian lay back down and turned to face the wall, curling into a fetal position, much like the child in her womb.

Julie Richards reached for the call button and Tracy quickly opened the door to the ultrasound room.

"Tracy, I need Linda to go to my office and bring Mrs. Macomb back here now."

Julie tried to comfort Jillian, pushing the hair from her face and touching her softly on the cheek.

"It's okay, Jill. Calm down. Your mom is on her way, sweetie." Dr. Richards held the trembling girl and talked softly, trying to reassure the frightened teenager.

"Jillian, it will all work out, you'll see. We will all figure this out together."

The door burst open and Sara Macomb rushed in, trying to make sense of the scene in front of her.

"What's wrong, honey? What's going on?" Sara's concerned voice filled the tiny room.

Hurrying to her daughter's side, she took Julie's place next to Jillian and held her little girl, rocking her gently back and forth. But she wasn't looking at Jillian. She couldn't tear her eyes from the monitor. She was staring at the unmistakable ultrasound image of a baby.

Chapter Sixteen

She's asleep." Sara closed the study door and went over to the window where Marc stood trancelike, staring into the moonlit yard.

He didn't say anything, but reached out and drew her into his arms, and bending low, buried his face in her hair and inhaled deeply, trying to draw comfort from her sweet familiar scent. The numbness slowly receded and though the shock remained, he knew they had to talk, to try and make sense of what was happening.

"Did she talk to you? Say anything at all to explain what's going on?" Marc asked.

"She's in denial. She won't say anything, except to repeat over and over that she's never had sex. She swears that Jamie is not the father. She claims she has no idea how she could be pregnant."

Sara leaned against Marc, the headache that had been threatening all afternoon, finally exploding behind her eyes.

"She thinks she is going crazy and rambles on and on about the dreams and some old woman she saw at Julie's office. I don't know what to think, Marc. Julie suggested we give her a few days to come to terms with everything. She wants to see her before the weekend to do a full prenatal check. Jillian was so upset, it was impossible to even think about doing it today."

Turning from the window, Marc moved toward his desk like a sleepwalker and reached down for the ultrasound image. Turning it over in his hand, he looked at his wife.

"I don't know what to think, Sara. I don't know what to feel. I can't fathom this. I can't understand how we would not have known, seen signs. Jillian is, or at least I always saw her as, the most open and responsive teenager I know. Has she ever given us reason to think she was experimenting with sex? She's too smart for something like this to happen."

"Listen, Marc, it's not just you. I'm confused, too. She is so adamant, insisting that she's still a virgin. I feel like we are living inside one of her nightmares. Do you think she really could be having a mental break-down?" Sara asked.

"No, honey, I don't."

"I am way too close to the situation to even try to evaluate this. I keep going over and over the last few months. I can attribute the tiredness to so many things…the last few months of school, exams, a boyfriend. I feel as if I've failed her. I'm a damn psychologist, Marc. I should have seen something." Sara sank into the armchair in the corner of Marc's office, tears flowing unchecked down her cheeks.

"Sara, you have to listen to me. We are not playing the blame game. This happens in a lot of families and it is not a failure on anyone's part. We're in shock right now, that's all. We have to give this time to sink in."

"It's hard, Marc."

"We are going to have to talk about Jamie, though. I am trying really hard to control myself, but I actually want to rip his head off. We need to talk to Jillian again. Do you think he broke up with her because she is pregnant?"

"No. That's just it. I don't think Jill ever knew she was pregnant. You should have seen her, Marc. She was inconsolable and almost primal with grief. She kept begging Julie over and over to take the test again. It couldn't be a baby. She never had sex. There had to be a mistake. Julie Richards didn't expect that reaction, I'm sure. It took both of us over an hour to calm her down enough to get her into the car to come home. Julie had to clear out her office and cancel the rest of her patients. It was hor-rible." Resting her forehead on the palms of her hands, Sara felt her throat constrict with the pain of trying to speak.

"God, I am so sorry you had to go through that alone."

"It's not your fault. I couldn't leave her for a second, not even to call you. All I could think was that I had to get her home. Julie Richards was a huge help in sorting things out. When she offered to call your office for me, I was relieved."

"Yes, I'm sure you were. Although, it was a long ride home for me, not knowing what the 'urgent' situation was. She said something like 'It's not life or death, but you need to go home now, Marc.' At least I think that was how she put it."

Marc walked over to the window.

"Damn. It's so much more than her being pregnant. This is our grandchild. A new life. All of our plans for our daughter's future have changed in one day. We have to make sure she knows we support her. We will figure out a way to make this work, because if I believe anything, it is that God has a plan for this family. We have to have faith and the rest will work out," Marc said.

"I'm a little upset at God right now." Sara hugged the throw pillow to her chest.

"Honey, it is going to be alright. We can't lose faith. I'm just not sure how we should handle the rest of it."

"You mean Jamie? I don't know, Marc. It's kind of hard to call him on the carpet, when Jillian won't even admit he's the father of her child. I think we need to take a deep breath and let our emotions settle. I don't trust either of us to confront him right now. And the relationship did not end on a very good note."

"Don't even remind me how that little bastard broke up with our daughter. Let's see how she is in the morning and we'll talk to her again. We are going to have to call Jamie's parents and meet with them. If Jamie is the father, they have a right to know. Their lives are about to change, too, even if they don't realize it yet. He is going to have to take some responsibility for this." Pacing now, Marc felt like a caged animal, not sure which direction to take in the tiny room.

"We need to stay calm. We also have to be realistic. What if Jamie is not the father? What if someone slipped her a date rape drug and she is not even aware of what happened. Julie pointed that out as a possibility. She said it happens often enough and there is no way to trace the drug in someone's system after several hours. Jillian may not even be aware of how this happened to her. She may honestly believe what she is saying. We would have no way to know. Maybe there's someone else in the picture that we're not even aware of," Sara said.

"This is our Jillian we are talking about." Marc threw the ultrasound picture back on the desk and pounded his fist against the wall above the fireplace.

"I know that. But Jillian is not acting like our Jillian right now and I'm scared." Sara forced herself from the chair and walked sadly toward the door.

She looked over her shoulder at her angry husband as she was leaving the room, but she was too exhausted to help him calm down.

"We may have to accept the fact that we really don't know our daughter at all," she said.

Marc did not look up.

"Go to bed, Sara. I'm going to stay down here for a while and pray for guidance."

"You do that, Marc. Pray for us all." Sara turned and left the room.

Chapter Seventeen

Julie Richards squeezed her car expertly into the private parking space behind her office. John Mitchell's silver Camry was already parked haphazardly across two of the spaces next to hers. She smiled and shook her head at his obvious lack of precision when it came to parking his car. And this from an OB/GYN who, by all accounts, was considered to be an expert in his field. Absent minded professor was a term that came easily to mind when Julie thought of the illustrious Dr. Mitchell.

Walking around to the passenger door, she reached in and grabbed Jillian Macomb's file from the seat. Balancing her briefcase, the file and a much too expensive cup of coffee from the coffee house down the street, she fumbled with her keys and managed to unlock the back door of the building without dropping anything. Walking through the back hallway, she poked her head into John's cluttered office.

"Hey, John, how was the day off?"

"Ha. I worked on the kitchen all day yesterday and if you can believe it, I feel like I have more to do now than when I started. This was supposed to be a labor of love. I am ready for the love part to start."

John Mitchell had bought an old Victorian house in Nashville and spent months gutting the previous owner's amateur update, painstakingly beginning the restoration process and hoping someday to return the house to its original glory.

"Keep up the good work, Dr. Mitchell. It will all be worth it in the end."

Julie unlocked the door to her private office and dropped everything onto her desk. Carefully taking a sip of the hot coffee, she walked over to the window, opened the blinds and looked out onto the courtyard. She had spent all night worrying about Jillian. The Macomb's had been patients and friends for over 20 years. She knew this was an agonizing situation for them.

She had never had a patient in such a state of denial as Jillian was yesterday. Her conviction was strong and Julie had no reason to doubt that Jill believed with all her heart that she had never broken her vow of chastity. So now, the question seemed to be, what next? In her present emotional state, they had to tread carefully. The ultrasound showed a normally developed fetus at approximately fourteen weeks gestation. That meant conception had occurred around the middle to the end of March, which was about the time Jillian first complained about the fatigue. That would make her due date around the first or second week of December, if Julie's calculations were correct.

On Tuesdays, appointments were usually booked only in the afternoon. Normally, she saw her first patient at one thirty, but today a few of the appointments cancelled yesterday had been rescheduled for later this morning. It was only a few minutes past seven. She had at least three hours to tackle the paperwork that had accumulated on the corner of her desk.

Linda had set the results of Jillian Macomb's quantitative HCG test on top of the pile. She had affixed a little blue sticky note to the top of the report with a bold question mark drawn in black marker. Mentally calculating that the HCG levels in the blood typically climb every day within the first trimester of a pregnancy, Julie would expect that Jillian should have levels well above fifteen thousand, judging by the development and measurement of the fetus in the ultrasound. Picking up the lab report, she started reading.

"What the hell?" Julie turned the lab slip over to make sure she was looking at results for the right patient. Jumping up from her desk chair, she rushed out of her office and across the hall to the lab. Both lab techs looked up as she pushed through the door.

"Who ran the HCG levels on Macomb yesterday?" Julie asked.

Kathy looked up from the tray of slides she was preparing and nodded her head toward Angie.

Angie answered at the same time.

"I ran that one. I told Linda I had concerns about the results. There was no detectable HCG in the quantitative sample. That patient is most definitely not pregnant. Or if she is pregnant, she's not far enough along in her pregnancy to register."

"Angie, I saw a very active fourteen week fetus on the ultrasound screen myself. I heard a very healthy heartbeat. Somewhere along the line yesterday, her results got mixed up with someone else. There was so much confusion in the afternoon. Please re-run the test now, and bring me the results ASAP."

"You got it, Doc. I can have it for you in about two hours, give or take."

"Good. I'm going to bring her back in for a prenatal visit and we can do a follow-up then if we need to. But these numbers most certainly do not belong to Jillian Macomb." Julie waved the yellow printout of the lab slip at the girls as she backed out the door.

"Trouble in paradise?" Dr. Mitchell threw a chart in the tray as Julie walked out of the lab.

"Only a little cloud cover." Julie smiled at him as she went back to her office to tackle her morning. Taking a sip from her now lukewarm coffee, she reached for Jillian's file and once again began to study the chart. Angie knocked and walking into the office, slid the second set of results on the desk in front of her.

"Crap." Julie slammed the second report back onto the desk. Glancing up quickly at the walnut clock, she figured that John Mitchell should be just about finished with his last morning patient. She could sure use some of his unbiased expertise right about now. She pushed the call button for John's nurse.

"Karen, is Dr. Mitchell with a patient? What does he have scheduled after that? Okay, when he is finished will you have him come to my office? Thanks."

Picking up the phone, she dialed the Macomb's home number.

"Hi, Sara, this is Julie Richards. How is Jillian this morning? Okay, I don't want to upset her, but when she wakes up, I need to run another blood test. You can come by the office anytime. She doesn't have to see me today. We can wait until Friday for the prenatal visit and give her a chance to let everything sink in, but I would like this new test run today."

The green light on the wall next to Julie's desk was blinking, indicating her first patient was gowned and ready for her.

"Noon would be fine. I'll let the lab know you're coming in. No, everything is okay. We didn't get results for one of the tests we usually run in house, and I'd like to have them before her appointment on Friday. We should have the rest of her test results by that time, too. Thanks, Sara. Are you and Marc okay? I know. Just try to hang in there and I will see you then. Call me if you need anything."

Julie took her lab coat off the hanger. Looking back toward her desk, she noticed with a frown that the pile of paperwork was still waiting for her attention. Her rendezvous with John would have to wait. Damn. Only Tuesday and it already felt like one heck of a long week.

Chapter Eighteen

The line for burgers was probably the longest one in the Campus Commons area, but Stephen didn't care. Grabbing an orange plastic tray from the end of the counter, he drifted over to the end of the assembly line. He was hungry and in the mood for greasy American junk food and the day had already proved too long and confusing to make one more decision, even if it was only a decision as simple as what to have for dinner.

He had been in the middle of a meeting with Dr. Macomb yesterday afternoon, when Marc took a personal phone call that had abruptly ended their planning session.

"Is she hurt? Okay, I'm on my way." Marc ended the call and quickly disengaged himself from their discussion.

"I have to go. You are more than capable of leading the fellowship portion of the meeting tomorrow night, Stephen. I should be available in the morning to go over revisions and any last minute questions you may have."

"Is everything okay, Dr. Macomb?" Stephen asked, as Marc grabbed his papers and jammed them into his briefcase.

"I'm not sure. I'll call you first thing in the morning to confirm a time for us to meet." Patting his pockets as he put on his jacket, Marc pulled out his keys and ran out the door.

Stephen hadn't heard from Dr. Macomb this morning. He asked around the Divinity School, but no one had spoken to him since he left the campus yesterday. Stephen had finally stopped checking for messages on his cell phone after lunch. He carried his tray to one of the small round tables that peppered the cafeteria and sat down. Summer session was in full swing, and though weekends were dead at the university, the weekdays were already bustling.

"Hey, Stephen, do you mind if I join you?" Arshad Ahmed sat down at the table before Stephen had a chance to acknowledge his question one way or the other. Like all the new fellows, he was eager to get the debates and discussions underway.

"Are you prepared for the meeting tonight?" Arshad asked.

"It is my understanding that it will be pretty informal tonight, sort of a religious rap session. And yes, as a matter of fact, I have several ideas for the year ahead, so I am looking forward to a meeting of the minds." Stephen stirred sweetener into his iced tea.

"Arshad, have you met Father Andrews from Holy Name Cathedral yet? I've only seen him celebrate mass on Sunday and I haven't had a chance to talk to him one on one. I understand he will be here for tonight's discussion."

"I haven't met the Catholic priest, but I hear he is ultra traditional. Four faculty, four practicing clergy, and first and second year fellows… this should be an interesting and lively debate and I, for one, can't wait." Arshad said.

Stephen finished his dinner and leaned back in the chair. He was tired today and, if last night was any indication, the dreams were not going to end anytime soon. If anything, they had become even more vivid and extraordinary. He yearned for one complete dream-free night of sleep.

"Arshad, have you by chance seen Dr. Macomb on campus today? I was supposed to meet with him this morning, but he wasn't in his office," Stephen didn't really expect an affirmative answer.

"I can't help you there, man. I have been chasing down Dr. Ranchalamun all day, so I get where you're coming from. Where do these guys disappear to?"

"It's a mystery. Well, I have to finish up a few things for tonight, so I guess I'll head over to the library. Catch you later."

Taking his tray to the conveyer belt, Stephen once again checked his phone for messages. None registered and no missed calls. Shoving the phone in his pocket, he couldn't help but wonder what had happened at the Macomb's. Whatever it was, it was enough to make the meticulous Dr. Marc Macomb fall off the face of the campus map. At least for today.

*   *   *

The lights from Divinity Hall spilled out onto the grassy common area. The night was warm and balmy and Stephen was optimistic about the coming year based on the attendees at tonight's meeting. All five fellows had been there, and the session had run well past the two hour allotment of time. Pushing chairs back in place and gathering used cups and discarded papers, the fellowship students, professors and clergy were gradually leaving the building and heading for home. Dr. Macomb had never shown up and Dean Smyth said only that it was something unavoidable that had kept him away.

Stephen was concerned and made a mental note to call the Macomb's house in the morning. He was gathering his notebooks when he noticed Father Andrews making his way to the vestibule of the building. Stuffing the last of his paperwork into his backpack, he hurried over to catch up with the departing priest.

"Father Andrews, it was so nice to meet you tonight. Stephen Jacobs, from Ontario." Stephen held out his hand to the robust Catholic priest. "I enjoyed the discussion tonight. I am looking forward to some lively debate this fall."

"Ah, yes, Stephen. Dr. Macomb speaks highly of you. Let me see if I remember … Early Christianity and New Testament?" Father Phillip Andrews took a handkerchief out of his back pocket and mopped the considerable amount of sweat from his brow.

"I am flattered that you remembered. I have been attending Sunday mass at the Cathedral for the last few weeks. You have quite a large congregation. I understand you have a contemporary service on Sunday evenings. I have always attended traditional services, but I'm very curious," said Stephen.

"Yes, well, the younger parishioners seem to enjoy it. A lot of waving of the hands and singing, drums, guitars… you name it. I suppose one must open one's mind in the twenty-first century. Anything to get the teenagers to embrace their faith, I suppose." Father Andrews sat on a folding chair in the vestibule of the Divinity Hall.

"Are you settling in, Stephen? I think it was a grand idea for the fellows to take up residence during the summer. You'll have a much better feel for the lay of the land when fall semester rolls around. Nashville is very interesting."

"I couldn't agree more. I've enjoyed meeting the fellowship students before classes officially start. Everyone seems anxious to get off the ground running this year. And I do enjoy Nashville. It is hot, though, compared to St Thomas. I have to admit I miss the lake."

"Yes, I imagine our lakes here in Tennessee do not compare favorably with the Great Lakes. Have you had a chance to spend time with Dr. Macomb and his family? They are wonderful people and very welcoming. It's too bad Marc had to miss this first meeting. I am sure Sara will have you entrenched in the Nashville social scene before you know it. Watch out for her…she has been known to have had her hand in quite a few weddings here in Nashville. You'd better watch your back," laughed the priest.

"I will be sure to turn up the radar. Father Andrews, I may call your office this week and schedule some time to talk with you about some personal matters. It's nothing major, but I'd like to talk through some things that are troubling me. Do you think your schedule will allow a few counseling sessions?"

"Call Rosemary at the church office tomorrow. I stopped carrying a day-timer long ago, since she always seems to rearrange my schedule, anyway. As long as she turns me around and points me in the right direction, I manage to show up exactly where I am supposed to be. I will be happy to meet with you. Nothing too serious, I hope?"

"No. I don't think so. I am just trying to work through a few things. I'd really appreciate your opinion. Well, it looks like everyone has packed up and gone home. So nice to meet you, Father. Let me walk you to your car." Stephen helped the priest from the chair and walked with him to the parking lot. "I think the year ahead will be very interesting."

Later, making his way to his apartment, Stephen let his mind wander to the dreams. He hoped the aging priest would be able to offer him insight and comfort. He felt that if he could just talk through everything, he would finally get rid of this preposterous idea that the dreams were premonitions of something in his future. Why on earth would he be the target of a prophecy?

Climbing the steps to his apartment, he decided that he was definitely going to call Rosemary in the morning to make that appointment with Father Andrews. He would also call Dr. Macomb if he wasn't back in his office by then.

Stephen opened the refrigerator and took out a beer. Settling on the sofa, he kicked off his shoes and grabbed the remote. Something strange was happening at the Macomb's. He could feel the weight of it settle in his own chest.

"Dear Heavenly Father…" Before he could fully formulate a prayer in his mind, he fell asleep, the reflection from the television splayed across the wall behind him.

Chapter Nineteen

It was already close to seven on Tuesday night when Julie unlocked the glass door of the lobby to meet Marc and Sara. Having sent the staff home after the last patient left at five thirty, they had the office to themselves.

"Hi. I'm sorry about the hour. I wanted a chance to have an uninterrupted meeting with you two and office hours just do not allow for that." Marc and Sara followed to the small conference room between Dr. Mitchell's office and hers.

"How is Jillian doing today?"

Marc ran his hand through his hair as he sat in one of the black leather chairs.

"I think she's okay. She is spending a lot of time in her room. She doesn't want to come out, or have a conversation, so it's hard to gauge how much of this has sunk in. I wonder how it is possible to be fourteen weeks pregnant and not have a clue." His anguish was palpable.

"When we left your office this afternoon, after the blood test, she stared out the window on the ride home and wouldn't say a word. I think she's waiting for you to tell her that this is all a huge mistake. I know she gave you permission to talk to us, Julie. Did she give you any insight at all?" Sara hated the pleading tone that crept into her voice, but found it increasingly difficult to keep up her guard with her friend.

"No. I wish I could say she had, but her stance was the same with me. No indication that she was sexually active or knew she was pregnant. But that's not the entire reason I wanted to see you tonight."

Julie reached down and pulled three bottled waters out of the under counter refrigerator. Handing each of them a bottle, she opened Jillian's file and pulled out the reports from the lab. She walked over to the window before she turned to face them.

"I have concerns about the results from her lab work. That's why I had you bring her in for the second blood test. Let me explain. Human chorionic gonadotropin, or HCG, is a hormone produced in pregnancy. I know you probably remember some of this from your own pregnancy, Sara. It's detectable in the urine, as well as in the blood, and it's what causes the positive response in a home pregnancy test. To measure the health of a pregnancy, we use a blood test for a quantitative reading of the hormone." Julie waited to make sure they understood and then continued.

"The actual levels are not as important as the fact that the levels continue to increase, because this hormone directly relates to the health of the placenta which nourishes the fetus. The levels in early pregnancy rise at a predictable rate and then toward the end of the pregnancy will begin to decline, returning to pre-pregnancy levels soon after delivery. I hope I'm not confusing you." Julie came back to the table and sat down.

"Typically at fourteen weeks gestation, I would expect the numbers to range from at least fifteen thousand to over two hundred thousand." Julie handed them each a copy of the results from all three of Jillian's tests.

Sara looked up from the report with some confusion. "Julie, can you explain? I'm not sure what I'm looking at. This report says negative for HCG. What does that mean?"

"It means that Jillian's tests showed no detectable HCG levels in her blood. None of the normal pregnancy indicators are present. It means that by all the scientific data available to me, her levels are incompatible with a viable pregnancy. Yet, we both saw a normal fetus on the ultrasound with a healthy heartbeat."

Marc stood up, leaning against the table. "What does that mean, Julie. Viable pregnancy? Is she pregnant or isn't she pregnant?"

"She is most positively pregnant. However, I am concerned about the possibility of miscarriage or some chromosomal abnormality. The results of her labs contradict what we saw on the ultrasound. I would like to admit her to the hospital for chorionic villus sampling or CVS. It is a procedure where we go in vaginally and remove a small sample of the placenta for further testing. There is a slight risk to the pregnancy, but at this point, I hesitate waiting three more weeks for an amniocentesis. Weeks we may not have, if the pregnancy is indeed at risk."

"Are you saying, that after all this, she may lose a baby she doesn't even believe she is carrying?" Marc asked.

"Yes. That is exactly what I am saying. Listen, your family has been through a horrible shock. I don't know how I would feel in your situation. But I am concerned about Jillian and the baby. The results of this test are crucial to ensuring the healthy continuation of her pregnancy. There is no way for me to predict the outcome without it. And because these results are so outside the norm, I have no reference from which to predict the possible risk for Jillian, either."

"Of course, she'll do it. How soon can we schedule it? How long before we'll have the results?" Sara asked.

"I would like to schedule her as soon as I can get her in. Possibly tomorrow. We should have the results in one to seven days. She'll have the test done as an outpatient at the hospital, and then we'll keep her for a couple hours after the test to monitor her for complications."

Marc reached for Sara's hand at the same time she reached to pick up her purse from the chair.

"Just let us know when you can get her in and we'll be there. I'm going to give you my business card, so you'll have my cell phone number with you. This has to be okay, Julie. She has to be okay. Do everything you can to keep her safe for us. Please." Sara handed Julie the card.

"You two know you can call me any time, day or night. I mean it. If she shows any signs of miscarriage or anything that you consider out of the ordinary, I want to hear from you. Immediately. Her physical exam was unremarkable, so I think we are okay for now."

"Unremarkable? Nothing about this situation has been unremark-able. All we can do is put this in God's hands and pray that everything works out. None of us can hope for more than that. Julie, thank you for your support. All three of us appreciate everything you're doing for us," Marc said.

"You two go home and try to get some rest tonight. I'll talk to you in the morning." Julie locked up behind them and watched from the doorway as they walked to their car.

The night was mild and muffled traffic could be heard in the distance. Students were still milling around, as it was only minutes after eight o'clock on a balmy summer evening. Before he opened the car door, Marc gathered his wife in his arms.

Pulling her even closer, he said, "I've never been so worried about anything, or felt as helpless as I do right now."

"I know, Marc. I'm frightened, too, of the unknown, the unthinkable. What are we going to say to Jillian? How do we explain this to her?"

Marc kissed the top of her head and bent to open the door.

"It is all going to work out. We stay strong in our faith and we will hold each other up through this. Jillian is stronger than we give her credit for. We have to believe that she will be fine."

"And the baby, Marc? What do we hope about the baby?" Sara looked over at him as he started the car.

"Before I formed thee in the belly I knew thee; and before thou camest forth out of the womb I sanctified thee, and I ordained thee a prophet unto the nations." Marc quoted the verse from Jeremiah 1:5, his voice catching on the last words.

"We have to trust God, Sara, and accept all of this. We have our faith. The outcome is in his hands. He will not let us down. We have to hold on to our faith. And pray."

"I know. I do accept it. And I have faith." Sara whispered. "But I don't have to like it."

Chapter Twenty

Jillian lay on the hammock in the backyard, swinging slowly, stretched between the old maple tree and the dogwood. She finally turned her face away from the house, knowing her parents kept peeking out the kitchen window. They may as well be sitting on the warm grass next to her. She had to plead with them to let her escape from her room or she would have gone stark raving crazy. She was ready to explode like the geyser that erupts when you shake a bottle of cola.

She felt like a human specimen under a microscope, waiting for someone else to zoom in on her. The test this morning was gross and even though it only took a few minutes, it seemed like forever. She couldn't wait to get out of that room at the hospital and into the car to go home.

"The only thing that hasn't been in my vagina is a penis!" she remarked when they finally did get into the car.

"*Jillian!*" Her parents responded in unison, which, looking back now, was almost worth every minute of the lecture that followed.

"Well, it's true. And you don't have to go advertising this to the whole world. If I am pregnant, which I don't see how I could be, it wasn't with Jamie, so you don't have to make a big deal out of this with his parents."

Sara swung around in the front seat until she was facing her daughter. "Jillian, if it wasn't Jamie, then who is the father? You don't just *get* pregnant."

"I told you before, a hundred times before, I did not have sex. This is crazy!"

"We are not angry, but we have to know. We are trying to understand you, but we need answers so we can make plans. Jamie and his family have a right to know. It is not just about the responsibility. What if all these tests show there is a problem with your pregnancy? What if Jamie and his family have the answers, or something you need for the sake of the baby? Your child, Jillian. You cannot keep pretending this is not happening." Her mom only stopped once to take a breath before she turned around to face the front.

Jillian caught her mother out the corner of her eye, as she gave her dad the *'say something'* glare.

"Jill, you know we love you. This has nothing to do with trust. We understand what it means to be young and faced with temptation. I teach college and see it in my students all the time, and your mom counsels people going through these situations every day." Marc finally spoke.

Oh great, here we go. Good cop, bad cop. Rolling her eyes, Jillian turned her head and looked out the car window. Watching the cars whiz by them on the interstate, Jillian fumed.

"I did not have sex with Jamie. I did not have sex with anyone. *I am still a virgin.* I don't know how this baby happened...*I DID NOT HAVE SEX!*"

"Jillian, you may as well know that I called the Tylers and they are coming over tomorrow to talk about the situation we find ourselves in. Jamie has to be aware before he leaves for college. None of us asked for this, Jill, but we have to deal with it. We aren't making you get married for God's sake, but we've got to have a plan. There are a lot of things to take into consideration." Once again, her mother turned to look at her, but Jillian closed her eyes and pretended to be asleep the rest of the way home.

According to the doctor, she was supposed to be lying down with her feet propped up higher than her heart, but she was finally able to persuade her parents it might be wiser to let her out of confinement for a few hours, rather than hear her moaning and groaning up in her room, and they finally agreed. So here she was, looking up through a lacy canopy of leaves, to the last bits of blue in the early evening sky. Her iPod was next to her in the grass playing something soft and dreamy. She let her mind wander.

She had seen the little blob again in the hospital. They had her hooked up to the monitor when they did their test. She had to admit that it really did look like a baby. Trying to keep her mind off the tube they had shoved up inside of her, she watched the little thing rolling around, clawing at her insides, looking for a way out. Boy, she knew the feeling. And regardless of what the nurses said when they were getting her ready for the assault, that test hurt. It wasn't just a little pinch, it hurt like hell.

Through a sleepy haze, she heard the phone ringing in the house. She was drowsy and the early summer breeze blew softly across her skin. She could hear birds in the background and the soothing waterfall that emptied into the backyard fountain. It felt like she was floating, but not quite. She felt the hammock swaying softly, adding to the illusion that she was suspended in air, weightless, and riding the soft summer clouds. The pleasant summer sounds fell away, leaving only peacefulness.

The light appeared gradually. She didn't think she was asleep, but then she never did when she dreamed. She may have tried to sit up, to call out to her mom, but she couldn't be sure. It was so serene that she really didn't want to leave this place. The glow was radiant, but it didn't hurt her eyes. There was someone coming toward her, bathed in this ethereal light, but strangely she wasn't afraid. It was a woman. She was beautiful.

"Am I dead?" Jillian asked.

The woman threw back her head and laughed, an unexpected and magical sound. Everything around her seemed to be happening in slow motion. The woman's skin was translucent, her hair long and golden, and she was dressed in flowing white. She didn't walk, as much as glide, toward Jillian. She reminded her of the good witch in the Wizard of Oz.

"No, sweet Jillian Grace, you are not dead. I can understand why you might feel that way. This seems very strange to you, I suppose. It seems we have not been very helpful in guiding you toward an understanding of the message. When I came to see you last time, you were frightened."

"I don't remember you. I would remember if you had come before, even if I am crazy."

"Angels take on many forms, Jillian. I'll show you, but please do not be afraid."

The fairy-like face melted into the wizened face of the old woman in the waiting room. Then she slowly faded away to be replaced by the many faces of people Jillian remembered only from her dreams, leaving her with snippets of words and prophecies to figure out when she was awake. As quickly as the images appeared, they were once again replaced by the beauty and light of the woman.

"Okay, now I'm freaked out. Do you mean she…you…are the old woman and you came to see me before? I like you a lot better the way you look now. Why are you looking for me? Why am I seeing all of you? Why am I having these dreams?"

Jillian sat cross-legged on the hammock now, bathed in the soft glow emanating from her visitor. She knew in her heart that she was safe and this apparition meant her no harm. She didn't want to run away, and she didn't know if she could, even if she wanted to. She felt weightless, as if she was floating. In the back of her mind, she had a fleeting thought that this vision might be proof she was crazy, but if you were sane enough to think you were nuts, maybe you weren't.

"I am here to prepare you. I am an angel of the Lord, a messenger. God has chosen you, Jillian. The time has come. You are not imagining this. You are a virgin and you are with child. You carry a son and he is blessed by the Lord. He shall lead the faithful to Paradise and the righteous to glory. He shall be despised by the evil ones, and those same evil forces shall be frightened of his goodness. They shall rise against him and a great war shall visit the earth. But he shall be triumphant and a symbol of eternal light. The world shall fall away and the heavens remain. It is written."

"Wait a minute. You want me to believe that I am pregnant and that it was planned. *By God.* Like Mary. How did I get pregnant? I was never with anyone. How did this happen? Why did this happen to me? I'm not some holy person. I am not special. I am just me."

"Oh, sweet daughter of the Lord. You are not the first one to walk this path. The chosen have been so chosen before the earth was formed or the sun rose in the sky. It has always been. You have carried this seed since before you were born. We will guide you, Jillian, you must believe."

"Believe that God sent you? I can't just walk into the house and tell my parents an angel came to me in the garden and told me I'm having a holy son. You better come up with a better plan than that. They don't believe me now, so I can just imagine what would happen if I told them about you."

"You will know when the time is right. The time is close at hand when they will believe you, Jillian. God has chosen a protector to guide you. You must know this is not an easy path. Things will happen that are beyond your control. You will be in grave danger for a time. Certain people will covet you and the child you carry. Follow your protector, Jillian. Trust him, for he will be shown the way. Follow your protector, Jillian, even when you are unsure. You must open your heart and believe in the power of the Lord. Nothing is impossible with God."

The angel put out her hand to touch Jillian's cheek. Feeling the softest whisper of a breeze on her face, Jillian put her hand up to touch the angel's fingers. Jillian inhaled sharply as the strangest sensation, a beautiful vibration, coursed through her body. She felt the child stir in her belly for the first time.

"I prayed every night, you know. I prayed when Jamie wanted me to give in to him, because I needed strength to say no. I prayed when he broke up with me, because I couldn't help but think there was something wrong with me. I prayed when Dr. Richards told me I was pregnant, because I knew that I had never been with anyone. I even prayed to make this baby go away. Now I don't know what to pray for." Jillian started to cry.

"You say I must accept what you tell me, that I have been chosen to carry this child for God. I am having a baby, and I know I haven't had sex with anyone. It seems the decision has been made for me, and I really have no choice but to believe what you say. But just so you know, I liked my life the way it was. So now, I have to pray that things will happen the way they're supposed to, because obviously I have no say in any of this."

"Praise be to God. These events shall come to pass. Let the peace of the Lord come upon you. Trust in him, Jillian. Open your heart and accept the strength you will need to carry out his word."

The angel started to move away, the light began to fade. Filled with an overwhelming feeling of sadness, and still in awe, Jillian slowly opened her eyes to find the last bit of daylight had faded from the sky. She didn't know what had just happened, because everything in her life was upside down. But the vision left her with a feeling of peace, a certainty that she didn't have to figure everything out right this minute. She put her hand on her belly, where she felt the baby inside of her moving to a rhythm all its own.

*   *   *

Jillian pushed her food around on her plate.

"How are you feeling, sweetheart?" Sara passed the platter of warm rolls to her across the dinner table. Dinner was late tonight, not at all unusual for them with their varied work schedules.

"I'm fine. A little tired, that's all." Jillian swirled her fork through the corn on her plate and pushed the chicken to the side.

"Dad, do you ever dream?"

"Everyone dreams, Jillian. I would have to say yes. Why?"

"I don't know. Do you ever feel like your dreams are trying to tell you something?" Jillian put her fork down and took a sip of water, waiting for his response.

"I don't know about that, Jill. I mean, sometimes I wake up and find that a good night of sleep clears things up for me, if I've been trying to work through a problem." Marc didn't want to push, so he waited for her to continue.

It seemed like ages since they had even the semblance of a normal conversation, so he was anxious to keep things moving along.

"No, I don't mean like that. I mean more than a dream. Like someone comes to you when you are asleep and tells you something is going to happen, or that you have to do something. Like a messenger. And you wake up and know they were really there. Or what they said to you is really true." Jillian looked at her father.

"Do you mean like a premonition, Jillian, or an actual person?" Marc was trying to follow her train of thought. "Has something like that happened to you?"

"Maybe. I don't know. It seems silly now when we are sitting here at the table. But sometimes I think I'm having visions. Don't worry, Mom, I'm not losing my mind. Yet." Jillian smiled at Sara, who had put down her fork and was watching her daughter closely.

"Jillian, since you brought it up, do you think it might have something to do with the pregnancy? Do you think that possibly, subconsciously, you are trying to work through your denial about the baby? That would seem a perfectly natural progression in this situation. A good thing." Sara could not keep the hopefulness from seeping into her voice.

"Mom, I don't think that at all. I know you can't believe this now, but I did not have sex. I don't think I am working anything out in my subconscious. I was just wondering about dreams. That's all. Can I be excused?"

"Jill, honey, sit and finish your dinner." Marc, trying to salvage the evening, felt as if he was walking on eggshells.

"I'm really tired tonight. I just want to rest. Tomorrow is going to be horrendous and I just want to sleep. Please reconsider having the Tyler's over tomorrow. It will just make things worse."

"Jill, we have gone over this. We'll come up in a little while to say goodnight." Sara said.

Jillian didn't argue, but carried her plate to the counter and left the kitchen.

"What do you suppose that was all about?" Sara asked.

"Something is troubling her. I mean besides the obvious. Do you think we should put off talking to Jamie's family for a few days? I mean until we get the results of everything?" Marc asked.

"What if something is wrong, Marc? We know our daughter is not promiscuous. Jamie has to be the father. What if the tests come back and something is horribly wrong. I think we need to make them aware, at least. We would want to know right away, wouldn't we?"

"Yes, I guess you're right."

"And besides, if everything comes back okay, we still have a lot of figuring out to do. I don't think we can put this off. The longer our daughter remains in denial, the harder this is going to be on all of us."

Chapter Twenty One

Jeff and Diane Tyler sat self-consciously in the Macomb's living room, waiting for Sara to come back from the kitchen with their drinks. Diane kept smoothing her skirt, picking at imaginary lint, obviously ill at ease about the events surrounding this sudden invitation by the Macomb's to discuss *something important*. She didn't like the sound of that.

Diane thought Jillian's parents were nice enough, but they didn't travel in the same social circles and quite frankly, Diane felt out of place. If she was totally honest with herself, she had to admit she was only half sorry that Jamie and Jillian had broken up. God, she hoped Jamie hadn't done anything to offend the Macomb's. She didn't need that on her plate right now. Her son sat there looking as if he was ready to take flight any second. Jamie assured his parents he didn't have a clue what this *important meeting* was about.

"Jeff, have you been affected by the layoffs at the plant?" Marc asked, trying to fill the awkward silence with small talk. Jeff Tyler worked at the auto plant in Spring Hill, about an hour south of Nashville. The recent recession had caused massive layoffs and there was fear the plant would close, putting hundreds out of work.

"No, Dr. Macomb… Marc. I think I'm safe for right now. There may be another wave of layoffs come fall, but for now we are looking pretty good."

"Here we go." Sara walked into the room balancing a tray of drinks and Marc jumped up to help distribute them to their guests, relieved that his awkward attempts at conversation were no longer necessary.

"Jamie, are you sure you don't want anything?"

"No thanks, sir." Jamie sat folded in the armchair next to his parents, knees bouncing, clearly nervous and anticipating the entrance of his ex girlfriend with dread.

"Here comes Jillian now," Marc said.

They all watched as Jillian resignedly came into the room, walking directly to the chair across from Jamie and plopping down sullenly. Marc could see she had been crying, but he doubted their visitors would notice.

Diane's head jerked up. "Hey, Jillian."

"Hi, Mrs. Tyler." Jillian mumbled the greeting with no expression.

She looked up once, trying to make direct eye contact with her parents, silently pleading with them to abandon this crazy idea of talking to the Tyler's. She knew there was nothing she could do to stop the inevitable. She had no way of knowing how Jamie would react, now that this whole can of worms was about to be opened.

The only other person in the room who knew the truth was Jamie. And he only knew the part about not having sex with her. This was not going to be pretty, and all she could do was sit there. There was no way she was bringing up her crazy dreams now.

"The tea is very good. I know you said you wanted to talk to all of us, Sara, but I have to say this waiting around is making me nervous," Diane said as she twisted the napkin around her frosted glass. "What's going on?"

"I'm sorry, Diane. This is an awkward situation and we weren't sure how to approach the subject with you." Sara said.

"Well, at least tell us if everything is okay. I mean, I know the kids broke up, but that happens, and if Jamie acted out, well, I'm sorry. This is uncomfortable for all of us." Diane looked everywhere in the room except at Marc and Sara.

"I apologize for the suspense. But this is very important ..." Sara stopped in mid sentence, looking at Marc, unsure of how to proceed.

Marc crossed the room and stood behind Jillian's chair. "First, we want you to know that Jillian has been against this meeting from the beginning, but as her parents, we decided it was in everyone's best interest for us to sit down and talk."

Jamie suddenly shot out of his chair.

"If this is about the breakup, I am sorry, Jillian. I told you I was, but you didn't want to hear me out. I should never have gone behind your back. I know I was a jerk, but I can't take it back." Looking imploringly at Jillian's parents, it was obvious Jamie was trying to keep his emotions under control.

"I was just frustrated. I didn't mean to hurt her." he said.

Jillian sat immobile in her chair, and did not raise her eyes or acknowledge Jamie as he spoke. She was mortified and the truth was, she wished she were invisible. She couldn't have made a sound if she'd wanted to. Her cheeks were flushed, her hair tousled, her hands folded in her lap. She was embarrassed about what was coming next, but was powerless to stop it.

"It doesn't have anything to do with the break-up Jamie, so calm down." Marc almost felt sorry for the kid. Sara walked over to her husband and laid her hand on his arm.

"Sara, you just have to say it," Marc said.

"Jillian is pregnant." Once the words left Sara's mouth, the silence was palpable, as if someone had completely sucked the breathable air from the room, leaving everyone gasping.

As if in slow motion, Jamie raised his hands in surrender and looked toward Jillian, backing away, the color draining from his face, tears of rage and indignation falling from his eyes.

"You lied to me! Tell them, Jill, tell them I never touched you. TELL THEM YOU NEVER LET ME TOUCH YOU!" he said.

"Jamie!" Jeff Tyler jumped from the sofa and went to his son, grabbing his arms to prevent him from leaving the room. Diane looked between Jamie and Jillian, trying to fully comprehend what she just heard. Jamie broke free from his father's grasp, looking wildly around the room for an escape.

"I never touched her. She said she was saving herself. I'm not lying. For six months, I wanted to and she said no! Who was it, Jillian? Who was worth it, Jillian? You lied to me. It wasn't me. Tell them, Jill. It was not me!" Jamie slid down the wall, collapsing in a heap on the floor in the corner of the room.

"We have to talk about this. You need to know she is fourteen weeks along and there may be a problem with the pregnancy. She had special diagnostic testing done yesterday and we just want you to be informed. You have a right to know about this." Sara stood behind Jillian's chair, caught up in the maelstrom her announcement had provoked.

She fought to regain her composure before she said anything else. She ran her fingers through her daughter's hair, the pulse in her neck fluttering like a bird. She looked at Marc and if it were possible, he looked even more flustered than she.

"We all need to stay calm. There was no easy way to tell everyone. We just found out ourselves. We aren't asking for anything, but we want you to be aware of the situation. We can work out details later," Sara said.

Marc walked over to Jamie and knelt on the floor in front of him. "It will be okay, Jamie. This will all work out."

"I never touched her, Dr. Macomb, and if she said I did, she is lying. I never had sex with Jillian. You can't pin this on me."

Jeff walked toward Jamie. "You heard my son, Marc. He may have hurt her feelings when he broke up with her, and I am not saying he did it right, but I believe him when he says he never touched her. He's got girls calling him all the time. There is no need for him to try to do something with your daughter if she said no."

Jillian sat rooted in her chair, never lifting her eyes. She was moving her lips silently, as if in prayer. Marc walked over to her as Jeff helped his son to his feet. Gently taking her chin in his hand, he forced her to look into his eyes.

"Jill?" Her eyes glassy, she met her father's anxious gaze and shook her head.

"I think we'd better leave." Diane, finally rousing herself from the shock of the announcement, stood up and turned to Sara. "I expect we'll talk tomorrow, once we all have had a chance to settle down. We'll talk to Jamie when we get home, but if I were you, I would start looking elsewhere. My

Jamie is going to college and if he says he's innocent, he is. You had better talk to your daughter. She's been awfully quiet over there."

Sara looked around the room. "It's natural for us to want to believe our children and no one is assigning blame here. We wanted you to know so plans can be made. The kids were together for a long time and most definitely at Easter when Jillian got pregnant. It's not easy for any of us to handle, but please don't deny the possibility that this may be your grandchild. It has been a shock for us, too."

"Marc and Sara, I don't mean to insult you, but we need to have a paternity test. I believe my son. And Jillian over there," Jeff said, pointing towards their daughter, "knows the truth, too. She hasn't said a word. We want a test." Jeff and Jamie were edging toward the door.

"If you want to take Jamie to our doctor's office tomorrow, Diane, I'll call and tell them you are coming in. I know they can do a paternity test. They have the baby's DNA from yesterday's procedure. If you feel it necessary, we can go forward with the test tomorrow. It's probably best, given the present circumstances," Sara said.

Emotionally exhausted, Sara could do nothing but watch as Jillian walked out of the living room and toward the stairway.

Diane set her glass on the coffee table, and watching as the silent teenager made her way across the room, she said, "Jillian, no one wants anything to be wrong with your baby. We hope everything turns out okay for you. But our Jamie says he's not the father and we believe him."

Jeff Tyler called to her from his son's side. "What do you have to say for yourself, girl?"

Jillian paused as she got to the bottom of the stairs and turned around, meeting Jamie's eyes for the first time since he arrived.

"It is written." Then she turned and walked up the stairs.

Chapter Twenty Two

Holy Name Cathedral on Broadway stood majestically against the backdrop of the blue Nashville sky. It was reminiscent of the cathedrals of Rome, with its intricate carvings, ornate statuary and the working bell tower. The impressive double wooden doors opened to a wide vestibule, where the marble floors had worn over the years to a rich and subdued patina. Another set of wooden doors opened to the worship hall which in itself was splendorous, with its soaring height and breathtaking stained glass windows. The smell of polished wood emanated from the pews in the sanctuary. The main aisle was flanked on either side with wide stately columns carved at the top and seeming to support the arched canopy of the ceiling.

Candle wax and incense permeated the air, providing an ageless solemnity that few new buildings could rival. Above the altar, the ceilings were painted with the images of the saints and the Holy Family. An overwhelming feeling of reverence immediately embraced all who entered.

Stephen made the sign of the cross and genuflected in front of the altar. Walking around to the sacristy he called out softly, not only because the cathedral demanded such respect, but he did not want to frighten the elderly priest. Father Andrews was behind the altar preparing for the weekend services.

"Stephen, come on around." The old priest poked his head through the side door and beckoned him to follow.

"I'm almost finished here," Fr. Andrews said.

Taking an elaborate ring of keys from his pocket, Father Andrew proceeded to the vestibule to lock the front entrance.

"Here, help me lock up. I hate that we have to take such precautions, but even in this holy place one can't be too careful. Let's walk around back to the rectory and get something to drink. Have you had lunch?"

"Yes, I'm fine, Father. Thanks again for seeing me today."

They followed the cobblestone path behind the church and walked up narrow side steps into the rectory kitchen. The magnolia trees shaded the walkway, but the summer heat was oppressive and the overweight priest was short of breath by the time he finished filling their glasses with ice and tea.

"Come, let's sit in the living room so I can close the doors and we can cool off. These old buildings are not the most energy efficient, I fear."

Father Andrews proceeded to remove the clerical collar from around his neck, and with his pudgy little fingers, unbuttoned the first few buttons of his black shirt.

"Pardon the informality, Stephen, but I am not going to be able to concentrate on a thing you say if I don't loosen up and get some air."

"Please, Father, make yourself comfortable." Stephen took a long drink of the cold tea. Now that he was sitting here in front of the priest, he was not sure how he was going to bring up the subject of the dreams. He didn't want to appear as if he was losing his mind. Faced with the long awaited opportunity of finally unburdening himself, he now questioned whether he had been blowing everything out of proportion.

"Let's start with the Lord's Prayer, shall we, Stephen? It doesn't hurt to invite God to be with us right off the bat to help guide us in the right direction." Both men bowed their heads and prayed.

"Now, young man, let's talk about what brings you to the cathedral to talk to an old priest on a beautiful summer afternoon."

"Well, Father, I'm not quite sure where to start. I am …" Stephen floundered.

"Why don't you jump right in? Beginning, middle, end. It doesn't matter because we will sort it all out as need be. Tell me what's troubling you, Stephen. You haven't been here long enough to be homesick, have you?"

Stephen smiled and shook his head.

"It's nothing like that, Father. I wish it were as simple as a phone call or a visit home. At least I could understand that and work through it. I am here because I'm having dreams."

"Dreams, Stephen? What kind of dreams?"

"Persistent dreams. Father, this is hard for me. I am analytical by nature, and I hesitate to even say this out loud, but these dreams are so real…I think they may be more than just…I think I may be having visions. I don't know how to figure it all out, or even where to start," Stephen said.

"Take it slow, son. We have plenty of time." Fr. Andrews put his glass on the table beside him and leaned forward, watching Stephen closely.

"When I am having the dreams, I can actually feel myself transported to different surroundings, experiencing the sights, smells, sounds. I have never encountered anything like this. All of the dreams have the same message, and it involves a young girl."

"Did you leave someone behind, Stephen? Could this be your way of dealing with loneliness?"

"No, it's nothing like that, I promise. In the dreams, this girl is in grave danger and I am the one chosen to protect her, to save her. It's very confusing, and perhaps I should be seeing a doctor instead of a priest, but these visions are too repetitive and too pervasive to be only the product of an over active imagination."

"Stephen, dreams are usually the mind's way of dealing with stress and uncertainty. Is there something about this move to Nashville that has you worried? Do you worry about your family back in Ontario, an old girlfriend perhaps?"

"No. It has nothing to do with the move. I know without a doubt that I am supposed to be here, in this place, at this time." Stephen took a deep breath and continued.

"In the first dream, the girl was stoned to death because she was unmarried and with child, and I was powerless to stop it from happening. It was as if I was being warned of what could happen to her if I didn't heed the message. It took place long ago, in ancient times, and was so lifelike, I could feel the heat of the Israeli sun on my skin. I could understand the native Hebrew dialect and I spoke it fluently." Stephen paused, closing his eyes, the scene running through his mind as if he were in that place again.

"Continue, Stephen. I'm not dismissing anything you are telling me, but it does sound a bit unusual. Could it be the stress of the impending program at the University, combined with the move to a new place?"

"Father Andrews, these are not just ordinary dreams. They are structured and very clear in their message. The girl is pure, a virgin, yet carries a child. Sound familiar? There is an old man who comes to me, calls himself the messenger, Gabriel. He charges me with her safety. I am warned that I must be prepared to act when the time presents itself, and have been given very explicit instructions that it is my role to protect her. To save her. But I don't know from what or even how I am to carry this out." Stephen was sweating now.

"Take a drink of your tea, Stephen, and let me repeat what you have said to me." Father Andrews summarized everything Stephen had told him.

"I know how it sounds, Father. I hesitated to come to you, or to anyone for that matter, because I know how it sounds. The dreams started before I left Ontario and have steadily increased in intensity. The message becomes more urgent with each dream. They are becoming more frequent, and I am powerless to stop them."

"I understand, Stephen, but perhaps it is too early to call them visions or prophecies. Be careful, son, that you do not get carried away and project upon yourself something that is not factual. I am by no means dismissing the importance or perplexity of your torment."

Father Andrews picked up his tea and took a long slow drink before setting the glass down on the table and looking once again at Stephen.

"I can see how easy it would be to get caught up in the moment, Stephen, when you consider that your business is searching for answers through the Old and New Testaments. I imagine that constantly exploring the history of the prophets, and their messages, plants seeds in the minds of you young students. Once planted, they are left to ferment and grow. You are impressionable, in new surroundings and filled with a thirst for answers as we all are. Christianity is a mystery, or series of mysteries, begging to be explored. And the fact that much of what you have explained to me so closely resembles the circumstances surrounding the Virgin birth, I am led to believe you are dealing with emotional overload right now."

Stephen let his head fall into his hands. "I have thought of that, and I have asked myself if it could explain all this. I don't know. Yes, I study Christianity and have always been immersed in it's history. But why would this start happening now? Why the same visions over and over with such a clear message?"

"You say the girl comes to you and she is pregnant. There is a messenger named Gabriel who proclaims you have been chosen to protect her. You know the story very well, Stephen."

"Yes, of course I do. But I also know these dreams are more than just the idle wanderings of my mind."

"Stephen, surely you will agree, that in this day and age, the babies born out of wedlock would fill this cathedral to the rafters. And probably half the girls don't know how it happened to them. I don't think you have to worry about a stoning today." Father Andrews took another drink of his tea.

"What can I do to help this girl? I know her situation is escalating, and I don't know how to stop it. I am supposed to act, but don't know when or how. I try to figure out what the message is, but obviously I'm not wise enough. I am left waiting for the next dream."

"Let the dreams come, Stephen, and accept them for what they are. The girl in your dreams must represent something happening in your life right now. If you will allow these things to run their course, you will soon settle in and be back to normal in no time. You need not try so hard to figure out the meaning."

"Respectfully, Father, I don't think this is something that will run its course. For whatever reason, I believe I have been chosen to protect this girl and her infant, and have been shown very clearly what will happen if I don't. I don't know how or why, but I know these things are going to happen. I cannot accept they are merely the ramblings of a tired mind. Throughout the history of the Old and New Testaments and even today, there are cases of purported visions and messages from God, document- ed by our own church."

"Okay, Stephen, I'll tell you what. I want you to keep a journal. Record your dreams for one week and come back next Thursday so we can talk again. I am not making light of this. I see how it affects you. The mind is powerful, young man, and you have a brilliant future ahead of you. Let's get this figured out so you can go forward and do what God intended for you."

"Thanks for listening, Father. I'll be around on Sunday evening for the contemporary mass. I promise I will consider what you said, and I will keep a journal."

Stephen stood and held out his hand to the priest. As he walked back to his car, he reflected on their conversation. When you looked at things in the light of day, it was hard to imagine the intensity of the visions. He could not fault the old priest for his opinion, or the way he handled the admittedly odd situation. If someone had come to him professing visions, he probably would have counseled them the same way, or might have been less generous and sent them packing to a mental institution by way of a straight jacket. But Stephen knew the difference between reality and fantasy, and he believed in his soul that these were more than ordinary dreams. And he knew they had something to do with Jillian.

He vowed that he would call Marc Macomb as soon as he got back to the campus. He had to find out as much as he could about the professor's daughter, so he could try to figure out the danger she was in.

Chapter Twenty Three

Stephen sprinted across the grounds of the campus and took the steps to the Divinity School offices two at a time. If nothing else, his time spent this afternoon talking with the Catholic priest had reaffirmed his conviction that his nighttime apparitions were more than mere dreams and were somehow connected to Marc Macomb and his family. He knew he had to tread carefully. If he came across as a lunatic, he would not only be banned from Professor Macomb's inner sanctum, but probably tossed out of the fellowship program on his ear. And with good reason.

Father Andrews did not come right out and infer that he was delusional, but he knew the old priest must have been thinking it. However, Stephen knew there was more to these apparitions than just an overactive subconscious at play. Talking about these matters in the light of day forced him to accept that these visions were not going to just disappear. He had agreed to keep the requested journal.

He decided to document his dreams from the beginning, putting into concrete form as much as he could remember. He wished now that he had started a journal at the onset, but he was optimistic he would be able to remember most of the details. That was his forte, after all. Research.

Stephen burst through the door to the faculty offices. Mrs. McCarthy sat in her usual post at the reception desk, ramrod straight posture, high collared blouse buttoned up to the neck… projecting a formidable figure. The Sentinel. She looked up at his less than restrained arrival, and then very deliberately looked down at the appointment calendar. Ever wary and protective of the professor's time, she quickly and proficiently weeded out all unnecessary interruptions to the sacred schedule.

"What can I do for you, Mr. Jacobs?" she said to him, peering over her glasses. Redirecting her gaze from a mound of paperwork, she deftly placed her finger in the middle of the stack, lest she lose her place. Pushing her glasses up on her nose, the gray haired woman waited resignedly for Stephen to state his business.

"Would it would be possible for me to schedule some time with Dr. Macomb later this afternoon. Our meeting earlier this week was interrupted and I really need to speak with him." Until that exact moment, Stephen had not realized he had been holding his breath, silently praying his newfound confidence in this mission would not wane.

Mrs. McCarthy pointedly turned to look at the black schoolhouse clock on the wall behind her desk. "It is already past three o'clock, Mr. Jacobs. Dr. Macomb will be out until Monday. Something unavoidable came up and he will not be taking any calls until then. Shall I leave him a message?"

"Is everything alright? I mean, he left in such a hurry and …" Stephen stumbled over his words, leaving his adversary a perfect opportunity to interject.

"Mr. Jacobs, I am sure I don't know anything more than I just told you. If you would like to set up an appointment for next week, I will be happy to schedule it. Other than that, there is not much I can do. Would you like to speak to someone else on the faculty?" Mrs. McCarthy leaned forward at her desk, waiting expectantly for Stephen to end his sudden intrusion into her sanctum.

"No thanks. I'll check back Monday and see what his schedule looks like then. Thank you for your time." Stephen started toward the door and turned around again, finding Mrs. McCarthy vigilantly observing his retreat.

"Does Dr. Macomb do this often? I mean… take time off during the week?" He watched her closely, trying to gauge her response.

"Mr. Jacobs, I am not in the habit of discussing the patterns of behavior of our professors."

"I'm sorry. I was just concerned and I…" Stephen said. The rest of his thought remained unspoken.

"No. In all the years I have been here, Dr. Macomb has never missed a day that wasn't planned well in advance. Is that all, Mr. Jacobs?" Mrs. McCarthy's demeanor made it crystal clear that their impromptu meeting had ended.

"Yes. Yes, that's all. Thanks again."

Stephen walked slowly across campus and back to his apartment. He was going to pay the Macomb family a surprise visit tomorrow, but he had to figure out how he could make it look like he wasn't barging in uninvited, when that was exactly what he was planning. There was something going on over there and he needed answers, because he believed he was somehow part of it.

Finally back in his apartment, Stephen threw his keys on the table and headed for the phone. He needed more than anything to hear a familiar voice, and was relieved when his mother answered.

"No, Mom, I'm fine. I was thinking about everyone and wanted to touch base is all. I missed being there for Cami's birthday. Are you doing okay in the house by yourself?"

Stephen walked around the tiny apartment while he talked to his mother. Standing at the window, he looked down on the street. It was getting dark and the light from the streetlamp cast a yellow pool of light on the sidewalk below. A stray cat jumped from the top of a garbage bin that sat waiting at the curb for tomorrow morning's trash pickup.

"How is Mandy feeling? Good. I'm glad she's doing okay. I know. I'm excited about the baby, too. Do we know yet if it's a boy or a girl?"

Stephen walked into the kitchen and put a cup of cold coffee into the microwave. Punching the reheat button, he grabbed the pile of mail off the table and went back into the living room. It felt good to talk to his mother. He needed the familiar sound of her voice to anchor him.

"I love you, too, Maggie Mae. Tell everyone I said hi and I will call them, I promise."

Stephen hung up the phone and pulling a notebook out of his brief-case, retrieved the mug of warmed coffee, then sat in the chair next to the window and began to write. He let his mind wander back to the first dream. Stoning an unwed mother was common in ancient times, even common today in certain parts of the world. The garb, the structure of the marketplace, and the attitude and language of the people in his first dream, were all concurrent with his knowledge of ancient Israel. Why ancient Israel?

Stephen's plan was to document everything he could remember before trying to analyze anything. Once he began writing, the details flowed easily from his memory to the paper. As the events surrounding the first dream became clearer to him, he couldn't write fast enough. Remembering back to that morning when he was too numb from the fresh horror of his dream, there was something else about the first vision hovering just beyond his recall.

Wait a minute. Flinging the notepad to the table next to his chair, he jumped up and ran into the bedroom. Swinging open the door to the closet, he rummaged through the mess until he came across his suitcase. Throwing it on his bed, he felt around the lining until his hand ran across the smooth outline of the small black stone. Removing the stone from its inadvertent hiding place, he turned it over and over in his palm. *A sign?*

Placing the stone in his pocket, Stephen went back into the living room and once again began to write.

Chapter Twenty Four

D r. Jackson Mullins pushed his glasses to his forehead and leaned in to view the slide that was inserted onto the stage of the microscope. Trying once again to adjust the fine focus, he backed away from the counter and marched across the lab, hurling his gloves into the biohazard receptacle as he passed by. Punching the extension on the intercom, he irately bellowed for his intern.

"Dr. Sorrento. Who prepared the Macomb-Tyler paternity specimen for pathology?"

"I prepared it myself, Dr. Mullins," Michael Sorrento answered cautiously, mentally reviewing the meticulous protocol he had followed. One thing he knew for sure, and that was, you didn't want to piss off Mullins.

"Get in here, Michael. Level two. Now."

"I'm on my way, sir." Dr. Sorrento finished charting the entry for the case he was working on and closed the file, mildly apprehensive about the source of the obvious frustration he heard in his mentor's voice. Not that it mattered much to him. He welcomed any excuse to get into the lab and away from all this paperwork. He had learned early on that charting was imperative, but mundane, grunt work and he yearned for more time spent in the lab doing research, no matter how he got there.

Donning the required lab gown and mask before entering the sterile environment, he pushed through the swinging doors and into the bright white glare of the lab.

"Dr. Mullins?" he called out.

"Dr. Sorrento, go to station three and tell me what you see. Start with the slide on the left. Male subject."

"Is this the paternity case we sent up this morning? What am I looking for?" Michael put on a pair of gloves and walked over to the microscope.

"Just do it." Dr. Mullins said through clenched teeth, every moment bringing him closer to a full blown recurrence of his ongoing battle with TMJ.

Jackson Mullins took his research seriously. Incompetence was not a word in his vocabulary and he refused to surround himself with inept practitioners. He had his eye on the Nobel Prize for his discovery of a new molecular theory that promised to reverse the development of mutated cells in the embryonic stage of development. He would not let anyone, or anything, smudge his perfect record. He was so close to his goal that he often worked the graveyard shift in the lab, perfecting his technique and furthering his research. It was an added bonus that he was able to escape the watchful eye of the daytime administration.

He was very well aware that there were colleagues in his field who questioned his methods of research. In his opinion, they were distrustful jealous fools who were short-sighted at best. He was tired of listening to all the mumbo jumbo about the ethics of the use of human stem cells for scientific studies. Hogwash. The protesters were the same fools who wanted a cure for genetically caused diseases yesterday. And what good was a tangle of discarded cells, anyway? The outcome for the stem cells was the same. Might as well have them put to good use.

He secretly yearned for the notoriety the Nobel Prize would bring him. Financially and professionally, he would be set for life. That he may have found a way to stop genetic diseases in the womb, or perhaps found a cure for cancer, was secondary. He secretly could care less what happened to the subjects of his research. For him it was the resulting glory.

The mundane job of running these lab tests for the hospital kept him in favor with the powers that be, and gave him unlimited access to the hospital grounds. He was afforded the proverbial keys to the kingdom in exchange for only a few hours of having to suffer fools like this inept and idiotic intern.

"I don't see any abnormalities. Am I missing something?" Looking into the microscope, Michael observed the specimen in the slide on the left and noted its image of the XY chromosomal make-up of the human male genome.

"Now replace it with the maternal slide." Dr Mullins barked.

Doing as he was instructed, Michael put the second rectangle of glass under the microscope.

"I see a normal XX chromosome with no abnormal looking cells." Puzzled, Michael turned to Dr. Mullins who was standing across the lab, flipping through the patient file.

"Now, if you would be so kind as to look at the specimen you prepared yesterday with the CVS of the placenta." Mullins threw the file down on the counter behind him and strode across the room, pulling up his mask and snapping his gloves into place.

Michael once more lowered his eyes to the lens.

"Whoa, what the hell do we have here?" Michael raised his head and looked at Mullins.

"I'm telling you, Dr. Mullins, I prepared this specimen myself. There is no way it could have been contaminated with anything. I've done hundreds of these and never had a failure....not one," said Michael.

"In that case, Dr. Sorrento, I suggest you congratulate yourself on the enormity of your first screw up. And get me a sterile specimen. Immediately. A full report of these results has been promised by Monday at the latest, and I have a backlog of other cases to review. A first year med student could have prepared this slide." Dr. Mullins was furious.

Angrily yanking the slide from the deck of the microscope, Dr. Mullins inadvertently hit the edge of the counter with the small piece of glass, snapping the slide into two jagged pieces. Michael reflexively reached out to catch the smaller fragment before it could fall and shatter on the floor. Managing to catch it, he jammed his hand into the side of the cabinet in the process.

"Oh, shit." Michael looked up.

Trying not to panic, he extended his hand toward Dr. Mullins. Slicing easily through his glove, the razor sharp fragment of the slide had deeply embedded itself into the fleshy part of his palm. As they watched in shock, Michael's blood oozed beneath the latex.

Mullins guided Dr. Sorrento to the lab sink, thinking not so much about the medical implications of the injury, but rather how the report could be worded to abdicate him of any blame in such a careless lab accident. That was all he needed at this point. An investigation of lab protocol would not be an acceptable intrusion.

"We must stop the bleeding, but we have to be cautious. We're going down to ER to have this x-rayed before we make any attempt to remove it. The glass is precariously close to the ulnar nerve which, if severed, could cause irreparable damage to your hand." Dr. Mullins cut the glove away, exposing the full extent of the penetration of Michael's palm.

"I don't think it's that deep. I think the bleeding is letting up." Michael looked at the glass protruding from his palm and taking deep breaths, forced himself to remain calm.

"Nevertheless, we are going down to the ER so they can evaluate the damage before we remove the glass. Be sure to document every step of the protocol you followed for the prep on that slide, Michael. I've never seen such a chemical reaction under the scope. We must analyze the biohazard risk to you in addition to the pathological. While I saw no abnormal cellular activity on paternal or maternal cultures, the CVS sampling was phosphorescent, a different matter altogether."

"I'll go over my notes later and get the report to you. But I swear I did not deviate from normal protocol," Dr. Sorrento said.

"We'll see."

As they discarded their lab coats and protective gear, Mullins handed Michael a sterile towel to stem the flow of blood and was already leading him quickly toward the elevator.

Chapter Twenty Five

Julie Richards replaced the phone in its cradle and drummed her fingers on her desk. If anything else went haywire with the Macomb case, she would scream. Head spinning, she looked at the clock on the wall above the door. Thank God it was Friday, and she only had patients scheduled in the morning. Opening the top drawer of her desk, she pulled out the plastic bottle of ibuprofen and popped two of the little orange pills into her mouth, followed by a long swig of water.

Jamie Tyler's visit earlier today should not have come as a surprise to her, but nevertheless she was caught off guard. When Sara called earlier this morning and described the scene that had taken place at their house the day before, Julie made it very clear to the girls at the front desk that they must rearrange the schedule to get him into the lab for a quick blood sample and out again as soon as possible.

Diane Tyler had been a nervous wreck when she arrived with her son, so the less time they had to spend waiting, the better. Julie had her nurse personally deliver the blood samples to the Division of Genetics over at the hospital and was promised a speedy turnaround.

Thinking back to her conversation with Sara about the confrontation with the Tyler's, she was forced to entertain the possibility that both Jillian and Jamie were telling the truth about his involvement in the pregnancy. She had never witnessed such adamant denial in a patient. Perhaps Jillian was suffering a psychological break from reality. Pregnancy at any age was a huge adjustment, but a teenager couldn't always be expected to have the experience or maturity to handle the situation.

Julie sat shaking her head. It was going to be a long weekend for both families. She still could not believe the call from the hospital lab. She had never heard of a single case where the geneticist screwed up a simple paternity test. Thank God, they had the tissue from the CVS sampling and it was still viable. Rubbing her temples with the tips of her fingers, Julie retrieved the contact numbers for both families from her rolodex. Picking up the phone, she dialed the first number, then replaced the receiver without completing the call as the green light in her office blinked, summoning her to her last patient of the day.

Chapter Twenty Six

The X-ray Technician on ER duty carefully aligned the x-ray tube to capture Dr. Sorrento's splayed hand on the table. Cathy Walker had been doing this for seven years and was constantly bewildered by the number of employee casualties that came through her door. Employee safety was an issue that was crammed down their throats at every department briefing, but there you have it. Interns were famous for their arrogant disinterest in mundane procedures, believing themselves infallible. Another one bites the dust.

"Okay, Dr. Sorrento. I know you're in pain, but try to hold still. I'm going to step out of the room and snap this last picture. As soon as I check these films, you can go back to the exam room and have this glass removed."

The x-ray would show the proximity of the deeply embedded glass to the deep nerves in his hand, and would help determine the safest method of extraction. Shifting uncomfortably under the weight of the lead apron, Michael heard the technician ask him to hold his breath, but he was preoccupied with the issue at hand. Literally.

If there proved to be nerve damage to his thumb and fingers, there was a probability he would be unable to carry out the necessary research for his PhD. How he would be able to get past that hurdle was beyond him. He couldn't believe he had grabbed that slide. He replayed the accident in his mind, but it all happened so fast that his reaction was automatic. Common sense would indicate the correct response should have been hands up and let it fall. But he didn't have time to consider the outcome. He acted purely from instinct. Damn.

"Okay, Dr. Sorrento. Hold your breath." Cathy's voice came through the overhead speaker, shaking Michael out of his reverie. His hand was throbbing now, and he was becoming lightheaded.

He heard the characteristic whir and click of the x-ray being taken. He felt the slightest pulsation in his outstretched hand, and then the unmistakable sensation of something falling gently into his hand. *Damn.* He was sure that positioning his hand for the procedure had caused the wound to begin actively bleeding again. Fearing the worst, Michael looked down at his palm.

What the hell was going on? Lying neatly across the palm of his right hand was the broken laboratory slide, its clean jagged edge casting a prism of light across his chest. As the glass fell gently to the x-ray table, Michael slowly raised his hand in front of his face.

The door swung open as Cathy breezed back into the room.

"Okay, Dr. Sorrento, you are good to go. I'll get these pictures over to the ER doctor right away." Cathy stopped in her tracks, gawking speechlessly at Michael's hand.

The large gaping slash across his palm had disappeared. They both stared in awe at the completely undamaged palm of his right hand.

Chapter Twenty Seven

Stephen lingered in his apartment Friday morning, going over his notes from the night before. The floor was littered with the remnants of late night snacks and caffeine breaks. It was quite obvious from the debris that his pacing route had taken him to the kitchen and back to his chair at least fifty times. Having spent the night fighting to stay awake, he finally gave in to exhaustion around three in the morning. He awakened at six, resolve intact. He knew his approach to Dr. Macomb would be more credible if he were less vague about his understanding of the dreams.

The journal was half filled with his recollections. The analytical half of his brain was attempting to establish order from the details. By force of habit, Stephen did so with careful documentation of facts. In order to keep an open mind, he decided to dissect each dream separately while he still remembered them vividly, instead of as a jumble of random thoughts. It was easier than he thought it would be. The visions were unusually clear and the language concise.

Studying the sequence of each dream gave Stephen a sense of control. Each dream had a recurring theme. The girl was with child. She was not married. She spoke of never having been with a man. She said she was a virgin. Possibly.

Being Catholic, an image of the Virgin Mary leapt immediately to his mind. And what of the message contained in the first dream? *It begins.* What begins? It was certainly the beginning of these dreams. In the first dream, the girl was killed and Stephen ran into the crowd to avenge her. Why? Was the first dream a prophecy of fact, or was it a warning of the dire consequences of not heeding the message?

The second dream was a plea for his help. But how could he help her, when he didn't know what he was helping her escape from? When is all of this supposed to happen? Being that he could not go back in time, it had to be a foretelling of an event yet to occur. Stephen tried to stay focused and keep his frustration at bay. His list of questions grew, but that happened often in his research. Many questions and fewer answers until, all at once, everything clicked and came together to form an educated hypothesis.

Stephen set the journal aside and leaned back in the chair, closing his eyes. The visions had a theological undertone he could not dispute. The similarities of his visions, to the supposed facts surrounding the message delivered to Joseph regarding the young Virgin Mary and the child she carried, were hard to ignore. But why him?

He had spent his adult life up to this point, trying to prove or disprove facts and hypothesis like these. The doubt that plagued him from childhood reared its ugly head now, shaking his belief system. He went through all the motions. Church on Sunday, confession, communion and the desperate hope that prayer was heard by God, trying to buy into the belief system so thoroughly ingrained in him while growing up.

His interest in the Divinity School had more to do with his intense need for research and a personal quest for answers, than an unwavering belief in the sanctity of organized religion. There were thousands of books written on the subject. He kept his inner conflict well hidden, and the necessity for debate in his research enabled him to do that easily. He would love nothing better than to uncover undeniable proof that the man named Jesus, who walked the earth centuries ago, was truly the Son of God. There was no doubt in his mind that the man, Jesus, had existed. But was he the Son of God, or a prophet?

After all, the Bible is a series of books written by men, about God, and the life of Jesus. Men are not infallible and most certainly through the ages, have proved to be self serving. That there was a higher power,

Stephen had no doubt. But to identify it? That was the question he wrestled with on a continual basis. So why would God choose him to protect this girl?

Despite his own quandary, Stephen had no intention of clouding this research with his personal belief system. Picking up the journal, determined to be objective, he continued to read.

There was always the messenger, Gabriel. The old man imparted such urgency to the situation, seeming to believe that Stephen understood the consequences. Listen to your heart, Stephen. In the last dream, the messenger mentioned the cabin. No one knew about that place but Stephen's father, and he was gone.

The abandoned cabin deep in the Northwest Territory was their secret. His father had estimated that it was over a hundred years old. It had probably been abandoned sometime during the last century, when Indian nations physically and violently fought for land that belonged to them, taking it back from the trappers and loggers who had infringed upon their territory.

Over the years, on the Jacobs annual male bonding pilgrimage, they had filled the place with the bare necessities, adding bits and pieces each year, always mindful to respect the land. It was their home base during their wilderness survival expeditions, and Stephen knew the woods surrounding it like the back of his hand. He and his father had permanently affixed well concealed trail markers, but Stephen could instinctively find his way without aids. There was no doubt in his mind that the cabin still lay untouched and no one else knew of its existence. The rough terrain and winter climate made it doubtful that anyone would ever venture close enough to discover it. That anyone had ever attempted to live there at all was a mystery to him.

Of course, if the dreams were a product of his imagination, which Stephen doubted, that would explain the mention of the cabin, but Stephen was more convinced with every entry in the journal that these visions were a premonition of things to come. But why were they set in ancient times? He could only draw a parallel between events of long ago, and what was prophesied to happen now. Visions and dreams had been respected in the Old World. Nostradamus continued to engage a following to this day with predictions and prophecies made in the mid 1500's. And Stephen, being well versed in the ancient history of religion, was receptive and intelligent enough to ponder these events with open minded wisdom.

Perhaps the most troubling and confusing image was the manifestation of Jillian Macomb. Her presence in his dreams was perplexing. Why would he have a horrific vision of her death by stoning, when he had never laid eyes on her until he got to Tennessee? The dreams started before he even met her.

Gabriel said that it would become clear when it was time for Stephen to act, that he would receive a message from the Most High. God? Is this what the visions are about? The only thing Stephen knew for sure was that the dreams were becoming more powerful and disturbing with each occurrence. The message was not clear enough for him to execute any concrete plan of action. He could not barge into Marc Macomb's home and whisk his daughter away to a cabin in the wilderness, to save her from some unknown force of evil. He could picture the headlines now.

He would find himself in jail before he made it to the end of the block, much less to the border. *No.* He had to allow himself to succumb to the visions and the message would become clear when it was time. He would be vigilant and begin to prepare. It was possible, that by being receptive to the dreams, he may finally get some answers to the troubling questions swirling in his mind.

In reality, he thought it would be appropriate to pay the Macomb's a casual visit. He would have to find a way to make the uninvited social call plausible, because he had to see Jillian. She was most definitely at the center of this mystery, the catalyst, and he felt the need to observe her state of awareness. Everything would be clear in its own time. He closed the journal and went to get ready. *It begins.*

Chapter Twenty Eight

Marc marched into the yard and slammed the side door to the garage, grateful for once that unlike the contemporary homes springing up around them, this small building was well separated from the house. Normally passive, he felt the overpowering need to throw something, smash something, and if there had been a projectile within easy reach, he would have done just that. Standing just inside the door clenching and unclenching his fist, he imagined himself a thoughtful man, a provocative thinker, but when it came to his daughter and the circumstances of the past week, he was at a loss. He felt ineffectual toward his wife's obvious distress and his daughter's frustrating ambivalence.

He would not fail them now. They would get through this ordeal and retain their family unity. That was his mission. A baby. Dear God, what were they going to do? That seemed to be the least of their worries at the moment. Of course, they would rally around and support their daughter, but Jillian's inability to accept her situation left Sara and him at a loss. How could they plan anything when their little girl refused to accept the fact that she was pregnant?

At the moment, however, he was more concerned about the results of all these tests. If Jamie was not the father, they would deal with that. But an abnormality with the baby? Their strict Catholic belief system gave them one option and one option only. The child would be born.

What of his daughter? At seventeen, she was old enough to make adult decisions that would impact her future. She was well informed about abortion, and Catholicism was an integral part of her upbringing. What if her life was at stake? Would he be strong enough to support whatever choice she made? These unanswered questions pummeled his senses, kept him pacing at night, bringing his temper and frustration to the brink of eruption. He had to force himself to keep these anxieties at bay and deal with one thing at a time.

Marc finally settled down enough to reach out and push the remote, and waited as the garage door rose slowly on its track. Getting into the car, he adjusted the mirror and began to slowly back out of the garage. He and Sara had decided that a late dinner of carryout pizza would be a good change from the bowls of cereal and sandwiches they had lived on since Sunday. Jillian was in her room again and neither he nor Sara felt much like going to the grocery. Out of the corner of his eye, he saw someone pull up to the front of the house on a bike. *Oh, great, just what they needed tonight, an uninvited visitor.*

Marc slowed the car at the end of the driveway and honked the horn. Wanting to catch the intruder before he went to the front door and rang the bell, he rolled down the window and called out.

"Hi, can I help you?"

The familiar cyclist sprinted to the car.

"Hey, Dr. Macomb! I was out exploring when I found myself in your neck of the woods. I hope you don't mind. I thought if you were home, I'd stop by and say hi. I can see you've got plans." Stephen found it difficult to concoct much of a reason for his intrusion, so he decided to keep his explanation as simple as possible. Running into the professor this way turned out to be a fortunate accident.

"Stephen. It's good to see you. Listen, we're not really up for company tonight, but I'm running into town to grab a pizza. Hop in. You can ride along and fill me in on what's going on at the University." Marc realized, with a guilty start, that he had all but abandoned his fellows this week. "I'm sorry I had to run out so abruptly Monday. I had something unexpected come up with the family that needed my attention."

"I think I will join you, if you don't mind the company." Stephen opened the passenger door and hopped into the car.

"Is everything okay now? I hope it was nothing too serious. I haven't seen you on campus all week." Stephen felt guilty trying to pry into Dr. Macomb's personal business, but if he was going to get the answers he desperately needed, he was forced to be outspoken. He was finding out quickly that he was not proficient at subterfuge.

"To be honest, I'm not sure how serious yet, Stephen. I can't go into details now, but hopefully by Monday I'll have some answers. I'm not trying to be vague. We are trying to get a handle on a very delicate situation. I'm sure that by next week at this time, whatever the outcome, it will have spread all over campus, anyway."

Stephen's heart was thudding against his chest wall. He was sure the color was high in his face. He knew that whatever Marc Macomb was alluding to, it had something to do with his dreams.

"Is there anything I can do, Dr. Macomb? After everything you and Mrs. Macomb have done to help me ease into Nashville life, I'd feel horrible if you didn't let me help your family in some way. You have my word that I would not betray a confidence." Stephen felt guilty for trying to wheedle information from this man. It was obvious the professor was distraught, but desperately trying to conceal it from him.

"Listen, Stephen, I'm not one to burden someone else with my problems. The truth is, our family has been pretty problem free until now, so we're learning to negotiate our way through this, one day at a time. I appreciate the offer, and believe me, I may call on you for help. But for right now, I would be thrilled to hear how the meeting went on Tuesday night."

Stephen gave him the lowdown from the meeting, causing both men to chuckle over remarks from the distinct personalities that made up the faculty and fellows. Marc pulled into the parking space in front of the pizzeria, leaving the car idling while he ran in to get the food.

"Be right back." Marc said.

Damn. How the hell am I going to find out what is going on in that house. Looking around the interior of the car, Stephen's eyes fell on the yellow hospital lab slip protruding from a stack of papers on the back seat. He glanced up in time to see the professor coming back to the car, arms loaded with hot food, and quickly jumped out to open the back

door so he could set the pizza down on the seat. It only took a few seconds, but Stephen was able to see the name printed across the top of the
hospital paperwork. Jillian Grace Macomb.

The men drove home in relative silence. Stephen talked a little about
St. Thomas and his sisters, and Marc shared a few anecdotes about life at
the University. They pulled up to the Macomb house and Marc stopped
the car at the bottom of the driveway.

"Hey, I picked up a sandwich for you to take home for dinner, Stephen. That place makes the best grinders. I wish I could invite you to join
us, but tonight is probably not a good night."

Marc handed Stephen the white carryout bag.

"Listen, any other time we'd welcome the visit. And I do owe you an
apology for not getting back to you after I jumped ship on Monday. We
just need to navigate through the next few days, then I'll give you a call."

Taking the bag from his professor, Stephen paused as he opened the
door to get out of the car. "I know this probably sounds corny, but I'm
here if you need anything, Dr. Macomb. If there is anything I can do....
anything at all."

Without saying a word, Marc waved him off and drove up the driveway to put the car in the garage. Neither man noticed Jillian, looking
down on them from her bedroom window, before she lowered the shade
and turned out her bedroom light.

Chapter Twenty Nine

D r. Beverly Castiglione couldn't stomach Dr. Jackson Mullins... she didn't care how many designations he carried after his name. As the director of Genome Research in Pediatrics at the hospital, she tried to be generous, but found him to be an insufferable old fool. Standing before her now, he blustered through the commotion, interrupting everyone and drowning out anyone who tried to speak. He cared only about his agenda. The five of them were crowded around the table in her tiny conference room at the hospital.

"I'm telling you, Dr. Castiglione, we must get the girl admitted to this hospital at once. I want her in isolation, using transmission based precautions, with only a handful of staff able to access her," Dr. Mullins ranted.

"Okay, calm down. Everyone calm down." Beverly looked around the table at the group of physicians who had gathered for this meeting so late on a Friday night.

"I want to go over this again, one detail at a time," Dr. Castiglione said.

"The hell with redundancy, we are wasting valuable time. I prepared three slides myself and every last one presented with the same mutation! Do you realize the implications of these results?" Dr. Mullins ranted, veins bulging on his forehead.

Beverly Castiglione had heard enough. Holding up her hand, she looked directly at the irate doctor.

"Dr. Mullins, I must ask you to restrain yourself for the duration of this meeting or you will be asked to leave. Before I authorize a phone call to that girl's distraught parents, I plan to ascertain that the course of action you requested is justified. Is that understood?"

Jackson Mullins sat heavily in his chair. Beverly allowed herself a congratulatory sigh of relief. She had finally put him in his place. Julie Richards was the Macomb family doctor and was quite visibly shaken, as was the young intern, Dr. Michael Sorrento. Understandably, the x-ray technician was still in shock.

"Now, if I may recap, Dr. Mullins, it is my understanding that Dr. Sorrento's wound was directly caused by a lab accident involving a slide prepared for a paternity test, with the CVS obtained from the Macomb girl's pregnancy. You considered the wound severe enough that Dr. Sorrento would most likely need surgery to remove the glass, is that correct?"

"We have been over this...."

"Is that correct, Dr. Mullins?" Dr. Castiglione interrupted him before he could go off on another tangent.

Unceremoniously rolling his eyes, Dr. Mullins answered, "Yes. The glass was embedded precariously close to the ulnar nerve. I was afraid that taking it out, without establishing the exact proximity to the nerve, would cause irreversible damage to the dexterity of his hand."

"Thank you, Doctor."

Across the table, Michael Sorrento, dazed and bewildered, looked up and Dr. Castiglione paused before she spoke again.

"Dr. Sorrento, are you okay?" she asked.

Michael nodded his head.

"You are sure that you felt nothing unusual before you went into the x-ray room?"

"Dr. C, I was in pain. Then, after the x-ray, all I felt was a slight vibration," said Michael, exerting obvious effort to keep his composure.

"I thought it was the x-ray machine doing its usual thing. And then all of a sudden I felt the glass laying in my hand, just laying there. I swear to all of you... it's a miracle. A damn miracle!"

His eyes welled with tears that threatened to spill at any moment. Voice quivering, he said, "One minute it hurt like hell and the next minute my palm was completely healed. Not even a scar, no mark at all. A miracle."

Michael held up his right hand, turning it around for everyone to see. Shaking his head slightly in disbelief, his awe finally giving way to the enormity of the events of the day, unspent emotion bubbled to the surface and he lay his head on the table and wept silently.

Dr. Castiglione could feel the atmosphere in the room shift slightly after Dr. Sorrento's impassioned and surreal recounting of the events leading up to this meeting. Afraid to let the momentum of information gathering subside, she quickly turned to her young x-ray technician.

"Cathy, I know you're upset and I understand that. Are you absolutely sure that all protocol was followed while Dr. Sorrento's hand was being x-rayed?" Beverly continued.

"Yes, Dr. Castiglione. I am very sure. I followed the same procedure for all three pictures," she answered softly. Rocking slowly in her chair, with arms folded tightly in front of her, Cathy Walker looked around the table at the physicians, like a doe caught in headlights.

"It's okay, Cathy. I have someone down there now, checking the machine that was used to x-ray Michael's hand, but until the investigation is complete, that machine is off limits."

"Dr. Sorrento, I've already called Admitting and we'd like to keep you for observation. At least for a few days. I know it may seem an extraordinary measure, but this whole situation has been of an extraordinary nature. If you notice anything unusual, any symptoms at all, in your hand or elsewhere, I expect you to call me. I have given the floor nurse explicit instructions that you are to be put through to me immediately." Dr. Castiglione reached out and touched his hand.

"Michael, I'm sure you realize this could turn into a media circus. I ask that everyone in this room refrain from theatrics and give us a chance to investigate thoroughly, before you speak to the press." Beverly had a sinking feeling that it was already too late. There was no way to stem the flow of hysteria that an occurrence of this magnitude was sure to generate.

"What should I tell my wife?" Michael murmured to himself.

"We will tell her the truth. There has been a mishap at the lab and you are fine, but we want to keep you under observation for a few days. She can certainly come by and see for herself."

"Cathy, I would like you to stay overnight for observation as well. By morning, we will have been assured that the x-ray machine is functioning normally and you will be able to leave. Then I want you to take a few days off to regroup."

"If you two haven't had dinner, I can have something sent to your rooms. Obviously, I can't keep either of you if you refuse to stay, but I would ask you to consider carefully before you disagree. Your health and well-being are of paramount importance to me and to this hospital. We don't know what organism we're dealing with, and until we do, I urge extreme caution. Dr. Sorrento and Miss Walker, you may both go to my office on the second floor and the staff will admit you and show you to your rooms. I'm putting you both in standard isolation on the fourth floor, west wing, so that you will get some rest. I'll be along later to check on you before I leave."

The remaining three physicians watched the duo shuffle quietly from the room. Dr. Castiglione held the first copy of the x-ray, clearly showing that the glass was deeply imbedded in Dr. Sorrento's palm, and had sliced through both nerve and muscle. Passing the x-ray to the doctors, she held up the last film, taken only minutes after the first. The final x-ray clearly showed the outline of glass as it lay innocuously across Michael's palm, no longer any damage evident in the structure of his hand. Setting the pictures on the table, Dr. Castiglione looked up.

"Dr. Richards, considering that the subject matter indirectly concerns your patient, you have been exceptionally silent this evening. You've heard all the statements and now I'd like to hear your opinion. As the Macomb girl's primary physician, your input would be appreciated." Dr. Castiglione looked at Julie expectantly. She assumed that Julie was taking everything in, analyzing the facts before she spoke.

Rousing herself from her meandering thoughts, Julie said, "This case has been unusual from the beginning, Bev, and I would be lying if I said I was not both amazed and concerned."

"Has there been any progress on the CVS testing, aside from the paternity test?" Julie looked pointedly at Jackson Mullins, waiting for his response.

"I will have a partial analysis by Monday. The rest of the report will be ready soon after. But I must tell you, I have never seen images of that nature on a slide." Jackson Mullins looked back and forth between the two doctors.

"Most unusual. Depending on the results of the CVS testing, I would like to suggest an amniocentesis be performed as soon as she is admitted. We must analyze the condition of the fetus. If the results of the amnio are normal, and we are dealing with contamination of the CVS, there will be hell to pay!" Dr. Mullins sputtered, his face turning bright red, as he jumped from his chair and pounded his fist on the table.

Ranting, the surly physician turned to Dr. Richards, "But I seriously doubt that's the case. I myself ran the tests, and the CVS was gathered using the normal protocol. We must get this girl admitted at once! Time is of the essence. We are finished here. You must call that family *now*."

Julie stood slowly, and facing Jackson Mullins, leaned her outstretched arms on the table. Through clenched teeth she said, "MY patient is a seventeen year old girl, who found out on Monday that she was going to have a baby. She is not one of your lab animals, Jackson. Your bedside manner leaves much to be desired and if you were not an expert in genetics, I would not let you within twenty yards of MY patient. I will be present for all tests and you WILL NOT enter her room without her parents or me at her side. She will be here for observation only, Jackson, not as the subject of one of your experiments." Julie glared at the doctor.

"This is preposterous! And I will not…."

"Am I understood, Dr. Mullins?" Julie interrupted.

"Just get her in here, Dr. Richards, and make sure she is in transmission based isolation. We don't want every fresh-faced, wet-behind-the-ears intern running in and out of her room." Jackson Mullins unceremoniously gathered his paperwork and hastily retreated, leaving the two female physicians behind.

Sinking into her chair, Dr. Richards exhaled loudly. Leaning her head against the back of the chair, she turned and met Beverly Castiglione's steady gaze.

"Insufferable old goat."

"Are you sure this is what you want, Julie? She is your patient and ultimately it's your call." Dr. Castiglione said gently.

"I am not sure where this is leading, Bev. I've never heard of the kind of CVS results that Mullins is delivering. First, I am faced with a lack of HCG in her blood and now this. I grudgingly have to agree that observation in isolation, and possibly bed rest, is prudent in this situation." Julie picked up the results of the paternity test and tapped them on the table.

"It's already past ten, so I'll call the Macomb's first thing in the morning. I'll agree to a modified transmission-based isolation, and even set up an amniocentesis as a precaution, BUT her parents must be allowed to stay with her. They'll gown up, but that's the extent of it. I'm not going to have them gloved and masked. They've been around her for the past three months of her pregnancy, and this whole ordeal has been stressful enough as it is. It's bad enough the staff has to gear up." Julie looked at the results of the paternity test once more, before setting the paper down on the table.

"Morning is fine. Jackson will have to sputter for a few more hours, and I'll agree to the modification for her parents, as long as the test results continue to support that protocol. For the time being though, you've got it, girl. What about the baby's father, Julie? Is there going to be an issue with him?" Dr. Castiglione asked.

Julie tapped the report with her finger.

"The only thing that Mullins was able to ascertain from the paternity test was that the male DNA sample we provided was negative. The DNA provided by Jamie Tyler was not a match. Father is unknown."

Chapter Thirty

Marc dragged himself into the kitchen the next morning and found Sara standing at the counter, phone dangling at her side. The overhead light was on, forcing him to squint into the brightness. She raised her head as he walked in and absently placed the phone on the countertop.

"Who the hell is calling at six a.m. on a Saturday?" Marc ran his hand through rumpled hair as his eyes adjusted to the light, finally aware that the color had drained from Sara's face.

"Honey, what's wrong. Who was it? Is it your dad?" he asked.

Sara worried constantly about her father. At seventy-eight, he stubbornly resisted all medical advice from his family doctor and did pretty much whatever he pleased. He was ornery as hell, and it had driven her and her sister Susie to the brink on more than one occasion.

Obviously dazed, Sara tried to focus her gaze on her husband.

"That was Julie Richards, Marc. They want us to bring Jillian to the hospital immediately. There's something wrong, Marc. I'm scared." Sara fell into her husband's arms and finally let go, grief and despair pouring out in waves of anguished sobs.

"What is happening, Marc? I don't understand what is happening to us."

"Okay, honey, now calm down. What exactly did Julie say? What did the test show?" Marc felt his pulse quicken as he led Sara to a stool near the counter.

He pulled a tissue from the flowered box on the side counter and handed it to his wife, setting the container down in front of her.

"She said she would go over everything with us when we got there, that it was too complicated to go into over the phone." Sara blew her nose and pulled another tissue from the container. "They are all in agreement that Jillian needs to be admitted now, and Julie said she would be waiting for us at the side entrance of the hospital.

"Who's 'they' Sara?"

"I don't really know. I think she said specialists in genetics. I don't remember."

"Is Jillian at risk, Sara? Did Julie say that Jillian was in imminent danger?"

"No. She said to try not to worry. Jillian will be okay, but we need to get there as quickly as possible. They will be waiting for us. She asked if we wanted her to send someone to get us. We should plan for at least a week in the hospital, maybe longer."

"Jesus Christ, Sara, what the hell are they talking about?" Marc reached frantically for the phone and punched in the number Sara had written down on the pad by the telephone.

"Damn. It went right to her voicemail." Slamming the phone down, Marc went to the back door and flung it open. Looking up at the morning sky, he mouthed a silent prayer and turned back to his wife.

"We are not going to frighten Jill. I want you to go take your shower, and I'll start a pot of coffee. Pack an overnight bag for both of us. We have to think about how we are going to approach our daughter with this. Everything will be okay. Sara, look at me."

Sara looked up at Marc, waiting expectantly for him to finish his thought. She couldn't think for herself right now, and suddenly everything was happening way too fast. Had it only been this past Monday that all of this was set into motion? It seemed like ages ago. She felt bruised and raw, far from in control. Her emotions had run the gamut, and she knew in her gut this was only the beginning. Marc was trying to be stalwart right now, and she needed that comfort from him at this point more than anything else. She knew her turn would come, and she would have to be the strong one, but for right now, she was content to let him take charge.

"I'll be up in a minute. You go on and get ready. We'll wake Jillian when we have everything organized. But not one minute before." Marc pulled the coffee filters out of the cabinet and turned the tap on to fill the coffeepot with water.

Sara paused at the top of the stairs, suddenly remembering what Julie had told her about the test results for paternity. She started to turn around, intending to go back down to the kitchen and tell Marc what she knew. The grandfather clock in the foyer chimed the quarter hour, and with a start, Sara hurriedly continued to their bedroom, anxious to get their little girl to safety. There would be plenty of time for the rest of it later.

Chapter Thirty One

Jillian heard the phone ring on Saturday morning. It was still dark, but she had already been awake for awhile. She was waiting for the morning light to splash across her bedroom floor before she made herself leave the cozy confines of her bed. She had pretty much stayed in her room since Jamie and his family left on Thursday. What a fiasco that was. She had wanted to reach out to Jamie, to tell his parents he was off the hook. It wasn't his baby, they didn't have to worry about it. It kind of made her mad though, when he called her a liar. In front of all the parents! She couldn't believe her ears.

She knew what he thought, because he called on her cell phone that same night and told her exactly what he was thinking. He said she was a two-timing bitch. He was going to tell everyone exactly what she was and that she could rot in hell. He couldn't wait to have the blood test to prove it, too.

She burrowed into the safety of her covers and pulled the pillow over her head, even now reeling from the embarrassment of his tirade.

"What do you have to say for yourself now, *Miss Goody Two-Shoes?*" Jamie was livid. "All that stuff about saving yourself for marriage. What a crock! You have no idea what you've done, you little liar! I never hated anyone the way I hate you right now. Say something!" he screamed into the phone.

She wanted to hang up, but she figured he would just call back, so she thought she might as well hear him out then and get it over with.

"Jamie, I never lied to you and I told them we did not have sex," said Jillian. "I never wanted my mom and dad to call your parents, but they wouldn't listen to me. It seems like no one will listen to me."

"You are so delusional! I can't even talk to you right now, I am so pissed. I hope you rot in your little delusional world. I hope you're happy for all the misery you've caused me. I had to listen to this crap *all night* from my mom and dad!" Jamie's ragged breath hung heavily in the silence that followed.

"I'm sorry, Jamie. I am really sorry. I can't explain any of this, even to myself. I am so sorry." Jillian started to cry, the last thing she wanted to do in front of him.

"Sorry! It's too late for sorry, you lying little... I'll find out who your lover is and you two will never live it down. I can't believe this!" Jamie hung up on her.

Jillian didn't know if he tried to call her back, because she turned her phone off and threw it across the room. She knew what everyone would say. Even her best friend, Evie. She really missed talking to her friend. This was supposed to be the best summer ever, and now look. Ruined. Just like her life. Evie was on vacation this week, but when she got back into town tomorrow, she would be bombarded with phone calls from all their friends, wanting to know the scoop. Jillian knew it. How was she supposed to explain things to Evie, when she didn't even know herself what was going on?

She lay on her back and ran her hand over the little bump on her belly. When she was standing up you couldn't even see anything, but when she lay flat she could feel it. She had another dream last night. Arianna came back to see her...she guessed she was an angel. If she was going to keep having this dream, she might as well at least try to go along with it.

"What's your name? I mean, don't angels have names?" Jillian finally thought to ask her.

"Yes, Jillian. I am called Arianna." The angel smiled at her. That beautiful smile again.

"Well, you probably already know about all the confusion around here. I mean, you being an angel, I guess you can pretty much see everything."

"Jillian, you must listen closely to me. Everything unfolds as it should. Do not be frightened when…"

"Oh, I'm not afraid anymore," Jillian interrupted. "I figure it can't get too much worse, can it?"

"I'm glad you are not afraid, Jillian. Everything has been set into motion, dear child. You must not fear, for the Lord is watching over you. You must be strong and know that God is with you. The child you carry has started his mission on this earth, even now. Be strong and trust in the Lord, Jillian."

Arianna faded away slowly, until all that was left was a hint of early morning mist, hovering sweetly, until the sun came up and it, too, slowly disappeared.

Jillian rubbed her belly in a soft circular motion. "Well, you heard it here first, little bump. Fasten your teeny tiny seatbelt, because I think we are in for a crazy ride."

*   *   *

"Jillian wasn't even upset, Marc. It was almost as if she was waiting for me. I mean…she was already awake, sitting on the side of her bed." Sara and Marc were in the hospital corridor, waiting for Julie Richards to finish drawing blood and getting vitals from Jillian. Dr. Richards asked them to wait in the hallway while she did her initial workup, but Sara thought it was more likely the doctor wanted to ask Jillian questions that their daughter may not want to answer in front of them. She and Marc were still reeling from the news that Jamie was not the baby's father.

"She took the news about being kept in isolation pretty well, don't you think?" Marc asked, thinking that Jillian actually took the news better than he did.

"Yes, but do you suppose any of this seems real to her yet? So much has happened in such a short time. I just wonder how she is processing everything," said Sara.

Julie came out into the hallway and approached them. She could sense the worry emanating from Marc and Sara as soon as she closed Jillian's door.

"Let's go down the hall to the staff meeting room, so I can brief you and give you the protocol for isolation." Julie smiled at the floor nurse sitting at her station, telling her that she would be right back with a list of approved visitors. "Until then, no one enters that room without my permission."

The meeting room was small and sparsely furnished. An old Formica topped table stood in the center of the room with several blue plastic chairs pulled haphazardly around it. The room was approximately eight by ten and judging by the lack of décor, no one spent much time there.

"I know you are beside yourselves, so I want to get right to the point and review what has transpired since I saw you on Wednesday for the CVS." Julie explained the paternity test and the subsequent lab results, carefully side-stepping the accident and the confusion surrounding the outcome of Dr. Sorrento's injury. All of the physicians involved had agreed, that until they could prove without a doubt that these issues were related, there was no sense alarming the family and throwing everyone into a state of mass hysteria. It would have to be addressed, but now was neither the time nor place to do it. The Macomb's would find out soon enough.

"Dr. Mullins ran the paternity test multiple times and felt it necessary that Jillian remain isolated until we get to the bottom of this. The slides he prepared with the placental material from the CVS are showing the same anomaly each time he prepares one. He is an expert in his field. We have no way of knowing at this point whether the sampling was compromised in some way, or whether we are indeed looking at a genetic phenomenon. We are going to request your permission to do an amniocentesis. I want to wait until her fifteenth week, which is slightly early for the test, but if there is a problem with the fetus, the sooner we get to the bottom of it the better. I am going to be setting up the ultrasound in her room, so we can measure the baby's progress and get a more accurate account of gestational age. When she is ready for the procedure, it will also be done in her room. I have a feeling she'll be ready by Wednesday."

"What are the risks? Can we be with her while you do it?" Sara was twisting her hair around her finger and was afraid to meet Julie's eyes.

"The major risk is to the fetus whenever we do an invasive procedure, and we try to avoid them, if at all possible. In Jillian's case, I have to agree with Dr. Mullins. We must get more information and we are not able to rely on the CVS alone this time. According to my external exam, the fetus is not showing any distress and both the heart-rate and growth pattern seem normal. I am sorry. There is no other way. If you'd like to be in the room for the initial ultrasound, that's fine."

"Listen, Julie, we both agree that we want you to do whatever it takes to keep Jillian safe. Is there any risk for her with an amniocentesis?" Marc asked.

"Right now, I have to say she is probably the most well protected person in this hospital. Isolation will help keep the minute risk of infection to a minimum, and theoretically speaking, the procedure for the mother is statistically pretty risk-free. Obviously, we would rather not perform any invasive procedure, but as I said, in this case there is just no other way for us to get the information we need. The benefits far outweigh any minute risk involved."

Dr. Richards went over the isolation protocol with them and explained the protective procedures that were in place. There was an outer chamber for gowning up before they entered the room and de-gowning when they left. They were to scrub their hands in the outside chamber before entering and upon leaving, but as parents were not required to glove or mask. Everyone else who entered was required to don full protection. Any discrepancies were to be reported to the nurse's station immediately.

"We can't let anyone in to visit until we have moved her to standard isolation or to a regular room. Hopefully this phase won't last long, but it is for her protection. Do you have any questions?"

Marc and Sara grabbed each other's hand and shook their heads. They understood the isolation protocol, but would never in million years understand what was happening to their family.

Julie stood and walked over to the door.

"Now, let's get you in there to see your daughter."

Chapter Thirty Two

Beverly Castiglione stopped by the staff lounge on the second floor of the hospital to grab a cup of coffee before going to her office. It had been nerve racking last night and was shaping up to be much the same today. The Macomb girl was safely ensconced on the fourth floor, east wing, in isolation, and both Dr. Sorrento and Cathy Walker were safely tucked away on the opposite end of the floor, in the west wing.

The results of the mechanical check on the x-ray machine were back and the machine was operating normally. No malfunctions were evident, and all radiation levels were normal. She was going to spring Cathy after lunch. She wanted a chance to evaluate her mental state first hand, before she was released. By all reports, both patients had a restful night.

Turning the corner into the hallway leading to the lounge, she stopped short. A crowd of hospital employees were silently gathered outside the door and as she approached, they parted slowly so she could enter the room. Everyone's attention was focused on the television broadcast of the morning news. Remembering the September 11 attacks on the World Trade Center, she shuddered at how they once again were gathered around the small television, hungry for every detail that it spit out. She was about to ask what was happening when her pager went off, vibrating in her coat pocket. Reaching in and glancing quickly at the number displayed, she saw that it was the hospital administration.

Before she turned to answer her page, she caught sight of the screen, a reporter standing at the front entrance of the hospital, microphone in front of her beautifully made up mouth. She didn't hear the whole report, but what she heard threw her off balance.

"We are reporting live from Bradford University Hospital, ladies and gentlemen, waiting for confirmation from the hospital spokesperson regarding what is being described by our sources as a 'Miracle Healing.' Stay tuned to News Channel 3 for updates as they occur. Amy Levine, reporting live."

Dr. Castiglione reached over and pushed the off button, as chaos erupted in the room.

"People. People. Calm down. Get back to work. We have PATIENTS here!" she said, while backing from the room, coffee long forgotten.

"Dr. Castiglione, do you know what they are talking about?"

"Dr. Castiglione, they said he was bleeding all over the place, and then he spontaneously healed with no sign of injury. Is it true?"

"Who was it, Dr. Castiglione? Is it true?"

"Jesus, Mary and Joseph, it is a miracle," wailed a little Spanish girl, whose nametag said *Maria*. Making the sign of the cross, she pushed her cleaning cart down the hallway, muttering what sounded like the Hail Mary to Beverly's untrained ears.

Momentarily paralyzed, she looked around, taking in a sea of expectant faces. She realized with a start that she had been right. It had proven impossible for this situation to remain contained within the walls of the hospital. She had just not been prepared for the speed with which the word spread.

"Now listen up, people. I have just been paged by hospital administration, so I have to go. I want all of you to report back to your stations and continue caring for the patients. As soon as I figure out what is going on, I will come back up and talk to you. *Do not* talk to the patients about this until we get to the bottom of it. Do you all understand?"

One by one, the staff nodded their heads and went back to their posts. Yes, ma'am, it was going to be one crazy day. She turned quickly and headed for the elevator. Administration was on the first floor and she had an ominous feeling she'd better hurry. She had just been informed that the emergency room and the streets outside the hospital were already beginning to fill with people desperate for a miracle of their own. Like a virus, the news was spreading quickly.

While she waited for the door to open, she glanced down at her watch, surprised to see that it was only nine o'clock in the morning. It had been less than twenty-four hours since the healing had occurred and she knew in her gut that things would not be the same around here for a long time. Her coffee long forgotten, the elevator started its slow descent.

Chapter Thirty Three

Amy Levine took off her microphone and headed for the news van. It was already proving to be a sweltering June day in Nashville. She knew her boss had sent her out here to cover this lame story because she jilted his son, but so what. She would take whatever airtime she could get these days. There was already a small gathering outside the door to the hospital, and she saw a security guard lead someone from the sidewalk to the parking lot.

Jeez, these people are dim-witted. Every religious fanatic within one hundred miles was going to be hobbling up to the hospital doors to be 'healed' before the day was over. That old security guard better be calling for backup before too long. This is a bigger story than the 1996 'Nashville Nun Bun' likeness of Mother Theresa that was found in a cinnamon roll at a local coffee shop. That one made the national news. People. They do like their miracles. Before she finished her train of thought, a patrol car pulled up to the hospital entrance and parked.

"Wake up, David, are you getting all this?" Amy turned to the cameraman as he swung from the front seat of the van, focused on the action, already filming.

"Maybe this won't be such lame assignment, after all. Give me a few minutes to get some notes together, and we'll start interviewing some of the people who are milling around. It may be possible to turn this into a special interest lead- in to the five o'clock broadcast."

By four o'clock, the police had put a barricade around the entrance of the hospital and the street was already beginning to fill with the hopeful, the sick, the lame, and the crazy. The 'end of the world' signs began to sprout, vying for an audience along with the ever present 'repent the end is near'. The sidewalks were crowded with wheelchairs and people carrying portable oxygen tanks, scraping along on walkers and crutches, mothers holding screaming babies and a multitude of other unfortunate specimens of humanity.

By six o'clock, the vendors were standing on the corners, hawking t-shirts and selling bottled water and stuffed animals, most likely left over from the past football season, and even a hot dog cart was making a circuit. The Red Cross had dispatched volunteers to try to keep some semblance of order and make sure the most infirm of the crowd did not expire and fry, right there on the sidewalk. All intersections were closed within six blocks of the hospital.

Every available security guard had been notified to report for a briefing in the hospital cafeteria, and the hospital called in all available medical personnel, as if disaster were imminent. The police had cordoned off the area in front of the university itself and completely blocked one street leading to Bradford University Hospital, for emergency patient and employee access only. All elective surgeries were in the process of being rescheduled. Chaos reigned.

Amy Levine answered her phone for the sixth time in an hour. "Rex, I told you I'm on it. We have it handled. We're supposed to get an announcement any minute now. Quit calling me. I have David filming non-stop and there is no way you can get anyone as close as we are right now. I'm hanging up. We'll send you live feed as soon as they send someone out. It is nuts here. Yes, I see the helicopters. I'm hanging up now." Amy flipped her cell phone closed and threw it on the front seat of the van.

Chapter Thirty Four

Stephen leaned his bike against the faculty building and ran up the steps, only to find the door locked. Things must be bad if someone had persuaded Mrs. McCarthy to abandon her post before five o'clock. He had left his apartment as soon as he saw the news, and headed over to the Macomb's house first, where he discovered no one home. Acting on a hunch, he called the hospital from his cell phone and asked for Jillian Macomb's room. After waiting for what seemed an eternity, the operator came back to the phone and said that her room was not accepting outside calls.

His voice cracking with unspent emotion, he thanked the harried woman and tried to make his way back to the University. Security was tighter than ever, and he said a silent prayer of thanks that he had remembered to take his photo ID card off the dresser. He had already pulled it out of his pocket three times since he made it back to the campus grounds. People were everywhere. He decided he would make better time if he left his bike at the library on campus, so he secured it to the bike rack and took off on foot.

Stopping to purchase bottled water from a vendor on the corner of 23rd and Peterson, he downed it in one gulp. The carnival atmosphere was intensifying. The heat was oppressive and swarms of people added to the already airless misery on the sweltering asphalt streets. It was getting late, close to five thirty, and he had yet to find a way in to see Dr. Macomb.

It was critical that he talk to him about the visions. He had no way to contact him....*Wait a minute!* Stephen stopped in his tracks. Holy Name Cathedral was just around the corner. If Stephen could convince Father Andrews to call the professor for him, he may still have a shot at talking to the professor tonight.

Turning back toward West Avenue and away from the University, Stephen pushed forward through the hot tangle of flesh, heading for the Cathedral, more convinced than ever that the prophecies were about to unfold. He wasn't sure how he was going to do it, but he already knew for certain that he was to protect Jillian at all costs.

*   *   *

"Bishop Tomlin, I know what is happening outside my own door! The parish is being bombarded with prayer requests and people from every religious persuasion demanding that we investigate this so-called 'miracle'. I can only imagine what the streets will be like tomorrow."

"I hear you, Father Andrews. Have you contacted the hospital and spoken with them yet about my visiting the young doctor who they claim was healed?" Bishop Charles Tomlin sat in the study of the Bishops Council House at the USCCB in Washington D.C., tapping his toes, anxious to get back to his committee meeting.

"Yes, but I have not been able to get through to administration. I am telling you, Charles, it is a madhouse here. Unlike anything I have ever seen."

Father Andrews peered out the rectory windows, to the street in front of the Cathedral.

"I am going to have to call in reinforcements, Bishop. I can't have the parishioners standing in front of the Cathedral, chanting and praying, with their rosaries out and candles lit. I have to let them in. It was ninety-five degrees out there today and not expected to be much different tomorrow. Imagine Easter Mass if you will, and that was only the size of the crowd today. I cannot even fathom what tomorrow will bring."

"I know, Phillip. I've seen the news reports, even here. I will try my best to return before Tuesday, although I suspect flights into Nashville may be hard to come by. Perhaps my esteemed colleagues will offer some advice on how best to handle the throngs. Listen, I have the secretary up here trying to commandeer a flight out tomorrow, on an emergency basis."

Bishop Tomlin looked up to see Monsignor Granger peering around the corner of the doorway, pointing to an imaginary watch on his wrist.

"I will call you as soon as I have something arranged," Bishop Tomlin said.

"We must handle this posthaste, Charles. It is going to get out of control quickly, and I don't have the resources to handle this. Our parish is aging and so is your pastor." Father Andrews tried a feeble attempt at humor, but this situation was far from humorous.

"I have even heard whispers about the National Guard."

"Don't go getting all melodramatic on me, Phillip. This, too, shall pass. I will be there as quickly as I can, and in the mean time, do what you can to hold down the fort. I must hang up now… they are holding the meeting for me."

"Godspeed, Bishop Tomlin." Father Andrews listened as the Bishop cut the connection. "Hurry home, Charles," he said into dead airspace.

Father Andrews sat in the darkened living room of the rectory. He could hear Mrs. Murray in the kitchen preparing his evening meal, before she left to walk the three blocks to her home. There had been no further news from the hospital, and the lack of information was causing frenzy in downtown Nashville. As the pastor of the Cathedral, he felt obligated to see to his parishioners, but he was only mortal and the crowds continued to increase. He knew they were waiting for some kind of statement from him, but their sheer numbers frightened him. He had called his deacons this evening and asked them to come in the morning, prepared to stay with him at the rectory until this matter was under control.

He looked up to see his housekeeper standing in the doorway.

"I'll be leaving then, Father. Your dinner is warming in the oven and I left the salad in the refrigerator. Will you need anything else tonight?" Mrs. Murray walked over to the side table and turned on the lamp.

"Won't do you any good to sit here in the dark now, will it, Father?

You need to eat before you start working on your sermon for tomorrow. I expect you will have a full house for all masses. And for once, the congregation will be hanging on every word."

"Thank you, Adele. What would I do without you?" Father Andrews got up, walking her toward the kitchen door. You be careful now. Is Joe coming to meet you?"

"He's already out back waiting for me. I'll see you Monday morning. But, if you need me before then…"

"I'll be fine. You go on and spend time with your family." The priest locked the door behind his housekeeper.

Once inside his study, as he was reaching to turn on the television news, a frantic pounding on the back door momentarily paralyzed him. Already on edge from the events of the afternoon, he roused himself, made the sign of the cross and cautiously headed toward the back door.

"I'm coming, I'm coming." He pulled the shade aside slowly and turned on the outside light, dispelling the early evening shadows from the porch.

Catching sight of the priest peering through the slit in the shade, Stephen called out to him. "Father Andrews! Father Andrews! I must speak to you. Please, Father!"

Stephen pounded on the door again for emphasis, worried that the parish priest would turn away and leave him standing on the stoop.

Opening the door, Father Andrews gasped as he caught full sight of Stephen. "Come in, son, come in. My God, what is the matter with you? You look terrible. Now come sit and let me get you something to drink, Stephen."

"Father…" Stephen started to speak, but the priest cut him off.

"No. You will calm down now and drink this. I am not going anywhere so we can talk when you have had time to catch your breath. Dear Lord, you are a long way from Ontario, Stephen. This heat will knock you out. Now drink."

Handing him the cold water, Father Andrews pulled out a chair at the kitchen table. "Sit right here while I go out and lock the gate. I have a feeling this is going to be an interesting evening."

Chapter Thirty Five

D
r. Castiglione stood behind the administrator of Public Relations at Bradford University Hospital, and waited for the press conference to begin. A makeshift press room, set up just inside the hospital entrance, was so crowded and filled with chatter, she wasn't sure how anyone would hear her speak, even with the microphones. It was almost eight o'clock on Saturday night and looked like it was going to be another all-nighter.

Taking a piece of gum out of her pocket, she removed the wrapper and popped it into her mouth, hoping to relieve the incredible dryness. She had been rehearsing her statement for over an hour, but was still dreading the inevitable questions that would follow. Speaking in front of a crowd, much less in front of a camera, was not her forte'.

Jackson Mullins was still upstairs in the lab, badgering the Macomb girl's personal physician about getting an early amniocentesis. So far, Dr. Richards was standing her ground. From the moxie she had demonstrated thus far, Bev wasn't too worried about leaving her alone with the barracuda. So she was stuck down here on her own, in the unbelievable position of explaining the unexplainable to a throng of insatiable hopefuls.

The hospital administration hoped that a timely and calm response to the public frenzy surrounding the rumors swirling through the community, would convince most of the crowd to disperse and go home. She hoped she could pull it off, because from the looks of the crowd gathered outside, that could take another miracle. The public relations staff had carefully prepared and reviewed her statement, encouraging her to project control of the situation at all times. *Easier said than done.*

All at once, silence. She suddenly realized that she had been introduced. Beverly smoothed her navy skirt and walked to the podium. Adjusting the microphone, she looked out and faced the hungry faces of the press.

"Good evening, ladies and gentlemen. I have a short prepared statement of the facts from the hospital, but will not be able to answer all of your questions at this time. As most of you are aware, we had a situation yesterday afternoon in which a physician, running a routine lab test, was injured on the job and taken immediately to the emergency room for care. During the course of his examination and treatment, the moderately severe wound spontaneously healed, leaving no sign of damage, either temporary or permanent. The physician in question is presently in isolation, being monitored around the clock, to make sure there are no hidden ill effects from the injury and subsequent cure. We are conducting further tests to determine exactly what contributed to his rapid recovery. We are all anxious to get to the bottom of this very unusual occurrence and will share our findings as they become available. Obviously, the knowledge we attain from this phenomenon could eventually prove to be of great benefit to everyone. But, having said that, we must caution you to refrain from jumping to unwarranted conclusions. The hospital is asking that you all return to your homes this evening. This investigation could take weeks, or even months, to conclude. We will make an announcement when we have answers, but until then, it's much too hot and dangerous for many of you to be standing out here on the street. Thank you."

"When can we see him?"

"Are you calling this a miracle? What was he working on?"

"We want to see this man!"

"That is all I am prepared to say at this time." Beverly picked up her note cards and turned to leave the podium.

The crowd continued to lob their questions at the administrator as Dr. Castiglione made a hasty retreat, and she felt guilty for jumping ship.

The truth was, none of them knew what was happening either, and they needed the results from the amniocentesis on the Macomb girl to take their investigation to the next level. She was proud of herself for not using the word 'miracle' once in her statement. Because, at this very moment, she realized that is exactly what she thought it was.

Chapter Thirty Six

What the heck is going on out there? You should see this! There must be a thousand people in the street in front of the hospital." Marc moved back from the window, letting Jillian and Sara closer to take a peek.

"Oh, my God!" Jillian was amazed and delighted at the spectacle on the sidewalk below.

The lights from the police cruisers reflected a mosaic pattern of blue crystal on the ceiling in the room behind them. People were huddled on the curbs, the sidewalks, and sitting in camp chairs. Candles were flickering, and although they couldn't hear them, it was evident from the swaying bodies and and the consistent movement of their lips, that the crowd was singing or praying in unison.

"Is that the girl from Channel 3 out there by the driveway? Over there by the blue van." Sara stretched her neck to see where Marc was pointing.

"Turn on the TV, Jill. Let's see if there's anything on the news about this."

Jillian reached over and grabbed the remote from the bedside table. Clicking the 'on' button, the wall mounted television sprang to life. "Which channel is Channel 3 on this thing? All the numbers are screwed up."

Marc took the remote from his daughter's hand and flipped through the channels until he came upon the scene duplicated outside their window. "Here it is. I got it!"

"Hey, I saw that lady when they were bringing me up to the room!" Jillian said. "She was in the elevator with us, don't you remember?"

Dr. Castiglione stood behind the reporter on the screen.

"Sshhh!" Marc turned up the volume on the television in time to hear the last few words of Dr. Castiglione's statement. As she turned and left the podium, the administrative spokesperson briefly took her place.

"That's all for now, folks. Please go home! Thank you for your patience with the hospital while we investigate this incredible phenomenon." The administrator also left the podium quickly, leaving questions hanging in the air. The camera panned back to the news van and the little blonde reporter lifted her microphone to speak.

"You just heard a statement from Dr. Beverly Castiglione, the Director of Genetics and Genome Research at Bradford University Hospital. To recap, there was a lab accident of some sort yesterday afternoon, in which a doctor was injured. The extent of his injuries has not been disclosed, but they were severe enough to require emergency treatment. We heard directly from Dr. Castiglione, that the wound did, in fact, heal spontaneously, and they are intensely probing the cause of this amazing event. We will continue our coverage of the 'Miracle Healing' and will bring you more information as it becomes available. This is Amy Levine, for Channel 3 News, live at Bradford University Hospital in Nashville."

*   *   *

"Wow." Sara watched the mass of people who remained undaunted by the pleas of the hospital administration and continued their vigil. "People won't leave, Marc, not as long as there is an ounce of hope that there has been a miracle. This is amazing!"

"I'm going out to the nurse's station to see if they can give us more details about what's going on. I'll be right back. While I'm out there, does anybody want a snack from the patient lounge? They have ice cream, Jill." Marc closed the blinds at the window and headed toward the door.

"I'll take ice cream, Daddy," Jill said.

"I'm good for now, Marc. I'll go out and get some tea later. Right now, I'm going to try to get this sofa bed set up for us." Sara picked up the bedding and moved it, so she could open the pullout.

"Why don't you walk around a little, and see if you can find me some magazines somewhere. I think there's a gift shop down by the cafeteria. As long as you have to re-gown anyway, you might as well burn off some steam or you'll go stir crazy before the night is over."

Marc entered the decontamination chamber outside the room, degowned and scrubbed his hands. He put the used gown in the bio hazard bin before he opened the door to the hallway, and was buttoning the cuff of his shirt, when he saw Julie Richards walking down the hall toward Jill's room.

"Hi, Julie, I was just going down to the nurse's station. Do you have the results from Jillian's ultrasound?"

Marc still found himself in somewhat of a daze when he remembered the beautiful images he had witnessed on the ultrasound monitor. Silently, he had watched the technician as he moved the wand carefully over Jillian's abdomen this afternoon. He would never forget the amazing impressions of the tiny child within his child, dancing and whirling to the sound of his daughter's heartbeat. He had no control over his emotions as the likeness of the baby that was projected on the ultrasound monitor formed an indelible image on the screen, and even more astonishingly, into his heart. It was the first time since all this started that the magnitude of this new reality sank in.

"Marc, I was just coming in to speak with you and Sara. It looks like we will be able to do the amniocentesis in the morning. According to the ultrasound, Jillian measures right at fifteen weeks gestation, which as I said before, is a little early, but I think the risk of waiting may outweigh the risk of going ahead."

"You think the baby will be okay?" Marc stopped her, putting his hand on her arm.

"That ultrasound was pretty powerful stuff, wasn't it, Marc? Even now, I never cease to be amazed when I see those tiny images for the first time. To answer your question, we are progressing cautiously. None of us want anything to happen to the fetus. There is a less than one percent chance of complications during this procedure and we have a team of experts going in there with her."

"I trust you, Julie. It will be okay. I know it will. I have faith in you and I have faith in God. Speaking of God, I hear he stopped by the hospital yesterday and performed a miracle."

Yes, can you believe all of this? It is amazing out there. I would say that your little family checked into this five-star hotel just in the nick of time. Parking is a nightmare, and from what I hear, it's getting worse by the minute. If they were hoping to put an end to the madness by having a news conference, they are going to be sorely disappointed."

"Has there been any word on the doctor who was injured?" Marc asked.

"As far as I know, he is resting comfortably." Julie wanted to tell Marc that the intern had been working on Jillian's paternity test when the accident happened, but thought better of it. They had enough on their plate right now without being subjected to irrelevant information.

"I'm going to check in on Jillian before I go downstairs to get some sleep. I think I'll stay in the doctor's lounge tonight, so just have the desk nurse page me if anything comes up during the night. Hopefully, we'll have some answers soon."

"Thanks for everything, Julie. I guess I'll head down to the gift shop and pick up some goodies for the girls. We'll talk tomorrow."

Marc walked down the long hallway and stepped into the elevator. He pushed the button for the first floor and as he stood waiting for the doors to close, the phone in his pocket began to vibrate. Looking quickly at the number, he was surprised to see he had missed six calls and several messages. With a sigh, he decided that it would be prudent to stop at the cafeteria after his visit to the gift shop, so he could listen to messages and sort out the jumbled mass of thoughts raging relentlessly through his head.

Chapter Thirty Seven

S tephen, I understand your passion, but think about what you are saying." Father Andrews walked once more to the window and peered out into the front courtyard of the church.

"I don't like the frenzied climate in the street. If anything, the news coverage has intensified the situation. Come with me please, Stephen. I must check the doors to the sacristy and make sure they are secured. I am quite worried about these crowds. We'll continue our discussion when we return."

Father Andrews walked through the kitchen with Stephen trailing close behind.

"Father Andrews, do you really want to go out there? It sounds pretty boisterous. I don't know how happy folks will be when they discover the doors of the church are going to remain under lock and key," Stephen said.

Stephen was worried about the priest, and his ability to move quickly, if he needed to remove himself from a sticky situation. It crossed his mind that perhaps he should stay with the old man until help arrived in the morning.

"Follow me, Stephen. There is a way. Now you must give me your word that what I am about to show you will remain confidential. I have a good feeling about you, son, and I normally would not do this, but desperate times deserve desperate measures, or something to that effect."

Father Andrews opened the door to the voluminous pantry. There were shelves on the rear wall that housed canned goods of every variety and caloric content, which explained quite a lot to Stephen about the size of his host. Walking to the back of the pantry, Father Andrews pushed on a wooden panel, revealing a hidden slide bolt on the side of the shelf unit and unlocked it quickly. With a slight tug, the whole shelf unit swung wide, revealing a doorway. Opening the door, the priest reached out and pulled the string on a naked light fixture that hung at the top of the exposed stairway.

"Watch your head, Stephen, and pull the unit back into place behind you. You can lock it from this side. The latch is along the side, set into the doorframe."

Father Andrews pointed to the side wall, and following his instruction, Stephen felt blindly until he found the bolt and slid the barrel into place.

"Father Andrews, this is very cloak and dagger, almost medieval. I can't see very far into the basement. Is there another light?"

Making his way gingerly down the dark and narrow stairway, Stephen had the feeling that if he tried to stand, his head would make contact with the very low ceiling, so he stood slightly stooped at the bottom of the stairs.

"There are some flashlights over here if I'm not mistaken, and if need be, there are candles and matches in a box under the bottom step. Wait a minute. I found the flashlights and, lo and behold, praise Jesus, they work. Let me grab one for you," Father Andrews said.

Flipping the light switch, Stephen fanned the beam across the room. The rafters were exposed and his initial suspicion of the low ceiling height was not too far off base, although he was relieved that it was possible to stand upright with about three inches to spare.

"There is a tunnel, son, that runs beneath the rectory and underground to the church. During World War I, the Bishop of Nashville decided the Cathedral might need an underground escape route and some hiding places. Saint Anne's, the original Cathedral in Nashville, was a makeshift military hospital in the mid 1800's during the Civil War, so I suppose the reigning Bishop wanted to make sure that any Cathedral built during his tenure would be ready for anything."

"This is really something." Stephen looked around the cavernous room and adjoining tunnels with awe. "Amazing. It's like an underground city."

"I suspect you would find many such rooms and passageways all over the south, son. The war forced people to make decisions. I'm sure there are secrets hidden within the walls of many structures in Nashville. People do what they have to do to survive, or to help others survive. Oppression is not so different in any century. Look at the years of religious persecution in your own studies of ancient religions, Stephen…the very history you study with such a vengeance."

The tunnel itself was narrow, much tighter than Stephen would have imagined, and had he been of ample girth like his tour guide, he would have found it quite claustrophobic. The passage curved slightly left toward the end of the trail and the damp stone walls suddenly gave way to a stone stairway leading up to another door. Thankful that Father Andrews knew which passageway to take, he was filled with a new respect and admiration for his counselor.

"We're here, Stephen. I'll go through first to open the chamber door, as it appears there is no room for both of us to maneuver. This small vestibule empties into the far left confessional just outside the sacristy. Before I open the door, we must extinguish our lanterns so as not to be visible from the front of the church. The stained glass will do well to hide us from the people outside, but I fear the beams from our lights bobbing up and down would give us away in short order."

The muted noise from the massive crowds of people permeated the heavy oak doors of the cathedral, reminding Stephen of the first dream. It seemed such a contrast to him. Here he was, standing in this tranquil place with the sound of holy water softly emptying into the baptismal font, the smell of beeswax and the soft flickering of candles in the darkened church offering peace, yet the mayhem reigned. The hope of many that miracles do exist, was wreaking havoc right outside the Cathedral doors.

Father Andrews made his circuit, quietly checking the locks and the deadbolts on the exterior doors, and setting the alarms and motion detectors, before they retraced their steps through the depths of the Cathedral and back to the rectory. It seemed surreal to be imprisoned within the eerie dark confines of the bowels of the church. Stephen felt uneasy in spite of himself. The damp earthen smell of the basement rooms and niches brought to mind the cave in his dreams, where Jillian had pleaded for his help. Filled with new resolve, he followed the bulky form of the priest through the labyrinth and back to the warm and cozy kitchen of the rectory.

"That was quite an adventure, Stephen, if I do say so myself. Now, let's have some of this spaghetti casserole Mrs. Murray put up for me and then we'll discuss your visions." Father Andrews chuckled as he pulled the steaming casserole dish from the oven and set it on the small table.

Turning back to the pantry, Father Andrews reached for a loaf of bread to add to their meal and then looked at his guest.

"Come, come, Stephen. I'm not laughing at you. We must find some humor in this situation or we'll quite possibly go mad. Let's eat. Shall we pray?"

The two men bowed their heads and gave thanks, then ate their meal in silence, both lost in thought. In the background, the sound from the television echoed the muffled din that seeped in from the streets outside. Stephen was famished and finished everything on his plate before leaning back in his chair to contemplate the priest and his present situation at the Cathedral.

"Father Andrews, allow me to make a pot of coffee while you finish." Pushing his chair from the table, Stephen took his plate to the sink and walked back to the pantry, opening the door. "I suppose I'll find what I need in the quasi pantry, won't I?"

"Yes, please. Help yourself. Coffee would be wonderful, as I don't see how we will get much rest tonight, anyway." Father Andrews blotted his mouth with a paper napkin and wadding it up, threw it onto his plate.

"I'm in awe at the virtual underground maze that exists beneath this Cathedral. I mean, you read about these things, but to actually see it is amazing."

"Yes, it is amazing. I vividly remember my introduction to the catacombs. I was alone, Stephen, and I believe that when I finally found my way back to the rectory, it was the first time I ever noticed a touch of gray in my hair."

"Would you like me to stay the night, Father? I really don't like thinking of you here alone should something come up. If the deacons are arriving in the morning, I'll feel much better about handing over the guard to them, so to speak. Do you mind?"

"I think that is an excellent idea, Stephen. I can't say I feel totally at ease with this happening right outside the door, and darkness does have a way of amplifying unusual circumstances. I will be glad when the Bishop comes back to town. He is much more decisive than I. Anyway, now that you have decided to stay, we'll be able to spend time in real conversation about your dreams. Shall we take our coffee into the living room?"

Already familiar with the room from his earlier visit, Stephen once again sat in the easy chair, setting his cup on the side table.

"Father Andrews, I didn't tell you everything about my dreams when I was here last time."

"I would expect that you held some things close to the vest, Stephen. It takes time to feel comfortable with whomever you choose to entrust with your thoughts."

The priest walked over and turned off the television. The absence of background noise only served to amplify the undercurrent created by the growing crowd outside the rectory.

"It won't be the first time I've not had the complete story at the start of a counseling session. Establishing trust is a complicated endeavor, but perhaps with the situation we find ourselves in tonight, well, just maybe the trust issue has been hastened along."

"Last time we spoke, you asked me to keep a journal. It's hard to believe it was only a few days ago. I did exactly that. I wrote down all I could remember from each dream, as far back as I could remember."

"Excellent, Stephen. And what did you discover?"

"Probably not what you intended I discover. I am more convinced than ever that what I have experienced is a prophecy of something that is going to happen. The first vision was only a warning, I believe… an image designed to convince me that the girl and her child will be in grave danger if I chose not to act. She will be persecuted in some way and perhaps even harmed. The woman and child are to be protected at all costs. An angry mob murdered her in my dream. They stoned her and were ready to kill me for trying to defend her honor. The intent of the first vision was to get my attention, and we both know how well it succeeded in doing just that."

"Okay, Stephen. But what is it that you are to protect her from? An irate parent? A jilted lover? This is the twenty-first century and these children are not looked upon as bastards anymore. We discussed this Thursday. There is no shame, right or wrong, in having a child out of wedlock. And why do you believe it is more than a dream? How do you know it's not something else that haunts you subconsciously and has seeped into your dreams?"

"Father, the last time I was here, you talked about how easy it would be to get carried away with the mysteries of Christianity, in light of the research I do. With all due respect, sir, I thought about just that, and I believe that's exactly why I have been chosen. Think for a moment about the virgin birth of Jesus through the Immaculate Mother Mary. She was a young girl, visited by the Angel Gabriel and told of an impending pregnancy and birth of a son. She accepted her vision and her fate without question, and agreed to do God's will at whatever the cost to her. Now fast forward to Joseph. Also visited by an angel and assured that his betrothed was being truthful about her pregnancy. Because he accepted and believed in his vision, and placed his trust in God, he saved his future bride from certain death. Mary was a good girl. If we are to believe that the Bible reflects the Word of God, she had known no man in such an intimate way. Is that not what Church Doctrine supports?"

"Absolutely, Stephen. But in those days…"

"We are asked to believe that she gave birth to the Son of God. Is it so hard for us to consider the possibility that it could happen again? God speaks to us and works through us in mysterious ways. We need only open our minds to the possibility and let him into our hearts. He has promised he will come again."

"Surely, Stephen, you are not comparing your visions to the birth of the Son of God. And who is this girl, Stephen. The one you are to protect? Are you saying hers will also be a blessed birth?"

"Yes. No. I don't know. How could I possibly know the answer to that question? I am asking you to keep an open mind, Father. We cannot presume to know what God has in mind for our future. Do you think that everyone believed Joseph and Mary about her fidelity? I would imagine, even in those days, there was suspicion and denial. Why is it so hard for us to open our minds to the possibility that God is sending us another message and we must be open to him? Look outside your very window, Father. There's your proof positive that people are starving for a sign."

"Okay, let's presume for a moment that you are to take this girl away, so as to protect her and her unborn child. What are you to protect her from, Stephen?"

"I'm not sure yet. I know that sounds ludicrous, but I know I will recognize it clearly when the time is right for me to act. I am not a fanatic, Father Andrews. I kept fighting the dreams and trying to rationalize every possible reason for them. Throughout the ages, people have been receptive to visions and the prophecy of God's plan. The Bible is filled with accounts of messengers and heavenly apparitions. We call them prophets. Why should we close our minds to that possibility in today's world, or give our visions any less credence? I need your help, Father."

"Oh, Stephen, what can I possibly do to help you, except listen to you and council you to be patient and pray for guidance as you work this out?"

"Father, just believe that I am not a lunatic and promise me you'll keep an open mind."

"You have my word, Stephen. I won't call the University hotline or anything like that. I do believe you're sane, although somewhat misguided. I will promise to do what I can to help you through this, Stephen."

"I need your help to get in touch with Marc Macomb. I need to talk to him"

"Do you think that's wise, Stephen? It's one thing to talk to me as your confessor, but he is your mentor and an esteemed professor of the Divinity School. Should you not wait until you have worked through some of these questions, before you bring all this up with him? He was instrumental in bringing you to Nashville. I trust you realize that he could just as easily send you packing."

"He's not been at the university all week, Father. I saw him briefly yesterday and he told me he was working through a family issue. I have reason to believe his daughter, Jillian, is in the hospital, as we speak. I called on a hunch before I came over here and asked for her room. I was told she wasn't taking calls."

"You what?" Father Andrews shot out of his chair and stormed across the room with a speed that belied his girth.

"Stephen, why on earth would you think Jillian Macomb was in the hospital? That is a flagrant disregard of their privacy! You are teetering very close to the line, young man. I know you are sincere and you believe in your visions, but this must stop! I can't have you stalking Professor Macomb and his family!"

"But, she is in the hospital. Father Andrews, listen to me. I believe everything that is happening now, including the miracle and Marc Macomb's daughter, are all part of what is happening in my visions." Stephen stood and gestured at the window.

"This is all connected and I have to talk to Marc Macomb. You are the only person I know who has a way to contact him for me." Stephen turned and sat once again, lowering his head to his hands, sure that he just lost his only hope of an ally.

The priest undoubtedly thought him deranged. When he looked again at Father Andrews, he was begging.

"Please, Father. Please call him for me, just to make sure everything is okay."

"Stephen, this has to sound ludicrous even to you. If Jillian has been admitted to the hospital, what on earth could that have to do with any of the madness outside?"

"Because, Father Andrews. Jillian Macomb is the girl in my dreams."

Chapter Thirty Eight

When can we go home?" Jillian was staring out the window, glowering at the people clustered on the streets below. "We've been here for two days and I feel fine. They got their test and I want to leave."

Sara came out of the bathroom, towel drying her hair. She walked silently over to Jillian and closed the blinds. The crowds outside had not shown the slightest inclination to disperse and their muffled noise was an ever-present undercurrent that seeped into the room. Sara looked at her daughter and smoothing the hair from her brow, she leaned over and kissed her on the cheek.

This was her baby, her little girl, and no matter what they discovered, they were in it together for the long haul.

Marc escaped earlier to get coffee and call his office, the inactivity already taking a toll on him after only two days. Yesterday had seemed unending, and they were all starting to feel the effects of being trapped within the walls of the isolation chamber. The amniocentesis had been traumatic for Marc and Sara, but it was the waiting that dragged everyone down. Not even the results could be as bad as the waiting. At least then, you would have something concrete to focus on.

"Dr. Richards is going to come in and talk to us this morning, Jill. If everything checks out, I think they will probably let us leave this afternoon, but you're still going to have to lie low for a few days."

Jillian catapulted herself onto the bed and threw her head against the pillow. She hated being in this little room with her parents and hated that everyone who walked through the door was wearing a mask and gloves. She felt like there was something wrong with her, and even though they explained it was to keep her from getting infected with germs from outside, she still felt like a lab rat. That needle they used for the amniocentesis had been humongous. Like a scene from some horror show.

It turned out to be only a little bit uncomfortable, but she could not watch them stick that thing into her belly. They all said they were proud of her, and she had tolerated the test with no obvious side effects. Except that she wanted to tell them she was going nuts. The baby was flipping around all the time now, and based on the way she was feeling, they all had to agree there was no reason to believe that anything bad was going to happen. She just wanted to go home and not have her parents at her side every second, watching every move she made.

Arianna came to her again last night in her dreams. She didn't know how her parents slept through her angel light, but they did. Jillian had been sleeping soundly and suddenly felt a draft, like the soft warm air that blows across your skin on a summer night. She sat up in bed and there was the faintest glow, a slight glimmer in the corner of the room that radiated outward and moved closer, until her angel was right there, standing at the foot of the bed.

"Arianna, I'm glad you came. I want to leave here. I want to go home. Isn't there some way you can speed things up around here?"

"Dear Jillian. I want you to listen carefully. I know you are getting impatient, but it won't be much longer. You must be very brave now, Jillian. Things are going to happen that you won't understand, but you must believe in God's plan for you and for the child you carry."

"I told you I would believe, and I do. And things are already happening that I don't understand. But Arianna, it's boring and when you aren't here, I'm a little nervous that I won't know what to do."

"God will provide you a guardian, Jillian, someone you can trust. You must believe that God has sent him to keep you safe. There will be much confusion and doubt, and even though he has been sent to comfort you,

you may not always be sure. He will tell you something that no one else could know. Only then, will you know that the time has come and you must follow him."

"What does that mean? What about my parents? Are they going, too? This is so confusing, Arianna. Can't you just tell me now what I need to know?"

"You will know, Jillian, when the time is right. Your parents will not go with you, but must stay behind until it is their time. You must trust that everything will be as it should be. The peace of the Lord will be with you."

Jillian had looked over at her parents lying spooned together on the sofa bed. Gross. They could hear her at home when she snuck down to the kitchen for a glass of milk, but were sleeping through this bright light and her whole conversation with an angel. She couldn't believe it.

"Can't we just wake them up, Arianna? Maybe, if they could talk to you about this whole baby thing, they would know that I'm not nuts and am telling the truth. It would only take a minute and then you could go back to heaven and report that everyone is on board."

"Jillian Grace, the message is meant only for you. Your parents will believe because they are filled with faith in God. Make no mistake. Their faith is about to be tested. But they will believe. I must leave you now, but remember this, Jillian…the time is close at hand and you must not falter. Your guardian is one of the chosen and you must follow him without fear. He will keep you safe."

"Arianna, I am a little bit afraid."

"Put your faith in the Lord, Jillian. Trust in him."

Arianna started to fade away, the glow in the room began to diminish and soon she was gone. Jillian knew that she might as well go back to sleep, because there wasn't anything she could do about any of this.

So now, she sat on the edge of the bed watching her mother got dressed, and could only hope that they would let her go home today. It was so hard to believe that it had only been a week since all this started. Her mom and dad had stopped asking her about the father of her baby, now that they knew it wasn't Jamie. She didn't know what she could say to them about that, but she did wonder when she should tell them about her angel. Arianna said she would know what to do, so she wasn't going to worry about it now.

Sara and Jillian heard the outer door open and the sound of the hand sink being operated. "How are my girls doing?" Marc's voice bounced into the room and he followed, balancing a tray of coffee and bagels.

"Have we heard from the doctor yet?" He walked over to the bed and kissed Jillian on the forehead.

"Julie said she'd be up before noon, but I haven't heard from her yet. How's crowd control out there? It still looks crazy." Sara took her coffee from Marc and added cream.

"Unbelievable, Sara. There are news crews all over the place and the story made headlines in the Tennessean and on the front page of USA Today. Crazy. The Bishop is flying back to Nashville today according to the paper, and the church will be sending over a team of clergy to investigate the so-called miracle. Did you know they have a special investigation team for miracles? I even heard a rumor in the cafeteria that some Government officials are arriving tonight to interview the hospital executives." Marc went to the window and tilted the blinds slightly, so he could observe the street below.

"Well, imagine the implications. Government officials would definitely want to investigate the spontaneous healing of serious wounds. Think about it, Marc. It is miraculous. My sister called… they've even heard about it in Michigan. I told her I would call her back tonight and fill her in on everything else that has been going on. I guess it's time to bring everyone on board. Were you able to get in touch with anyone at your office?" Sara spread cream cheese on a bagel and handed it to Jillian, who was busy flipping through the channels on the television.

"I left a message for the Dean and also for Mrs. McCarthy. I can only imagine how the University is handling this influx of people. From what I understand, they have security beefed up and are only allowing the faculty and students, who live or work on campus, access to the grounds. They have several check points set up. Everyone has to flash their University ID and sign in to enter and exit the buildings. No cars in or out past a certain point, and they are searching all delivery trucks for reporters or anyone else trying to get closer to the scene of the miracle."

"God, Marc. How are we going to get home?"

"We'll be okay. They have one access road set up for admissions and a separate road for discharges from the hospital. I had several messages on my cell from Father Andrews over at the Cathedral, but I can't get through on the direct line to the church to return his calls. Can you imagine what his day must be like? I know I have his cell number, but its back at my office. I'm hoping Mrs. McCarthy can snag it for me. I want to call Stephen Jacobs, too. I think I'm going to have him come in tomorrow and help me catch up on some of the paperwork I've fallen behind on. If we can even get into the office, that is. He offered to help when he stopped by Friday night. I feel bad about giving him the brush-off. The poor guy is probably bored and homesick and wondering what the hell is going on here."

"I'm glad you are going to call him. You can use the help and he's a nice kid. You need to go to the office, Marc. You left in such a hurry on Monday. I'm sure everyone is frantic and wondering what's going on with you."

"You're right. But I have a feeling that the 'Miracle Healing' has taken the heat off the Macomb's, at least short term."

Sara was folding the sofa bed back into sofa position, when a sharp knock sounded at the door.

"Good morning. Can I come in?" Julie Richards poked her head around the corner of the partition and was pulling her gloves on as she rounded the corner.

"How's my favorite patient this morning?"

"I'm ready to go home, Dr. Richards."

"I'm sure you are. No cramps or leakage from the test yesterday? The nurses said everything looks great as far as your vital signs. Let's take a listen."

Julie picked up the stethoscope and listened to Jillian's chest, then placed the Doppler on her abdomen so they could all hear the steady swish, swish, swish of the baby's heart.

"The baby's heartbeat sounds good and strong." Julie stood up and faced her patient. "I'd like to have a short meeting with mom and dad, to let them know what the tests are showing us so far, and then we'll talk about when you can go home. Sound like a deal?"

Chapter Thirty Nine

Marc and Sara waited for Julie at a table outside on the fourth floor balcony, overlooking the park behind the hospital. Crowd control was evident everywhere by now, and the playground and gardens across the street were eerily silent. As part of the university and hospital grounds, that area was off limits to the public for the immediate future. Sitting on a covered portico, the ceiling fans brought welcome relief from the blistering heat. It wasn't even noon and the day already promised to be sweltering. They could still hear the sounds of hymns being sung, and the rhythmic cadence of fervent prayers coming from the crowd, but the continuous pleas to be cured were muted. It felt so good to escape the confines of the small room, that neither of them minded the sheltered heat of the piazza.

Julie Richards came out and joined them, Jillian's file in hand.

"Are you okay out here? I know it's hot, but I figured we'd have more privacy. Who in their right mind would want to be out in this heat if they didn't have to, right?"

"It's fine, Julie. It actually feels good to be outside, and it's not that bad here."

"If you're sure about that, I'll get right to the point so you can get back inside. I don't know quite where to start, so you'll have to bear with me while I try to explain what's going on with Jillian's case."

First, and most importantly, I don't want you to be alarmed, because on all accounts, the baby and Jillian seem to be doing fine. But having said that, I must also tell you that I have never seen a pregnancy follow this course. I have pursued every tag or line of research I can possibly track, and have a team of interns following every plausible, or even, implausible lead. There is nothing to explain Jillian's test results."

Fat silent tears rolled down Sara's cheeks and she reached out to hold Marc's hand. "I'm scared and confused, Julie. If Jillian is doing fine and the baby is doing fine, what is the problem? I am just so tired and worried."

Clearing the obvious emotion from his throat, Marc said, "What is it about the results of the tests that concern you? What exactly are you researching?"

"I am going to explain everything I know so far. Let me just say that Dr. Jackson Mullins is an expert in genome and genetic research here at the hospital and has published papers on various subjects having to do with genetics. He is one of the leaders on the case, so you have some great people involved in Jillian's care.

"Last week, when we did the Chorionic Villas Sampling, the CVS, the results were inconclusive. We assumed the sampling had somehow been contaminated, because the sample presented with a strange characteristic that we had not seen before. To put it simply, an atypical molecular glow was observed. While Dr. Mullins was able to conclusively eliminate Jamie Tyler as the biological father of the fetus, no tests for genetic abnormalities could be performed with any clarity. We feared the sampling had been altered in some way, incompatible with reliable test results."

"So the contamination of the first sampling led to the amniocentesis," Marc said. "Is there a chance that Jamie is the father after all? I mean, would the amniocentesis clear that up without a doubt?"

"No, there is no chance that Jamie is the father. The DNA ruled that out completely. And yes, the amniocentesis will definitely affirm the original results of paternity. Let me try to show you. Bear with me, I am not an artist. DNA is the molecular makeup that all humans have in common, but at the same time, it proves that each of us is unique. You've both seen the double helix model of DNA."

Julie opened a notepad and fished a pen from the pocket of her lab-coat.

"Sort of looks like a spiral staircase. Let's separate the double helix into two strands. A strand and B strand. Here is the double strand for the mother and here is the double strand for the father." Julie sketched a rudimentary design of the double helix.

"There is a chain of four nucleotides on the A strand of the helix that complement the four nucleotides on the opposing, or B side. These are the steps of the staircase so to speak. Sequencing of these nucleotides is what gives Marc blue eyes and Sara brown. It's the subsequent combination of the parent strands that cause a new DNA sequence to occur, thus creating a new genome, or new sequence of hereditary material that becomes the double helix or DNA makeup of the fetus. In evolution, the genomes can change, but these mutations usually happen over the course of several generations."

"I think I understand the basics." Sara said.

Flipping the pad closed, Julie said, "Close enough. In Jillian's case, it is simple chemistry to trace her DNA to the fetus. Every female passes her mitochondrial DNA (mtDNA) to the fetus. That is the line that geneticists usually look at very closely, because mtDNA is passed down from generation to generation. In Jillian's case, the paternal DNA is showing signs of mutation. Something we've not seen before. Ever. And couple that with the lack of HCG, or human chorionic gonadotropin in her blood to sustain a pregnancy, we have a medical mystery on our hands."

"What does all this mean? Jillian seems fine and you said the baby seems fine." Marc was relieved and worried at the same time. And his confusion was evident.

"I don't know what it means. That's what we are working on now. Dr. Mullins is in the lab right now, preparing new slides for sequencing. Dr. Castiglione is the Director of Genome and Genetic research at the University and is also involved in every step of the process. We are hoping the information we obtain from the amniocentesis will give us the clues we need to find the cause of this phenomenon."

"And what happens then?" Marc asked.

"Remember, the CVS may have been corrupt and the amniocentesis may provide normal results. But we are still trying to understand the lack of HCG. I have to tell you, if I hadn't seen the baby with my own two eyes and heard the heartbeat, I would say this pregnancy was impossible."

"Wow. But she is pregnant. I mean, we have all seen a presumed healthy baby, right? You have two miracles in one hospital, Julie! What are the odds of that?" Marc was only half joking.

"How is the doctor who is providing us with all the intrigue? Has he shown any problems or abnormalities since being healed?"

"He is being discharged soon. He asked the PR department not to put out a statement to the press until after he is liberated. The poor guy has been poked and prodded so much this last few days, his original injury must seem like a piece of cake. Even the virtual ambush by the public and the media must seem attractive to him, after his last few days with us," Julie said.

"Does he know what he's walking into? The crowds are fierce out there, and if he's released and people know about it, they'll feel a sense of entitlement. They'll want some kind of physical contact with him. It's human nature. This is all so incredible," Sara said.

"I do know that security is intense for him. His plan is to lay low for a few days, away from the hospital, to see if things will die down after he's gone. He wants to get back to interning, but that would be detrimental for both him and the hospital right now, and he's aware of that. We aren't sure how the story leaked, but those things have a way of finding their way into the public domain at the speed of light. This, too, shall pass." Julie closed the file and looked at the couple sitting in front of her, wishing she had some concrete theory to offer them.

"How are they going to explain his release to the public?" Marc asked.

"Dr. Castiglione is going to give another press conference to let everyone know we are still working on the case. What can you do? The truth is the truth."

"Maybe by then, they'll have something figured out." Marc wiped beads of perspiration from his brow.

"Hey, I do have a little trivia for you. I didn't want to say anything to you until things calmed down a little, but coincidentally, he was the intern working on the paternity test for Jillian. Jillian's slide was actually the one that broke when he was working on the case with Mullins. There is some thought that whatever agent caused the contamination of her slide, may have had something to do with the healing. Just a hypothesis at this point, but it's a small world."

"Dear Lord, can this get any more complicated?" Sara asked.

"Listen, it is quite a coincidence, but also an interesting fact to share with your grandchild some day. He can say he was indirectly involved in the 'Miracle Healing.'" Julie smiled at them, relieved that she had finally shared this information with the Macomb's, no matter how irrelevant.

"Can we take our daughter home now?" Marc pushed up from the table and went over to the railing. "We just want normalcy for a while, Julie. If she feels fine and the baby looks fine, everything else will work out one way or another. You have everything you need for your blueprint, and nothing is going to change the DNA, whether she's home or at the hospital."

"Yes, Julie, I can bring her to your office whenever you need to check her, but this isolation, and the circus outside, is starting to wear on all of us." Sara was precariously close to tears again, and looked at Julie with pleading eyes. "We just need a break. This past week has been more than any of us were equipped to deal with."

"I wanted to keep her until we got the preliminary results back from the amniocentesis. I'll tell you what. I will discharge her, but you have to promise to be within reach at all times. Do you still have your hospital pager, Sara?" Sara nodded. "Dr. Mullins will have a fit, but the truth is, I can't find a reason to keep her under lock and key. This isolation protocol was a little over the top anyway, but better safe than sorry. It may take months to find answers, and by that time, the baby will be here. You're going to have to bring Jillian to my office every week for an ultrasound and blood test. If there is even one minute change in her condition, or if Dr. Mullins finds something threatening in the test results, she is going to be referred to a high risk pregnancy specialist and plopped right back into the hospital."

"You got it, boss." Marc hugged her. "We do appreciate everything, Julie. We'll watch her like a hawk. Anyway, it looks like you will have your hands full here with the whole miracle phenomenon. Good luck with that."

"Thanks, we'll need it. I'll be up in a few minutes to sign her discharge papers. I'm going to call security to escort you down the back elevator, but listen, be careful out there. You don't live that far from the University, and I don't know how far this craziness has spread. Weird things are happening everywhere. Marc, bring your car around to the physician's entrance and I'll let them know you're coming. You'd better skedaddle before they get wind that Dr. Miracle is leaving us today. Oops, don't repeat that. You did not hear that from me."

"Hear what? Boy, take a look at those clouds moving in from the west. It looks like there is going to be going to be one whale of a summer storm. Those poor people on the street are in for some rough weather. I wish everyone would just go home." Julie followed the Macomb's into the hospital, as thunder rumbled in the distance and lightning arched across the morning sky.

Chapter Forty

Dr. Mullins grasped the tube of amber liquid between his thumb and index finger, and holding it up to the light, examined it closely. *Liquid gold.* He had started the procedure for preparing the amniotic sample for DNA extraction and was anxiously waiting to begin. He was working in a Level II clean room and had forbid anyone to enter. No more mishaps by inept fools.

His intention was to put the pieces of the puzzle together, one step at a time, to figure out where the breach in protocol had occurred that inadvertently caused the spontaneous healing of Dr. Sorrento's hand. Mullins chuckled to himself. He had to give the bumbling intern credit. His clumsiness may one day be compared to Isaac Newton sitting under the apple tree. Except that the name associated with the process would be Jackson Mullins, MD. PhD. FAAP. FACMG. He could see it now. A discovery of such magnitude would certainly go down in history.

He hated the fact that the Government felt the need to send a representative from the National Science Foundation to hang around in the visitors lounge. If that weren't bad enough, the Bishop of Nashville had landed today. Investigate a miracle. He had no time for these petty interruptions, but Beverly Castiglione smugly informed him that he was to make time to be interviewed while he waited for the DNA tests to begin in earnest. Did they all expect a 'eureka moment'?

Well, he planned to be well compensated for his work. He was a pioneer in his field and no one would hinder his success, nor forget his name. It would all happen on his time schedule and not one minute before. He had to let them discharge the intern, but he made sure to collect enough blood and serum samples to last a millennium. He believed Sorrento was only the effect anyway, and Jackson Mullins was intent on finding the cause.

He was more than a little frustrated. The CVS contamination was absolute and the exact results were replicated every time he prepared the slides. He followed each procedure exactly as Sorrento had documented it on the day of the 'miracle'. Many times. Every ingredient even remotely key to the CVS testing had checked out unexceptionally, with no contamination, so it was the CVS sample itself that was ruined.

He had no choice but to try and duplicate the paternity test with the amniotic fluid he obtained yesterday. Borrowing one little drop would not interfere with the genetic testing, and no one would be the wiser about his little digression.

Dr. Mullins carefully opened the tube of amniotic fluid and extracted a drop with a sterile pipette, before he placed the cylinder back in storage. Placing a single drop on the end of a sterile swab, he gently swiped the slide and allowed it to air dry. He wanted to observe raw amniotic fluid under the microscope, before the more complex tests began. Once it had dried completely and the glass slide was in place, he lowered his eye to the lens.

Amniotic fluid had certain characteristics when allowed to air-dry on a slide. The crystals that formed on the glass would be fern-like in appearance. Dr. Mullins focused and refocused the lens. He felt the hair stand up on the back of his neck. *This can't be happening.* Quickly moving across the room, he withdrew the capsule containing the amniotic fluid from the Macomb girl, and willfully calming his shaking hands, once again withdrew a single drop of the fluid from the encapsulated tube.

Removing a sterile slide from the drawer, he placed a swab on the open end of the pipette and watched it absorb the drop of liquid from the small tube. Smearing the new slide, he once again waited impatiently for it to air-dry before placing it under the microscope, and lowering his eyes to the lens.

It was never the procedure. It's the fluid from the girl. Jackson flew across the lab, leaving the clean room through the airlock, throwing his gloves aside as he tore through the chamber. He was intent only on obtaining a clean amniotic sample from another patient at the hospital for comparison. Hurrying over to the Level I lab, he headed straight for the cart holding the new draws, grateful that no technicians were in sight. He gloved up quickly and withdrew a random tube from the fluids that had been drawn this morning.

Unlocking the drawer that held the sterile syringes, he went to a work station and removed the stopper from the tube. Inserting the needle, he withdrew 3cc's of the amber liquid and capping the syringe, placed it in his pocket, and returned the tube to its rightful place on the tray.

Heart slamming against his ribcage, he could hear the lab technician coming around the corner. He knew he had to leave the area before he was spotted and forced to explain his presence. He did not want to be caught with his hand in the proverbial cookie jar. Sliding behind the partition of the work station closest to the door, he was blocked from her view. Lowering himself quickly onto a stool, he bent over a microscope, in the event she looked over and spotted him. *Damn. He had left the drawer open that housed the syringes.*

The lab tech walked over to the cart and pushing it down the aisle, picked up the clipboard and started to reach for a tube when she noticed the drawer.

"This is the second time this week. Where is that guy? This time he gets a piece of my mind."

Mullins heard the jangle of keys as the tech slammed the drawer shut, locking it, before she turned and angrily walked further into the lab.

Just enough time to make my exit. Mullins slid around the partition and made his way through the double door, paying no attention to the heated exchange going on in the lab behind him. Retracing his steps, he moved back into the airlock, carefully following protocol. He hurried back into Level II to begin his control test.

Chuckling to himself for the second time that day, Jackson Mullins was already sure of what he would find when he prepared the new slide from the anonymous donor.

Chapter Forty One

Monday morning dawned with the Cathedral awash in the soft light of a spectacular sunrise. Already hot and muggy, Stephen could feel the tepid air pouring from the air conditioner, as it struggled to remove the humidity from the rectory. He had agreed to stay with Father Andrews until the Bishop arrived this afternoon. He didn't mind, really. His impatience to talk to Marc Macomb receded a little when he saw the critical impact the 'miracle' situation was having outside the church on Sunday morning. He found himself literally at ground zero.

Yesterday had been a war zone, and the old priest had found it almost too daunting a task to say mass. The National Guard had been called to Nashville to keep the crowds in check, and water stations had been set up on almost every corner, each with a guardsman standing close watch. The heat was grueling and the number of people filtering into the city increased on an hourly basis. The Guard was successfully backing the crowd further away from the doors of the Cathedral, and by the time the eight o'clock bell chimed in the tower, Father Andrews was able to say mass to a packed house.

The Bishop had approved the addition of several daily masses, which helped appease the throng of people that were lined up and waiting to get into the Cathedral. Everyone would get their chance to hear mass and receive Holy Communion. The Sacrament of Penance had been streamlined and was held before each mass with the congregation as a whole.

Communion wafers were being shipped by the thousands, directly to the Cathedral from the supplier. Every Catholic parish within one hundred miles was reporting an unprecedented number of worshippers.

Deacons were in demand and being pressed into service, whether readily available or not, to help lighten the load on the parish priests. A statement issued from the diocese assured the faithful that the occurrence in Nashville was under immediate investigation. People were strongly cautioned against forming conclusions about the event until the results of the inquiry were complete. They were urged to keep their faith focused on the present and to be mindful of their fellow man. The Church as a whole would not be commenting further on the supposed 'miracle' until the examination of the facts was complete and the findings scrutinized.

Stephen woke to the smell of frying bacon and realized he was famished. The amazing Mrs. Murray must have somehow made her way through the barricade and into the kitchen. He stretched languidly and rose from the bed, pulling off the soiled linens as he headed to the shower.

"Stephen, come down to breakfast when you've finished. We shall have a short meeting before you leave." Father Andrews called through the door.

The last few days had been taxing and he had been impressed with Stephen's ability to roll with the punches, and quietly amused at his inept fumbling, while serving as an impromptu altar server at several of the masses yesterday. Father Andrews finally decided that Stephen's passion and belief in his dreams deserved his respect, and in light of the craziness happening all around them, it would not be appropriate for him to judge the boy prematurely. God did indeed work in mysterious ways.

Taking the stairs two at a time, Stephen looked somewhat rested when he appeared at the kitchen doorway.

"It smells great in here."

"Stephen, I'd like you to meet Mrs. Murray. She is the boss around here during the week, and she takes very good care of us as you can plainly see. I am proof of how good she is in the kitchen." Father Andrews patted his ample middle and motioned Stephen over to join him at the table.

"Nice to meet you, I'm sure, Stephen. Now you two eat a good breakfast. No telling what today will bring." Mrs. Murray filled their plates, then left the kitchen to see about the laundry.

"Bishop Tomlin was able to wrangle a seat on an Army helicopter, and will be here early this afternoon. Can you imagine? Flights coming into Nashville are hopelessly delayed. If you want to leave the city though, you've got it made. This convergence is unprecedented." Lifting his fork to his mouth, Father Andrews looked closely at Stephen.

"I am filled with gratitude, young man. I could not have managed the sudden influx of the faithful to the Cathedral yesterday without your unwavering reinforcement and support. The deacons will be here shortly to help manage the masses today, so you will be able to leave after breakfast."

"Thanks, Father. You haven't forgotten…"

"As a matter of fact, Stephen, I wanted to talk to you about that. I've called and left several messages for Dr. Macomb, both on his cell phone and at his house, begging an audience for you. I have not heard from him, but even if he had tried to call the church office or the rectory, he would have had problems getting through. The last message I left for him included my cell phone number. I hope to hear from him soon."

"I can't thank you enough, Father Andrews. I won't bombard him, I promise. I won't stalk his family and I am not a nutcase. I promise I won't betray your trust in me, and I will take things slow."

"I know you will. I cannot explain why, Stephen, but I am willing to entertain the idea that all that is happening now is not random coincidence. The message arrives in many forms, son, and who are we to question?"

"Why don't I help you get things lined up today before I leave? I thought I might attempt to make it over to the apartment to get my mail before I head to the campus. It will probably take me forever, but you have my cell number in case Dr. Macomb calls. I truly appreciate your help, Father."

"Play it close to the vest, Stephen. You may not be able to find such support out in the secular world. The School of Divinity may prove to be an ally, or just as easily, an antagonist. For all the hype, people don't always believe what they can't see. Take care of yourself out there, Stephen."

"Well, being that I hadn't planned to stay with you for two days, I brought nothing with me… so I guess I'm ready to head out. If you are sure you'll be okay, I'll go ahead and leave now."

Father Andrews stood with Stephen at the back door, placed his hand on the young man's bowed head, and bestowed a blessing. Removing the medal of St. Anthony of Padua from his own neck, the priest placed it around Stephen's, praying that St. Anthony would keep him safe on this faith journey.

"Go with Christ, Stephen. Godspeed."

Stephen stood with the priest for a moment, then wordlessly turned and walked out the kitchen door, shutting it quietly behind him. Father Andrews stood without moving, trying to gather his thoughts into some semblance of order, before he turned to face the day ahead. Cocking his head to one side, he paused and listened to the deep rumble of thunder in the distance. Peeking out the window over the kitchen sink, he watched as the dark clouds moved in from the west, hanging heavy and low in the morning sky. He flipped the light switch on the wall as he walked by, throwing light into the darkening room, as he made his way slowly to his study to prepare for the arrival of the Bishop.

Chapter Forty Two

It was after twelve o'clock on Monday afternoon before Dr. Castiglione finally made it back to her office. Her plan was to sort through the barrage of paperwork that had parked itself on the corner of her desk. Taking her glasses out of her pocket, she picked up the chart at the top of the pile and started to read.

It seemed like a week had passed, instead of just a few days, since the 'Miracle Healing' had taken place. Had it only been Friday when the intern Sorrento had the accident in the lab? He was leaving the hospital this afternoon with no fanfare, just sneaking out the back door, with an undercover escort assigned to him from the Nashville Police Department. It had been a unanimous decision that he would not come back to work for awhile, and was on paid leave until all the hoopla died down. A visiting nurse would be sent to collect blood and urine samples every few days, but from every indication to date, they expected no decline in his condition.

Looking over the test results again, Beverly was as mystified now as she had been on Friday. The poor guy had given at least a pint of blood and had gone through an extensive physical exam on Saturday, with not even a scar to show from his injury. If she had not seen the before and after x-rays, and talked to Mullins first hand, she would say he was trying to pull off the caper of the century. Turning to her window and looking out onto 23rd Avenue, she was still amazed at the unsettled confusion on the streets below. Hopefully, when news of his release reached

the streets, the crowd would diminish and things would eventually
return to normal.

A thunderstorm had just passed through Nashville, and she had been
worried and upset at the condition of the people below. Some of them
were beyond sick and had been out in the heat for two days. At first a
trickle of humanity and now a wave, for the most part, it was a quiet
hopeful group that remained after many attempts to have them disperse.
Very few people had been admitted to the hospital, a trend that would
surely change as the days wore on. The sun was trying hard to poke its
way through the clouds after the storm, and steam wafted up from the
blacktop in patches, bringing to mind an old B movie.

Looking at her watch, she took out a notepad and started to jot down
notes for the meeting tomorrow with the Bishop of Nashville and a local
representative of the United States Government. The National Science
Foundation was also sending its own scientist to investigate. Evidently,
legitimate miracles were in demand. Everyone wanted answers and the
hospital executives planned a closed door briefing for tomorrow afternoon at three o'clock. She tried not to think of the implications of such a
meeting, and instead turned her attention to the next case on her desk.

The buzzer on the intercom sounded, startling Beverly from her reverie. "Yes, Carol?"

"Dr. Richards is here to see you."

"Okay, send her through. And Carol, hold my calls for now."

Julie Richards closed the door behind her, and instead of sitting in
the only available chair in the office that wasn't covered with paperwork,
began pacing.

"Have you talked to Dr. Mullins yet?" she asked.

"No, I was hoping you had something to tell me. I just started to
review Jillian's chart." Beverly set the Macomb chart down on her desk,
watching her colleague closely. Concerned at her uncharacteristic ner-
vousness, Beverly asked, "What's going on here, Julie?"

"I discharged Jillian Macomb," she said pointing toward the open
chart. "I told her parents she could go home this afternoon. There was
not much else I could do. She feels fine, the ultrasound is normal and

the baby's heartbeat is perfect. I just wish I could get through to Mullins to see if he has all the testing underway. Now that I have released her, I wonder if I did the right thing."

Beverly stepped out from behind her desk and motioned to the empty chair. "Sit."

She waited until Julie was seated before she sat across from her and began to talk.

"Calm down, and do not second guess a decision you clearly made based on the facts you have available to you. I'm sure the parents are unnerved by all the commotion at the hospital right now. And Julie, between the two of us, was it that important that Jillian be kept in isolation? She's been out and about for the first four months of her pregnancy. I'm looking at the results of blood work clearly showing your patient is supporting a pregnancy that, by all of the medical data presented here, should not even be viable. And yet the ultrasound is normal. You can't keep this teenager on bed-rest until the birth, when everything is progressing as it should."

"I know. I have gone over and over all of this in my mind. What about the meeting tomorrow afternoon? Is Jillian going to be mentioned at all? I finally told the Macomb's that it was her slide that Dr. Sorrento was working on when he got injured." Julie bit her lower lip.

"Her case will certainly come up, but only as the case that was being processed when the injury occurred. Mullins is repeating the paternity test this afternoon, using an amnio sample and trying to duplicate the results of the first test. My hunch is that something contaminated the original sampling and caused some kind of chemical reaction which produced our 'miracle.' Listen, you know as well as I do, Mullins will be on the fame and fortune research wagon for a long time with this one."

"He'll have a fit when he hears she's gone home."

"Don't worry about Jackson Mullins. I'll handle him. You do not need his permission to discharge your own patient. Have you eaten yet? Let's go down to the cafeteria and grab something. I haven't been home since Friday night, so I better eat here. No food in the fridge at the condo, and I probably won't be able to venture out until all of the excitement dies down. At least for another few days." Dr. Castiglione grabbed her office key and they walked out together.

"She's healthy, Bev, in every way. I wish I knew what was going on around here."

"Don't we all? Jillian Macomb will be fine. She has supported this baby to the second trimester and is showing no signs of termination. I would say odds are in her favor that she will make it through to the end of term. Besides, her mom is a psychologist and her dad is a professor. They are intelligent people, more than familiar with the medical field. They know what to watch for. She's home. She'll get more rest there than she would around this madhouse. You need to relax and follow your gut. Come on. You can check with them later to see how she's doing. It's going to be okay."

"I know. I'm letting all this other stuff spook me. Let's eat. Wonder which chicken dish the cafeteria staff has conjured up this afternoon."

They left Bev's office and walked toward the elevator.

As the elevator door was closing, a furious Jackson Mullins called to demand yet another blood sample from the Macomb girl. Carol put him through to Beverly's voicemail. It took several minutes for the call to end, the red blinking message light on her office phone signaling the second, more violent storm of the day. The rage of Jackson Mullins.

Chapter Forty Three

By Monday morning the streets of Nashville were overflowing with every imaginable nationality and religious persuasion of beleaguered humanity. Stephen wound his way through the crowd, which had increased dramatically since his arrival at the Cathedral on Saturday afternoon. He tried to keep a steady pace, stopping only occasionally to offer aid to someone whose plight was too intense to ignore.

The heavily patrolled avenues resembled a war zone, and in an amazingly short amount of time had become obstructed with wheelchairs and stretchers. The sight of parents desperately trying to comfort their terminally ill children affected him the most. The fear and frustration in their eyes had been replaced with an inner light, born of hope. Faith in miracles. And they were not leaving anytime soon.

Slowly threading his way toward his apartment, Stephen's thoughts wandered back to the dreams and he wondered how the message would affect his carefully planned future.

Preoccupied, he momentarily lost sight of what was happening around him. It had taken almost an hour to travel the first few blocks from the Cathedral. He finally felt that he was making progress, when the sound of pure grief stopped him in his tracks. He felt a tug on his belt and turned to find himself looking into the eyes of a young boy, no more than ten or eleven years old.

"Please, mister. I can't get her to wake up. My mom won't wake up," the boy said.

Following the child the short distance to the corner, Stephen knelt in front of the wheelchair carrying the boy's mother. He pushed the hair from her eyes and hesitantly reached over to feel the pulse in her neck. She seemed to be unconscious, and although he was no expert, he realized immediately that her time on earth was nearing the end.

Turning back to the youth, Stephen asked the weeping child, "What is your name, son?"

"Johnny Boone." The boy bravely tried to control his tears and looked at Stephen, his eyes filled with despair. "Is she gone, mister? Is my mom dead?"

"No, Johnny, she's still alive, but she is very sick. What's wrong with her, can you tell me that?"

The small boy reached out for his mother's limp hand.

"They say she has Lou Gehrig's disease. We came here for a miracle, mister. We live in Columbia, about forty miles away. It's just the two of us, and I brought her here for the miracle. The doctor said she was going to die, but I believe in miracles and I know she'll be okay. Can you help us? Can you get us over to the hospital?"

Stephen stood and slowly scanned the mass of people blocking the route to the hospital. He peered through the crowd and could see guards manning the roadblocks in tight formation. He felt helpless, yet he knew that if he turned and walked away from this young boy, the woman would surely die right there on the Nashville streets, in the midst of thousands of hapless strangers who were all waiting for that same miracle. He could only imagine the horror this child would have to endure. He turned back to the boy.

"My name is Stephen, Johnny Boone. Now listen carefully to me. We are going to try and get the wheelchair over to the University campus. I'm a student there and I have my ID. They will only let people through who can prove they belong, so I'm not sure how this is going to work. Stay close to me and we'll see if we can get you through."

Stephen decided that instead of turning toward the medical center, he would retrace his steps and try to gain access on the west side of the campus. The crowds were less intense further west of the Cathedral, but he worried about the time it would take to cover the distance with a gravely ill woman and small boy in tow. Johnny walked obediently at his side and never once questioned him, or the direction they were taking.

Pushing the wheelchair, it took over two hours to retrace their steps the few blocks back to the Cathedral, and another hour, through the crowded streets, to get to the guard post that had been established in the parking lot of Feldman Hall.

"State your business, sir." The guard on duty was young, but serious, as he stood at attention and closely scrutinized the trio, paying particular attention to Stephen and the woman in the wheelchair.

Stephen reached into his back pocket and removed his ID card. "I just left Father Andrews at the Cathedral, and am on my way to the medical center with this woman and her son. You can call Father Andrews, or you can call Dr. Marc Macomb at the Divinity School. I have clearance for the entire campus. Here is the number for the Admin offices of the Divinity School. Mrs. McCarthy is the receptionist. You can read her my ID number and she'll vouch for me."

Taking the card from Stephen, the guard moved to call the office from his cell, to gain clearance for them. His radio snapped to life simultaneously, with a static call for help from another guard, several yards away. They could clearly hear the angry sounds of rebellion from where they stood.

"Roger. Unit 2 responding." More static. "Unit 4, can you fan out and hold my position?"

The guard threw the ID card back to Stephen, and once again looking at the woman, wrote something on a checkpoint card before handing it to him.

"This will only get you across campus. You are on your own when you get to the hospital. Better move on and get out of here fast. We've got trouble on the line. Good luck."

Stephen and Johnny ran the few yards across the open parking lot in front of the Feldman Building, pushing the wheelchair, and were well on their way across the campus when they heard the first shot. They both instinctively crouched as low as they could, while racing across the open expanse of the common area.

"Almighty God, guide us." Stephen wasn't sure if he had prayed out loud.

A spray of gunfire resounded behind them, and Stephen continued to pray as he pushed the unwieldy wheelchair toward the medical building without stopping. A bullet hit the huge oak tree to the right of them, spraying bark and dirt in their direction.

"Jesus Christ." Too late, Stephen realized they were perilously close to the crossfire.

Sirens screamed in the distance, and the sound of men on bullhorns reverberated across the normally tranquil field. The scene was surreal. His mind reeled with the sudden realization that they had been only seconds away from missing their opportunity to enter the campus before it was put on complete lockdown. Even more frightening, he realized just how close they had come to the violence. Had they arrived one minute later, they would have been caught in the middle of the fray.

"Hang in there, Johnny. We're almost there."

His breath came in harsh ragged gasps, and he could only imagine how terrified the child must be. He looked down to see the boy running to keep up, weeping quietly, holding his arm close to his side, bloodied where a wayward bullet must have grazed his pure flesh.

"Johnny, are you okay?" Stephen pulled him behind a magnificent magnolia tree and quickly examined his arm.

"Can you keep going? It's only another block to the entrance of the hospital." Stephen frantically foraged through the pouch attached to the wheelchair. Finding a soft cloth, he quickly tied it around the wound.

"It just burns, is all. It's hardly bleeding. Please, Mr. Stephen, my mom." Stephen reached up, his fingers quickly finding the place on her neck where a tiny pulse tiredly fought to continue beating.

"What's your mom's name, Johnny?"

"Theresa. My mom's name is Theresa."

"Okay, Theresa. We are almost there. Let's get you some help." Forging straight ahead, the battered trio hurriedly rounded the last corner, and came face to face with a line of National Guard, three deep around the entrance to the hospital.

"Please sir, you have to let us through. This woman is in bad shape and her child was caught in the crossfire back there."

Stephen gave the uniformed guard his ID and the signed checkpoint card, while Johnny pulled his mother's drivers license from the pouch on the back of the chair.

"Wait here while I verify your ID card. Campus is on lockdown and you are going to be detained. No one can leave or enter the campus. We'll take the kid and his mother through to the emergency room, but the chair has to stay here. Never make it through metal detection. Bomb threat just came through."

Stephen got down on one knee and looked at Johnny.

"You are going to be fine now. Do what they tell you, and they'll take care of you and your mom. You are a brave boy, Johnny. A very brave boy. I'll try to check on you tomorrow. Now go."

Johnny locked his arms around Stephen's neck.

"Thanks, mister."

"You go on now. You'll be okay. Remember this. It says in the Bible that 'If you have faith even as small as a mustard seed, you could say to this mountain, move from here to there, and it would move. And nothing will be impossible to you.' You have come a long way on your faith Johnny Boone. Keep your faith."

Two well-armed guards came through the line with emergency technicians and a gurney, and they carefully lifted the boy's mother from the wheelchair. Tubes and medical apparatus followed in a blur of activity. Stephen watched as they led the duo away and gave Johnny a thumb up when the child looked back at him. He turned to the guard and stood patiently while they frisked him, then led him over to a detention tent while they verified his information.

He sat on the ground in the corner of the tent and looked around at the other students and faculty who waited with him. Covered with grime and sweat, his shower this morning seemed an eternity ago. Stephen closed his eyes and prayed that brave Johnny Boone would be safe, and could handle whatever the outcome of this day.

Chapter Forty Four

The marker ricocheted off the wall and hit the side of the filing cabinet with a loud clatter, shattering on impact before coming to rest on the tile floor of the lab.

"That stupid bitch." Jackson Mullins was furious and if the veins bulging from his forehead weren't evidence enough, the pool of black ink seeping from the demolished marker at the base of the filing cabinet would suffice as proof positive.

He slammed the phone into the cradle after he unloaded yet another heated tirade onto Dr. Castiglione's answering machine. *I cannot believe they discharged the girl. What the hell are these incompetent people thinking?*

He marched quickly across the lab and picked up the small tube of blood he had managed to wrangle from the lab tech. *At least they had the foresight to draw blood before the girl left the hospital.* After placing the glass slide under the microscope, he moved his chair back slightly and began to write in his journal, careful to document every step of the procedure as he performed it.

He examined the specimen on the slide. So odd. The maternal blood sample still showed no HCG. Amazed that the fetus had survived to this stage of the pregnancy, he removed the DVD of the ultrasound from his smuggled copy of the Macomb girl's file and inserted it into the machine. Pushing the play button, he watched as the fetus came to life, moving gently in the girl's womb, the heartbeat strong and solid. *You have the answers locked inside you, my little man. And I will find the key.*

He removed the DVD from the machine and shoved it back into his personal, albeit illegal, file of this case. He had to get the disc back to Castiglione's desk before she and that birdbrain, Julie Richards, figured out it was missing. But he wasn't too worried. It could be days before they discovered it was gone, and by then he was sure he would be able to smuggle it securely back into the file.

After he'd left the first heated message on Beverly's voicemail, he had bolted from the lab, ready to force his way into the director's office to give her a piece of his mind. All three of the incompetents were gone, including the receptionist. He couldn't believe his luck. Thank God, he knew where that old buzzard, Carol, kept the extra key to the office. He had helped himself and walked right in. Smack in the middle of Dr. Castiglione's desk was the Macomb kid's file. *Easier than taking candy from a baby.*

He had surreptitiously taken the chart to the doctor's lounge and used the copy machine, copying every last scrap of paper in the file. Then he leisurely made his way back to Beverly's office, and with still no sign of the AWOL trio, let himself in. He replaced the file and returned the pirated key, putting it back into the peppermint tin, second drawer down, on the right side of Carol's desk. He figured he could get the ultrasound copied and back into the chart in due time. Everything was falling into place. That is, until he had gotten back to the lab and actually read the chart and discovered the girl had been discharged.

Swallowing his frustration and forcing himself to concentrate solely on the task at hand, he once again looked through the eyepiece at the girl's blood smear. No glow. Noting his findings in his file on the case, he documented the maternal blood sample as normal. The paternity test sample taken from that poor kid the Macomb girl was dating did not match the amniocentesis sample, proving beyond a doubt that Jamie Tyler was not the father.

The mystery in this case was the paternal DNA strand. The abnormal reading had to originate with the biological father of the fetus, or with the new genome created from a combination of the mother's and the father's DNA. And Julie Richards had let the precious living specimen walk out the doors of the hospital an hour ago. *Damn.*

He duplicated the paternity test, using the amniotic fluid from the anonymous donor that he had taken earlier in the day. He followed the exact procedure, using the exact components, in the same sequence that Sorrento had documented in the original lab file. He took another drop of the fluid, and allowed it to air dry on the slide, as he had done with Jillian's sample earlier. As he suspected would be the outcome, the results of both tests were normal. No glow. No phosphorescence. The 'miracle' had nothing to do with Sorrento or the paternity test he had been performing when he was wounded. The substance that had caused the wound to heal originated with the fetus.

Jackson Mullins jumped from the stool and quickly walked back to retrieve the slide that held the DNA sampling from the Macomb girl's amniocentesis. Heart beating wildly in his chest, he realized that he was holding in his hand the raw source of the 'Miracle Healing.' *I am the sole witness to a unique DNA sequence mutation.* An unknown paternal DNA, combined with the known maternal DNA, has produced a live fetus with a distinctive genome that is able to survive and sustain itself, in the womb, with no Human Chorionic Gonadotropin. *Amazing.* Even more amazing was the effect of the combined properties. *Spontaneous healing?*

What was sustaining this pregnancy? Who was the source of the paternal DNA? Therein lays the answer to the so-called 'Miracle Healing.'

He knew what he had to do. Jackson Mullins gingerly carried the precious DNA slide over to the microscope, hyper-aware now of what he actually held in his hand. Bending toward the glass, he saw the glow even before he lowered his eye to the lens. Slowly raising his head, he once again removed the slide from the stand and turned robotically to the counter behind him. He set up the lab's video recorder and positioned it carefully, wanting to capture the next sequence of events on film to review later.

Rolling up the sleeves of his shirt, he removed his gloves and scrubbed from fingertip to elbow at the utility sink. Only after the execution of a meticulous surgical scrub, did he don clean gloves. Removing an alcohol swab from the drawer next to him, he swiped his arm, cleaning the skin from just above his left wrist to his elbow.

He closed his eyes, envisioning each step necessary to carry out this experiment alone. Secrecy was of paramount importance to him, as he was determined that no one would know of his discovery until he was absolutely sure of the results. He would not share the credit with anyone. This was *his* moment of glory. His alone. He was about to realize his heretofore elusive claim to renown.

He took time to document each step aloud on the recorder and then opened the drawer containing sterilized instruments. Selecting a number 10 scalpel, he unsealed the sterile pack and exposed the knife, carefully picking it up with his right hand, and reaching for the specimen slide with his left.

Sliding down to the tile floor into a sitting position, using the cabinet for support, he arranged the prized slide next to him on a sterile towel and was finally ready to begin. Sure and steady, he held the scalpel in a palmar grip and placing the knife against the inside of his left forearm, skillfully sliced through the tender skin, applying the necessary pressure, while cutting through the muscle and peripheral arteries.

Sweat beaded on his forehead, his breathing labored with the intense pain. He felt lightheaded and nauseous, but willed himself to remain in control. He had a fleeting thought that it would have been so much easier had he numbed the area first, but Sorrento didn't have that luxury when he was wounded so Mullins decided to mirror the original sequence of events as closely as possible.

He reached out and felt for the specimen slide on the towel at his side. Carefully handling the slide that carried the DNA of the Macomb fetus, he lifted it to his forearm and inserted the small piece of glass, past skin and muscle, into the gaping wound he had just created with the scalpel. Throwing his head back in agony, it took every bit of resolve he possessed not to cry out.

Jackson Mullins took the towel and wrapped his arm loosely, leaning his head against the cabinet behind him. Before losing consciousness, he watched with eyes clouded by pain, as blood flowed freely from the fresh wound, bright crimson finally mingling with the black ink of the marker, forming a murky pool of his own life fluid on the floor beside him.

Chapter Forty Five

Jillian sat at the kitchen table, spreading peanut butter on a slice of wheat toast. She was trying not to think about the long ride home from the hospital. It had taken over two and a half hours to go one and a half miles, most of the time at a crawl. Her dad always said he loved the location of their house because he could sleep until seven, work out for an hour and still make it to work by nine. That was before the 'miracle.'

She had done her best to ignore the scenes being played out in the once familiar streets of Nashville, trying very hard not to look out the car window, but it was impossible. The number of people camping on the side of the road was increasing hourly and, judging from the news broadcast on the car radio, the migration of the infirm showed no signs of slowing any time soon. Her dad told her the army guys were with the National Guard. It looked bizarre to see them walking along the side streets, holding guns at their sides, marching right along with people holding their sick babies and others pushing wheelchairs. The characters brandishing cardboard messages really spooked her. *'Repent, the end is near.'* Old wide eyed souls were spooking everyone around them, totally believing what they had scribbled on their homemade signs.

The Red Cross had relief stations set up under little white tents and, in addition to water, they were distributing sunscreen. It was brutally hot. The rain this morning made it even worse and the humidity smacked Jillian in the face as soon as she left the air conditioned hospital. She was just glad to be home.

"Hey, Jill, how are you feeling?" Sara came into the kitchen as she flipped through the mail, her hair twisted into a clip on top of her head.

"God knows how the mailman made it through, but he did. I heard on the news that the post office is not promising daily delivery to this area until the crowds disperse. Listen, honey, when you finish eating, I want you to go upstairs and get some rest. I have to lay down. I have a splitting headache." Sara took two ibuprofen followed by a glass of water.

Jillian looked closely at her mom for the first time in a long while. There were dark smudges under her eyes, and she was usually so positive and excited about everything. She looked worried and tired now, and almost seemed to be moving in slow motion. Jillian felt a pang of guilt and focused on her toast, tearing little edges of crust off and dropping them to her plate.

"That's okay, Mom, you go on. I'm tired too. I'll clean up my mess and I'll probably go up to my room and watch a movie." No way did she want to watch the news again.

"Where did Dad go?"

"He was going south, into Brentwood or Franklin, to stock up on groceries. It doesn't look like things are going to quiet down around here any time soon. We may be homebound for awhile."

Sara walked over and kissed her daughter's forehead.

"I'll call up when dinner is ready. Try to rest, Jillian. This has been hard on you and you have to take care of yourself for the baby."

Jillian finished eating and stacked her dishes in the dishwasher. She grabbed a yogurt from the fridge and checked the back door to make sure it was locked. All this craziness was getting to her. While climbing the steps to her room, exhaustion finally hit hard, and the last few steps may as well have been fifty. She shuffled into her room and closed the blinds, erasing the sunlight that spilled across her bedroom floor. She flopped across the bed and for the first time since the dreams started, she was the one calling out to her angel, hoping she could summon Arianna at will.

"Arianna. Can you hear me? I need to talk to you. I'm afraid of every-thing that is happening around us, Arianna. It's all out of control. Am I part of this? The miracle and this baby... Arianna, are they all the same? I'm frightened." Jillian started to cry.

She had not recognized, until that very second, the turmoil that had become part of her life. She realized that she believed that all that was happening was related in some way to her and this pregnancy. How could it not be? She didn't know what to make of any of this.

"Please, come to me, Arianna."

She lay back on the yellow quilt and absentmindedly rubbed the soft skin of her growing belly. She felt herself dozing off and heard nothing but the whisper of the air conditioning, blowing cool air into the room through the vents.

"Child. Do not be afraid. The Lord God has chosen you, among all women, to bring forth new hope for the world. Your child is blessed by the Father and the Son and the Spirit that dwell in him. You will bring forth the final light of revelation for those who believe the Word, and he who believes shall not perish, but will dwell for all eternity in the house of the Lord."

"It doesn't seem real. Why me? I'm not some holy roller, Arianna. I am just me. Something bad is coming soon, I can feel it. I am afraid and I don't know what I am supposed to do. I am so tired. So tired." Jillian tried to sit up in her bed, but lay back instead, feeling heavy with fatigue.

"Sleep now, child. The time is close at hand. You have been called upon to be a faithful servant of the Lord. You will follow the steps of those who have come before you. You shall be the mother of the last generation. The blessed generation that will dwell in the house of the Lord. No one knows the day, the hour or the second that these things shall come to pass. But the Father who knows all, will guide you well. Be still and sleep now. Put your trust in the Lord. There is no truth but His."

Jillian fell asleep, knowing at last, that all these things were true.

Chapter Forty Six

Sara frowned. Reaching over to the nightstand in the darkened bedroom, she blindly felt for the phone's handset, anything to stop the ringing. She pushed the answer button, finally able to silence the intrusive sound. Half asleep, and still groggy from her headache, she mustered up the energy to speak.

"Hello?"

"What the hell is going on in Nashville?"

"Oh, Susie. I know. Can you believe all this?" Sara raised herself to a sitting position in the rumpled bed, and took a drink from the glass of water she had pushed precariously close to the edge of the nightstand while fumbling for the phone.

"I'm so glad you called. I was going to call you tonight. So much has happened in a week's time, that I haven't had time to think, much less talk to anyone."

"Is everything okay? You sound like I woke you up."

"No. Yes. I mean yes, you woke me up and no, I don't know if everything is okay."

Sara broke down at the sound of her sister's voice, the turmoil of the last week spilling over. She told Susie everything. She told her of the pregnancy and the bizarre results of all the tests. She explained Jillian's denial of having any knowledge of the act itself. She sobbed through the description of the ultrasound images and the trauma of seeing her daughter in isolation. She had been so frightened having to watch her endure the amniocentesis. She cried through the telling of the freak accident at the hospital and the phenomenon that followed. The agony of recounting the events of the past week doubled her over in grief, her mourning a palpable throbbing pain in her heart…to the core of her being.

"I am coming to you now." Susie jumped into action mode, beside herself with worry.

Her only sister and best friend in the world had been trying to handle this unimaginable pain by herself. And she never knew, never even had an inkling of what was happening to their little family.

"No, Sue, you can't. It's a madhouse here, and I doubt you can even get through. Marc said that the interstate is backed up to the Kentucky border from the north, with people trying to get close to the miracle. And forget about trying to book a flight into Nashville right now. I'll be okay. I think just hearing your voice was a relief. It has been so hard with no one to talk to about everything. Marc is going through his own hell."

"Oh, sweetie, how is Jillian taking all of this?"

"I'm not sure. She seems to have accepted the pregnancy, but she won't talk about the rest of it. I know she went through hell with Jamie, but she doesn't even talk too much about that. All this miracle stuff has been a huge distraction for all of us."

"I'm just going to check a few things out, okay? It may be that I can't make it, but let me talk to Tommy and see if he can think of a way. Just let me try. I'll feel better if I at least try. You need reinforcement right now, and I need to see you and Jill, and that brother-in-law of mine."

"Okay. You are an angel, Susie. Everything will be okay, won't it? I mean, Jillian is going to be okay, right?" Sara, on the verge of tears again, wiped her burning eyes on a tissue and tried to smile.

"Everything is going to be fine. Now, let me go and talk to Tommy. I'll call you back later. My husband is much more analytical than we are. Where is Marc?"

"He went to the store to get food. He was going to come right home, but God knows how long that will take with the crowds the way they are. There is no way you can even pretend to imagine what the streets are like right now. He has been trying to get through to his office by phone, hoping one of the new fellows can bring some of the work he needs to finish. If anyone can make it through, that is. They have cancelled all classes at the University, at least for this week. But my husband needs something to take his mind off of everything that is going on."

Eyes welling with tears once again, Sara whispered, "Someone was shot on campus this morning. Killed. And two people injured. You just can't believe what is happening here, Susie."

"Dear Lord, Sara. It's been on the news, but I had no idea how this was impacting you. Please make sure you keep your doors locked and pay attention. You guys are not that far from the campus."

"We'll be okay. Call me later. I think I hear Marc at the door. I love you."

"I love you, too. Take care of yourself." Susie ended the call, but Sara held on to the phone until the beeping stopped and the handset went silent.

*   *   *

Marc pushed the back door open and set the first of a dozen grocery bags on the countertop. It was dark and quiet in the house. *The girls must be asleep.* He finished unloading the trunk of the Malibu and began unpacking the refrigerated food, leaving the pantry items for Sara. He had to take back roads, traveling down to Franklin to shop. The stores any further north were almost depleted of their stock and, on top of that, were having problems with deliveries. He did the best he could with what remained on the shelves. If this kept up for any length of time, he wasn't sure what people would do for supplies. It was going on four days since the 'miracle' and three days since the population had exploded.

He had tried to reach Father Andrews by phone while he drove across town, but had no success. He finally got through to Mrs. McCarthy, and gave her a list of what he needed from the office. Normally unflappable, he could tell she was quite shaken by the violence that had occurred outside Feldman Hall that morning. The uncertainty in her voice hit a raw nerve with Marc. The fact that she had even attempted to show up for work this morning proved dedication and valor far beyond the call of duty.

"Mrs. McCarthy, I want you to listen to me. Pack up and leave that office now, and don't return to work until you hear directly from me. It is ludicrous that you are even there today. Are there any other staffers working with you?"

"Not many, Dr. Macomb. Dean Smyth just left, and the few secretaries from Admissions who made it in are the only people still here."

"Okay, listen to me. Forget about everything. Don't even worry about the list. Just lock up and get everyone out. It's not safe for you to be there alone, and with classes cancelled, everything can wait. The campus was put on lockdown this morning after the disturbance, but you should be able to leave now. Don't wait too much longer. There is no telling what will happen over the next few hours. I absolutely do not want you there at dusk."

"Dr. Macomb, someone is at the door, pounding and ringing the bell. Dr. Smyth locked us in when he left. I don't like this," Mrs. McCarthy said warily.

"Damn. Peek out the window in my office. Don't open the door unless you know who it is. I'll wait on the line." Marc felt helpless and was worried sick about the women, stranded and alone in the office.

"Oh dear, it's just that Jacobs boy. He was here looking for you on Friday, nosing around, wondering about you. There were several messages on the voicemail when I got here this morning, from him and from Father Andrews at the Cathedral."

"Thank God. It's okay, Mrs. McCarthy. Let him inside and lock the door behind him. Can you quickly gather the items on the list, while I talk to Stephen? Let the women in Admissions know that you're closing the building and they must leave with you. I'll have Stephen escort you all to the guard posts. Give him the phone now and let me speak to him."

Mrs. McCarthy opened the door and quickly motioned Stephen inside, locking the deadbolt behind him. Handing him the phone she set to work immediately, her fear replaced with purposeful resolve. She went upstairs to the admitting office to gather the three women who were working there and then unlocked Dr. Macomb's office and began to collect the materials on his list.

Stephen waited until Mrs. McCarthy left the room before he started to speak.

"Hello?" Stephen said.

"Stephen, its Marc Macomb. I am so sorry it has taken so long to contact you. I tried, but the confusion around here is far-reaching. I know all about the excitement on campus this week. Sorry you had to face that."

Stephen stood in the reception area for a minute, holding the phone in his hand, finding it hard to believe the subject of his intense search was finally available to him on the other end of the line.

"It has been quite eventful, Dr. Macomb. I'll have a lot to share with you later. How is your family holding up?" He worried now about what to say to the professor. He realized that God was opening a door for him, but he didn't have to bust through it like a bull. Everything would unfold in its own time.

"It's a long story. I have to ask a huge favor of you. Mrs. McCarthy is gathering some research material for me as we speak and there are several women still in the building with her. Would you escort them to the guard checkpoint so that they can get off the grounds before something else happens on campus? I hate to think of them trying to maneuver past all the guard-posts by themselves. I understand classes have been canceled for the rest of this week."

"Of course I will," said Stephen, mentally noting that his role of campus guardian seemed to be escalating naturally. "The campus lockdown has been lifted, but only until six o'clock. That's two hours from now. Then they are putting a strict curfew in place. No one in or out until eight in the morning. And they mean business."

"I'm sure they do. After you see the women to the gate, is there a way you can get the research material to me?"

"Sure, Dr. Macomb. It may take awhile, but I can do that."

"And Stephen, I know this is an imposition, but would you agree to stay with us for a few days? My office is in a room over the garage, and there's a small bedroom up there with a bath, so you would have your privacy. To be totally honest, Stephen, I could use the help. This whole 'Miracle Healing' has thrown me for a loop. If you were here we could work uninterrupted, somewhat removed from the madness. There are other circumstances involved, but I'll share those with you when you get here."

Stephen closed his eyes. Jillian. He knew the prophecy was beginning to unfold and he was powerless to stop it. This was the opening he had been looking for, the path laid out before him. He stood rooted to the floor, not moving or speaking, his mind suddenly blank.

"Cat got your tongue?" Mrs. McCarthy came up behind him and nudged him with arms full of books and papers.

Jolted from his trance, Stephen looked into the eyes of the four women waiting to lock up and leave the building.

"Of course I will, Dr. Macomb. Yes, to everything. I'll stop at my apartment and gather a few things after I escort the ladies off the campus. I'll get there as soon as I can. It may take several hours, depending on how fast I move through the traffic. What number shall I call if I need to contact you?" Stephen motioned to one of the women for a pen and wrote the number across the back of his hand.

Hanging up the phone, he turned to the four dedicated, but anxious, females. Bowing slightly at the waist he said, "After you, ladies."

Stephen said a silent prayer as he once again passed the bullet scarred oak tree and continued to retrace the steps he had taken earlier in the day with Johnny Boone and his mother. Late afternoon shadows fell heavily across the campus…not a word was spoken as they walked quickly away from the familiar and into the unknown.

Chapter Forty Seven

Julie Richards looked at her watch and was surprised to find that it was well past six o'clock on Monday night. It was officially one week since Jillian Macomb had walked into her office for her first exam. And almost that long since she had been able to keep regular office hours. She was determined to assume her responsibilities and finally relieve her partner. John Mitchell had been a champ for keeping her most critical patients on schedule, but she had to put in a personal appearance tomorrow or half her practice would disintegrate.

The strain of the past week was beginning to catch up to her. Rubbing the back of her neck with practiced hands, she tried to work out the kinks before she faced the long trip home. She made a mental checklist of patients she had on her schedule for tomorrow and put the last of her hospital files in her briefcase. *I need to check with Beverly before I leave, to see if she has heard anything from Mullins.*

"Crap." The call went right to Dr. Castiglione's voicemail. Julie decided she could just as easily walk over to the pathology lab and talk to Dr. Mullins, herself, on the way to her car. He was pissed at her anyway, so she might as well get the inevitable first confrontation behind her. Maybe she could soothe his wounded pride by reassuring him that he would get his precious specimens from Jillian on a weekly basis.

The labs were located in a secured corridor on the first floor which required authorization to enter. Julie pulled the lanyard from around her neck, and taking her ID card, swiped it through the card reader that opened the door to the unit.

Because the pathogen being studied was of unknown origin, Mullins was working in a bio-safety level II lab. She hoped she could get his attention without having to go through the whole airlock procedure. The labs were arranged in a circle around a central control desk which housed locked files containing the information on each research project currently underway. Each lab had been assigned as Level I or II, indicating the bio-safety risk of the research being carried out within.

The Level III and IV labs were located in a basement unit, separated from the hospital. Julie found Mullins lab easily. His name was on the placard on the tile wall in the main hallway, just outside the airlock. Directly beneath, he had posted a No Admittance -Work In Progress sign. The airlock obstructed any view into the lab itself. Steeling herself for the fury about to be unleashed, she pushed the speakerphone button next to the door and called to the doctor.

"Dr. Mullins, it's Julie Richards. I'm getting ready to leave for the day, and thought you may want to confer on Jillian Macomb before I do." Julie released the call button and leaned against the tile wall, waiting for a scathing reply. A few minutes went by. Nothing.

"Jackson, listen, I know you're upset about her discharge, but I promise you will have everything you need from the patient. The climate in this hospital is not really conducive for rest right now, and she is in a fragile mental state. She had to be home."

There was still no response from inside the lab.

"Jackson, I know you are in there, so please acknowledge." Silence. *For Pete's sake.*

Julie walked over to the central desk and checked the wallboard. Posted prominently on the wall in front of the central workstation, it charted all activity in the research area. Every physician and technician was required to sign in and out every time, to ensure the uncompromised safety of the unit. The research budget dictated that the central desk was not manned on a continual basis, but usually clerks were stationed there for two hours at the beginning and end of each shift, to file and document the progress of posted operations. Wall mounted cameras picked up activity in the hallways, between the labs and the elevator, and were monitored by security 24/7. The speaker system was tied to the main alarm system, so if ever there was a breach in bio-safety precautionary measures, once the protocol was set into motion, it was only seconds before the necessary containment procedures were put into place.

The wallboard showed that Jackson Mullins had checked into the lab at 9:45 that morning and signed out for one hour at lunchtime. According to the chart, he signed back in at 1:30 and had not signed out again. By his own account, he was still working. Anyone conducting research in any of the bio-safety labs was mandated to acknowledge contact by speakerphone within five minutes.

This safety procedure had been put into place several years prior, when one of the senior lab technicians had a heart attack while doing research. The No Admittance sign had been posted and, assuming he was caught up in his research and ignoring the phone, no one thought to penetrate the lab when he did not respond to communications. By then it was too late. From that incident on, failure to comply with the acknowledgement mandate was met with swift disciplinary action, including the loss of research privileges. Julie knew he was egotistical, but even Jackson Mullins knew the risks and would not take a chance like that. *Damn.*

Looking up and down the empty corridors, Julie decided she had to go in and check on Mullins. She signed in at the wallboard, marking her entry time as 6:45 p.m. Even though her hospital privileges extended to the labs, she very rarely had reason to enter. Making one more unsuccessful attempt to reach him by speakerphone, she carefully opened the door to the airlock and placed her briefcase and personal belongings in a locker. She wasn't about to barge into the lab... just poke her head in to make sure he was okay. Still, she had to follow procedure and gown up, and she was ticked off and surprised that he was vindictive enough to ignore her, even if it meant jeopardizing his privileges.

Finally ready, she opened the door slowly so she wouldn't startle him.

"Jackson?" She called out quietly, not wanting to disturb his train of thought if he was in the middle of something. Still no response. She couldn't see him, so she entered the lab, quietly closing the door to the air lock behind her. She noticed that the microscope had obviously been in use, so she walked toward it carefully, avoiding physical contact with the equipment. She didn't want to be chastised for contaminating anything he may have been working on. Everything appeared orderly, but it was evident to her that he had stopped in the middle of his study. She turned to face the opposing counter, thinking that he may have entered the biological safety cabinet, which could explain why he hadn't answered her page.

Then she saw the blood. A huge amount of blood lay pooled on the cold tile floor of the lab.

Not again. "Jackson?" Julie, anxious and alarmed, dazedly backed away. There was no sign of life in the lab. There was no sign of Jackson Mullins.

Lightheaded and breathless, she escaped the close confines of the lab. Disrobing in the airlock, she threw her gown and gloves into the basket behind her, not stopping to gather her briefcase or purse. She ran through the hallway, racing to the central station, where her shaking fingers fumbled to grasp the marker from the slatted tray beneath the wall board.

Visibly trembling, she forced herself to take the time to put her initials under the out column. Grabbing a spool of yellow biohazard tape from the emergency cabinet behind the clerk's desk, she simultaneously pulled her cell phone from her lab-coat pocket. Frantically, she dialed Beverly Castiglione's number on her way to the elevator, stopping only long enough to stretch the fluorescent tape across the door of Mullins lab in the shape of an X, leaving the spool of tape dangling from the end of the last strip.

Chapter Forty Eight

Jackson Mullins tightened the pull-string around the pants on the set of scrubs he had confiscated from the surgical supply cabinet. He carefully placed the syringe he held in his left hand into the pocket of his newly acquired scrubs. Adjusting the surgical cap on his head, he walked quickly through the maze of hallways on the first floor, heading toward the emergency wing.

The intensity of repercussions resulting from the announcement of the 'Miracle Healing' had escaped him until this very second. Holed up in the lab, he had been only peripherally aware of what was going on around him. The halls were teeming with activity and hundreds of patients lined the walls in the emergency room, some crying out, some screaming in pain and distress, most just staring ahead, waiting for their turn to be seen. They had finally closed the ER to admissions and were rerouting patients to Maury County and beyond, as the Nashville hospitals were filled to the brim with the casualties of illness and heat.

Jackson weaved in and out of the mass confusion, desperately trying to avoid notice until he found a viable subject and was able to discreetly carry out the next step in his unauthorized and very unlawful experiment. *I don't have time to go through the red tape. Consent. Forget it. Every last person in this ER would be begging to participate, if they knew what I carried in my pocket.*

He scanned the crowded corridors, trying to spot the right candidate, glancing quickly at charts placed haphazardly in the bottom of the gurneys. It was vitally important that the subject be sick enough to need admission, so he could chart the progress of his treatment. It had to be someone who was not presently aware and would retain no knowledge of what he was about to do. *Damn. I wish there was time to do a trial protocol and perfect the delivery of the serum, but there's not. I have to go with what I have now. I can't afford to wait.*

"Dr. Jackson Mullins, please pick up line 4."

"Paging Dr. Mullins to line 4. Code Purple."

"Dr. Mullins. Code Purple."

You have got to be kidding. Alarmed that his absence from the lab had been discovered so quickly, he couldn't believe they had issued a Code Purple on him. *Damn. The blood. He should have taken the time to clean up the blood.* When he regained consciousness on the floor of the lab, he had been beyond elated. Euphoria enveloped him the moment he had become aware. There was no evidence of the self inflicted trauma to his arm. He could think of nothing but moving immediately to next step in his plan.

But now, for his lack of patience, he was rewarded with his name sandwiched between two Code Purples. The hospital used this archaic method for alerting employees that a staff member had been injured and was unaccounted for. Everyone would be on the lookout for him now. *An injured him.*

A sense of urgency overwhelmed him, but he managed to remain outwardly calm. He had hoped to have the luxury of time as he carefully chose the subject of his next experiment. Turning the corner of the ER, he paused outside a curtained area. Though he heard no sound coming from within, he peeked behind the curtain. He could have fainted with relief as adrenaline continued to course full steam through his system. A small boy slept in a chair pushed next to the bed of an obviously terminal female patient. She wouldn't be going anywhere soon, and from the look of things, he knew he had to work fast. Jackson glanced at the chart and noticed big red letters across the top. ALS. Amyotrophic Lateral Sclerosis- End Stage. Always fatal. Lou Gehrig's Disease was a death sentence. Theresa Boone was 43 years old and had come to this hospital in search of a miracle. *Perfect. I am about to give you one.*

Pulling the syringe from his pocket, he walked over to the bedside, keeping his eyes on the boy. Moaning aloud, the little one stirred once. Jackson froze, but the boy settled back to sleep, reaching automatically for his mother's hand.

No time to swab the skin with alcohol. *If this works you won't need it anyway, darlin'.* Pulling back on the plunger, he positioned the needle over the wasted muscle of the emaciated woman's thigh. *Here we go. Now.* Looking at the clock on the wall behind her bed, Jackson Mullins mentally documented the time. 7:22 p.m. As he withdrew the needle he glanced at her face for the first time, startled to see her eyes wide open, as a single tear made its way down her temple, landing on the pillow beneath her head.

"Just a little something to help you rest, Theresa." He smiled at her as he backed out slowly, his eyes locked with hers, until he pulled back the curtain and left the room.

"Dr. Mullins?" He swung around abruptly, capping the syringe behind his back and sliding it quickly into his pocket.

Noticing the nametag on the nurse's sweater, he answered.

"Yes, Miss Jenkins?"

"Are you okay? There's been a Code Purple called on you. Did you not hear the intercom?"

The young nurse looked closely at him, examining him for possible physical injuries with experienced eyes.

"No, I'm sorry. I left the hospital for some fresh air and am just now returning. I'll see to it right now. Dear me. There is so much confusion around here."

"Yes, it's been this way for awhile now. If you're sure you're okay, I have to get back to patients. Call extension four, Dr. Mullins, and let them know you're okay."

Watching the young nurse disappear into the fray, Jackson Mullins rolled up his sleeve exposing the soft unblemished skin of his left forearm. He walked back toward the lab, gently rolling the syringe inside his pocket as he started to whistle, barely able to contain his giddiness as he contemplated the significance of the last hour. Theresa Boone. The next miracle.

Chapter Forty Nine

While pondering the past few days, Father Andrews lumbered through the sanctuary exchanging the burnt out candles with fresh new votives. The smell of melting wax was thick in the air of the chapel and wafted out into the main vestibule with the slightest breeze. The faithful had filled the sanctuary with candlelight, putting dimes and quarters into the money box in exchange for favors from the Most High. Deacons had taken shifts staying with him, and would begin to alternate preaching the gospels at all masses, though he feared they would soon have to streamline the Mass to accommodate the sheer number of people and their growing demands on the parish.

His voice was hoarse and his throat raw and scratchy, the result of his attempts to make himself heard above the shuffling and sniffling of the injured and lame that filled the church, lining its aisles for some promise of a physical remedy in the form of a miracle. He looked out onto the congregation occasionally, amazed and surprised, at how one supposed manifestation could result in such an outpouring of hope and faith. All it had taken was a miracle.

The Bishop had landed in Nashville several hours ago and was inching his way toward the parish as quickly as the Army Reserve could make it happen. Father Andrews had spoken to him briefly, and he was already showing signs of impatient crankiness. He was sure to be exhausted and hungry when he arrived and, bless her heart, the ever vigilant Mrs. Murray had a casserole ready to heat in the microwave as soon as he walked through the door.

It was already close to nine o'clock and the streets were relatively quiet, as the exhausted people who lined them quietly fell into their nighttime routine. Father Andrews gave a passing thought to the hygienic conditions out there, which surely would cause a new set of problems if something was not done quickly to alleviate the situation. The church, from necessity, had hired a few of the willing public to care for the restrooms in the front of the church, keeping the stalls and the sinks stocked with fundamentals, and to prevent malingering among the faithful gathered outside the church doors. These temporary hirelings were more than happy to escape the sweltering summer heat, even if it meant cleaning the stalls used by the ailing public. *This too shall pass.*

Genuflecting before the altar, he made the sign of the cross and decided to walk through the gated courtyard to return to the rectory, instead of making his way through the underground tunnels. He smiled when he remembered young Stephen's look of surprise as he was introduced to the catacombs. Thinking of Stephen, he mouthed a silent prayer, hoping the young man had finally contacted Dr. Macomb. He looked at his watch and noted the late hour, trying to decide if he should call the professor again. So much had happened today, he couldn't find the time, but for the attempts he'd made earlier this morning. Well, perhaps tomorrow, before the Bishop stirred, he could try again. He would call Stephen tonight though, to make sure he had arrived safely home.

Climbing the steps to the back door, Father Andrews contemplated Stephen's dreams and wondered once more at the message they foretold. Were they only the wanderings of a youthful and impressionable mind? Who knew? Nashville was the home of Country Music and look at the difference in less than one week. The area around the hospital was now being referred to in the press as the Miracle Mile. He locked the back door of the sanctuary behind him, and walked into the rectory to wash his face and prepare himself for the arrival of Bishop Tomlin.

Chapter Fifty

Camellia Jacobs expertly pulled the Chevrolet Z-71 into the public parking lot behind the Greyhound station roughly two miles from Stephen's apartment. The old truck had over two hundred thousand miles showing on the odometer, but on the road had proved to be a sturdy and reliable ride. Her little blue sports car was in the shop getting body work done, the result of a little fender bender that happened while she was reporting on a house fire in St. Thomas. Good old Mr. Phillips.

Her editor at the newspaper didn't blink twice at the suggestion that she come to Nashville to visit her brother. After all, Stephen lived right smack in the eye of the 'miracle' maelstrom. He tried to keep them updated on the latest news from the University, and was her 'reliable source' for most of the first hand information she had been able to gather. Old man Phillips was chomping at the bit before she even finished asking him to send her out on assignment.

Mom's preacher friend, Reverend Jennings, had this fine grey truck hibernating in his garage. He hadn't driven it in several years and handed her the keys without a second thought as soon as he heard she was leaving for Nashville.

"You'll need something substantial for this trip, Miss Camellia." Reverend Jennings called everyone Miss or Mister. It didn't really matter how old you were.

"I appreciate your offer, Reverend, but I don't know what I am heading into. I can't promise what the driving conditions will be and I understand the traffic is murderous. What if something happens to the truck while I'm traveling?" Cami was telling the truth. From what Stephen had been describing to them, she estimated the trip would take at least four times as long, and be at least twice as hazardous, as the normal journey.

"Now you listen here, little Miss. That old truck has been sitting in my garage just waiting for an adventure. I wouldn't have you driving into that fracas with that little sports car of yours. No ma'am. Margaret Mary's daughter is going to be safe, and that machine is as reliable as they come. Four-wheel drive and power everything. And it has a huge gas tank, with a second one for good measure. We'll leave the bed cover on so you don't have to worry about unwanted guests hopping aboard, and you'll still have plenty of room to stow your gear. No ma'am. You can't go wrong with that truck." Reverend Jennings threw the keys on the kitchen table and turned around to leave.

Cami threw her arms around his neck from behind and gave him a squeeze.

"I'll be careful with it, I promise."

"Now you go on and get ready, Miss Camellia, before your mom gets back from the store. I want you to stop by the church tomorrow before you leave now, you hear?"

"I'll be there. Thanks again."

Smiling at the memory, Cami grabbed the backpack off the front seat and threw the strap of the Sony Altra 350 camera around her neck, as she turned off the engine. Resting her head on the steering wheel, she took a few deep breaths and rehashed the sights and sounds she had experienced on her way to Nashville. Stephen had not exaggerated about the mayhem. The shots she caught on camera could be rivaled only by the AP photos staring back from the front page of the Sunday paper. As soon as she found an internet hookup, she would get some of these back to Phillips.

It had taken over 36 hours to drive 650 miles…the last 24 hours spent crawling from the state line of Kentucky to the bus station in Nashville. She'd made better time driving through the night, and had been able to catch catnaps during the day, until she crossed over into Tennessee. At that point the landscape changed drastically. Nothing Stephen had said could have prepared her for this.

Every cell in her body screamed for her to stop and help the people lining the side of the highways, as they summoned every ounce of strength they possessed just to put one foot in front of the other, to keep moving forward. Cars abandoned because of the congestion, they struggled on, painstakingly finding their way to Nashville. How could she choose to help one out of a thousand without causing a riot?

Those walking along the road seemed almost catatonic and very seldom glanced up, as the never ending line of vehicles snaked toward the city. Those on foot seemed to be making more headway, as the constant stop and go made the trip anything but smooth for the steel caravan. As surreal as it was, the sight of the little white crosses springing up on the side of the road affected her the most, testament to the hundreds of sick and exhausted people who had found the end of their journey on the edge of a highway while searching for miraculous intervention.

She had tried to reach Stephen Sunday morning after church, to let him know she was on her way. His voicemail was evidently full, so she couldn't even leave him a message. The last time she talked to him was Saturday morning, when he was on his way to talk to the Catholic priest, and he sounded flustered or absentminded, as if he wasn't really listening to what she was saying. She knew her brother well enough to know when something was troubling him. Oh, well. She had his address and his phone number, and had a map of Nashville streets. *Surprise.*

Cami offered a silent prayer of thanksgiving that she had ended the first leg of her journey unscathed, adding a small postscript prayer, hoping that Reverend Jennings meant what he said about not caring about the condition of the truck when it was returned. Climbing down from the cab, she tossed the long term parking pass on the dashboard, and patted the side of the truck where a long deep gash bore witness to the grueling journey behind her. She put the keys in her front pocket with her cell phone, and started walking among the homeless and the seekers, all blending seamlessly into the ever changing landscape of the city.

Chapter Fifty One

Stephen climbed the stairs to his apartment and fell through the door. It was almost midnight when he looked at the clock in his kitchen. Time ran together now. He had left Father Andrews at the rectory before noon and so much had happened since then, that it was all a blur. Taking his cell phone from his pocket, he looked around the kitchen until he spotted the phone charger on the counter under last Thursday's bills. He made a mental note to go down to the lobby and grab the week's mail before he left for the Macomb's.

Peeling off his shirt, he walked into the bathroom and turned on the shower to warm the water while he shaved. He had to wake up. Physically and mentally, he could not go another step until he ate and had some sleep. As much as he wanted to get over to see Marc Macomb and Jillian, he knew he did not have the strength to act until he refueled. Looking at his reflection in the mirror above the sink, dark blue eyes staring back at him, tired and puffy, he wasn't sure if removing the three day growth of beard had made things better or worse.

Stephen stood in the shower and let the spray rain down on him, thankful he had the luxury of soap and water. Remembering the journey from the campus to his apartment, it was quite evident that most of the people in the crowded streets did not. *What is going to happen in the days and weeks ahead?* Stephen believed that eventually people would return to their homes. He could not fathom what would happen if things didn't improve quickly. People were dying on the side of the road, for Christ's sake.

Stephen finished showering, and then, somewhat refreshed, wrapped the towel around his waist as he walked into his bedroom for a change of clothes. Finding nothing clean, he threw a pile of nasty looking laundry into the washer, and headed to the kitchen to heat a can of soup and to call Dr. Macomb.

He stood at the counter with his phone tethered to the charger and punched in the doctor's number. He figured he should leave a message to let the professor know what was going on.

"Hi, Dr. Macomb. It's after midnight and I just made it back to my apartment. I'll pack up and leave early in the morning for your house. If you tried to get through earlier, I apologize… I lost power to my phone. I will see you tomorrow. It will probably be early in the afternoon, if I make good time." Stephen ended the call, thinking it ludicrous that a two mile journey could now possibly take as much as half a day to complete.

He finished eating while leaning against the sink, then went in to watch the local news while he waited for the washer to finish its cycle. There was Amy Levine from Channel 3. Did she never sleep? She had been covering this story since Friday night when news of the miracle leaked. She had to be running on pure adrenaline. Turning up the volume, he sat on the sofa and listened to the recap of the day's events.

"We are reporting from outside Bradford University Hospital, waiting for the latest information from the administrative spokesperson. What we know at this point; they have not found the source or cause of the 'Miracle Healing' and continue to test all resources. Bishop Tomlin of the Archdiocese of Nashville and representatives of the United States Government are scheduled to meet with hospital officials Wednesday afternoon, and we are promised a press conference sometime after that. Meanwhile, the shooter from the ambush this morning at the University has been detained and the victim's next of kin have been notified. As soon as we have the name of the deceased, we will let you know."

The studio anchorman's image flashed on the screen and, in his polished suit, every hair meticulously in place, he asked the reporter about conditions in the street.

"All I can tell you, Bob, is that we continue to monitor the situation from the van at ground zero, but from all reports that have come my way, people continue to pour into the city on day four of the 'Miracle Healing'. The Davidson County Police Department and representatives from the National Guard are urging all citizens to remain in their homes, if at all possible, until further notice. This is Amy Levine reporting live from Bradford University Hospital in Nashville."

Stephen hit the mute button and went to throw the clean load of clothes into the dryer, then repeated the whole process with a load of towels and underwear. He went back to the sofa to lie down, waiting until he could throw the last load into the dryer, before going to bed for some much needed sleep. He figured he'd better be up by seven to head over to the Macomb's, but at least he wouldn't show up with a duffel bag full of dirty socks.

As he lay there, eyes closed, his mind drifted back through the day and how close he had come to real danger. It seemed almost dreamlike now. He wondered about young Johnny and his mother, and how they were doing. Once he had delivered Mrs. McCarthy and her coworkers past the guard posts at the University, he tried for over an hour to get through to the hospital to check on the Boones, but was unable to connect. The phone lines were overburdened and his cell phone went dead. There was no way they would let him into the building. He finally talked one of the guards into taking a note to the ER desk to be given to Johnny, but had no way of knowing if it was ever delivered. The most he could hope for was to ask Dr. Macomb's wife, Sara, to use her hospital privileges to make contact with the emergency room and find out how they fared. Things hadn't look so promising when he left them at the checkpoint. He was worried about the boy being alone in the city.

Stephen was drowsy and lightheaded, and could feel himself being pulled down gently into the vortex that led to his visions. Unable to stay awake any longer, he fell through the opening willingly, hoping for answers that would guide him through the next step of this journey.

The vision came to him at once and was stunning and beautiful. The messenger Gabriel stood in the clouds over a sea of crashing waves, a halo of light surrounding him, his robes billowing in the wind. The girl was nowhere to be seen, but it was very clear to Stephen that the vision was all about her and what was to take place. As Gabriel raised his arms to the sky, a sound like thunder tore through Stephen's soul, and without Gabriel saying a word, Stephen knew all that he was destined to know. He knew of the child and its mother, and how he was to protect them both.

He watched the world as he knew it cease to exist, and he saw the future of man and was both awed and terrified. He knew nothing of the time or the hour that these things would take place, but he knew without any lingering doubt, that he had indeed been chosen. Gabriel turned away from him and raised his arms once again. The clouds parted, and scenes from the heavens filled the sky with light. Stephen saw his father's face clearly and desperately tried to reach out to him, but he could not raise his arms and the beautiful face of his parent disappeared, replaced by a majestic ring of angels. He watched as the radiant beings circled the opening of what could only be the gates of heaven, but was unable to see their faces, for the brightest of stars surrounded them.

The Messenger lowered his arms, the beauteous vision faded, and Stephen was filled with a deep longing he could not fathom.

With his arms pointing downward toward the churning sea, the Messenger opened wide his hands and the waters beneath his feet parted to unleash the pit of hell. Captured within the void were sounds of despair and longing and sorrow and pain, the likes of which Stephen had never imagined possible. From the depths of the abyss rose black angels, unfurling mighty wings of hatred and despair. The strength of evil was never to be underestimated. Stephen understood clearly now. Their faces were hidden by evil black clouds swirling and boiling around the opening of the low place. No fire was evident in this hell, only the absolute absence of light for all eternity.

Gabriel turned once again to Stephen and the void disappeared, leaving behind a tranquil sky and calm sea... no trace of the ultimate joy from above or the devastating suffering below. He looked to Stephen only then, his arms held out as if to invite him into an embrace. Stephen fell to his knees, knowing he had been given a glimpse into Heaven and Hell.

He began to pray, wordless wrenching sobs of fear and sorrow, knowing that he stood at the precipice of good and evil. He begged forgiveness, and for strength to carry out these next acts with courage and faith. Had he been witness of what was to come? He knew in his soul he would die to keep them safe, but who were the child and the virgin? Who was Jillian Macomb?

Chapter Fifty Two

I t was only a whisper, but as sweet as the sweetest music he'd ever heard. When the boy first woke, he batted absently into the air around his head. It had been so long since he felt the soft touch of another human, that he didn't recognize it and tried to swat the featherlike intrusion away. His sleep glazed senses thinking at first that it must be a fly or some other insect coming to rouse him from his dreams. When he finally made contact with the source of the soft insistent stroking against his hair he froze, afraid to move and break the spell.

"Johnny."

He heard his name again, his throat almost closing as he choked back the hot tears he had held inside for so long now, his mind finally registering the sweet pain of recognition. Lifting his head slowly from the bed, Johnny Boone found himself holding the fragile hand of his mother, as she moved her fingers gently through his hair for the first time in over six months.

"Mama?" He realized then. He watched her eyes flutter open with surprise, and she looked straight at him as she worked the muscles of her mouth to form his name. Before she fell once again into an exhausted sleep, he swore he saw the corners of her lips turn up into the long forgotten shape of a smile.

Chapter Fifty Three

I t was just a vial of blood." Jackson Mullins sat on the corner of the conference table, swinging his leg and buttoning the wristband of his collared shirt. "Really, Dr. Castiglione, do I look injured to you?"

"Dr. Mullins, if I weren't desperately in need of the results from the research into Dr. Sorrento's healing, you would be put on administrative leave faster than you can say 'miracle.'"

"I explained to you that I left the lab because I needed a break. After the vial smashed to the floor, I realized I had not taken my eyes from the telescope for several hours. My intent was not to frighten anyone or turn this into a major ordeal. I should have taken the time to clean up the blood, but I was frustrated and had a numbing headache. I needed fresh air. I forgot to sign out. Pure and simple. I had no idea some errant fool would barge into my lab unannounced and cause such a ruckus. I had dinner and then headed back to the lab for a few more hours. I've had a good night's rest and today is a new day."

"You scared the hell out of Julie Richards." Beverly Castiglione took off her glasses and sat in a chair at the head of the table.

"Don't get me started on that incompetent woman." Jumping to his feet, Jackson Mullins blustered as he strode toward the door.

"She had no business discharging that girl. I may have to bring her back in, and that will prove to be even more disruptive to the family, don't you think?"

"Have you made any headway, Jackson?" Dr. Castiglione rubbed her temples as she followed the doctor's retreating back with her eyes.

"I am starting to gather some interesting results, but of course it's much too early to report anything conclusive." Mullins paused with his hand on the doorknob, turning slowly to look at Dr. Castiglione, waiting for her to dismiss him.

"The meeting is tomorrow at 2:30. The Bishop will be present, as will the Government Officials. I hope you have something more to offer, Jackson. Anything. Everyone is getting antsy and the furor on the streets has not receded at all. We need answers or they will send their own experts over to investigate." Beverly straightened in her chair and looked directly at him.

"They will have their answers soon enough. Until then, my lab is off limits to everyone." Jackson turned and left the conference room without another word.

Chapter Fifty Four

I t felt good to sleep in her own bed and Jillian woke refreshed Tuesday morning, rising earlier than usual, and ravenous. She could smell the coffee from the kitchen downstairs, a sure sign her father was up and moving. Her mother and he had worked half the night, turning the apartment above the garage into a guestroom for Stephen Jacobs. She watched for a while, as they carried boxes of Christmas ornaments and old magazines and catalogs from the university, stacking them in the unfinished space in the attic.

"Why don't you just let him stay in the extra room upstairs in the main house?" Jillian asked as her mom plopped face down on the unmade bed.

"Your dad thinks Stephen needs his own space, and besides, we're not sure how long he might be here with us," Sara answered, her voice muffled.

Turning over to face the ceiling her mother said, "He will probably like the privacy out here."

Marc walked back into the room from his adjoining office and looked around the space. "It looks presentable, don't you think?"

Sara raised herself from the double bed and grabbed the set of sheets she had carried up from the house. "Here, Jill, help me with these. You take that side." Shaking the linen out into a billowy cloud, Jillian helped make up the bed.

"How long do you think this will go on, Mom? I mean the people and all?"

"I'm not sure, honey. We just have to wait it out like everyone else. I hope something happens soon, though. I'm not sure how much longer people can last on the streets the way things are." Sara sounded sad.

Jillian had gone to bed soon after, and finally snug in her own bed, lay listening to the comforting sounds of her parents moving back and forth between the house and garage, until she finally fell asleep. Now, waking up in familiar surroundings, she yawned, stretched again and finally pushed herself out of bed. She found the pair of shorts she had thrown on the floor the night before, and leaning against the dresser, put them on with a clean t-shirt. She heard the back door slam and followed the sounds of her parent's bantering to the rooms above the garage.

"Good morning, princess." Marc said as he walked past her and into the apartment with a small nightstand in his arms.

"Hey, it looks great in here, Daddy. Maybe when Stephen leaves, I can move up here and..." Jillian paused, remembering the baby and Arianna, and all of the things that would never be the same.

"Honey, it's okay. Don't be sad." Sara came from the bedroom into Marc's office and smiled, determined to be cheerful.

She opened her arms and gestured toward the newly organized space.

"It amazes me that your father ever got any work done in here with all the garbage that was laying around. At least now it's presentable. Are you hungry, Jill?" Sara asked.

Putting the furniture polish in the cabinet, she tossed the last of the old newspapers into the trash bag and turned to face her daughter. "Come on. I am finished and I'm famished."

"Mom, I was thinking I would call Evie today to see if she can come over for a while. I miss her a lot, and I really want to tell her about everything that's been going on. Before she hears about it from somebody else." Jillian leaned against the doorway twirling her hair around her finger.

"Honey, I know you're missing your best friend and I think its okay, but I should call Dr. Richards and make sure you can have visitors. I don't want you to do anything that may prove to be a setback for you or the baby, and I especially don't want you to have to go back into the hospital."

Sara knew the time was fast approaching when the news would hit the campus and she was trying to brace herself for the impact. The most important consideration right now had to be Jillian and how everything affected her. Sara instinctively knew that her daughter felt isolated and alone, and believed a visit from her best friend, after almost two weeks of turmoil, would go a long way toward making her feel like a normal teenager again, whatever that was.

"I'll get in touch with Julie after breakfast and then you can call Evie to see if she can come over and spend the night."

"I agree. Let's get some noise and normalcy back into this house," Marc said.

Marc glanced around the apartment and finally satisfied, turned back to his office.

"Sara, have you seen my class schedule?" he called over his shoulder, raising the shade on the window above his desk.

Sara rolled her eyes in his direction and went into his office, where she found Marc studying something out the window overlooking the front yard.

"Hey, Sara, there's an army jeep at the curb and someone is walking up to our front door. What the heck?" Marc leaned in to get a closer look as Sara rushed over to the window and stood next to her husband, looking down to the yard below.

"Marc, it kind of looks like…"

"I'll be damned. It's your sister. It's Susie." The three of them raced toward the door, Marc taking the steps two at a time.

*   *   *

"I can't believe you made it. And you made it in 24 hours, Susie." Sara started to cry again. She couldn't believe her sister had pulled it off. Feeling relief that was palpable, Sara, at that very moment, realized how much the presence of her older sister meant to her. She knew that having her there would help them all get through these next few weeks.

"And what an adventure it turned out to be." Susie laughed, at the same time noticing that the stress of the last few weeks, had etched itself deeply on the faces of her sister's family.

They were sitting on the screened porch, drinking iced tea and enjoying the soft breeze from the overhead fan. Susie pulled her feet underneath her on the porch swing and patted the flowered cushion next to her, for Jillian to sit.

"Let me tell you how everything happened. Bless my husband." Susie looked up dramatically, made the sign of the cross and continued her story.

"After I hung up yesterday afternoon, Sara, I called Tommy at the office and told him about everything that's been going on down here. We have been watching the news reports, obviously… after all you can't turn on CNN or any of the cable news stations without seeing graphic images of all this. Never in a million years would we have guessed what you three are going through. I've tried so many times to get through to you, never dreaming any of this was happening. Anyway, Tommy said it was obvious I had a bee in my bonnet and knew I would not rest until I made my way to you. He does know me well."

"I love you, sissy." Sara smiled, but the tears kept coming. Jillian sat next to her aunt, laying her head on Susie's shoulder.

"Well, my Tommy got on the phone right that second and called his corporate office, explaining that we had a family emergency. They said they couldn't get clearance into Nashville with the corporate jet, but could land in Smyrna, which turned out to be a greater blessing. One of Tommy's old National Guard buddies is still on active duty and stationed at the Smyrna airport as a helicopter training supervisor.

"You are not telling me you took a helicopter from Michigan?" Marc threw his head back and laughed, for the first time in a long time.

"No, you moron. I took a corporate jet to Smyrna, *then* a helicopter to that little park across from the University Hospital. They have it cordoned off from the public, and the National Guard and Davidson County Police Department are using it as a headquarters. Tommy's friend had a jeep waiting for me at three in the morning and here I am. The longest part of the entire trip was from the park to your front door. About four hours."

"You are one remarkable woman, Susie. You have no idea how glad we are to see you." Sara looked at her sister in amazement.

"Well, I would have been here sooner if you had clued me in about what was going on." Susie looked at all of them, then pulled back and took Jillian's chin in her hand. "How are you feeling, little one?"

"I'm okay, Aunt Susie. I'm getting fat, though. Look." Jill raised her t-shirt so they could all see the little bump that seemed to have grown overnight.

"Well, we have lots to talk about. How about if I go in to unpack and freshen up? Sara, show me where I'm sleeping, honey, and then we'll visit. I have so many questions about this 'Miracle Healing' and everything else that's going on in Nashville. It's unbelievable, the things I saw on my way in. It's even more mind boggling from the sky."

The women got up and put their empty glasses on the tray.

"Aunt Susie?" Jillian called to her aunt as the two sisters walked through the door and into the kitchen.

"Yes, love?"

"I'm glad you're here."

Chapter Fifty Five

I went into their room to give the little boy a note. One of the guards at the post outside the emergency room must have brought it in last night and left it at the nurse's station. We're so shorthanded, Dr. Castiglione, you know how it is." Aubrey Parson had been an ER nurse with the hospital for over five years.

Short and stocky, with dark hair gathered into a clip on the top her head, she had always been a no-nonsense practitioner dedicated to her patients. It took a special personality to operate under fire all day long, everyday, never able to anticipate the devastation that would come barreling through the automatic doors at any given time.

"We were swamped last night, and when I checked on the Boones, the little one had climbed onto the bed with his mommy and they were both asleep. I knew he was exhausted. He'd been keeping vigil since they came through the door. I left the note on the bed next to the little guy without waking them up and got out of there. Her vitals looked a little better on the monitor, but I just didn't have the heart to disturb them. So I skipped the full check and let them sleep. I mean, we all know it's just a matter of hours until she's gone."

"Evidently, not anymore." Beverly studied the nurse, but could not bring herself to issue a reprimand for not waking the Boones in order to do a shift change check on the dying woman's vital signs. The administration counted on the staff to use compassion and common sense in the present situation, and with the ALS diagnosis and the condition of this patient when she was admitted, Bev probably would have made the same call. The attending had chosen not to have her moved out of the ER and transferred her into a private exam room instead, feeling her demise was imminent. They were to call Social Services for the boy today.

"When the little guy came running out into the hall this morning, he was so agitated and excited that we thought she had passed. He was pulling me and waving his little note and saying something about a mustard seed and his friend, Stephen. I thought he was hysterical because she was gone." Aubrey paused for a minute to regain her composure.

"I tried to slow him down. I wanted to get an aide to sit with him while I attended to his mother's body, but he kept pulling me, and then he started laughing, so finally I just went with him."

"What happened next?" Beverly Castiglione was taking notes and trying to concentrate on the facts, instead of on the implications of what Aubrey was relaying to her.

"Their room is located in the far corner of the ER. I opened the curtain just enough to let myself in and still give them privacy. Also, I didn't want to upset any of the patients waiting in the hallway. I figured she was gone. So I followed him in, and Johnny was still pulling me and laughing. Then I saw her."

Aubrey paused and closed her eyes, remembering.

"The bed had been raised into a sitting position and there she was. I'm telling you, I almost passed out. They must have removed the oxygen from her face themselves, because she was looking right at me and smiling. I mean, she looked weak, but she held out her hand to me and she was smiling. She actually raised her arm and held out her hand to me."

Aubrey stared off into the distance, once again reliving the moment when her patient looked at her and murmured in a tight whisper, "Hi, I'm Theresa Boone."

"Have we confirmed the original diagnosis with Maury Regional?" Beverly closed the notebook.

"Yes. That was the first thing we did when we admitted her. The boy had her medical history with them. That kid is amazing. Only ten years old, and he knew the names of every doctor she had seen and every medication she was on. He said he brought her for the miracle. And I'll be damned if he didn't get her one."

"Okay, Aubrey. Easy on the 'M' word. Hang tight and I'll call you the minute the examination is completed. I'd like you to be the one to get them settled upstairs in a room when we're ready. I have a feeling it's going to get even more crazy around here as soon as word gets out, and they'll need someone they're familiar with to help with the transition. I have the Chief of Neurology coming over to do a complete exam and workup on her. We can compare the results of his exam and the blood-work and vitals we took yesterday afternoon with the results of the last exam performed by her primary care doctor. If you would take the boy down to the cafeteria to get him out of the room for awhile, that would be a help. But I want you to stick to him like glue."

"No problem." Aubrey turned to leave the room.

"Aubrey?" The nurse paused and turned to look back at Beverly. "You see people come into the ER all the time. Are you sure she was that bad when she was admitted?"

"I promise you, Dr. Castiglione, she would have been trached and put on a respirator as soon as we got her yesterday, but there was a DNR posted on her chart. She had a living will and a next of kin somewhere in South Carolina that we were supposed to call to come for the boy. I think maybe the ex-husband, but whoever it was had same last name. We tried to contact him to get things moving, but the number had been disconnected. Department of Children's Services was going to be called for Johnny this morning. Her life could have been measured in hours. Or less. That much I know for sure."

"Okay, Aubrey. Thanks again." Bev dismissed the nurse but she stood for a moment without leaving.

"Doctor Castiglione, can I ask you a question?"

"Sure, go ahead."

"Do you believe in miracles?"

"I wish you'd asked a question I had an answer for Aubrey. I don't know. I just don't know."

Chapter Fifty Six

Cami pulled the scrap of paper from the pocket of her blouse and followed the numbers on the buildings until she was standing in front of Stephen's apartment. A woman and a small group of children were huddled on the corner, about thirty feet away, watching her closely. The streetlamp bathed them in soft light, and she noticed one little guy smacking his arm to ward off insects that had been drawn to them by the glow. As she glanced their way, she saw the woman hesitantly break away from the group, and clearly embarrassed, she gestured to Cami.

"Miss, excuse me. I'm sorry, and I can't believe I am asking you this, but do you have any food you could spare? My husband has been standing in line at the food tents for hours, but he hasn't come back yet and my little one is so hungry."

The woman, whom Cami assumed to be the mother, moved aside and she saw a little girl of about seven sitting on a blanket in the middle of the sidewalk. Soft fuzz where her hair had been, she had obviously been ravaged first by cancer, then by the chemo that would hopefully save her.

"I have granola and small bags of trail mix. Will that help?" Cami fished in her backpack and handed the little plastic packets to the woman. "There should be enough there for the boys, too. At least it should help until your husband gets back with some real food. Do you have water?" Cami moved a little closer to the family.

"Yes, ma'am." The woman pointed to a small cooler the boys were using for a bench. "It's not as hard to find water. They have stations set up all over the city."

"I'm Cami," She held out her hand to the woman. "Where is your family from?"

"My name is Laura Wellborn. We're from Georgia and we came as far as we could by bus. Then we walked. I moved us back here off the main roads of the city last night. I know we're not supposed to be in the residential area, but there is so much sickness around and we have to be careful with Ramie. She gets sick so easy now. "

"I understand." Cami looked around. "It seems pretty quiet around this building. I doubt anyone will say anything to you. Laura, would it be okay if I took a picture of your family? I'm a reporter from Canada and I would love to be able to use it in a human interest piece. I promise I'll send you copies of all the photos. There are so many people here searching for a miracle. Laura nodded and scooted the boys to the side so the camera could spotlight all of them."

Cami stood in front of the little girl. Focusing her lens carefully, she tried to capture the innocence, lost in pursuit of the elusive miracle they desperately searched for. A miracle that may never come for them. She had no way of knowing it then, but as she snapped the last shot, the sun came up behind her. Bringing with it a halo of soft light that illuminated the child's face, it reflected star-like prisms from the sole tear that made its way slowly down her baby soft cheek to the sidewalk below. Shaken by the beauty of the image reflected in the screen on her camera, Cami stood slowly. She smiled and wordlessly turned away from them to make her way back to Stephen's front door, not trusting her emotions. Raising her hand behind her to acknowledge their thanks, she silently rang the bell to his apartment.

*　　*　　*

Stephen's muscles were cramped and he opened his eyes slowly, feeling drugged and disoriented. He could hear the incessant buzzer and remembered the dryer, but the noise sounded too loud. He was on the floor, still on his knees where he had fallen after the vision. The buzzer sounded again, this time louder, still more insistent, almost desperate. Fully conscious, Stephen finally recognized the sound. The doorbell. He had never heard the doorbell in all the weeks he'd lived here. No company ever graced his apartment. Who now?

He stood slowly, stiff and sore from laying in the same position for several hours. He couldn't see the front door from his window, but saw a small group making camp on the corner. It looked like a family without a father. Whoever was at the door was not going anywhere until he answered… that much was clear. Taking off the towel he'd draped around his waist last night, he flung it into the basket that was sitting on top of the dryer and reached into the machine for a clean pair of shorts.

"I'm coming, I'm coming." Before he opened the exterior door, he pulled the curtain aside on the vestibule sidelight. There, like a mirage, standing outside on his stoop, was his little sister. All five foot two of the tiny warrior, Cami stood there with a smile plastered from ear to ear. He unlocked the door and she leaped into the building, throwing her arms around her big brother.

"Surprise!" Cami sang out, as if she was jumping from behind a chair at a birthday party.

"How did you ever…" Stephen could not find the words.

"Are we gonna go into your place, or just stand here in the lobby squawking like a couple of Canadian geese?"

"Let me take that." Dazed, Stephen removed the bulging backpack from his sister's shoulders and led her into his apartment. He closed the door and turned to look at her.

"Cami, how did you get through?"

"I tried to call you several times. Do you not *ever* listen to your voicemail?"

"God, Cam, there has been so much going on. I don't even know where to start."

"Listen, it's only six o'clock in the morning and it appears we have all day, so start at the beginning. If it's any consolation, I can totally pick up on the confusion around here. And that is even without the benefit of my investigative prowess."

"I'm not even sure I remember the beginning anymore. Damn, Cami, I cannot believe you're here. I didn't even offer you anything to drink. Come and sit down. Are you exhausted?"

"Stephen, if I want something to drink, I'll get it myself. And it feels good to move around. It took over 36 hours to get here. Unbelievable. Now tell me, what on earth is going on. Oh, and by the way, brother, you look like hell."

Stephen laughed. This was his baby sister, his fearless confidante. He wasn't sure how she would react to everything he was about to tell her, but he was so glad to have someone who would be in his corner. He knew this without a doubt in the world. Cami was his lifeline.

She watched her brother closely as he explained everything that he could remember about the visions. She looked into his eyes as he told her about the prophecy, the miracle that had taken place at the hospital and his feeling that everything was connected in some way. She was certain Stephen believed everything he had told her and that was enough for her.

"What's next, Stephen? How are you going to convince Dr. Macomb that his daughter is in danger? Do you even know for a fact that she is pregnant?" Cami's instincts were keen and her reporters mindset was beginning to take over.

"I'm not sure. And no, I don't know that Jillian is pregnant but I suspect. She was in the hospital and was released yesterday. Marc called and asked me to bring research materials to their house. He wants me to move into the apartment above his garage until the uproar over the miracle dies down, so we can continue our research for the coming semester. And he'll want to research the miracle, too. Find the basis in fact. It hasn't even been a full week since this started Cami and…"

"Say no more about that. I've experienced the ramifications, first hand, since Sunday night when I got to the Kentucky border. Someday we'll talk about all of this in detail, but right now let's figure out what you need to do."

Cami got up and walked over to the television, the volume still muted from the night before. She stood for a moment watching in silence before turning to her brother.

"I think you should go. Whatever force is guiding you is not going to forsake you now. It's a little unnerving though, Stephen. I mean I have to be honest. You are going to have to tread lightly. If I didn't know you as well as I do, I might be sneaking towards the exit door right now. And if you were telling me about a dream you had involving my daughter, I don't know what I would think."

"I know, Cami, believe me, I know. When I talked to Father Andrews, he all but said the same thing. You two are the only ones I've shared every detail with. But it's all true. This is not how I imagined I would begin my career at the University. And the first dream came before I even left home. Believe me, I never even laid eyes on a picture of Jillian Macomb before I got here. Yet there she was, the girl in my dreams. The one I am destined to protect."

Stephen leaned back, closing his eyes to the memory. "I thought Mom was going to have a coronary trying to wake me up the morning of the first dream. I know it scared her. Hell, it scared me. It was a powerful way to grab my attention."

Camellia stood and clapped her hands together. "Let's get you packed."

"What about you, Cami? I can't abandon you, can I? You just walked through the door."

"Listen, Stephen, I'm a big girl. Here's the deal. I'm going to stay in your apartment and do everything I can to help you from here. I have to be at ground zero. Where the story is. There is a Pulitzer out in the streets of Nashville right now, and I am going to do everything in my power to find it. I mean, just in case the world doesn't end. Anyway, I promised Mom and our big sister that I would take care of you, and that is exactly what I aim to do."

Hands on her hips, Cami surveyed the apartment.

"This will work perfectly for me. I can set up shop here and hook up to internet…you do have internet?"

"Yes, I have internet. Not wireless, but I have it. I mean, I'm usually on campus, so I haven't needed all the bells and whistles here. But I have a printer that doubles as a fax. You have to push a button to change one from the other, though."

"That's okay. I'll figure it all out, and this will work fine. So, forget about me. Stephen. No need to worry about me. But, do tell me what you're thinking. About a virgin birth and all. It's hard not to draw comparisons to the first one, you know."

"I know what you're thinking. I go over and over the same things constantly. I mean…this is my area of expertise. This is what I do. I study the history of the Christian faith. But for the past to manifest itself in the flesh and blood of the present? I just don't know. Is this a message from God? A second chance, or the end of the world as we know it? There are similarities, but Cami, to even think that this might be happening, boggles my mind. Even though people profess to believe in the birth of Christ, will they accept the idea a second time? And what about me? How do I fit into the divine scheme of things?"

"Well, brother, I guess you'll know soon enough, because it sounds like your visions are becoming more insistent. And a baby takes nine months to be born, so that time frame is definitely finite. And there is the 'miracle' to consider. It sort of puts people in the mood for listening, don't you think? And here you are, smack dab in the center of the maelstrom. Just take things slow, Stephen. Please. You've had time to come to terms with all of this, but the rest of us are still on page one."

"I know. I am trying to be patient and let myself be led. I don't want to scare the hell out of anyone."

"Well, now that you mention it, Stephen, it seems to me it wasn't all starlight and snowflakes for the Holy Family, either. There was the small matter of King Herod to consider. He killed all the male infants in the vicinity. Who is there today that would feel threatened by the significant consequences of a second virgin birth?" Cami's eyes were bright, her cheeks flushed with the excitement of trying to unravel the mystery of events yet to unfold.

"There is that little detail. I have been over the danger element in my mind a million times. I am under no illusions that this journey will be easy or safe. I can only believe the visions were accurate when they fore-told a great danger for the young mother and her newborn. And I am to protect them."

"I can't think of anyone more trustworthy or well suited for the job. Go get yourself packed. Got any teabags around here?"

"Yes, on the shelf next to the stove. I'm going to hop in the shower. Try to work out a plan of action for yourself while I get ready, so at least I'll know what you're up to. How long are you staying?"

"I'll stay as long as I need to. Do you have any problem with me camp-ing out in your apartment while you're at the Macomb's?"

"Of course not. I'm glad you're here. Just be careful, and promise we'll touch base every day. It's dangerous around here with everything that's going on, and I'll want to know you're okay."

"I have a feeling that you're the one who needs to be careful. Now go and get ready. It's going to take you all day to get to the other side of town." Cami pushed her brother into his room and pulled the door shut behind him.

She went into the kitchen and found a blue mug with BIBLEMAN written across it in white letters. She smiled as she filled it with water and put it in the microwave. Stephen had been enamored with the history of the church and it's people since he was a boy. She couldn't remember a time growing up, when he wasn't asking questions or poking around the library with his nose in the history books. He took it all so seriously.

She knew in her heart that he believed everything he had just shared with her. She hoped for his sake that the people involved would come to the same conclusion. But the truth was…either Jillian was pregnant or she wasn't. One thing Cami knew for sure. She would never doubt her brother. She was in.

When the microwave sounded, Cami put a tea bag into the mug and dipping it up and down in the hot water, went back into the living room, turning up the volume on the television. A female reporter from the local news station was broadcasting live in front of the hospital, bringing the viewers up to date on the latest developments, when some-one walked up to her with a small slip of paper. Glancing down briefly, she read the note and looked up quickly, then looked back down again, turning the paper over in her hand as if to ascertain its authenticity. She paused for only a moment, and then looked straight at the camera, her skin growing visibly pale under her makeup. She started to speak, her voice unsure, sounding much different than the professional tone she had used just a few seconds earlier.

In the background, Cami could hear the flow of water in the shower stop as it was turned off. She heard the telltale squeak of the shower curtain as her brother pulled it open and it scraped the metal rail. She was aware of the newswoman droning on in the background, as the cameraman panned back to show a full view of the hospital.

She stood up at some point, vaguely aware that the mug she had set on the floor by her feet had overturned, and the hot tea had fanned out across the floor in a steamy liquid pool. Heart beating loudly in her chest, she walked trancelike over to the closed door of Stephen's room, lifted her closed fist and pounded on the door.

"Hold your horses, girl. I'm almost ready. I'll be out in a second." Stephen said.

Finding her voice, Cami called through the door.

"Stephen, I think…."

Bare-chested, with hair dripping wet, Stephen flung the door open wide and caught his baby sister as she sagged against the doorway, her hands covering her mouth. Looking over her head into the living room, he watched as Amy Levine looked straight into the camera, holding tight to her microphone, but not saying a word. The look in her eyes was enough. It was true. A second miracle had just been confirmed.

Chapter Fifty Seven

Jackson Mullins wanted to dance. He was elated beyond measure when the news of the ER miracle filtered its way through the corridors of the hospital and landed at his door. He had been anticipating this moment. They were admitting his unsuspecting subject after Neurology did a complete workup on her, and he was waiting in pathology for her precious blood to be sent up for testing. It was all he could do to restrain himself. Patience. He must be patient. All would come about in good time, of that he was confident. He still had the small problem of how much progress to report to the vultures at the meeting this afternoon.

Dr. Castiglione had warned him an hour ago, that this latest development was sure to increase the pressure on the hospital for results from his research. She felt certain that he would be forced to allow more than one outside specialist into his lab. The U.S. Government? The Catholic Church? Fat chance he would ever concede to that on his watch. No, he must have a plan. He would not share his newly confirmed knowledge of the source of the miracles. They had no reason to suspect that the precious liquid surrounding the Macomb fetus was bringing about such glorious chaos. And he intended things to remain that way.

He carefully placed the recorded footage of his own personal 'Miracle Healing' into his briefcase, along with notes and his private documentation of the unauthorized experiment he had performed on the Boone woman. He was still giddy with the success of the two conclusive trials. Not one indication of failure. That was unprecedented.

Three separate incidences of catastrophic, near fatal or maiming diagnosis…his own self inflicted wound included, with 100% cure rate. All of this happening within moments of exposure to the serum. No side effects. Nothing that would contra-indicate that his discovery had resulted in a complete recovery in each case. At this point, he felt certain there would be no injury too severe or profound that would not benefit from exposure to the fluid. Subsequent blood work performed on him and Sorrento had come back normal, as he suspected would also be the case with Theresa Boone.

The ramifications were magnificent. He could already envision a day when there would be no death from horrific diseases. No fatalities sustained during war. For whichever country paid the highest price, of course. And to imagine, after years of trying to find his way out of this hellhole, after years of begging, almost pleading, for every research dime…all of this, quite literally, had fallen into his lap.

Thinking ahead to other applications for his discovery, his mind was consumed with fantasies of eternal youth and life everlasting. His research was still in its infancy, and at this time, he, Dr. Jackson Mullins, held the only key. Fame, fortune and the proverbial fountain of youth, were perhaps only the tip of the iceberg. There was nothing to stop him. Kings and presidents, the rich and famous, would all be willing to pay whatever the asking price for this powerful discovery.

Mullins was grudgingly considered by his peers to be a genius in the field of genetics. His mind was wired in such a way, that facts and possibilities which were obvious to him, others never saw or could not imagine. He understood that as the first documented mutation of this magnitude, the interest surrounding the birth of this child would be unprecedented if the true documentation was revealed. And he was neither a fool nor a bumbling mastermind. This was his time to shine. His alone.

Amniotic fluid, harvested from a pregnant womb, is ripe with fetal cells and amniotic stem cells cast off from the growing fetus. Mullins 'liquid gold' was being produced by a tiny miracle maker and his teenage mother…and she had no idea of the importance of their very existence. No one must be allowed to even guess at the true source of these miraculous events.

He had every confidence that he would find a way to make sure that this little family unit was within his reach at all times. He had five months to figure out the logistics of his plan. The child would belong to him. A lifetime donor of the DNA his dreams were made of.

First things first. He sat down at his desk and methodically resumed making notes for the meeting this afternoon.

Chapter Fifty Eight

Father Andrews crept quietly down the stairway, hoping to catch Mrs. Murray before she went about setting the table in the kitchen. Bishop Tomlin was still sleeping and if Andrews had any luck at all, that would be the case for several more hours. He was already exhausted from the two hours last night that he had spent in the bristling company of the esteemed Bishop.

After listening to Tomlin elaborate on every conceivable inconvenience he had endured during his hastily arranged departure from the Council House in Washington D.C., Father Andrews had been sure that each story would be the last, and the long night would finally come to an end. Not so.

No, Charles Tomlin was just getting started. After a hastily laid out dinner which did not come close to meeting either the Bishop's satisfaction or taste, Phillip was treated to an informal inquisition concerning his own personal behavior of the past week.

"Tell me, Phillip, could you have done nothing to arrest the hysteria that has built upon itself out on the streets of Nashville. Surely, there must have been something that could have stemmed the flow of unrestrained delirium. Perhaps you could have delivered a cautionary word as the pastor of the Cathedral?" Bishop Tomlin stared at Father Andrews…the implications in his tone were obvious. The insinuation was that he had caused the multitudes to gather on the steps of the Cathedral, never mind the alleged miracle.

"Well, Bishop Tomlin, perhaps I am not experienced when it comes to disillusioning people from the hopes and dreams that sustain them. I believe, dear Charles, the solution to this mayhem that we find ourselves in the middle of, has more to do with the will of the Almighty than anything you and I could possibly propose as a solution. People are starving for hope, Charles. And we must feed their souls."

"Well said, Phillip. But suppose that this 'miracle' which so easily slides from your tongue, is found to be a hoax? Possibly nothing more than the heightened imagination of overworked emergency room workers. What then?" The Bishop bent to remove his shoes and Father Andrews hastened to push the stool closer to his visitor's chair, so he could raise his feet.

"You are the Bishop, Charles. I'm sure that when you are finished with your examination of the facts, and have time to interview the people involved, you will be able to interpret the information well enough to have a good feel for the authenticity of these claims. I, for one, see no reason to doubt the hospital administration. Something incredible did happen in Nashville last week, Charles, whether it be a miracle or not."

Father Andrews went to the side cabinet and poured two glasses of red wine. Handing one to Bishop Tomlin, he sat in the chair directly opposite him and waited patiently for the tirade to continue. It had been his experience in the past that it served no purpose to argue with the man. You were duck soup, whether proved right or wrong. He settled in, trying unsuccessfully to stifle a yawn.

"I assure you, Phillip, I am well aware of the facts presented to date. Let me remind you that the eyes of Rome are now upon this Cathedral, as are the eyes of the rest of the world. The manner in which this is handled by the church, particularly here in the local parish is of paramount importance. I will not be made a laughing stock, Phillip. As the pastor of the Cathedral, you may do as you please. I have plans for my future in the church hierarchy and I would like to remind you I am still your superior."

"And I am quite happy and content right where I am, Charles. It would honor me greatly to see you advance to the prestigious role of Cardinal Tomlin, for which you are well suited. You have the stomach for it.

I do not. I am afraid that I have neither the ambition nor the desire, to leave the people of this parish. And for that reason alone, I will agree with you that this needs to be handled carefully."

"Good. I am glad to see we are on the same page, Father Andrews. It gets cold in Alaska in the winter. I'll say good night now." And with the veiled threat of reassignment left hanging in the air, Bishop Tomlin finally stood and left the room. It was going to be a long week.

This morning the air inside the rectory was oppressive with the presence of the royal pain. Father Andrews came upon Mrs. Murray laying out place settings in the dining hall. The dark paneling and heavy drapery suited his mood this morning.

"Bless you, Adele. However did you know that the kitchen would not suffice?" He shuffled behind her into the kitchen, where he poured a fresh cup of coffee into the mug she had laid out next to the coffee decanter.

Peeking out the window above the sink, he wondered at the increased volume of the crowd so early this morning. The last few days had been relatively peaceful considering the atmosphere, with the crowds remaining quiet later than usual, until at least seven, before starting in with their morning chants and prayers. Father Andrews was sure that he only imagined the anxiety level outside the Cathedral intensifying. He was consciously trying to prolong the silence inside the rectory and held out hope that an extended repose for Bishop Tomlin would improve his disposition this morning.

Mrs. Murray walked back and forth through the swinging door that divided the kitchen from the dining hall.

"I've been around the block enough to know that when Bishop Tomlin visits, we move into a different mode. I know what to expect, Father. You always give people the benefit of the doubt. Hoping they will change. Change is not so easy for some, especially those unwilling to see they are in need of it." Mrs. Murray carried a vase filled with summer flowers into the dining hall and placed them in the center of the table.

"It smells good in here, Mrs. Murray. Anything to tide me over?" Father Andrews walked over to the stovetop and lifted the corner of a towel that covered a pan of croissants, fresh from the oven.

"Go ahead, Father. Bishop Tomlin won't be down until at least eleven and I planned brunch for you then. Pour yourself some juice and have a few croissants while they are hot. That should do you fine until he makes his appearance."

"You are an angel, Adele. An absolute angel. The hospital is sending a National Guard driver over at 1:30 to take him to the University for a meeting." Father Andrews sat in his favorite chair at the kitchen table, spreading strawberry jam on the buttery roll. He took a bite, closing his eyes as he chewed, and thought once again about the conversation last night. *Alaska. Humph.* He picked up the remote and turned on the small television suspended under the cabinet next to the sink.

Hoping to hear news that the weather would be less brutal to the people still gathered outside the doors of the Cathedral, he saw instead the image of Bradford University Hospital jump out at him from the screen. *Good Morning America?* Taking another bite of the warm pastry, Father Andrews stopped chewing and raised his eyes to heaven. Scrolling across the bottom of the screen, under the heading BREAKING NEWS, the tickertape announcement of a second miracle spread across America.

Chapter Fifty Nine

S tephen hopped off his bike, finding it much easier to press through the congested areas of the city streets on foot. He could not help but notice a renewed fervor in the air. People were joyful and expectant as the news of the second miracle spread steadily through the streets of Nashville.

Even the hardened guards, exhausted by hours of overtime spent pacing in the brutal heat, seemed energized and exhilarated. Stephen suspected that was due more to the reinforcements that were on their way to relieve them, which must seem to them a miracle in itself. This morning, the President of the United States declared Nashville a national disaster site for the purpose of allocating food, supplies and additional troops. Stephen could feel a charge in the air, an electric forewarning of things he knew were about to happen. The prophecy had begun to unfold and he knew it was only a matter of time before he would be compelled to take action.

As he slowly made his way toward Jillian, the sequence of events that had played out over the past several hours ran through his mind unchecked. Stunned, he and his sister had listened in amazement to news of the second miracle. Cami was silent for once and had looked at him with huge eyes, as the truth of all he had shared with her became clear at that exact moment, any unspoken doubt washed away. They simultaneously fell to their knees and began to pray, both lost in the sweet agony of the prophecy, both afraid to believe, but even more afraid not to.

"Stephen, this is a sign that things are going to happen soon. You must leave right this minute. I'll be fine and I'll be here if you need me. Promise you'll let me know how things are going and you'll stay in touch." Cami squeezed his hands, almost afraid to let go.

Would she ever see her brother again? "I will be praying for you, Stephen. Please don't let anything happen to you"

"It will be okay. Thanks for believing in me. It means a lot, Cami. As soon as I know something, I'll call you. And listen, call Mom and let her and Amanda know that you got here safely, but aside from what we know of the miracles, it's not time to share anything else with them. I don't know how I know that, but I do." Stephen grabbed his backpack from the chair in the kitchen and was unplugging his phone from the charger, when it rang in his hand.

"Hello? Calm down, calm down. Johnny? I see. I know. Where are you now? Yes, I'll call you later at this number. God bless you, Johnny. I am so happy for you. Yes, I know. Faith is a powerful thing." Stephen sank into the chair, motioning for his sister to come to him. Holding her hand, he disconnected the call and put the phone in his shirt pocket.

"Stephen, what is it? Was that the little boy you told me about? What happened?" Cami knelt in front of her brother as he raised his eyes slowly, clearly stunned by the words he heard spoken at the other end of the phone.

"Theresa Boone was the second miracle, Cami. Johnny's mom is *walking* this morning. *Walking.*"

Cami started to cry, the emotions of the morning boiling up and over with no way to stem the flow. She laid her head on Stephen's lap and sobbed as her brother's trembling hands patted her, trying to calm her, looking beyond her into the dream world of the prophecy. Finally, tears spent, Camellia stood and holding out her hand, pulled her brother out of the chair, shaking him from his own reverie.

"Praise God, Stephen. Now look at me. You get yourself over there, ready to fight to protect that girl and her baby. There *is* a baby, Stephen, you and I both know the truth. We can draw whatever conclusions we want to, but these miracles are no coincidence. I have faith in you, and for whatever reason, you have been chosen to be the catalyst for this prophecy. You can see this through. You have guidance from above. Whatever happens, I will be here, believing in you, brother."

Camellia propelled her brother toward the door.

"While you're gone, I'm going to plow through some of your history books and do some research of my own. God, Stephen. To think you used to be so boring."

His last glimpse of his sister was from the second floor window of his apartment, her hand pressed flat against the glass as she watched him leave.

His mind refocusing on the present, Stephen finally turned off the main road and hopped easily back onto his bike, grateful for the relief it provided from the combined weight of his duffel and the precious papers for Dr. Macomb. Having escaped the pandemonium of the main roads, he followed the winding maze of streets leading to the Macomb's and found himself on their little street, where it was peaceful and quiet in contrast. It was hard to believe that only a few blocks away the mayhem continued, unchecked.

He wondered if this would always be the case, or would news of yet another miracle cause an even greater influx of people to migrate to the neighborhoods surrounding Nashville, just as blood seeks its way to the heart through a jumble of veins and arteries. He shuddered to think of the consequences if the truth concerning the child Jillian carried was discovered.

Old magnolias lined the street and carried their flowers proudly, as if daring anyone to interrupt their summer ritual. It was now after four o'clock and Stephen was hungry and tired, emotionally drained and ready for sleep. At last he found the little cape cod, peaceful and inviting, nestled in the trees and flowerbeds, like a long lost friend peeking out at him from a treasured hiding place. He rode up the long driveway and stopped behind the house, tethering his bike to the tree beside the garage, not sure where he was to stay, but looking forward to getting settled.

"You must be Stephen."

Stephen jerked around, startled, nerves still raw and on edge from his journey. An older replica of Sara Macomb straightened from her kneeling position in a bed of flowering impatiens.

"Sorry I scared you. I'm Aunt Susie." Removing her glove, damp and dirty from tending to the garden, she extended her hand to him. "I needed to work off a little pent up energy, so here I am, enjoying the garden."

"Pleased to meet you, I'm sure." Stephen held out his hand, jumping back involuntarily when the touch ignited a spark between them.

"Wow. That was some handshake. Now, just look at how handsome you are." Susie, hands on hips, looked him over slowly.

"Come on, then. Let's go in and get something cold to drink. Marc has been pacing after you like a worried hen, and Sara has chicken ready to throw on the grill. And I'll bet I can wrangle up some appetizers for us. I'm starving and, from the looks of you, you could use a little something to hold you over until dinner." Susie stood and brushed the dirt from the knees of her jeans, then reached up and hooked her hand into the crook of Stephen's elbow. "And I don't know about you, honey, but I sure could use a glass of wine right about now."

They walked toward the back door, leaving the driveway to follow the cobblestone path that Marc and Sara had laid themselves several summers ago. Fringed by impatiens and hosta, moss had filled in the cracks and the effect was warm and inviting. And safe.

"Company's here!" Susie's voice rang through the yard and the screen door on the back porch flew open as Marc and Sara bounded into the yard to greet their visitor.

"Stephen. So happy you made it. I think Marc was ready to call out the guard to help find you." Sara wiped her hands on a towel she carried from the kitchen and offered him a hug. "Let's get you something with ice in it. I'm sure you're parched. Then Marc can show you where to put your things. I hope you'll like your space. Jillian has been eying it, I think, so watch your back." Sara turned and went into the house with Susie to see about drinks.

Marc held out his hand to his houseguest and clapped him on the shoulder. "Sara's sister got here this morning. We didn't know she was coming, but it was a welcome surprise for us. It's been such a tumultuous week.

And here you are. This is above and beyond the call of duty, Stephen. I am so glad you agreed to come. I hope this isn't too much of an imposition."

"I'm happy to be here, Dr. Macomb."

"You must call me Marc."

"Marc. Believe me when I tell you that being here is much more appealing than staying at my flat. My place is not far from the main roads and people have started migrating closer to the building. I'm not complaining. But it is quite a constant dose of the new reality. And besides, without knowing how soon the campus will reopen, I could use a little intellectual stimulation. It seems there is much to discuss," Stephen said.

"I'm sure you've heard of the second healing at Bradford by now. How are the people on the streets reacting to the news? Oh, damn, forgive me, Stephen. Never mind. All that can wait until you at least get settled. The truth is, I'm going a little stir crazy cooped up with the women. I can't wait to delve into… you look wrecked, and here I am rambling on as if you are the last lifeline to the normal world. I'm sure you could use a shower before dinner, after being out in this brutal heat for the better part of the day."

Stephen smiled. "It's okay, Marc. I know how you feel. It will be good to have a sane discussion about the new circumstances and what it all means. I'm afraid I am beyond exhausted though, and if I were to try and carry on a lucid conversation tonight, I don't know how much sense you'd make of anything I had to say."

"That's okay. I am on strict notice from Sara. I am to let you catch your breath tonight. I am not oblivious to what you have been through, believe me. The excitement at the hospital defies all logic, and I am chomping at the bit to explore… no more. See how I let myself go off on a tangent? Let's go in now and get something to drink. It will all be here tomorrow. After dinner though, I do want to bring you up to speed on some personal issues we have been dealing with."

They both turned at the sound of the screen door opening, Sara standing on the stoop.

"Come on, you two. Marc Macomb, you look guilty as sin. Now leave him alone and both of you come and get something cold to drink. Leave the poor man to catch his breath."

Chapter Sixty

Jillian licked the whipped topping off her finger while she watched her mother clean the strawberries she had taken from the freezer earlier this afternoon. She liked to watch her mother work in the kitchen. She was able to do such magnificent and delicious things with food. Jillian hated the thought of chopping and cleaning and stirring, but watching her mother at the sink made her feel that all was right with the world. She sat on the stool, leaning against the counter, and dipped her finger once again into the bowl.

"Jillian Grace, get your fingers out of the topping or there won't be any left for dessert," Sara scolded. "Why don't you go in and set the dining room table."

"Aunt Susie already set the table before she went upstairs. I'm starving. How long is Stephen staying with us?"

"I'm not sure. Dad needs some help and they can't get to the campus, so it may be a while. Believe me, it's much better for your father to be occupied, and I'm sure he and Stephen will have much to discuss with the latest news from the hospital. Dinner will be ready in half an hour. Now scoot, before you ruin your appetite."

"Does he know about me?"

"Not yet. Daddy will talk to him after dinner. Sweetie, it's okay. We are all going to be okay. The baby is a good thing, just a few years ahead of schedule that's all."

Jillian slid off the stool and walked into the living room. She hadn't talked to any of them about Arianna and her message. They had hardly talked about the baby at all since they came home from the hospital. It was almost as if they were all pretending that everything was the same as it had been before this happened.

Everyone thought she was nuts anyway, and at first Jillian thought she might be crazy, too, but in her heart, she knew that everything the angel said was true. How else could she have this baby inside of her? At first it didn't seem real, but now with all the miracle stuff going on at the hospital, Jillian knew that everything Arianna had told her was really going to happen. And she accepted it. She was scared, but in some way, excited to be part of it.

She looked around the room as if seeing it for the first time. The sofas with their plump cozy cushions and the fireplace where her mom put candles in the summer, made the room feel inviting and safe. Jillian picked up a framed photo of the three of them taken last summer at the beach. Little had any of them suspected what a change the very next year would bring. She looked closely at her image in the picture, her head thrown back, laughing at something her dad said, her long summer skirt blowing in the wind.

Why did God pick her for this baby? She looked so ordinary. Clueless. She wondered what their eyes would show if someone snapped a picture of the three of them today.

Jillian felt the baby rumble inside of her. She knew it was kind of early for her to feel it move so much. But she could, like a slow rolling in the pit of her stomach. She figured it was God's way of reminding her she had an important job to do. She was almost half way through her pregnancy already. She had to talk to her parents about Arianna soon, because the angel made it sound like things were going to happen any minute. Once things were set in motion, life as they knew it would change forever. She needed to prepare them.

She could hear Aunt Susie upstairs, wandering around the guestroom. She loved her so much. Her aunt never made her feel silly or strange, and never once asked her about the father of the baby. She just laid her hand on Jillian's belly and closed her eyes as if she could feel the baby, too.

She was glad Aunt Susie was here. She would believe her about Arianna. Maybe she was part of the plan and would help her parents understand the truth.

"I just talked to Uncle Tommy and he said to give you a big hug." Aunt Susie came down the stairs and breezed into the living room, plopping herself on the sofa next to her niece. "Later on when things settle down, let's have a chat about everything that's going on with you, pumpkin. This whole situation is kind of scary for you, I would suppose."

"I'd like that, Aunt Susie. Maybe we could go for a walk after dinner, if Mom lets me out of the dishes."

"Nice try, Bean. I have a better idea. Why don't we do the cleanup together and then we'll go? It won't be so hot once the sun starts to set and I'm not used to this weather yet." Susie tossed a throw pillow at her niece, and then got up to help her sister in the kitchen.

* * *

Stephen was still tired, although somewhat refreshed, after he had taken a shower. The room above the garage was comfortable, and he had taken an extra few minutes to unpack his duffle bag and get organized. The space was large enough to be comfortable and housed a queen sized bed. There was a private bathroom stocked with towels and an extra set of linens. A small dresser had been arranged under the window next to the bed, and natural light found its way into the room, even this late in the afternoon. An overstuffed easy chair had been pushed into the corner with a floor lamp for reading, and a small café table and two chairs were positioned against the wall at the foot of the bed. Just outside the bedroom there was a small hallway with a closet on each wall. It opened into the office area which was roughly the size of the two car garage below.

Stephen took a minute to call Camellia before he made his way through the office and down the stairs to the garage.

"Howdy, brother. Everything is fine here. I talked to Mom and she's a little freaked out, but I told her everything probably sounds worse on the news than it actually is over here. I figured God would forgive a little white lie. I promised her you'd call when you got settled so, Stephen, call her soon. Before anything else happens."

"I'll call her when I get back to my room tonight, I promise. I'm exhausted, sis. I have to hang up and go down to dinner."

"Have you seen Jillian yet?"

"No. I'm sure I will at dinner, though. Listen, Cami, thanks again for everything."

"Knock it off, Stephen. Just take care of yourself and call Mom. Love you."

Stephen shook off the guilt that tugged at him for not calling his mother to check in. He knew she'd be frantic with mother-worry over the constant stream of news pouring out of Nashville. If it was possible, he felt even guiltier knowing that he couldn't share his own involvement. She would hear about it soon enough. He finished putting his clothes away, then turned out the light and headed for the house. He realized then... he had been stalling to prepare himself for his next encounter with Jillian.

Chapter Sixty One

Beverly popped an antacid prior to leaving her office, but unfortunately it had done little to quell the queasiness she felt at the prospect of presiding over this meeting. She stood at the door and greeted each of the attendees as they filed into the room and took their places around the conference table. This was her standard opening procedure for meetings and gave her time and perspective to observe the casual interactions between participants, and to make mental notes that often proved critical to her decision and policy making. The second so-called 'miracle' this morning added an exaggerated urgency to the gathering, and she tried to prepare herself for the intensity that was sure to come.

As the last person made his way to his seat, she quietly closed the door and moved into the room. She found it very interesting that Jackson Mullins had chosen to sit at the head of the table. She moved to the other end of the room and introduced herself once again to the group.

"I'd like to thank you all for agreeing to this meeting. In light of the most recent developments, I know we are all anxious to get started, so let's begin by briefly introducing ourselves and the institution we represent.

Looking to her left, she said, "Let's start with you, Kathleen."

As she listened, Beverly took personal notes in shorthand, used often over the years. Next to each name, she jotted notes describing personal characteristics and nuances, which helped her quickly identify each person and her immediate impression of them.

"Certainly, Dr. Castiglione. Ladies. Gentleman." Nodding a general greeting to the assembly, the slight woman stood and looked around the table at each person while speaking, as she did when presenting opening arguments to a jury.

"I am Kathleen Sullivan, an attorney on staff at Bradford University Hospital. I am here to represent the interests of the hospital, and to make certain that the public is informed of the circumstances surrounding the events of the past week, in such a way as to be truthful, but not cause panic. The safety of our patients and staff, of course, is of the utmost importance."

Daniel Barker was seated to Kathleen's left. He stood slowly, all six foot four inches of him. Dressed in a dark suit and white shirt, he looked every inch the part of a CIA representative. And he wasn't saying much. "Daniel Barker, CIA. I am here as a representative of the United States Government. Normally, I would not be sent to investigate such an occurrence, but Washington is quite interested in the stir this situation continues to generate…and the possible ramifications regarding National Security, should it prove to be more than a random occurrence." He sat down as slowly as he had stood up.

If Daniel Barker was intimidating, the woman to his left was anything but. A bundle of raw energy, she almost leapt to her feet when the roll call progressed to her. Beverly sensed that the bubbly exterior was only a cover and she would be the more aggressive newcomer, with every antenna up, and ready to absorb every minute scrap of information.

"I am Dr. Judith Sabot. I am with the National Science Foundation. We are a governmental agency that, quite assuredly, has already supplied federal funding for much of the research this fine hospital is currently involved in. We keep close and constant contact with the professional community to identify the areas of research which will most likely produce tremendous results. I am very curious about the outcome of this mystery in which we find ourselves immersed, and the potential of the future findings of any research that is being undertaken relative to these phenomena."

Julie Richards was next. She wasn't sure if Dr. Sabot was finished, but got a signal from Beverly to stand and introduce herself. She had a feeling, that if unrestrained, Dr. Sabot would continue talking indefinitely. Looking hesitantly to her right to make sure that Judith had resumed her seat, she stood and introduced herself.

"Dr. Julie Richards. I am an internist, specializing in woman's medicine, on staff at the hospital. One of my patients was indirectly involved in the first occurrence, as it was her CVS being tested at the time Dr. Sorrento was injured." Julie sat quickly, not willing to go into details about her patient's history.

Confidentiality and privacy issues continued to gnaw at her, even though she knew HIPPA required her to disclose information to the Government, whether or not she had the permission of her patient. She would wait until she was absolutely forced to concede.

If Jackson Mullins was intimidated by the presence of the Government agencies, it was not evident in his demeanor.

"I am Dr. Jackson Mullins, a specialist in the field of Genetics and Genomic research at University. I must admit that I find it premature to bring in the Government, when nothing substantial has presented itself in this case. The research is in its infancy, and to be quite frank, everything presented so far has been most ordinary. I am quite confident that by the end of the day, when all is said and done, we shall find nothing but an unexplained mystery, which came about by some combination of Dr. Sorrento's own genome system and a contamination of chemicals used to run a simple paternity test. End of story. As far as the second so-called phenomenon, we have yet to substantiate the original diagnosis of the Boone woman. ALS is very hard to diagnose and often resembles other treatable ailments, which don't present such a dire consequence." He sat down.

Son of a bitch. Beverly Castiglione felt the hair on her neck stand on end. If she knew anything at all about human nature, she knew for a fact that Jackson Mullins was hiding something. He knew more than he was willing to admit to anyone at this table, including her. She added a word next to his name. *Dangerous.*

"Sherry Donaldson, ER Attending. I was the attending on duty when Dr. Sorrento was brought down, and again yesterday, when the second 'mir...' um, case was admitted. I saw both patients prior to, and after, their...recoveries." Sherry sat down immediately.

The Bishop of Nashville surveyed the room over his glasses before he stood, painstakingly slowly. It was obvious he would not be rushed or cowed by anyone at this table.

"I am Bishop Charles Tomlin, representative of the Catholic Diocese of Nashville. I was attending a conference of Bishops in Washington, D.C., when I got the call from the pastor of Holy Name Cathedral, Father Phillip Andrews, concerning the happenings here. Had I known we would be joined today by such impressive representatives of the U.S. Government, perhaps I could have accompanied them on a Government jet to Nashville, instead of risking my life on an Army helicopter. Well, that is neither here nor there. I am here now."

Taking time to brush imaginary lint from the sleeve of his cassock, he straightened and once again addressed the gathering.

"We are skirting around the word 'miracle', as if the thousands of people on the streets have not been chanting and carrying on, bringing their illness and disease to Nashville, for a repeat performance. I was very skeptical myself, I must admit, until word of the second occurrence was brought to my attention this morning, via the little blond newscaster, who seems to have joined ranks with the homeless camped outside this hospital. It is preposterous that this nonsense has been allowed to grow out of control. The faithful expect the church to conduct a full investigation of these events and we will want to interview everyone involved."

Showing obvious displeasure with the whole ordeal, the Bishop of Nashville sat heavily in his chair and waited while the rest of the introductions took place. Beverly could not help but smirk to herself. *Jackson Mullins may have a run for his money with this one.*

Dr. David Kendrick did not stand, nor did he introduce himself. The neurologist, who had examined Theresa Boone, was not anti-social or shy, but saw no reason to get emotional or embellish the facts.

"I have examined Mrs. Boone. Unless I see something from prior test results that prove to me that she presented upon admission, the symptoms congruent with the devastating diagnosis of ALS, there is no possible explanation that would satisfy me. She has apparently gone into a complete and total remission. I thought perhaps she was misdiagnosed in the beginning, but I spent hours on the phone discussing her case with Dr. Peter Winchell in Columbia, Tennessee.

He is an expert in the field of neurological diseases, and I respect his opinion. We have presented here, a medical mystery of the most profound nature. I have requested the complete protocol of the treatment that was followed, and will await the results from pathology before I introduce a conclusive opinion. But I must caution this group. From what I have witnessed today with my own eyes…this woman is as healthy as any one of us sitting at this table."

"Thank you, Dr. Kendrick. Our Chief of Neurology, for any of you not familiar with the hospital staff or departments." Beverly looked now to Dr. Sorrento, who had been quietly listening to the introductions. "Michael, would you introduce yourself and then we can get started."

Michael stood. He hesitantly rolled up the sleeve on his right arm and splayed his hand, palm side up, for all to see.

"I am Michael Sorrento, serving as an intern in pathology at the University Hospital, and currently on leave of absence. I was directly involved in the first miracle. I call it a miracle because there is no other explanation for what has happened to me. I am not delusional and have photos, before and after my hand was healed, and the x-rays to back it up. My injury was severe, close enough to a major nerve to cause permanent and debilitating damage, considering my choice of career. Yet, I spontaneously healed in less than an hour, with no ill effects of a physical nature. Not even a scar. Spiritually, now that's another story."

Looking at the Bishop, he continued, "With all due respect, Bishop Tomlin. I am not a zealot and have never been overly religious. And, for the life of me, cannot figure out why this happened to me. But, by the grace of God, it happened. A miracle. There is no other explanation."

Turning to the neurologist sitting on his right, Michael Sorrento continued.

"Dr. Kendrick, I know you find it hard to believe that a person could be healed in a matter of hours, or even minutes, and not show any signs of the injury." Michael Sorrento once again held out his unblemished palm for the neurologist to examine. I brought the photos with me, and the x-rays. This happened less than a week ago, Doctor."

Beverly put her hand on Michael's shoulder and gently suggested he sit. "We are all searching for answers here. So let's get started."

Chapter Sixty Two

Doctor Sorrento, you told us that the CVS slide from the Macomb girl was the one that broke and imbedded itself into your palm, is that correct?" Judith Sabot was asking questions this time. Each representative was reading through their questions one at a time, hoping that a different perspective may throw some light on the murky details. A timeline had been drawn on the board and they were walking through the events of the past week for the third time, starting once again from the first known instance of a spontaneous healing.

"Yes, ma'am. Dr. Mullins called me down to the lab because there was an irregularity with the slide."

"And when you say irregularity, what exactly do you mean?"

Jackson Mullins sprang to his feet and slapped the pen he was holding down on the table. "This is preposterous. We have covered this information twice now, and I see no reason to go over it yet again." Raising his arms to the ceiling, he all but shouted at Beverly Castiglione, his jowls shaking and face reddening. "We have been here for over three hours, pondering and questioning every aspect of the days leading up to the present. I would like nothing more than to retire to my lab, where I can make real progress. This is getting us nowhere."

"Jackson, sit down. We have *all* been here for three hours. We will take a break when Dr. Sabot finishes her round of questioning, and not one minute before. We may find the one thing that has been overlooked that will get us closer to an answer. This may not work itself out entirely in the lab, Dr. Mullins. We are not only interested in finding the answer to this mystery, but also in the health and welfare of the people camped outside the hospital doors. Now, please take your seat so we can move on." Beverly looked at Michael Sorrento. "Go ahead, Michael, answer the question."

"It glowed, ma'am. It glowed. There was abnormal phosphorescence in the sample of material on the slide. I was injured before we could redo the test." Michael Sorrento sat back in his chair, reliving those moments in the lab. "I really thought my healing had something to do with the material on the slide."

"And do you think that now, Dr. Sorrento?"

"No. As soon as I heard about Mrs. Boone, I knew. It was a miracle."

"Dr. Mullins. Were you the pathologist who ran the blood tests on Theresa Boone when she was admitted?"

"No. The lab techs do the routine testing." Rolling his eyes, Jackson Mullins sighed heavily as he recovered his pen and began to scratch at the pad of paper in front of him.

"So, we are to assume that these lab reports are accurate, that her blood tests were normal and what one would expect, for a patient in her condition."

Sherry Donaldson, the ER attending, spoke up. "Yes. We did the usual blood gasses and counts and all results came back within the range we expected, based on her condition upon admission."

"No mention of any phosphorescence?" Dr. Sabot raised her brow, and Sherry Donaldson shook her head.

"No glow. There was no report of anything out of the ordinary in her blood test results."

"If Doctor Sorrento was discharged Monday afternoon and Theresa Boone admitted Monday night, is there anything else these two cases have in common other than the day of the week? Did they share the same ER room, the same lab?"

"No, ma'am. Dr Sorrento was in a cubicle in the front of the ER, and we decided, for privacy sake, that Mrs. Boone and her child would rest better in the far corner, where there was less noise. We knew the end… we *thought* the end was near," Sherry said.

"One more question for Dr. Richards. You said that Jillian Macomb was involved indirectly. I understand there was a paternity test underway when the accident happened. Am I correct?"

The sound of a notebook slapped violently against the table caused a chain reaction as everyone was jolted immediately out of their reverie.

Jackson Mullins exploded. "I cannot sit here doing nothing while this insane questioning drags on. What is the point of this?"

"Jackson, would you restrain yourself? I will be forced to take disciplinary action if these interruptions persist. This is your last warning. Now sit." Beverly Castiglione glared at Dr. Mullins, before softening her gaze to look at Dr. Sabot. "I am sorry, Doctor. Please continue. I assure you, there will be no further interruptions from the far end of this table."

Julie Richards pulled her eyes away from Jackson Mullins and focused on Dr. Sabot's question. "Yes. We were testing paternity on a patient of mine."

"And this seventeen year old patient was at approximately fourteen weeks gestation when the CVS was performed. A paternity test? Isn't that a bit unusual, Doctor Richards, to perform a test that carries with it an inherent risk to the fetus, for the sake of paternity?" All eyes were on Julie Richards and she shifted slightly in her seat. She had no choice, but to explain her decision.

"There were extenuating circumstances. I had reason to believe that the pregnancy and the health of the mother were at risk. The paternity test was performed because the genetic material was available, but it was secondary to the other tests we were running."

"Normally, I would not pry into such a sensitive subject, and of course, Dr. Richards, I understand your hesitance in sharing the specifics of this case, but what were the extenuating circumstances?"

"There was an issue with low HCG levels in the mother's blood. The ultrasound showed a healthy fourteen week fetus, but her levels were extremely low. I was worried that the pregnancy was not sustainable."

"So you ordered a prenatal test that might further endanger the fetus?"

The room grew quiet and Julie looked at Beverly for guidance. With a slight incline of her head, Bev encouraged her to continue.

"Yes. I was worried about the health of the mother. A young teenager. There were indications that the fetus might have been in danger, and possibly the mother as well. I needed to be sure the pregnancy was genetically sound."

"The range for HCG is huge at fourteen weeks gestation. How could you be sure she wasn't simply testing on the low end of the scale? You said the ultrasound showed a healthy fetus."

"Dr. Sabot, I was dealing with a patient who did not even believe she was pregnant. Jillian Macomb has no memory of being in any situation that would cause her to conceive. Her boyfriend at the time concedes that fact, and the paternity test subsequently ruled him out as the father of the child."

"With all due respect, Dr. Richards, Jillian Macomb is not the first, and will not be the last young girl to be naive when it comes to birth control, or to deny her sexual activity. Low HCG does not, in itself, warrant an early invasive procedure. Was there something else, Dr. Richards?"

"Jillian Macomb came to my office ten days ago presenting, by ultrasound, the image of an apparently healthy fourteen week male fetus, that she had absolutely no knowledge of prior to that visit. We did the appropriate blood work and urinalysis at that time, and even had her return to be tested again. I was not completely forthright when I said she had low HCG. What I should have said was that she presented *no* HCG. *Zero*.

"The blood tests performed at the hospital lab concurred with my findings, and we admitted her for further testing. By all accounts, Jillian Macomb should not be sustaining the pregnancy. The results of her labs indicate that it should be impossible. But, not only is she sustaining the pregnancy...the fetus thrives."

No one spoke. The doctors were lost in their own thoughts, each considering the magnitude of the events taking place at this hospital. They tried to make sense of implications that defied the normal rhythms of life and death. The lay members of the panel were just as confused, quickly realizing that what had happened was monumental and life changing.

No one, with the exception of Agent Barker, paid any attention as Jackson Mullins gathered his belongings and made his way to the door.

Startled, they all looked up when the light from the brightly lit hallway suddenly flooded the somber room. On its well oiled hinges, the door closed softly behind Mullins, leaving Beverly Castiglione standing frozen at the end of the table. She cleared her throat.

"We shall adjourn until tomorrow morning at ten o'clock. I think we all need to process. Please do not discuss the details of this meeting with anyone, especially the press, until after we meet here tomorrow. We will decide as a group how to deliver news to the public. Try to have a restful night. Your cars will be waiting outside the main entrance of the hospital.

Everyone rose and made their way to the door. Bishop Tomlin did not move, for once silenced and humbled by what he just heard. When he finally pushed himself up from the padded chair, he moved quietly to the other side of the room and rested his hand lightly on Julie Richards shoulder. He didn't speak when she turned to face him. As he looked into her eyes, they both realized at that moment…the first miracle had occurred long before Dr. Sorrento sliced his hand on the broken glass of the slide. The first miracle was growing in the womb of a little virgin girl in Nashville.

Chapter Sixty Three

Father Andrews lay prostrate on the floor of the sanctuary, in front of the altar. Unable to form the words to pray, he simply released the deep, soulful menagerie of thoughts that tumbled haphazardly from his mind, and directed them toward heaven. His head was filled with images of all he had witnessed these last weeks. He could not count the number of times he had been called upon to anoint the sick and the dying, the baptisms he had performed or the sins he was asked to pardon in confession. The list grew with each passing day.

The church was sending young untrained seminarians and transitional deacons… those close to taking the final vows of priesthood. The over burdened parishes needed help to keep up with the influx of faithful that continued to pour into the city. Father Andrews felt the energy and believed these happenings were truly the work of God. What did it all mean?

His random thoughts eventually settled on his conversations with the young scholar, Stephen, and his visions and the prophecy they contained. A brief exchange with him this evening by telephone had both relieved and unsettled the aging priest. Stephen was staying at the Macomb's and was to have a private conversation with the professor later that evening, finally sharing the message contained within the visions.

"Dear Lord, help me to understand the boy. Shall I believe him in his earnestness? He may truly be Your disciple. Who am I to argue with the truthfulness of his visions, in light of what is happening around us? The foundation of our Church is built upon the mysteries of faith. The teachings

of Your Son, born on earth as a mortal man, to spread Your Word, Father, have sustained us for centuries. Is it so difficult to believe that You, in Your divine wisdom, would send another to lead us to the salvation promised to us at the end of time? Are these current events apocalyptic? As Your humble servant, I pray You to guide my tongue and show me the way to serve You best. In Jesus Holy Name. Amen."

He continued to lay for another moment, straining his tired ears to hear sounds from the crowd outside the building. The guards who continued to push them further away from the doors of the Cathedral, had finally become immune to the begging and pleading of the poor souls trying to find comfort within its walls. Eventually, he hoisted himself off the floor, and shoulders sagging under the weight of overwhelming responsibility, he turned one more time to look upon the sanctuary, then dimmed the light and walked toward the door to the courtyard.

It was almost ten o'clock by now, and wondering when the Bishop would return to the rectory, he walked past the television without turning it on. He had no stomach for the newscasts any longer, because it was usually more of the same. The evil elements of society had begun to rear their ugly heads, preying upon the infirm and the hopeful, caring nothing about the miracles happening just a few yards away. In some places, a carnival atmosphere had begun. Music and spontaneous eruptions of lewd behavior were displayed on the same corners where weary parents stood, trying desperately to shield young eyes from sights no child should see.

The local law enforcement officials were stretched to the limit, holding things together as best they could. They began sending busloads of agitators across state lines to the north or south, wherever they could unload them, only to have the same scoundrels make their way back to the city, causing havoc wherever possible along their route.

Phillip went into his room, walked to the wardrobe and removed his clerical collar. Taking his robe from the hook on the back of the door, he went into the bathroom to wash his face and prepare to retire. He heard the back door open and knew Bishop Tomlin was back, but turned out his light and stretched out across his bed. *Dear God, forgive me, but there is always tomorrow.*

He had just dozed off, when suddenly the sound of the bell chime on his cell phone roused him out of a sound, dreamless sleep. He reached for the clock on his night table, and squinting his eyes against the blue glare illuminating the dial, saw that it was only twenty minutes past ten. He must have passed out almost immediately upon landing across the bed.

"Hello, this is Father Andrews."

"Father, it's me. It's Stephen."

The old priest wrestled himself into a sitting position. "Stephen, are you okay? You sound rattled. Hang on for one second." Father Andrews stood and walked to the chair on the other side of the bed, picking up a glass of water from the table and taking a drink before he spoke into the phone. "I'm sorry, Stephen. I was a little groggy and had to sit up. How did it go?"

"I know the hour is late, Father. I just talked to Marc Macomb."

"And…were you able to share with him anything about your dreams, Stephen?"

"Father Andrews, he just told me that his daughter is pregnant and that she swears she has never been with a man. They don't believe that's true, but they do believe that she thinks it's true. It is all coming to pass, Father."

Phillip Andrews stood quickly and paced the perimeter of the small room. "Dear God, Stephen. Do you have any idea what this means?"

"The visions are real, Father Andrews. And if the visions are real, she is in great danger."

Father Andrews could hear panic in the voice of the young man, a heavy burden placed on him at such a young age.

"First, Stephen, you must listen to me. Do not tell anyone what you believe just yet. God is not going to let anything happen to you, or to the young girl. You have been chosen for a mission, the magnitude of which I cannot even begin to wrap my head around. The implications are astounding. Regardless … the knowledge of the child's origin coupled with the miracles…I cannot even begin to comprehend the danger to the girl should this be made public."

"I know, Father. I am not sure what I should do. I can't just storm into their living room and tell them I am taking her away. They would think I was berserk. They would have me arrested, or worse. She's only seventeen."

"Not much older than the Blessed Mother, Stephen? I know what goes through your mind because I am thinking the same thing. You must try to rest, Stephen. From the sounds of it, things will start to happen soon. The Bishop returned from a meeting at the hospital a while ago, and I will talk to him in the morning. He has been known to pontificate, so it should be fairly easy to get a pulse on what is happening over there. I think it is all connected, Stephen. God is calling everyone to attention."

"How do I tell Dr. Macomb? They are still in shock. Look at everything that has happened to their family in the past week." Stephen was calming down, forcing himself to take deep breaths, trying to analyze the situation. It was important that he prepare a reasonable argument for the parents of the young girl he knew must be hidden from danger.

"Stephen, I am not going to discuss your visions with anyone, not even Bishop Tomlin, until you instruct me to do so. You forget, Stephen…it is not up to us to figure out when you are to act. You, my son, must turn to your messenger, Gabriel, for guidance. The importance of the prophecy cannot be denied and you must continue to believe. Trust him with your life, Stephen, and he will lead you."

"I will call you tomorrow, Father. Thank you. I don't know what I would do without your council."

"It seems I should be the one to thank you, Stephen. God be with you, son."

Father Andrews gently disconnected the call and for the second time that day lay prostrate in adoration of his Lord and Savior. *"Let the heavens and earth rejoice, let the sea roar, the fields and trees be joyful, as we wait in hope before the Lord. For the Lord cometh."* He rose and went to the Bible, opening it to Psalm 96, which he had just prayed, and taking the ribbon, marked the place so he could find it quickly in the days to come.

"For the Lord cometh."

Chapter Sixty Four

Stephen steeled himself as he dialed his mother's number, anxious that he would be unable to disguise the stress and fear that were spreading from the tightness in his chest to a place deep within the pit of his stomach. His mother knew him too well. The last thing he wanted to do was frighten her, and he hoped hearing his voice would carry her through whatever was to happen in the days and weeks ahead.

"Stephen, is that you?"

"Hi, Mom. First, I'm sorry that I haven't called. I have no excuse. It's just that things have been a little topsy-turvy here lately." Stephen paced back and forth across the little room, rubbing the back of his neck.

"I am too happy to hear from you to scold you for not answering any of the messages I left. Are you well, Stephen?"

"I'm fine, Mom. How are Mandy and Rob? God, I miss you all, and it has only been a few months. It seems so much longer. How is Mandy feeling? Is she as big as a house yet? I am sure Rob is still on cloud nine. And what about you, Grandma?"

"Your sister is fine. And yes, Mandy is getting bigger by the day. She doesn't want to know what she's having, so I can't tell you if it's a girl or a boy. We are all having fun guessing, though. And she feels great. Rob has decided to paint the nursery blue, regardless of the gender, and he is behaving like a typical daddy- to- be. And, I am getting used to the idea of having a new baby around the house. I wish your father could be here to share the joy."

"How are you, Mom? I know you worry."

"You mean, because two of my children are in the middle of God knows what in the States? I am okay, Stephen. Of the three of you, I know you and Cami are the best suited for this adventure. I am concerned that things will spin out of control, though. From the news reports, it looks like a war zone down there. CNN is covering the story almost twenty-four hours a day. The images are shocking, Stephen. I find myself scanning the crowds, trying to spot you."

"That would be like looking for the proverbial needle in a haystack. It is unbelievable, Mom. I am actually happy that I didn't know ahead of time that Cami was coming. I would have been worried, too. The roads get worse by the day, so she should expect to hunker down here for the duration."

"There is no stopping that girl, once her mind is made up, Stephen, and you know it. Listen, son, I want you to tell me everything you know about the miracles. Are they? I mean, is all this real?"

"As far as I can tell, Mom, they're authentic. I'm sure Dr. Macomb and I will study the facts at length. The Divinity School at the University can't help but get involved. Cami told you I'm staying with the Macomb's for a while and she is staying at my flat, so we are both off the streets. Please try not to worry, Mom. It's hard to call sometimes, but I will try to do better about answering messages."

"I know you will. Listen, you be careful and I'll tell Amanda you send love. Are you really all right, Stephen?"

"I'm okay. I love you. Don't believe everything you hear coming out of Nashville, promise?"

"I love you, too. I'll try not to jump to conclusions, but I'll still watch for you on the television. Now you be safe, Stephen."

"Bye, Mom."

Stephen put the phone on the dresser and sat in the easy chair, his head thrown back. A profound sadness that went far beyond the phone call from his mother began to envelop him. He knew this was only the beginning of his journey, but he had no idea of the destination. He closed his eyes, knowing he should pack it in and go to bed, although sleep would be impossible with the constant swirl of random thoughts churning in his head. Dinner had been uneventful. He had expected a lightning bolt of revelation when he saw the girl, but it never materialized.

Jillian had walked into the dining room and sat across the table from him, charming and funny, a beautiful child. And she was a child. Barely seventeen years old and unassuming, with an innocence about her that was evident. When she looked at him for the first time, had he noticed a slight furrow to her brow, as if she was trying to place him? Or was it just his already overworked imagination?

During dinner she mentioned having wild dreams. Stephen dropped his fork, sending it clattering to the floor, and he hoped his stunned expression would be attributed to embarrassment at his own clumsiness. But, did she know? Perhaps he was not the only one having visions. Did she know she was carrying this most holy child? And if she was having visions, did she believe in them? She must, by now. There was much to work through in a short amount of time.

Stephen raised his head from the back of the chair and saw Gabriel standing before him. Sitting upright, he rubbed his hands over his face, trying to clear his vision. He knew he was awake, and yet he saw the messenger standing there as clearly as he had seen Dr. Macomb earlier in the evening, when Marc stood in his office and explained Jillian's pregnancy.

The angel raised his arms to Stephen and nodded his head slowly. Although he appeared both with and without substance, Stephen had the feeling that if he reached out to touch him, his hand would encounter only air. As Gabriel stood before him, Stephen knew the time had come for him to surrender completely to the task set before him.

"Three days, Stephen. You must prepare for a journey in three days. The girl is in danger, as is the babe she carries in her womb. Do not believe the promises of powerful ones. You will have many allies, Stephen, and many enemies. The evil ones will try to convince you to follow them. Do not make the mistake of falling into the bottomless pit of their lies. You have been consecrated by Heaven for this journey of faith. Choose wisely, Stephen. It is in your hands. On the third day beyond today, you must leave with her and follow your heart, Stephen. It is written that for all of the faithful on that day... the beginning of the new world shall commence. Do not look back, Stephen."

His messenger silently disappeared. Stephen had pushed himself as far into the chair as he could, panting, unable to catch his breath. His forehead was beaded with sweat, his cheek wet with unnoticed tears. Only three days. *Saturday.* Finally, he was able to move himself the few feet it took to throw himself to his knees beside the bed. Pure agony and confusion poured from his throat as he groaned with anguish under the oppressing weight of his despair. *Choose wisely, Stephen.*

Chapter Sixty Five

Jillian crossed her room and looked out the window toward the garage, thinking it strange that Stephen was living there. When she saw him at dinner, she wondered for a moment if he was her protector, trying hard to remember if Arianna gave any clue as to who it would be. As hard as she tried, she only remembered her angel saying that when the time came, she would know. This was all so confusing.

She had told Aunt Susie about the dreams, about Arianna. Her aunt politely listened as Jillian told her story, then put her arm around her shoulder and said something about hormones and being pregnant.

"But, what if I'm not imagining? What if it's true and this is a special baby. I know you adults don't believe me, but I have never been with anyone, and I wouldn't lie to you, Aunt Susie, especially you. I'm not afraid to tell the truth. It would be easier for me if there had been the sex part. At least, I would understand what is happening to me."

Susie had stopped at the end of the driveway and turned Jillian around to face her.

"Honey, I think that's why Arianna is here for you, and you alone. It sounds like your subconscious is trying to help you work it out. Now listen, don't worry your little head about it. You just let nature take its course and we'll worry about all the other stuff later. You are going to be okay. Now scoot on into the house and go to bed. I'm going to sit here on the stoop for a minute and enjoy the cooler air."

"No smoking, Auntie." Jillian turned and started up the drive.

"Good night, Bean."

She felt her Aunt Susie watching her until she went into the house and closed the door, leaving her aunt in the garden alone.

Jillian went into the bathroom and ran water in the tub. She took off her clothes and stood naked in front of the mirror. When she turned sideways she could see the little bump. She ran one hand over her belly and one across her tender breasts. She lay in the tub, the tepid water closing around her tiny frame. Closing her eyes, she dreamed of summer days, when she and her girlfriends would lay awake for hours, talking about boys and clothes and tennis and school.

"Jillian, your days of rejoicing are here. Do not be sad, little one. You must prepare yourself now, for the time is at hand. On the third day, you must close your eyes to the world and listen only to him, Jillian. He will speak words that fulfill the prophecy and you will go with him. Do not be fooled by false prophets, Jillian. Listen only to him. You shall be given a sign when the time is right. A love so strong you have never known. Follow him gladly to the ends of the earth and the Lord will bless you for the rest of your days."

The water felt cold on her skin and Jillian depressed the plunger to drain the tub. She got out and wrapped a towel around her shivering frame. Three days. At least then she would know. After pulling her nightgown over her head, she opened the window a tiny crack and crawled under the covers, trying to get warm again. Closing her eyes, she thought she smelled the smoke from a cigarette drift up to her window from the yard below. She smiled to herself.

As she floated off to sleep, she remembered what she meant to ask her angel.

"Is it Stephen, Arianna?" She fell asleep, not knowing if Arianna had answered, and never heard the thunder in the distance, as huge wet drops of rain hit the pavement below.

Chapter Sixty Six

Mullins held the amber liquid up to the light in his scantily furnished apartment. He silently cursed at the thought of yet another meeting that he would be forced to endure at the hospital. He had watched closely yesterday at the way they were slowly adding things up and, try as he might, he had been unable to divert their attention from the girl. Well, they might suspect that her pregnancy was the first miracle, but they didn't have a clue that she and the child were the *cause* of the miracles. *At least not yet.* He knew it was only a matter of time before one plus one equaled two. He was no longer dealing with only the imbeciles from the hospital. He must formulate a plan quickly.

He opened his briefcase, removing the memory stick that documented his own miraculous recovery in the lab. Unable to resist watching it once more, he inserted the small card into the portable video camera, and scrutinized the footage one more time. Enthralled by the unbelievable images that were displayed before him, he reluctantly removed the video card and placed it in a paper grocery sack, along with his journal and his notes from the research he had completed over the course of the past week.

He replaced the original documentation with false reports that he had painstakingly prepared through the long dark hours of the night. The truth must never be discovered. He would not let this powerful discovery slip from his grasp. He had only begun to anticipate and savor the expected rewards from the prestige and power that were rightfully his. He would see this through. The girl and her babe were his discovery, and he would find a way to harvest the fruits of his labor. And hers. He laughed to himself as he picked up the paper sack containing the true evidence of the miracles, and gently placed the priceless vial of fluid in the pocket of his shirt, where he could feel it resting over his heart. He knew what had to be done.

Chapter Sixty Seven

Beverly Castiglione pushed through the swinging doors and walked into the hospital without looking back. The interview with Amy Levine had mercifully ended, but she had three more statements promised to other news affiliates that were to be delivered before the end of the day. The press conference had been brutal this morning and by unanimous consensus they had decided that the ALS cure had to be addressed. There was no way to sweep an event of that magnitude under the rug. Even temporarily. Little Johnny Boone was telling their story to anyone and everyone that would listen. His proud mommy was actually showing improvement in her muscle control on an hourly basis. It was entirely possible she could walk out of the hospital on her own by tomorrow. Unbelievable.

The meeting this morning went much as she expected. Dr. Mullins was to examine Theresa Boone and do the pathology on her blood and tissue samples, while Dr. Kendrick would order an EMG, MRI and CT scan through the Neurology department. Dr. Sorrento agreed to be readmitted to the hospital to be reevaluated by Dr. Sabot from N.S.F., and she also expected to interview Theresa Boone and Jillian Macomb.

Little Jillian. In retrospect, her case could have been considered a miracle from the beginning. Although, if Bev was completely honest with herself, it was Sorrento's dramatic healing that pushed everyone's mind onto the miracle train. Jillian may not have been mentioned at all, if Sorrento had not been prepping her slide for testing that day. They had taken the cautious route, looking at Jillian's case as a medical anomaly, and had acted appropriately.

If the Sorrento and Boone healings had not been so spectacular, Bev wondered, would they have considered the pregnancy of Jillian Macomb anything more than a mystery of science? A mystery that would be studied and analyzed for years, if it indeed produced a viable healthy child, but nothing more than a medical enigma.

Julie Richards reluctantly agreed to contact the Macomb's and have Jillian readmitted to the hospital. All present at the meeting were in agreement that an isolation protocol was unnecessary at this point.

"Julie, why don't you let me call the Macomb's for you. They may be upset and I don't want you to bear the brunt of their distress."

"Listen, Bev, I'm the one who let her go home in the first place. At least she's had a few days of normalcy. They knew there was a chance I would have her readmitted. I hope they understand that it can't be helped in light of what is happening. They are reasonable people."

"Okay, but if you change your mind, let me know. When are you going to call?"

"I'll do it first thing in the morning. I'd like to get things organized here first, so they aren't kept waiting for a room. She can be admitted during the weekend, and we'll be ready to start testing on Monday. At least we don't have the isolation to contend with this time. That would throw them over the edge for sure," Julie said.

Bishop Tomlin had already informed the Diocese that there was enough evidence to warrant a complete investigation of the healings by the Church. The process had been quickly set in motion. Beverly would allow the Church access to the patients for an interview if the patients agreed, which she had no doubt they would.

"My dear Doctor Castiglione, The Holy Father is waiting impatiently for news out of Nashville. Of course, the Church must remain skeptical because of the delicate nature of these events, until we have thoroughly examined the evidence and interviewed those involved. I must confide in you...I sense an undercurrent of excitement about this prospect. There has never before been such startling evidence in one place, at one time, that so clearly defies earthly explanation. You understand the importance of this, I know. The faithful gathered on the street are clamoring for Vatican involvement. Even though we must proceed with caution, the spiritual nature of these occurrences simply cannot be ignored."

Daniel Barker advised her this morning that the CIA would require a command post on the premises from which to operate while they waited for results of the various investigations. They had called in yet another Government expert to go over the pathology reports that Mullins had already documented, and to oversee the rest of the immediate testing. They requested lab clearance and the authorization to perform their own studies. The information garnered from these meetings evidently gave Daniel enough data to consider this a Government security matter.

"We'll need several offices and clearance to the lab area. Is there a secure location that can be cordoned off from the routine lab work of the hospital?" Daniel Barker leaned against the wall in the conference room. He was not making a request and she knew it. He was issuing an order from the United States Government and his droll attitude did nothing to mask that fact from her and everyone else in the room.

"The Level III & IV labs are located in the basement. They are reserved for infectious disease and quarantine cases and, therefore, are limited access sites. They're separated from the hospital by an airlock corridor. I can let you have access to several of those labs. They are rarely in use and, quite frankly, I would feel better if you weren't hanging around upstairs causing a disruption in the daily routine of the hospital," she said.

Barker was lost in thought. The scope of possibilities obtained from the latest round of information gathered in the meetings astonished even him. He was privy to enough classified material that he should be hardened to anything new. The idea that they were on the brink of discovering a substance that caused instantaneous healing had implications that he could not fathom, the scope of possibilities too broad.

"That sounds acceptable. We need to get our base established by this afternoon. Two of our research scientists are being flown in by helicopter, as we speak. They should be landing in about three hours. They will need the appropriate specimens and all documentation to date, from each of the patients, ready and waiting for them when they arrive. I trust you will be able to accommodate that request, Dr. Castiglione?"

"I'll do the best I can, Mr. Barker. Will you require an office in close proximity to the lab?" When he nodded, she made a note in her file and moved on.

Of course, Mullins was spitting and sputtering, and left the meeting in a huff for the second time is as many days. Beverly suspected that he was not being honest with them about the preliminary test results, but she was saving that fight for another day. Now that the United States Government was involved, Mullins would ante up the truth or pay the consequences. She had enough on her plate and refused to play nursemaid to his wounded ego.

The meeting had finally ended and the interview with Amy Levine, quickly followed by the press conference, left her emotionally drained.

By eleven thirty that morning, Beverly had closed the blinds in her office and kicked her shoes under the desk. Laying her head on the cool unforgiving surface of her desk, she was confused and not a little bit frightened. She felt her well ordered world spinning out of control. *This is impossible. How the hell am I expected to formulate a plan, when I don't even know what is happening? Dear Lord, help me. Guide me. Give me the words to explain things that I can't even begin to understand.*

She lifted her head from the desk and picked up the phone.

"Carol, put me through to the nurse's station on four, please."

Sandra Weston was the most levelheaded nurse Beverly could think of to carry out the necessary maneuvers quickly, without the need for lengthy explanations.

"Sandra, this is Dr. Castiglione. Do you have two doubles open on the east wing? Check with west and see what they have. You may need to move patients to accomplish this, but I need two doubles beside the old triple ward, at the far end of four, in the east wing."

"Wow. That's a tall order, considering capacity. Does this have to do with the miracles, Dr. Castiglione?" Sandra asked. She had seen a lot of comings and goings in her twelve years on ward four, and she was sharp, not the least bit naïve.

"On the QT, Sandra. I need a double for Sorrento, so his wife can stay if she wants to. I need beds for Theresa Boone and her son, and the ward for a pregnant teenager and her parents." Mentally going through her list, Beverly felt as if she was organizing the University Hospital Hotel.

"Teenager? What does a teenager have to do with the miracles? Did something happen that I'm not aware of?"

"Sandra, nothing new, I promise. I need this accomplished within the next two hours. Do whatever you have to do, then call me when you have it organized. And Sandra, the less said the better. I know you can pull it together. I am counting on you."

Chapter Sixty Eight

tephen, you must prepare yourself. You may be involved in something much larger than you can even comprehend. Bishop Tomlin woke early this morning. I was still in my nightclothes when I heard him getting ready to leave for the hospital." The old priest was breathing hard, trying to catch his breath.

"Calm down, Father Andrews. It will be okay. Tell me what happened."

"I heard him on the phone, Stephen. He was talking to the Vatican. They are sending a group of investigators to Nashville to challenge the miracles. I heard him suggest that Jillian Macomb's pregnancy was the first unreported miracle…and possibly the most important."

"Okay, Father Andrews, I'm listening. What will they do? How will they proceed?"

"They usually start with the Diocese, and if they find cause to investigate further, they send in a team of scientists and religious experts from Rome. Bishop Tomlin must have decided he could forego the Diocesan investigation, in light of the urgency of the situation. Rome had already been alerted and has been monitoring the events, and judging from the parts of the conversation I was able to decipher, must have concurred with the Bishop's decision to move forward with a full investigation. They feel appropriate actions are necessary, and they are acting post haste. It is usually a long and arduous process, Stephen. They seem to be cutting right to the chase. I am not sure how it will progress."

"Are you sure he was talking about Jillian?"

"Absolutely, Stephen. You must find a way to talk to Marc Macomb about your visions. I haven't told you the rest. The CIA and the NSF are involved with their own investigations. They are now considering these happenings to be a Government security issue. Think of it, Stephen. Whoever lays claim to the powers of this phenomenon will surely rule the world."

"How do I find words to convince him that his daughter is in danger? I had another vision last night, which left no doubt that I must act soon. Very soon. The wheels are already in motion. Pray for me, Father."

"Be careful, Stephen. It is so much more than I imagined."

"Father, listen carefully to me. I am going to need your help. This is what I want you to do."

Stephen spoke hurriedly, but the implications were clear. The old priest hung up the phone, pausing only briefly to say a silent prayer for guidance. Hurriedly dressing, he set out to put in place everything needed to complete the mission with which he had just been entrusted. His doubt vanished, and he understood clearly the course he was destined to follow. He had been called to bear witness to the word of God, and he would humbly follow and do whatever was required of him.

Chapter Sixty Nine

Marc turned up the volume on the television in his office. The hospital administrator was being interviewed on Channel 3 about the second miracle. Although she urged people to stay home and not travel to Nashville, Marc feared her plea would fall on deaf ears. He was growing increasingly worried about their proximity to the hospital. With the second miracle making headlines, he wondered if they should consider heading north to Rochester, Michigan, to stay at Tom and Susie's house until things returned to normal here. The prospect of fighting their way out of the city was no less daunting than trying to fight their way in. The window of opportunity had long since passed.

Sirens could be heard almost continually now, with reports of several break-ins in the neighborhoods surrounding the University. People were increasingly despairing. Marc wondered at the desperation which caused people to abandon their homes and livelihoods to come here and stand in the Nashville sun for hours on end, just to be in close proximity to these unexplained events. Not to mention the deranged souls, who talked of little else but the end of the world to anyone who would listen.

The landscape of Music City was changing by the moment. The Red Cross had been forced to set up tents on the field of the football stadium, which now resembled a small city. People needed shelter, and this proved the most efficient way to provide it to the lucky ones who happened to be in the vicinity when the doors opened. Images of the Katrina aftermath came to mind, but Nashville had been vigilant with its disaster planning, and though chaotic, at least the process seemed organized. Katrina had been a vivid lesson in how to handle such a catastrophic event.

The Christian churches had combined resources and each denomination was well represented at the Community Center, utilizing the meeting rooms as worship halls, while the City Auditorium was housing the European contingent, and Jewish, Muslim and Middle Eastern communities flocked to the makeshift temple to pray.

Hotels in Nashville and surrounding cities were already operating at full capacity, and for those new stragglers who continued to stream into the city by the hour, prospects for lodging, even paid lodging, were dim. Families who lived in the area had opened their homes to friends and relatives from distant places, and the stress was beginning to take its toll on overworked electrical systems in the city. Several brownouts had already occurred and the threat of a complete blackout was real. The brutal heat had burgeoned into an increased demand on already overworked power grids across the state. It was proving almost impossible to contain the borders of Tennessee, with many walking through fields and farmland on foot for days, to get to Nashville.

"It gets worse every day, doesn't it?" Stephen walked into the office as Marc reached over and turned the television off.

"Yes, it does. Sometimes I wonder if we should think about packing it in for the duration. I'm beginning to believe the city won't be back to normal for a very long time. But then I remember that this is the very thing we've committed to study, and I am as fascinated by the 'miracles' as everyone else. I just have so much on my mind these days. It has become impossible to focus."

"Modern theology is proving to be every bit as fascinating as ancient history. I wonder if the miracles documented in the Bible were subjected to the same degree of dissection and skepticism that we find it necessary to apply today." Stephen leaned against the door and closed his eyes.

"Give me an example?" Marc sat at the desk and waited for Stephen to continue.

"The Wedding at Cana, for instance. Mary instructed Jesus to help the host of the wedding because he had run out of wine. Turning water

into fine wine. The first documented miracle of his ministry. Do you suppose those party-goers spent much time pondering the origins of the fine
wine that was saved for last, or did they simply accept the miracle as such
and continue their celebration of the wedding?" Stephen pushed himself
from the doorway and took a seat across from the professor.

"There has been much debate through the years on the accuracy of the
accounts of the miracles in the Bible. I agree that events which occurred
in the past were met with less skepticism, and respectful reverence was
accorded the scholars and prophets, but even Jesus inspired jealousy and
hate. If these modern miracles prove to be authentic, they will be met
with much the same reaction, I'm afraid." Marc paused briefly.

"At the end of the day, people want validation of their faith, Stephen.
If those in authority wish to dissect the miracles, more power to them.
All the more reason for us to rejoice when the findings are announced. If
they are truly miracles as we suppose, they will not be undone, no matter how stringent the tests." Marc Macomb sat back in his chair, hands
cradled behind his head.

"And what of vision and prophecy, Marc? What of things we can't see
or put our hands on to touch. Dreams were readily accepted as prophecy
in the time of the Old Testament. As true directives handed down from
our Father in heaven. How would those messages be received today? On
faith? Or would the prophet be ridiculed and reviled?"

Marc turned to look at Stephen. "Continue."

"Are you able to open your mind and heart to the possibility that such
things still occur? That modern philosophers and prophets are being
drowned out in the din of mass media with which we barrage our senses
on a daily basis?" Stephen stared straight ahead, not trusting himself to
look at Marc.

"Stephen, I do believe in prophecy. With what we have experienced
in Nashville these past few days, how could I not believe these things are
possible? I may not believe that all of the self proclaimed prophets who
stand on every street corner of the city have a direct link to heaven, but I
absolutely trust that if we open our minds to the presence of God through
all that is happening, He will speak to us. And I do believe in the Word of

God that has been handed down through the prophets. What of you? Are you receptive to the idea?"

The last thing Stephen wanted was to give Marc Macomb the impression that he was a lunatic, but the urgency of his visions and the situation they found themselves immersed in, could no longer be ignored. Marc's child was involved in ways Stephen couldn't even understand. For a moment, he was silent, choosing instead to cross the room and stand at the window, his back to the professor.

"The first time I had the dream, I thought it was only a nightmare. I'd accepted the fellowship position and was getting ready to come to Nashville…leaving the next morning, actually. I had no understanding then of what was to follow, or where the visions would eventually lead me. How could I possibly have known how forcefully they would propel me, how much I would be expected to trust in them? I've only recently come to accept the messages in faith and allow myself to believe." Stephen turned, and seeing confusion and worry in Marc's face, was unsure of how to proceed, but realized there was no turning back now. The time had come.

"Professor, we need to talk." Stephen hesitated, breathing deeply, trying to slow the rapid beating of his heart.

"Why don't you sit down, Stephen, and start at the beginning. I'm listening." Marc Macomb did not take his eyes from the young man's face as he pointed to the chair. He listened carefully as Stephen earnestly recounted his dreams and visions, describing the prophecies and pleading for acceptance from Marc.

The late afternoon shadows worked their way across the yard, and still Stephen spoke, sharing the urgency of his call to action. Finally weary, his voice a whisper, he put his head in his hands and wept at the release.

Marc was silent for several minutes, not yet trusting himself to speak. He watched the boy and knew that he had shared what he believed to be the truth. There was much to be considered. This young man was talking about his daughter, his flesh and blood. Miracles aside, was Stephen mad? Had he unwittingly invited a psychopath into his own home? What now?

Marc clenched his teeth, his jaw working. Stephen raised his head and looked at him, begging tolerance and belief.

"I don't know how I am supposed to respond, Stephen. You must admit this is being thrown at me all at once. It's a lot to digest. You tell me that this is the end of the world as we know it? How am I supposed to react? Shall I march downstairs immediately and hide my daughter from you? Do I call the police and have you escorted off my property? Or, might I take you at your word, in light of all that has happened recently? In light of all that has happened with my daughter? There are so many unexplained truths and circumstances."

"Professor Macomb, I know this is hard to accept. I fought it myself for much too long, until things began to happen that forced me to acknowledge the truth, and for whatever reason, I have been chosen to act. I promise you, I would never hurt Jillian. You have my word that is not my intent. I will not do anything to harm your daughter. I have not invited this upon myself."

"I believe you're sincere, Stephen. But if you do cause harm to her, I will not be held responsible for my actions. I will protect my family at all costs."

"As I would. All I ask is that you keep your mind open, and be vigilant. Jillian is in danger, Marc, as is the child she is carrying. And when the time comes, remember this…I would give my life to keep her safe. I have been charged with her protection."

"I am not sending you away tonight, Stephen, but I am watching you. Not a word of any of this to the women. I need time to think things through."

"Thank you, Marc. I promise you this. You will be the one to tell me when the time is right."

The cell phone on Marc's desk began to ring and he reached out to answer, watching Stephen as he did. "Okay, yes. I'll be right down."

Forcing calmness he did not feel, Marc looked at Stephen, who was obviously spent, exhaustion creeping across the boy's features.

"I'll bring you something to eat later. That was Sara calling us to dinner. I'm sure you'll understand, in light of everything that has just transpired, if I ask you to stay up here tonight. Tomorrow is another day, and I need time to process everything we have discussed."

"Of course, Marc. I'm sorry I've frightened you, but you have to know there is not much time left before we will be called to act. Things will begin to happen quickly now." Stephen remained where he was and watched as Marc made his way to the top of the steps.

"The security system is armed at night, Stephen," Marc said.

"That's good. That's good." Stephen heard the door close at the bottom of the stairs and knew he was alone.

Chapter Seventy

I don't know why Stephen didn't come down, Marc. I hope he knows he's welcome. I hate to think of him sitting up there by himself every night." Sara was sitting up in bed, book open on her lap, watching her husband get ready for bed.

"He was tired, Sara. I took him a plate. It's been an eventful few days for the kid. Anyway, he hasn't been sleeping well. Dreaming." As Marc pulled down the shade, he looked across the yard at the light in the room above the garage.

"That's odd. There must be something in the air. Your daughter has been at it again. Tossing and turning. Susie said she heard her cry out last night, and went in to find her sitting up in bed, just staring. She was still sleeping, but sitting up straight."

Marc turned back the covers and got into bed, sliding close to his wife.

"Remember last week, when she asked us about visions. We kind of brushed it off. Anything like that? Does she remember anything about her dreams? " Marc asked.

"That's the funny thing, Marc. I think she remembers more than she lets on, but she doesn't want to talk about it. Maybe she's starting to remember what happened to her. I mean the pregnancy. I don't want to press. When she's ready, she'll talk. It will all come out."

Marc pushed back the covers and got out of bed.

"Honey, where are you going?"

"Just going to peek in on Jill and check the doors again. I'll be right back."

Marc saw light peeking from beneath his daughter's door, and knocked lightly before he opened it. She was awake, softly rocking in her chair.

"Hey, little girl, just thought I'd check on you before I go to bed. How are you feeling, Jill?

"I'm okay, Daddy. What's wrong? You're acting kind of dopey."

Marc threw his head back and laughed.

"You are feeling fine, I can tell. I'm just worried about you. The world must seem like a crazy place to you right now. Mom said you were still having dreams. You want to talk about it?"

"I'm not sure what you mean."

"Remember, last week you asked me if I ever had a vision. If I ever thought that a messenger was trying to tell me something."

"Yes, I do. You and Mom thought maybe I was remembering who had sex with me and how I got pregnant." Jillian began rocking faster, becoming upset and unsure of the direction this conversation was taking. Marc put his hand on her arm to soothe her.

"I know we did. I'm not saying that right now. I know you don't have the answer to that question. I'm asking if you want to tell me about your dreams, your visions. I really want to hear about them, Jillian."

"I know you and Mom think I'm crazy, but I'm not. Did you ever know something was going to happen, and you couldn't do anything about it? But you had to trust that everything was going to be okay?"

"Jillian, I am asking you, now, to tell me about your messenger. You said last week that someone came to you in your sleep and told you things. What things, honey? I really want to hear about it."

"Daddy, I..."

The door swung open suddenly, and Susie was standing in the hallway outside the door, with cold cream on her face, her hair bunched into a shower cap.

"Marc, I need to see you for a minute. I want to show you something." Susie turned and moved from the doorway, leaving Marc and Jillian to stare after her, open mouthed.

"Susie, can it wait a few minutes? Jill and I are talking."

"Marc, I think now is better." Susie called back over her shoulder

"I'd better go see what the crisis is. I'll come back in a little while and, if you're awake, maybe we can talk then."

"Okay." Jillian said.

As Marc kissed Jillian on the forehead, he heard Susie's impatient whisper in the hallway.

"Marc," Susie hissed.

"I better go." Marc, motioning in the direction of the empty doorway, shrugged his shoulders and smiled at his daughter. He blew Jillian a kiss and left, shutting the door softly behind him.

"Daddy? Her name is Arianna. My angel. She said I have to go away. I have to go with my protector." Jillian called after her dad.

But Marc was already gone.

*   *   *

"What's going on, Susie, and what the heck do you have all over your face?"

"Never mind me. Look out the window. That same car has been in front of the house all evening. After dinner, when I went up to my room to get my magazine, it was there. I didn't think anything of it then, but I just went out back to get some fresh air and it's still sitting there. That's five hours."

"Maybe someone just parked it there."

"No, Marc. There's a man sitting in the front seat and he's watching the house. He's not trying to hide the fact, either. He just lit a cigarette."

"Okay, Susie, let's calm down. I'll ring the police and see if they still have a patrol car assigned to the side-streets. They can check it out. You stay in the house, and I'll re-set the alarm. I'll wait down here for the police. Now scoot. Don't scare the girls. And wash your face, for Pete's sake."

Marc turned off the light above the kitchen sink, and went into the bedroom to tell Sara not to wait up for him. She was curled on her side, already asleep. He went to the living room, pulled aside the window shade, and watched as the man in the car got out and leaned against the back fender. Susie was right. He wasn't trying to hide it. He was watching their house.

*   *   *

"Damn it, Barker. You could have warned us you were putting surveillance on their house. You scared them half to death. What the hell are you people thinking? This is Nashville, for God's sake." Bev slammed the phone in the cradle and looked over at Julie Richards.

"The U.S. Government is afraid the public might find out that Jillian Macomb's pregnancy is the first miracle, and storm their house. They want to safeguard the girl, so they have someone parked in front of their house until she comes back to the hospital. They just neglected to inform any of us. What did Dr. Macomb say when you talked to him about readmission?"

"He wants time, at least until tomorrow morning, so he can break it gently to Sara and Jillian. The poor guy was up half the night waiting for the police to show up and question the suspicious character in his front yard. He was not happy. And now, he's more confused than ever."

"I'm so sorry, Julie. The Government evidently has an agenda of it's own, and I'm obviously not in the loop. Tomorrow is Saturday. Do you think you can convince Sabot and Mullins to wait twenty-four hours for her to be admitted?"

"Those two can start interviewing the others. The Macomb's need time to process this. The last thing we need is a hysterical teenager, and two overwrought parents pacing the halls. We'll send a car for them in the morning. I'll personally escort them. One more day at home will make all the difference to that family."

"You got it. Tell me what time and I'll schedule the car."

Chapter Seventy One

"What do you mean…they think she's part of everything that's happening at the hospital? Are you talking about the miracles?" Sara started to cry as soon as their bedroom door was closed. She began pacing, trying to dispel the weight of the fear that was growing in her chest.

"Yes. Julie said they have traced the beginning of the events back to Jillian. Not to the first healing, but to the actual pregnancy itself and the fact that she is even sustaining a pregnancy at all. They are also unable to identify the mutation of the paternal DNA."

"Marc, what are you saying to me? I don't know how much more I can take. I thought we were home for good. Or at least until the baby is born."

"Sara, I need some time to think this through. Honey, please don't panic. We're dealing with something neither of us understands. Reflect on it, Sara. Think about the miracles, the pregnancy. Jillian swears she has no idea how she got pregnant. Maybe we should entertain the notion for one moment that she is telling the truth."

"Marc, what are you saying? That Jill is a virgin? Please don't expect this of me. Do you know what you are asking me to believe?"

"I'm asking you to have faith, Sara. For today, I want you to have faith and pray. I need to go up to my office and try to make sense of this. Please, don't say anything to Jill or Susie until I come down. It's going to be okay."

"If what you say is true, Marc, it may never be okay again."

Marc saw, in his wife's eyes, a consuming anguish that she couldn't share with him. He knew she loved Jillian with her whole being. But, a father's love is just as strong. He crossed the room and held her then, their fears mingled with the bitter knowledge that they had no control over what was being asked of them.

* * *

Marc's pounding fist shook the door to Stephen's room. "Stephen. Wake up."

Startled, Stephen sat up in bed, groggy and still half asleep.

"Stephen. It's Marc. You have to get up. I brought coffee and we need to talk." Marc stood at the bedroom door, pounding on the polished wood, waiting to hear sounds from within.

"Okay, I'm up. I'm up." Opening the door, he saw Marc standing there, immediately noting the raw emotion etched across his brow.

"Has something happened?" Stephen asked, instantly alert.

He listened as Marc related the details of what had transpired the night before, only interrupting once, when Marc told him about calling the police to investigate the car parked at the curb.

"I heard the commotion around two this morning. I looked out and saw the patrol car and, to be honest, thought you might have called about me. I knew our conversation had shaken you and figured I would just wait until I heard a knock on my door. It never came, and I fell asleep," Stephen said.

"Dr. Richards is coming by tomorrow morning to give us a ride back to the hospital. They want to readmit Jillian. It seems that the Government is sending their own specialists to do independent testing. They suspect the alleged miracles started with her pregnancy."

"You and I both know that's the truth. Are you asking what I think about you going back to the hospital, or are you telling me you finally believe me?"

"Yesterday, you said that your visions had to do with the end of the world as we know it. You said Jillian and her child are the new beginning. The beginning of what? Are we talking about the end of time, Stephen? I need to know what to expect from all this. I need insight, because right now, I don't know what to do. Yesterday, you tell me you're having visions about my family, and today I find out that the Government wants to examine my little girl and her unborn child. I don't know which end is up." Marc's agony was palpable.

"We have to be prepared to do whatever is asked of us by God." Stephen said.

"Oh, come on, Stephen. Be realistic." Marc threw his hands in the air and turned away.

"I am to take Jillian away to keep her and the child safe. No one, not even you, her parents, must know where we are going. It happens tomorrow, Marc. Gabriel said tomorrow."

"Do you expect me to hand my seventeen year old daughter over to you, a virtual stranger, because of some fantasy you have conjured up in your head? Stephen, if I were to send her into hiding, I would go with her. I would need to know that she was okay. I should be the one asked to protect her, not you." Marc was flushed, his anger and frustration apparent.

"Marc, I'm sorry. The last vision was very explicit. I am sorry that you and Sara must stay behind. I only know what the visions have shown me, and even I don't know what comes next." Stephen never wavered, his voice strong and sure.

"You listen to me, Stephen, and get this straight. There is only one plan in place right now. Tomorrow morning, a car is coming for my family and it will take us back to the hospital. Even though Julie Richards cushioned the news, I know it is not a simple request. It's a mandate. Do you see that car parked in front of my house, Stephen? That belongs to the CIA. The Government is not fooling around. And unless you can offer something more concrete to guide me in a different direction, I plan to leave for the hospital tomorrow, as planned." Forcing himself to calm down, Marc visibly restrained the urgency he felt.

"Marc, I can only tell you what I see in my visions. I accept God's will. It is for Him to guide us."

Marc turned from the doorway and noticed Stephen's backpack leaning against the wall.

"You are prepared to leave?" He asked.

"I am prepared for whatever God asks of me." Stephen said.

"If this is the beginning of the end, Stephen, you are going to need more than a backpack to sustain you." The silence stretched tightly between them as Marc weighed the few options before him.

"Take your shower, then come down to the house for breakfast. Sara and Susie are worried that you are starving up here. Not a word about any of this. Until we leave for the hospital tomorrow, it's business as usual. I'd like you to help me gather what I need for the trip. Once again, it seems my office must be temporarily relocated."

Stephen watched Marc walk across the yard and disappear into the house. He noticed the car at the curb and watched the lone occupant get out, stretching his legs. He saw the gun holstered across his shoulder, and knew the Government would not be easy to deal with. His stomach tightened as his jaw clenched with new resolve. The time was at hand, and he was ready. He dialed his sister's number, and relieved at hearing the sound of her voice, sank heavily into the chair.

"Hello. Stephen, are you okay?"

"Cami, I need your help. Please listen carefully, because after this, I won't be able to contact you. We only have one chance to get this right."

Stephen laid out his plan, cognizant of the importance of what he was asking his sister to do. He was aware there would be many dangers for all of them in the days and weeks ahead, but he knew his sister would not be afraid. Stephen placed his phone on the desk and went in to shower. He would not hear the sound of his sister's voice again for a very long time.

Chapter Seventy Two

Jackson Mullins knew the Macomb family was being watched. Driving by their house that morning at seven, he had seen the car out front and recognized it immediately for what it was. Barker had the house under surveillance. The Government. He spat out the window, neither speeding up nor slowing down, but had continued to the end of the block and turned the corner. He glanced in the rearview mirror and saw the paper sack on the back seat of his car. The future of mankind was sitting right there, in a plain brown wrapper, and there was plenty more where that came from.

The houses in Nashville that hadn't survived the economic downturn were abundant. Lease signs had popped up on every other block, offered by desperate owners unable to sell their overpriced homes. When he finally found what he was looking for, he had been amazed at how easily he had been able to fool the ditzy little Realtor, coercing her to rent the furnished house to him for a month, all cash, no questions or paperwork. She had been amply rewarded, of course, and could be easily disposed of, should it come to that. How easy it had been to arrange a meeting with a total stranger at the empty house. Of course, she came alone, as he knew she would, too afraid a partner might steal the deal before she could tie it up.

The lot was wide and private, set behind a forest of trees at the top of a hill, with a panoramic view of the city below. He smirked as he pushed the remote and pulled into the attached garage as soon as the wide door swung open. The illegals he'd hired off the streets of Nashville had been sitting at the table of the furnished bungalow, playing cards, until they heard the garage door open. Lured easily to the suburbs by the promise of shelter and cash, it wasn't hard to persuade the little gang to stand guard over his soon-to-be houseguest.

Looking at them with barely disguised contempt, Jackson motioned to the garage as he tossed them the keys to the trunk. "Food."

As soon as they left the kitchen, he unlocked the door to the finished basement and went down the steps, taking care to lock the door behind him as he descended into the darkness.

Chapter Seventy Three

Jillian watched him closely during breakfast. She tried not to be obvious, but she was determined to figure out if Stephen was her protector. He caught her looking at him more than once, and quickly turned his head or looked away. The weird part was that she could feel her dad looking at both of them, like he was trying to find the missing piece of a puzzle. She knew that expression. It was the same one he wore when he was doing research, or grading papers from the University and trying to decipher the meaning behind the words his students had written.

Aunt Susie made her famous blueberry pancakes and Jillian was starving. Her mom wasn't eating much and really didn't talk at all. She just kept turning her juice glass around on the table and moving her pancakes from one side of her plate to the other. Aunt Susie was jabbering a mile a minute and it was funny, because she almost seemed to be flirting with Stephen, and his ears were turning red. He might be kind of old, but he was still very handsome in a man sort of way.

"Mom, is it okay if I call Evie this morning to see if she can come over and hang out? I'm bored, and you said she could spend the night last night, but I never called her." Jillian caught the look that passed between her parents and put down her fork, her temper flaring. "You said I could."

"I know, honey, but we need to talk to you about something that has just come up." Sara looked at Marc and then glanced quickly at Stephen and Susie.

"Let's go up to your room, Jillian. Your mom and I need to sit down with you..."

"And tell me what? Arianna already told me about my baby. She came to me in my dream and called my son a gift of hope for the New World. She even told me what his name will be. His name is Benjamin and he is a blessing of light from God. Those who believe will be led into Paradise. His name means 'son of my right hand.' Isn't that what you wanted to know last night, Daddy?"

"Arianna?" Aunt Susie turned around with the pancake flipper still in her hand, and looked at all of them in confusion. "Those are your hormones talking, baby. What is all this nonsense? Would someone please tell me what is going on?"

Marc raised his hand. "Not now, Susie. Jillian, please let's just go upstairs and talk this through."

"You asked me last night about my dreams. You wanted to know the truth. Well, this is the truth whether you want to hear it or not." Jillian bolted from the room, running up the stairs and slamming her bedroom door.

Sara looked at her sister with wide eyes.

"Susie, they want us to take her back to the hospital. They think the miracles may have started with her pregnancy. The Government wants its own doctors to examine her and ask her questions." Sara held herself, rocking back and forth in her chair, her throat tightening around the words as she struggled to make sense of everything that was happening.

Stephen had been silent, listening in shock as Jillian's words sank in, echoing everything he had been told by Gabriel. He raised his head, and meeting Marc's eyes, rose from his chair without a word and left the house, heading for his room above the garage.

"Are you two going to allow it? Have her treated like a guinea pig under a microscope? The hospital thinks that the healings started with our Jillian? Her and that little baby? I don't know about this, you two. Are they saying that she is somehow involved with these miracles?" Susie was incredulous.

Marc reached across the table, covering the women's hands with his own.

"Listen, Sara. You need to go up and comfort her. Tell her they only want her back in the hospital for a little while and try to calm her down. I have some things to discuss with Stephen. I'll be back down in a few minutes. And Susie, we aren't sure what to believe. We haven't been given much choice in the matter."

"There is always a choice, Marc. You are her father. There is always a choice." Susie got up and started to clear the table, butter from the pancakes hardening in the pool of syrup on Sara's plate.

* * *

Sara opened Jillian's bedroom door and walked over to the bed, climbing in beside her daughter. Lying next to her, she scooped the unyielding body of her little girl closer to her and whispered softly into her hair.

"Sshh. It's okay, baby. It's all going to be okay."

"I really don't want to go away, you know. I'm scared." Jillian scooted closer to her mother's warm body, feeling Sara's heart beating strong against her back.

"Oh, honey, they only want to make sure you're okay. They think you are special, that your baby and you are a miracle. We have to go back to the hospital because they want to check you, to see if they can understand everything that happened." Sara breathed in her daughter's scent, her soothing voice gently moving the fine hair that lay against Jillian's cheek.

"It's not for us to understand, Mom. This is from God. Arianna says it is his gift of promise to the faithful. I don't want to go away, but I will. Arianna says I must trust his word and I promised I would. I'm just afraid to be alone, that's all." Jillian turned to face her mother.

"Jillian, Daddy and I will be with you. We won't leave you for a minute. I know you feel alone right now, but this will all be over soon. We'll be back here with Aunt Susie, all together and snug as a bug. Dr. Richards is worried that if people find out about you, you may be in danger."

"I will be in danger for a little while, but where I have to go, you can't come. Don't you understand, Mom? You can't come. I'm not sure yet who my protector is. God will give me a sign that I should go with him, and only him. Please try to believe me. My baby is the promised one, the covenant of the New World."

"Jillian Grace Macomb, I don't know what to say when you talk like this. Daddy and I will stay with you for all time. We are your protectors and we won't let anything happen to you. We won't send you off with anyone."

"Mom, listen to me. When the time comes, you must know I will be okay. Promise me you will know."

"Jillian, I know you will be okay. Now stop this talk, and just lay here with me for awhile before we start to pack for the hospital."

Jillian and Sara lay together for a long time, until finally Sara closed her eyes, falling asleep against the sweet soapy smell of her daughter's skin. Jillian watched her, never moving her eyes from her mother's face… except once, when she checked to see that her bulging backpack was by the door where she left it.

Chapter Seventy Four

Y“ou heard what she said, Marc. Benjamin. Who is seated at the right hand of the Father, and came to us in the flesh?”

“Stephen…”

Pounding his fist against the wall, Stephen turned to Marc in anger and frustration, “*Who is seated at the right hand of the Father?*”

“Jesus.”

“How amazing that God, in his compassion and glory, would once again bless this world with a holy child. That He should reach beyond the Holy Trinity to bless us, his beloved children, with a sign that we should so easily understand. Make no mistake, Marc. This child has been sent by God, through your daughter, to lead us into Paradise. A symbol of hope. He has given us this chance to redeem ourselves through a simple act of faith. How can we not embrace this gift, and believe?”

“Stop it. Stop.” Marc held up his hand, as if he could physically stop the flow of words he didn’t want to hear.

“No. I won’t stop, because the answer is right there in front of you and you refuse to see it. Your daughter has been chosen. She is the great wonder in the heavens. She is the woman clothed in the sun, with the moon at her feet. She is to birth the child that will lead us all to salvation. You heard what she said, Marc. She did not come up with this by herself. Open your ears. Open your heart.”

“I can’t let this happen.”

“You don’t have a choice, Marc. It has happened.”

"I have to think. I have to have time to think."

"There is no time. Tomorrow is the day. I promised I would not take her until you said the words to me, and I will live by that promise. Sometime between now and tomorrow, Marc, I know that God will send you a sign."

"Stephen, you can help me gather work to take with me to the hospital, because until God sends me that sign you keep talking about, my only plan is to go with my family to the hospital tomorrow, where they will be safe."

Chapter Seventy Five

Mrs. Boone, this is Dr. Sabot. She is with the National Science Foundation. You are causing quite a stir in the medical community this afternoon, Theresa." Beverly Castiglione wrapped the blood pressure cuff around Theresa's arm and waited as it began to automatically inflate.

Theresa held out her hand and squeezed Judith's hand with a strong steady grip.

"Sorry. I know I'm crushing you, but it feels so darn good to be able to do that. It's nice to meet you, Doctor. Of course you know that the Lord healed me. It was a miracle, pure and simple, and my little guy Johnny over there gets credit, too, for getting me this far."

Johnny looked up at the women and smiled, before turning back to his lunch.

"He's excited he has his own little television on his bed over there. He's not gonna want to go home, I'm afraid. Everyone has been spoiling him."

"Theresa, I was hoping you would answer a few questions for my records. Of course, I'm sure you've already been over most of this, but it would certainly be helpful for me to hear your own account of the events," said Dr. Sabot.

"Honey, you go right ahead. You all have been so nice to us already, me and Johnny are happy to answer anything you ask. Of course, only God has the real answers, but I'd be happy to oblige."

"Great, thanks. I know you were only vaguely conscious when you were admitted to the hospital, Theresa. Is there anything special you remember about that day?"

"Honey, the last thing I remember before the hospital, is when Johnny got us off the bus in Nashville. It was so dang hot and I was thirsty. The poor little guy tried to feed me water with a dropper, to wet my tongue, you know. I couldn't swallow very good by that time. Because of the ALS. He had to deal with the wheelchair and all those people. I never saw so many people in one place in all my life. Thank the Lord, he met that Stephen fellow, because the next thing I remember was waking up here at the hospital, with Johnny sleeping in a chair pulled up close to the bed. His little head was right next to me and he was holding on to my hand for dear life. Like that was the only thing keeping me alive." Theresa smiled at her son and leaned her head back against the headboard.

"Oh, and then that nice doctor came in and gave me a shot in my leg. He said something funny about helping me rest, and I remember thinking to myself, if I got any more rested I would probably be dead, but of course I couldn't say that because I couldn't talk anymore," Theresa said, rubbing her thigh.

"My mom couldn't walk or talk, but then she had the miracle and now she can do everything. She's going to take me to the zoo in Nashville before we go home." Johnny opened the plastic cup of ice-cream on his lunch tray and turned back to his cartoons.

Theresa beamed at her son.

"It wasn't long after I got that shot that I felt a tingling in my fingers, a real funny sensation, and then I saw I was petting on Johnny's hair while he slept. You know, at first I thought I was dreaming, because I always used to do that to his hair before I got sick. He used to fuss at me about it. But not this time. I tried to say his name to wake him up. I saw him swat at the air, and then he looked at me, and right then I said his name a little louder, and he got so excited he ran out of the room to find the nurse."

"Theresa, when did this doctor come in and give you the shot? Did he tell you his name or did you see his name on his lab coat?" Dr. Sabot looked up briefly from the chart.

"No, he was wearing those blue scrubs and he was trying to back out of the room, real quiet. I don't think he knew I was awake until just before he left and he caught my eye. I don't think he really wanted to wake us up."

"Did he say anything to you?"

"Just 'something to help you rest.' That's all he said. And my name. He knew my name."

"Okay, Theresa. Do you know anything about this Stephen who helped you get to the hospital?"

"You'll have to ask my little Johnny about him. I don't remember any of that time. But I sure would like to thank him, if I could. If it wasn't for him, I don't know what would have happened to us out there. He was a real angel to my little guy. A real angel."

Theresa yawned and sat back against the pillows, closing her eyes for a minute.

"It's funny, you know. Last week at this time, I couldn't even move one muscle. I couldn't swallow...I couldn't hardly breathe on my own. I was all but dead. It's a miracle all right, a real miracle."

Judith went to the counter on the wall across from the bed and looked through Theresa Boone's chart. Scanning the pages, she compared the entries to the notes she had just taken. Closing the chart, she walked over to Johnny, who was flipping through channels, looking for something to watch other than the news.

"Hey, Johnny? I just want to ask a few questions about your mom, okay? Right before your mom woke up, were you awake when the doctor came in? The one who gave her the shot?"

"No, ma'am. My mom woke me up when she said my name, but I didn't see a doctor."

"What about Stephen? Who is he, Johnny, and where did you meet him?"

"He helped me. I saw him on the street and he looked nice, so I asked him to help me. He brought us through all the people to get here. We had to run, and people were shooting and he saved my life. See my arm?" Johnny rolled up his sleeve and showed them the large dressing the emergency room nurse had applied to his wound.

"Then he told me about the secret and how it worked. I know why my mom is healed. Stephen told me about faith and a mustard seed moving a mountain, and all you needed to do was to believe. I believed with all my heart and it worked."

The two doctors exchanged a quick glance.

"Okay, you two, that's it for now. I'll be back later to check on you, to make sure you have everything you need," Beverly said as they moved toward the door.

* * *

Once in the hallway, Judith and Beverly stopped just outside the Boone's room.

"Bev, I don't see any order for an injection in the woman's chart. The ER attending was Sherry Donaldson? Didn't she say that the Boone's were in the far corner of the emergency area?"

"Yes, she wanted them to have privacy."

"I want the security camera footage for every hallway in the ER on Monday night, and I want the drug inventory and staff assignments." Judith frowned, trying to remember something she had heard mentioned at the meeting.

"Okay, I'll have it sent up to my office. It may take a few hours, but I'll call you when I have everything. What are you thinking?" Beverly was already planning ahead, trying to formulate a strategy that would get things moving quickly.

"I don't know yet, but I want to find out who our mysterious doctor is. Any contact information on Stephen?"

"I think Johnny has a number for him. I'll round everything up and meet you in a of couple hours in the conference room. I'll call you when I have everything ready." She turned and walked back into the Boone's room.

As Judith Sabot approached Dr. Sorrento's door she hesitated, mulling over the new information she'd attained from Theresa Boone. Cursing herself for not requesting the security tapes the minute she set foot in the hospital, she wondered if other 'not so pertinent details' might also have been overlooked in the frenzy surrounding these phenomena.

Quickly gathering her thoughts, she knocked lightly on the door to Dr. Sorrento's room, promising herself she would not make the same mistake twice.

Chapter Seventy Six

It was after nine o'clock on Friday night before Beverly was able to gather all the requested information and have it ready for Daniel Barker and Judith Sabot. She did not have to wait long for them to meet her in the conference room. Judith sat beside Barker and waited for Beverly to close the door, before turning on the monitor and starting the first reel of the security tape.

The mayhem caught on the filmed footage was significant. People in distress lined the halls of the emergency room, and staff was moving constantly, trying to minister to everyone at once. After watching three hours of the security feeds, Beverly suddenly put her hand on Daniel's arm.

"Wait. Right there. Rewind the video. He's walking away from the camera, I can't see his face. There. He's going behind the curtain where Dr. Donaldson said the Boones were waiting. What time is showing on the feed?"

"Seven twenty-four p.m. on Monday night." Daniel said.

"Okay, he's coming back out." Beverly watched tensely, trying to recognize any small detail that could help identify the figure in the grainy footage.

"There's a nurse heading his way. Damn, she's blocking his face from the camera." Daniel was on his feet now, almost face to face with the monitor.

"Move, damn it." As if she could hear him.

"Patience, Daniel." Judith Sabot leaned closer to the image on the screen as the nurse finished speaking to the man. As she turned away, his face filled the screen.

Beverly stared in disbelief at the monitor in front of her.

"Oh, my God," Bev's hand flew to her mouth.

Barker had magnified the image now frozen on the screen. The face looking back at her was one she knew all too well. Jackson Mullins. Wearing blue scrubs, he was walking toward the elevator. It was the night he had been missing from the lab.

Beverly turned to say something to the Government agents, but Barker was already on his way out the door.

Chapter Seventy Seven

Mullins pushed through the holly bushes that formed a hedge around the back of the Macomb's yard, cursing under his breath at the stiff and unforgiving foliage. He knew that all pretenses were over. It was only a matter of time before they figured it out, the secrets he kept. The damn Government meddling in things they didn't understand, like scavengers. The magnitude of this single discovery had the potential to change the course of history and alter the fate of mankind. He was not content to be relegated to a footnote. The key to world power was in his breast pocket and he was only minutes away from claiming the source as his own.

He calculated an hour until sunrise, dark clouds obscuring the moon perfectly for this mission. He focused on the yard and noted the garden, memorizing the flowerbeds and the hammock floating eerily between two old trees. He listened carefully to the night sounds. The screened porch would be easy enough to infiltrate before sunup, and from there he would patiently wait for his chance to enter the house. His covert observances of the last few mornings led him to believe the professor would soon open the back door, amble slowly down the long driveway to the front of the house, coffee cup in hand, to retrieve his morning paper. He would have easy access to the house during that time. Easy enough, even for an amateur.

The car at the front curb never left its post, the agent slouching within, casually observing the comings and goings of the occupants of the house. The guard had been put in place to avert any emergency situation that might arise involving the girl, obviously not expecting any breech of the property. The yard was fully enclosed, and once leaving the driveway for the path, lush landscaping obscured the view from the street.

Mullins skimmed the perimeter of the yard, careful to stay close to the hedge and the privacy fence, lest someone rise early and look out one of the windows. He had worked feverishly the past few nights, removing planks from the fencing behind the garage, leaving just enough room to slip through easily and slip out again with his prize. The thick ivy hedge formed a dense cover in front of the fence, so in the event anyone did wander behind the garage, they were unlikely to notice the gap, especially after he carefully replaced the planks, fitting them snuggly into their previous spaces and securing them with twine.

The woods behind the house afforded the Macomb's their cherished privacy, and quite conveniently, offered the same to him. His borrowed car was parked in front of an empty wooded lot on the street behind them, and he counted on getting back into the vehicle with his precious cargo before anyone even noticed it was there.

Before he slipped across the yard, he donned surgical gloves, and then quickly moved to the steps leading to the back porch. Reaching for the handle of the door, he was relieved to discover it was unlocked. He knew he could slice the screen ever so slightly to gain access, and brought a scalpel should that be necessary, but not alerting the good professor to his presence before the time was right was crucial to his plan.

On the previous morning, he heard the door on the screened porch emit a grating squeak. It probably went unnoticed by the professor, but that small obstacle was easy enough to remedy, and he came prepared. Quietly taking the can of 31W from the pocket of his windbreaker and carefully squeezing the lubricant on the offending hinges, he pushed the small can deep into the bushes and pulled the door gently toward him.

He moved silently to the far corner of the porch, crouched behind the glider, and felt the unfamiliar but reassuring weight of the gun resting against his right hip. He was willing to wait patiently, watching for the light in the kitchen, the signal that he had five minutes until the professor walked past him on his morning jaunt to the front of the house. Mullins would then be able to slip through the unprotected back door. He smiled at the relative simplicity of his plan. We really are creatures of habit now, aren't we?

Chapter Seventy Eight

"Marc, when you go down to get the paper, will you put those in the mailbox?" Marc leaned into the laundry room doorway, as his wife opened the dryer and pointed to a stack of envelopes on the counter in the kitchen.

"What time do we have to be ready for Julie?" Sara turned her back to Marc while she transferred the laundry, uncertainty and fear running rampant in her mind.

"She said the car would be here around eight thirty, depending on how long it took for them to navigate the side streets. Are you ready?" Marc glanced at the clock above the sink.

"Yes, I guess I'm as ready as I'll ever be. I have to wake Jillian, but I thought I'd wait until seven thirty. I don't think she had a very restful night." Sara already looked bothered.

"Listen, honey, we have to believe that everything will be okay. The sooner we get to the bottom of this, the sooner we can come home." Marc grabbed his coffee and disarmed the security system, opening the back door and walking through the screened porch and into the yard as the sun broke through the early morning sky. It was going to be a beautiful day.

Sara bent and grabbed the last towel. She pressed the clean fabric to her face and inhaled its sweetness before adding it to the neat stack on top of the dryer. Calculating the time remaining before they had to leave for the hospital, she threw a load of sheets into the dryer and set the timer. She vaguely heard the door open in the kitchen and called out.

"Back so soon? I knew you'd forget the mail."

*   *   *

Stephen watched from the window as Marc walked slowly up the driveway and went back into the house. It seemed only a few short hours ago that they parted, having worked long into the night, an unspoken truce declared, gathering literature and research material for Marc to take with him to the hospital. Both were preoccupied and uneasy, but they forced themselves to stay on task.

Today was the day that Gabriel had commissioned Stephen to save the girl. He had no idea how or when this would happen. He thought briefly of Father Andrews and Cami. He thanked God they were stalwart warriors in his camp.

He'd tossed and turned for most of the night, unaware of the time that he eventually dozed off, and even less aware of what had finally roused him from his dreamless, restless sleep. He got up slowly, sitting on the edge of his bed for awhile before ultimately falling to his knees, praying for strength and the courage to do God's will. Instead of finding comfort, he was filled with overpowering doubt. Were the visions only a figment of his overactive imagination? What about the miracles? The pregnancy? So many of these recent circumstances pointed to the validity of the prophecies and he had to have faith that God would lead him. Today was the day he was to put into motion everything he had been asked to do. Now was not the time to falter.

"Gabriel? I know you are watching over us this morning. I feel your presence. Guide my hand, Gabriel, and bless us all. Please give me a sign that the time has come."

*   *   *

Walking back toward the house, Marc looked around the yard. For a brief moment he longed for the days that he and Sara would once again bemoan the crabgrass, or talk about plans for a family vacation. Outwardly everything looked the same. He had to have faith that everything would one day return to normal. Even the recent past paled in light of the dreamlike world in which he presently found his family immersed. It seemed so unreal, this talk of Jillian and a miracle. How had they come to be cast as major players in this surreal drama?

Marc opened the screen door to the porch and stopped. He backed up, opened the door again, then let it close, catching it before it slammed. Preoccupied, he hadn't noticed the silence on his way out. Shaking his head, he walked into the kitchen, tossing the newspaper onto the counter.

"Hey, Sara? Did you oil the hinges on the screen door? Honey?" Marc crossed the kitchen, going straight to the coffee pot and refilling his mug. Not expecting to find the kitchen empty and quiet, he glanced over at the laundry room, surprised to see the door closed. Sara never closed the door to the laundry room. It had always been a bone of contention between them, and he often found himself uncharacteristically annoyed when she started a load of laundry right before dinner. That was his time to unwind, sip a glass of wine and listen to the evening news. He always looked forward to the tranquility of that part of the evening, to Sara's recount of the day's events, and their shared laughter at some of the predicaments Jillian found herself caught up in. Those were the glorious days of normalcy. He smiled at Sara's small unexpected act of kindness this morning and walked over to flip on the television.

The weather report sprang to life and he smiled again, thinking how lucky they were, that in spite of the present circumstances, they had love and the comfort of a strong marriage, even after all these years. Turning his back to the news broadcast, Marc found himself heading across the kitchen toward the closed laundry room door. Not quite understanding why, he actually longed for the swishing, clanging and clinking sounds of laundry in progress. He turned the knob, pushing the door open.

He wasn't prepared. Confused, he stepped back, not fully comprehending the scene before him.

"Good morning, Dr. Macomb. We meet again." Jackson Mullins stood against the wall, holding Sara against him, his left arm wrapped tightly around her throat, his right hand forcefully pressing a gun to her temple.

Marc stood paralyzed. The only thing moving was his heart, slamming against the wall of his chest, even his breathing momentarily on hold. He could feel his face on fire with the sudden rush of blood pounding through his head, keeping rhythm with his pulse. His Sara imprisoned, soundlessly pleading with him, terror reflected in her eyes. The gun chafed a raw spot where it was pushed against her skin, a drop of blood already trickling, weeping from the wound. These things he saw, but could not understand. A moment. An eternity.

"Aren't you Dr. Mullins? What are you doing?" Marc finally found his voice, wishing it were fierce and threatening, instead of breaking in fear and anguish. His knees were a liquid pool and he held the doorframe to keep from collapsing to the floor.

"Marc, he wants…." Sara was straining against his elbow, but Mullins squeezed harder, jabbing her in the side with his knee. The gun scraped the skin from her temple, the blood now a steady flow.

"Calm down, pretty one. My aim here is not to kill you, although I will if I must, in order to get what I came for. I will do whatever must be done." Mullins looked at Marc with steely calm. "I am here for the girl, Jillian. She is my discovery, you see. My power. Not the imbeciles from the Government, who only want to dissect her. As if they could ever find the answers to their questions. I see no reason to allow their bungling ineptness. I refuse to let them interfere."

"But, Dr. Mullins, I don't understand. We are going to the hospital with Jillian. You will be able to…." Marc reeled with the sudden realization that this horror was real. This man intended to kidnap his daughter. Looking around wildly for some way to divert him, a way to escape this nightmare with his family intact, the sight of Sara, bleeding and held captive by this monster rooted him to the spot, his bravado all but evaporating.

Mullins rammed Sara's head into the wall and she cried out, her legs giving way beneath her.

Marc rushed forward without thinking, reaching out involuntarily to catch his wife, his coffee mug crashing to the floor.

"Stop! You're hurting her. I beg you to stop now. Please release her. You can tie me up if you want, hold the gun to my head. Please, just let my wife go. I beg you, please."

"*I WILL KILL HER.*" Jackson jerked Sara to her feet and with his head, motioned Marc to move from the doorway.

"Let's go into the living room now, nice and slow. If you try that again, dear Dr. Macomb, your precious wife will die. Do you still not understand that I've not come for you? It's not you I want. Nor your precious Sara. You are both expendable to me. Worthless. Only the girl. She is the one who holds the key to the miracles, she and the child"

Marc backed out of the doorway, walking through the glass and coffee spreading slowly across the floor, leading them to the living room, never taking his eyes from Sara's face. On the way through the kitchen, he could still hear the meteorologist rambling in the background, talking about rain. It was seven fifteen. The car at the curb may as well be a million miles away. He forced his knees to steady, and suddenly realized that he was helpless to stop this chain of events from unfolding.

Chapter Seventy Nine

Stephen looked over his shoulder as he left the office above the garage, grabbing the backpack from the chair in front of the desk, and heading for the stairs. He planned to wait with the Macomb's as long as he could, at least until the car from the hospital came to carry them away. He felt uneasy, off balance and at loose ends. He warily descended the garage steps, the hair on the back of his neck rising…a sudden unexpected watchfulness taking over his senses.

Sunrise cast its golden glow on the garden, the yard beginning to come alive with the morning sounds of nature. Stephen could smell the faint fragrance of honeysuckle, and something else. An acrid smell. He noticed her then, sitting on the hammock with her back to him, smoke from her cigarette spiraling toward the pale sky. She turned slowly at the sound of his descent, not surprised to see him, but resigned.

A faint smile played at the corner of her lips as Aunt Susie acknowledged him with a whisper. "Good morning, Stephen. You mustn't say a word. I have two a day, one in the morning and one right before I go to bed. One of many small vices. Of course, everyone knows I do it, but they pretend they don't. Out of respect for me, I suppose. Come here and talk with me for a minute."

Stephen sat on a small wooden bench, setting his backpack on the ground beside him. "It's still so early, Susie. Do you know what time they leave?"

"I heard Marc tell Jillian she had to be ready by eight thirty, so I suppose another hour or so. Jill was still asleep when I came out. I always wait until Marc goes down to get the morning paper, then I know it's safe to open the front door and sneak out without setting off the alarm. I often end up here in the yard. It's so peaceful in the morning."

"Yes, that it is," Stephen said.

"What do you think of this fiasco, Stephen? I hate the thought of Jillian stuck in that hospital, locked up like some lab specimen. Whether her pregnancy does turn out to be a miracle, or they find out something entirely different, it won't change anything. I wish everyone would just leave this family alone. They have already dealt with so much this past month." Susie pushed her cigarette into the wet soil and straightened, pulling her robe tightly around her.

"Time will tell, Susie. It is not for me to say."

"What do you think of all this mumbo jumbo about the baby? I swear, that girl always had an imagination, and now her hormones have revved it up a notch. Arianna. She used to have an imaginary pet when she was a little girl, a monkey named Sam."

"Perhaps, in light of everything that is happening around us right now, we would do well to keep our minds open, Susie. I believe her. She is telling the truth." Stephen stood, brushing dew from the back of his jeans.

"Oh, dear Lord, Stephen. Not you, too? Go on now, and get yourself some coffee. I'm going to stay out here for another minute or two. Maybe I'll break my own rule and have another cigarette. I have a feeling today is going to be a doozy. I'll be there in a little while. I want to see my niece before they cart her off to God knows where."

Stephen opened the screen door and set his backpack on the floor just outside the kitchen. He grabbed a mug from the tray by the coffee maker and filled it with hot coffee, smiling when he saw a serving platter in the middle of the kitchen table, heaped with muffins. Sara was so kind. She reminded him of his own mom. He helped himself and began to peel the paper from a pastry, when he noticed the mug lying smashed on floor in the middle of the laundry room doorway. Stepping over a puddle of coffee, he moved closer to investigate. The washer and dryer were running, but he saw no one.

He set his food on the table, and was reaching for a paper towel to wipe up the mess on the floor, when he heard it. An unintelligible noise came from the living room. To his ears, the sound was muffled and anxious. With dread and uncertainty, Stephen moved cautiously across the kitchen toward the hallway that led to the living room. He heard it again. He stayed in the shadow of the hallway, inching his way closer to the open doorway. He tried to remain collected, though his own nerves were now on edge. He knew that emotions would likely be running high this morning, and was not sure what familial scene he would possibly stumble upon. He certainly did not want to intrude on their last morning at home, but something was off. He could feel it. Was this the sign he had been waiting for?

His heart in his throat, his mouth was dry as he edged closer to the source of the incoherent sounds. A thump from the second floor stopped him in his tracks and he stood frozen, raising his eyes to the ceiling. He could hear bits of a heated conversation on the second floor, directly above him, and though the voices were muffled, there was no mistaking the anger.

He flattened himself against the wall, feeling somewhat melodramatic as he inched toward the doorway. He turned his body silently, pressing his cheek against the cool painted surface and slowly moved his head back just far enough to enable him to see into the room. His mind fought to make sense of the scene before him.

Marc Macomb was sitting in a dining room chair, bound at the ankles, with his hands tied behind him. He desperately strained against the rope, trying to free himself from his bondage, groaning through the silver duct tape that covered his mouth and surrounded his head. Positioned in such a way that he noticed Stephen's slight movement in the doorway, he frantically motioned to the stairway with his eyes.

Forcing himself to move, Stephen crossed the room in seconds, gesturing for Marc to be silent. He tore through the tape around Marc's head, ripping it from his mouth so he could speak.

"That doctor from the hospital, I think his name is Mullins. He's crazy. He's up there now with Sara, and he is going to take Jillian away.

He has a gun, Stephen." Marc whispered, frantically fighting against his restraints.

Stephen took it all in, the blood draining from his face.

"Marc, calm down and listen to me. I'm going to untie you, *but you have to stay where you are.* You have to stay in the chair. He mustn't know you're free. If he comes down here and sees you've moved, it will be bad for the women." Stephen worked desperately to loosen the bonds.

His hands were shaking and slippery with sweat, as he fumbled to untie the knots that seemed welded in place, while keeping his ears trained on the commotion upstairs. He gently replaced the tape across Marc's mouth and straightened, putting his finger to his lips.

"I will try to divert him, Marc. Be watchful and be ready to move. And pray." Stephen retraced his steps to the hallway and waited, sweat stinging his eyes, for Mullins to bring the girls downstairs.

Chapter Eighty

Julie Richards leaned her head against the headrest in the back seat of the Hummer winding its way through the streets of Nashville toward the Macomb's house. The militia was slowly moving people back to a radius of one mile in every direction from the hospital and University, so all arriving or departing patients were no longer ambushed by miracle seekers right outside the hospital's doors. That had been a nightmare.

The National Guard created a one lane artery that ran the circumference of the structures, with a check point at each road that intersected it. It made for slow going, but amid the unrestrained chaos prevailing for the past week, this was welcome relief. Once the vicinity outside the hospital cordon was reached, the car crawled along. Further from the hospital, the less dense the crowds. There were tent cities everywhere you looked, but for the most part, people who lived there went on about their routines as if this were normal.

Bev had reached her at five o'clock this morning and instructed her to call the minute she had the Macomb's with her and they were on their way back to the hospital. Julie couldn't help but think of her private practice, and worried that it would be non-existent after things got back to normal. She had neglected so many of her patients since all of this started. She tried not to think about it, the years she had spent building her life. She knew she wasn't the only one adapting to this new reality. She hoped her partner could hang in there a few more days. Bev Castiglione was almost frantic when she called this morning, and Julie could only try to imagine the Director's new reality.

"Listen, Julie, that CIA agent, Daniel Barker, wanted to send his own car to pick up the Macomb's and I refused. So please call me the minute you're on your way back. Then I can let him know that everything is going according to plan. We've had some unsettling developments with personnel, and the sooner everyone is under one roof and accounted for, the better."

"Okay, Bev, no problem. I told them eight thirty and my car should be here to pick me up any minute. I have my cell phone with me. What's going on?" That was all they needed on top of everything else. Personnel problems.

"I'll explain once you're here and everyone has checked in. The CIA has a car parked in front of the Macomb's. The agent stationed there is expecting you, so don't be alarmed when he follows you back. Be careful."

"Okay. By the time we load up, I'd estimate we should be back to the hospital by twelve thirty, give or take. I'll call the minute we're on our way. I suspect the CIA guy following us will do the same."

"Thanks, Julie. I'll see you at lunch and I can bring you up to speed then."

"And, Bev, please tell Barker to back off. This is a regular family we are dealing with and they've been through the ringer lately. The Government will get their information in due time. I don't want my patient subjected to any more stress than we have already heaped on her."

Julie looked out the window and noticed the streets of Nashville had sprung to life. Just another day in Music City. The clock on the dashboard read 8:01 a.m.

Chapter Eighty One

Mullins backed Sara against the wall outside Jillian's room, his face only inches from hers. She felt his hot breath on her face and her stomach heaved at the smell of him.

"You are going to go in and wake the girl. You are to tell her that she is going with me and then you will throw together some of her things. Five minutes."

"Please, Dr. Mullins. She's just a baby. She will be frightened. Please. She'll be in the hospital. You can...."

Mullins pulled Sara's hair, her neck snapping back against the wall. She cried out involuntarily in anguish and pain.

"I am going to stand out here in the hallway while you get her ready. Don't try anything, Momma Bear, because I'm not taking my eyes off either one of you. I will use this gun without one moment of hesitation if you try anything. Then what? How will you ever hope to see your little girl or meet your grandchild, if you are dead? Do I make myself clear?"

Sara nodded as he let go of her for the first time since he entered the house. She forced herself to calm down and tried to keep her hands from shaking, as she attempted to wipe the dried blood that had formed a crusty trail on her temple.

Mullins motioned Sara into the bedroom and she walked slowly to Jillian's bed, turning back once to look at him as he stood guard by the open door. She could hear Marc downstairs, his rage and grief muffled by the tape she had been forced to wind around his mouth. He must have realized the futility of fighting his bonds and fell silent, for which she was momentarily grateful. Her little girl would be fearful enough, without the sounds of her father's obvious distress in the background.

She sat on the edge of the bed and touched Jillian gently on the shoulder, bending to kiss the top of her head.

"Jillian. Honey, wake up. Sweetie, wake up." Sara rubbed her daughter's back softly, trying not to startle her, trembling with despair and swallowing her tears. She was beside herself with terror and cringed at the knowledge that she was unable to protect her child.

"Mom. I want to sleep. I'm tired." Jillian moaned and tried to turn over, pulling the blankets tight under her chin.

"Jill, you have to get up now." Sara pulled back the covers and stood next to the bed. She was powerless to stop the flow of tears as she looked down at her daughter and realized just how vulnerable her baby girl really was.

Jillian opened her eyes then, her vision still blurry from sleep, confused as she scrutinized her mother's face. Her mind slowly registered Sara's tears and the dried blood from the wound on her temple. Mingled together, they formed a ragged, rusty trail down her mother's cheeks. She sat up suddenly, reaching for Sara.

"What happened to you, Mom? How did you get hurt?" Jillian looked at her mother in shock, not able to comprehend what she saw.

"I'm okay, honey, just get up now. You have to get up and get ready to go."

Sara tried to block her daughter's view of the doorway. She wanted desperately that Jillian not be frightened by this madman with a gun.

"Let me help you get your things together. Do you have to use the bathroom?"

"Mom, what happened to you?" Jillian cried, reaching out to touch her mother's face.

"Stay where I can see you, Mom." Mullins bulk filled the doorway as he yelled his warning into the room and, for the first time since waking, Jillian realized they were not alone.

"Mommy." Jillian screamed at his sudden appearance, hiding her face in Sara's shoulder.

"Why is that doctor here? I thought Dr. Richards was coming to pick us up. Why is he up here in my room? Make him go away." Sara heard the hysteria building in Jillian's voice.

She stepped forward, pulling Jillian behind her as she did. "You are scaring her. Is that really necessary? We will do what you say, but she has to use the bathroom. Privately. I'll stay out here where you can see me and I'll get her things ready. But she has to go."

"Leave the door open. Little girl, don't try anything foolish or I will have to hurt your mom. Do you get it?"

Sara turned back to Jillian and cupped her chin in her hand.

"It's okay, Jill. He won't hurt you, I promise. You must do what he says. Go on now. Brush your teeth and get dressed. Please, sweetie, it's okay." Sara handed her daughter the clothes that were hanging on the back of the rocking chair.

Jillian watched Mullins out of the corner of her eye, as she reached for the clothes her mother handed her. Visibly shaken, she walked into the bathroom to get dressed.

"Hurry up. We don't have much time." Mullins looked at his watch. It was 8:09 a.m.

* * *

Marc reined in every ounce of self control he possessed, forcing himself to remain seated under the pretense that he was still shackled and defenseless. He heard the girls upstairs, their fear permeating the air, a cold heavy cloud that had settled over his entire being. He glanced at the doorway, where Stephen lay in wait, and prayed that a plan would present itself to one of them.

Marc closed his eyes, hoping to relieve the pressure in his throbbing head, but was instantly alert when he heard the madman and his precious hostages descend the front stairway. He shot a glance toward Stephen, who stood silent and still, just beyond the doorway.

"*Daddy? What is happening?*" Jillian cried out, frozen in place when she saw Marc.

"Never mind the theatrics, little girl. We are running out of time. Now go get another chair from the dining room for Mommy, and be quick about it."

Mullins sneered as he pushed Sara into the living room, never moving the gun from her head.

"Mom," her voice breaking, Jillian watched in shock and horror as Mullins shoved her mother into the room. She tried to understand what was happening to her family, her mind unwilling to absorb the harrowing scenario being played out in front of her.

Sara, forcing a reassuring smile, nodded to her.

"It's okay, baby. Do what he says. Everything will be okay. Just listen to him."

"We don't have much time. We must be ready for our next guest. *Now move*," Mullins ordered Jillian, through clenched teeth.

She backed out of the living room, turning only as she entered the hallway leading into the dining room. She pulled the heavy wooden chair from the table and was dragging it across the hardwood floor, when she looked up and saw Stephen, standing pressed against the wall outside the living room.

Jillian stopped suddenly, an audible gasp erupting involuntarily from her throat. Stephen recognized her panic, and holding up his hand, mouthed comforting words to her, motioning her into the living room with his head. *It's okay.*

"What's going on, little one?" Mullins started toward her.

"I dropped it, that's all. It's heavy. I'm coming." Jillian quickly recovered and dragged the chair into the room before Mullins had time to cross the threshold.

"That's a good girl. Now put the chair over there, facing your dad, but not close enough for them to touch." Mullins waved to the area of the living room where Marc was sitting.

Jillian moved the chair and Mullins pulled Sara over to it and forced her to sit.

"Take the rope on the sofa, Jillian, and tie your mother's ankles to the legs of the chair."

"Mommy, I...."

"*DO IT!*" Mullins spit the words at her and Sara reached out and touched her daughter's hair.

"It's okay, Jillian. Do what he tells you. You must listen carefully to me. He won't hurt you. He wants you and the baby to be safe, so he won't hurt you." Sara tried to soothe her daughter, wishing with all her heart that she could do something to stop this monster from going any further.

"Tie her hands. Then I want you to take that roll of tape, Jillian, and wind it around her mouth. I am watching every move you make, so if you don't want anything to happen to your parents, you'll do exactly as I say."

"You are the devil, you know. You think you have the power, but you're wrong. You can't hurt this baby because he is the promised child. The gift of hope. His name is Benjamin and he will lead the righteous to glory," said Jillian, her quivering voice charged with conviction as she tied the rope around Sara's wrists.

Jackson Mullins threw back his head and laughed.

"Is that right? Let me show you the real miracle, little girl." Mullins pulled the vial of amniotic fluid from his shirt pocket and held it up for her to see.

"Do you know what this is? No, of course not, how could you? This is a tiny bit of DNA. A little drop of amniotic liquid gold, taken from you and the little fetus you have swimming inside your womb. This, my dear, is the stuff the miracles are made of."

"That just looks like pee. You don't have anything. You know why? This is not yours to have. This is a child of God. That's where the miracles come from. Not from you."

Jackson held the vial, mesmerized by the fluid, dropping his arm slightly so that the gun pointed toward the floor.

"Well then, we shall just see what happens when I harvest the amniotic sac and your child before you deliver. Perhaps you don't have anything to do with this creation. You may be as expendable as your parents here. We shall see where the real science lies. Perhaps it is only the child that I need."

"You can take me. You can do whatever you want to me. But you won't ever have this child."

"You silly little girl. Do you people not realize that, if not me, the Government is in line right behind me? The Church, too, with all its pompous fools. Even my comrades in the Middle East are closely monitoring these events. Just imagine the supremacy to be attained by the one world power holding the key to the healings. No death on the battlefield. No needless carnage. Possibly eternal youth. Do you think I am the only one who will want this little bundle of joy when the truth comes out? We are talking about control of the universe."

"God will not let you win. You are the evil one. You are the Beast."

Jillian was taunting him now, moving around the room in such a way that he was forced to move with her, gradually standing with his back to the hallway door. Jackson put the vial back in his pocket and waved at Jillian with the gun.

"Get back over there and stand by your parents."

"I'm not afraid of you, mister. My protector will not let anything happen to me."

Stephen sprang, praying that Jillian had just sent him a signal. He knocked Mullins off balance, but not hard enough to disarm him. Mullins recovered quickly from the surprise attack, kicking at Stephen, the adrenaline pumping fiercely through his veins, lending him strength that belied his age. He refused to be stopped. He and Stephen fought for the gun, and then a loud *pop*, glass from the living room chandelier raining to the floor. The gun's retort was muted, and though it carried a silencer, sounded deadly. They struggled in a confused tangle of limbs. Stephen made a fist and punched at Mullin's ribs, while Mullins in turn grabbed a handful of Stephen's hair, yanking his head forward and trying to raise the weapon at the same time.

Jillian crossed the room within seconds as Stephen pounced, falling to the floor behind her mother's chair, and watched, breathless, as her father sprang to life. Toppling the heavy dining chair, Marc lunged toward Jackson Mullins, pulling the tape from his mouth as he made contact, a primal scream wrenched from the depths of his soul.

Fighting desperately for the gun, Marc and Stephen together tried to wrestle Mullins to the floor.

Jillian was panting, her slippery fingers working the flimsy knots from her mother's wrists, trying frantically to free Sara's hands quickly. Bending together, they labored to untie the thick knots from her ankles. Finally free, Sara ripped the tape from her mouth and grabbed Jillian by the hand, pulling her toward the front door and the safety of the Government agent parked in front of her home.

Another muted retort from the gun. *Pop.* Then total silence.

Sara's hand was on the knob, futilely pulling at the door. In her terror, she had unwittingly locked the door that Aunt Susie had unlocked just a few minutes earlier upon leaving the house.

"Do not move another step or I will kill your mother." Mullins was breathless, bent almost double, but his voice was unwavering as Sara and Jillian slowly turned back to the living room. Marc had fallen on his back, a dark red stain spreading across his chest, a crimson pool beneath him.

"*Daddy!*" Jillian screamed. Wrenching free of Sara's grasp, she ran across the room and knelt at her father's side.

"Look what you did to him!" Throwing herself across Marc's body, Jillian moaned, begging for help. "Arianna. Help us, Arianna."

The shock of the blast had sent Stephen crashing to the floor, his head making contact with the door jamb. He was on his knees now, dragging himself to Marc, whose body lay lifeless and pale in the middle of the room.

"Look what you've done, you monster. *You killed my daddy!*" Jillian was sobbing, her rage uncontained, her hands and face covered in her father's blood.

Mullins motioned to Stephen with the gun.

"Get away from him. Now. Who the hell are you?"

Stephen ignored him and glanced at Sara, who had fallen to her hands and knees and was crawling to Jillian's side. Oblivious to Mullins, she struggled to pull her daughter from her husband's chest. She ripped the buttons from Marc's shirt, exposing the gaping wound, and was trying desperately to find a pulse in his neck.

"*You bastard!* He's gone. *My husband is gone.*" Cradling her husband and daughter in her arms, Sara rocked back and forth, keening and sobbing in her sorrow.

Mullins motioned to Stephen with the gun. "Get over there behind them, where I can see you. It would be just as easy for me to kill you both right now, as it would be to tie you up, so you decide. I have no time left to play games." Mullins said.

Stephen bent to help Sara to her feet, his head bruised and swollen where he'd hit the corner of the door. Ignoring the pain, he placed his hands lightly around her shoulders, trying gently to separate her from Marc and Jillian.

"*Leave me alone!*" Sara screamed, yanking her arms from Stephen's grasp, turning once again to hold onto her family.

Mullins raised the gun, pointing it toward Sara's head.

"You give me no choice, Momma Bear." Mullins straightened, his back to the doorway, and facing the group huddled together on the floor, raised his arm to fire the gun. Stephen dove headlong into Sara and Jillian, pushing them away from Marc's body as he threw himself on top of Sara, knowing that Mullins would not harm Jillian or the baby. His outstretched body shielded her from the bullet's path. He braced himself for the impact of the shot and held his breath, begging God's forgiveness at his failure to successfully complete his mission. He closed his eyes and waited, hoping it would be over quickly, fervently praying that Jillian and the child would be safe.

What seemed an eternity was in truth only seconds. Stephen cast a backward glance toward Mullins, and caught the glimpse of a shadow crossing the threshold of the living room doorway. He heard a sickening thump, followed by a whoosh of exhaled air, as Mullin's body smashed to the floor, his chest landing across Marc's body, the gun skidding across the floor.

Stephen bolted for the gun, while a dazed and shocked Sara rose slowly to her knees, reaching once again for her daughter. Too numb with exhaustion and shock, she could do nothing more than follow Stephen's gaze with her eyes.

Standing in the doorway was Susie, the cast iron frying pan laying forgotten at her feet, as she tried to make sense of the carnage and havoc that had been wreaked upon her family.

Chapter Eighty Two

Julie hung up her phone and looked at her watch. Before she had time to dial the hospital, the blackberry rang in her hand.

"Dr. Richards here."

"Hi, it's Bev. Are you almost there?

"I'm glad you called. We ran into a detour about a mile from their house. I just tried calling the Macomb's to let them know I would be there closer to nine o'clock. No answer. I'm sure they are busy with last minute details."

"Okay. Just checking in. Barton is on the warpath. Mullins hasn't shown up yet this morning, and the Government researchers are trying to set up shop down in the Level III and IV labs. He wants copies of all Mullins' research to date. Do you, by any chance, have another number for him? I've tried all three of the numbers we have on file, and his pager. He was so mad yesterday when he left the meeting, that I have no doubt he is pouting to prove a point. Barton sent someone to his apartment this morning, but he'd already left."

"No, I don't have contact information for him and I don't want any, thank you. He is one big pain in the..."

"Gotcha. Okay, be careful. Let me know when you are on the way back to the hospital, so I can stop Barton from breathing down my neck. He is positive that Mullins knows more about this case than he is letting on, and I have to agree with him. I'll have him notify the agent on site that you'll be there shortly."

"Okay. Thanks, Bev."

"See you this afternoon. Be safe." Dr Castiglione ended the call.

Julie picked up her phone and tried once more to reach the Macomb's. The phone rang, unanswered. Oh, well. They had a right to some private time. She would be there soon enough.

Chapter Eighty Three

Get that bastard off my husband!" Sara sprang into action and ran back to Marc, pulling, tugging on Mullin's limp body, trying without success to move him.

"It's okay, Sara. Let me do it." Stephen stepped in and grabbed Mullins under the arms, dragging him over to the floor in front of the sofa, unceremoniously turning him onto his stomach and pulling his hands behind his back.

"Jillian, honey, hand me the rope over there." Stephen tried to distract her from her father's body.

"His precious vial broke. There's glass all over Marc." Sara knelt next to her husband and began to collect the fragments that had fallen on his chest. Her hysteria finally subsiding, she wept silently as she ministered to her husband's body.

"Doesn't anyone besides me think we should call the police?" Susie was still standing in the doorway, shock and confusion etched on her face.

Stephen finished binding Mullins and hurried to where Marc lay on the floor. He bent over him, putting his finger on his neck to feel for a pulse. He looked at Sara and shook his head slightly.

"Come over here, Susie. You need to sit down. I want you all to focus on what I say and keep an open mind about what I have to tell you. I know we've been through hell this morning, but once the police are involved, events will be set into motion and we will lose total control. Jillian has been talking to you about her dreams. I, too, have had dreams about her and about the child she carries. These prophecies started long before I came here and met you. I have been chosen by God to protect your daughter, Sara. You must let me take Jillian away, to a place she and the child will be safe from harm," Stephen whispered.

"Stephen, I am begging you, please stop talking this nonsense! How much more do you think we can bear? I have just lost my husband, Jillian's father. What are you trying to do to us? *I can't listen to any more of this right now!*" Sara pushed him away and gathered Jillian and Susie to her.

"Jillian is telling the truth about the baby and her dreams, and she is more involved in the miracles than any of us can even imagine. Her child is a gift to mankind and will lead us to the Promised Land where we shall glorify God, forever. The world as we know it, Sara, will be no more." The conviction in Stephen's voice intensified with each word.

"Even if that were not the case, even if you can't believe me, Mullins was right about everyone wanting her. Think of it. She holds the key to the miracles. Do you really think she and the baby she carries will be safe with the Government? The Church? God has mandated she be taken into hiding until the time of the baby's birth. I am to be her protector. " Stephen held out his hand to Jillian.

"He is the one Arianna told me about, Mom. She said I had to go with him and I would be safe. She said there would be a sign that we could trust him." Jillian looked at her father again, and then at Stephen. "Do you think this is the sign?"

Leaning against the armchair, Jillian began to cry in grief and anger and fear. Stephen lowered his hand, unsure how to answer or to comfort her.

"Now it's your turn to listen to me, Stephen Jacobs. Enough with all this stuff about the end of the world, and miracles and all that other baloney. Just look where it's gotten us. We should be marching right out that front door to that CIA guard, to make him come in here and take this Mullins character away. We need someone to see to my sister's husband. Don't you think they know how to protect us? That's what they are trained to do." Susie was trying to wipe tears from Sara's face, and finally pulled her sister's head against her shoulder. "Both of these girls have been trau-matized and need to be checked over. It's a wonder my little niece hasn't gone into labor."

Stephen could hardly disagree with Susie, and found himself wondering how the sun could have risen and the world go on as if none of this was hap-pening. It seemed impossible, but it was true, and he knew in his soul that he had to try to make them understand. *Gabriel, I need your help here.*

"Your husband and I are theologians, Sara. I'm not implying that he believed everything I am telling you is the truth, but his mind was open to the possibility that there is more to all that is happening. I promised him I would not take Jillian without his permission, and I intend to honor that promise by passing the decision to you, Sara."

"It's easy to settle then. I will not let you take my baby away. I don't even know you! I want you to get out of my house." Sara flew across the room, pushing at Stephen's chest, trying to move him toward the door.

"When Julie comes, we are leaving for the hospital with her, and then you will have to go away." Collapsing in a heap on the floor at his feet, Sara gave in to her overwhelming grief and confusion.

Jillian rose slowly, the blood suddenly draining from her face. Lifting her small hand, she pointed towards Marc. "*Daddy?*"

Stephen followed Jillian's finger and looked over to where Marc's body lay.

"Holy Father in Heaven. Sara, it's Marc, *he's moving!*" Stephen left Sara where she lay and hurried over, kneeling at his side.

"Marc, it's okay. We're here. Susie, can you bring some water please?" Stephen put his hand under Marc's head, and lifting him gently, held the bottle to his lips, letting just a drop of water wet his tongue.

"*Marc.*" Sara came to him, kissing his face and brushing his hair from his forehead. "Honey, we're here. We're getting help for you." She looked up at Stephen, and then back to Marc.

"No." Marc whispered. "No help. I'll be okay." He reached out for Jil-lian and she sank to her knees next to him and held his hand.

"Marc, try to listen to me. Please, let me take her now. It's our only chance to keep her safe."

He waited for Marc's reply, watching the family and knowing the moment had come…this was the chance he'd waited for. It all came down to these next moments.

"Marc, you scared the hell out of all of us." Susie stood above them, wringing her hands. "And by the way, Stephen, our friend over there, Mullins, he's coming around, too." Susie detected faint movement from Mullins, who was now squirming on the other side of the living room.

Marc looked up, trying to focus on Stephen's face. His throat was hoarse and dry, but he could speak.

"Stephen, Mullins was right about one thing. Everyone will want my daughter. How do I know I can trust your own intentions?" Marc tried to sit up, fighting against the dizziness that forced him back to the floor.

"Marc, you were gone. And only by the grace of God, fluid that came from your own grandson caused a mortal wound to heal before our eyes. You are alive and speaking to us. That is a miracle. That's the sign you begged for and all the more reason to praise God by honoring his word."

Stephen raked his fingers through his hair, wincing when he made contact with the battered flesh on his head. He caught Jillian's eye and she nodded, kissing her father's cheek and pushing herself to her feet.

"Mom and Dad, I have to go to the bathroom. I want to clean myself up. I'll be right back." She was still shaken as she climbed the stairs, her father's blood drying on her hands. She prayed for Arianna to help her carry out what she was certain lay ahead.

Chapter Eighty Four

Julie Richards walked up to the car by the curb, knocked on the dark glass and waited patiently as the guard rolled down his window and reached for her business card.

"Hi. Sorry we're late. It shouldn't take too long and we'll be on our way."

She turned and headed for the Macomb's front door, noticing that dragon leaf begonia, her favorite annual, was ripe with blooms and lined the front walk. She hated to uproot these people again and take them back to the sterile confines of the hospital. The truth was, she didn't like a lot of what was happening lately. So much of her practice was cause and effect, and that theory had quite effectively been tossed out the window, once the first miracle occurred. Of course, she was thrilled for the recipients of the miracles, but at what cost to the rest of the world?

She noticed that the curtains in the front windows were still pulled tight against the night. The Macomb's would probably keep things closed up as if they were going on vacation. *What a vacation.* She tried to imagine the planning that must go into leaving home for such an unknown period of time. Julie was quite sure every last houseplant of her own had shriveled up and died by now. Thank God, she had no pets. She wondered if the Macomb's did. Stepping onto the porch, she lifted her finger to push the bronze doorbell.

Chapter Eighty Five

The sound of the doorbell caught them all off guard. Susie took control, suddenly realizing she was the only one who had not been physically battered that morning.

"I'll get the door. It's probably that Dr. Richards, come to get you all. Thank God. You people better stay away from the door or you'll scare her half to death. All three of you look like death warmed over. No pun intended, Marc." She cast a glance over her shoulder at an unhappy Mullins, who Stephen had gagged and tethered to one of the dining room chairs.

Marc was sitting up now in the easy chair, slowly regaining strength, and Sara sat on the arm next to him, unwilling to leave his side. Occasionally, she forced him to take sips of water from a plastic bottle. Jillian was still upstairs and when they hollered up to check on her, she answered she was fine, but wanted to rest. They all agreed she could stay there until some kind of decision could be made.

Susie took one moment to gather her wits, then pulled the door open and met Julie Richards face to face.

"Come in, now. I'm Aunt Susie, Sara's older sister." Closing the door behind her, Susie turned the deadbolt into place. "It seems we can't be too careful this morning." She took Dr. Richards by the arm and steered her toward the living room.

"Before you go in there, I need to warn you that we've had quite a morning, so you'd best prepare yourself. I'm going to get you settled with the family and then I'll get coffee for you and Sara, but you need to sit down and let them fill you in. It's one doozy of a story. We have had another guest this morning. Uninvited. One of yours, I believe." Susie led Dr. Richards to the living room, her curiosity spiked, but nothing on earth could have prepared her for the scene that was waiting inside the door.

* * *

Mullins was straining against his bonds, mumbling against his muzzle in a murderous rage, his dignity beyond battered. It was all Julie could do not to go over and hit him on the head again when she heard the whole story. She opted for tranquilizing him, taking a syringe from her bag and unceremoniously jabbing it into his thigh. She figured it couldn't kill him, as he seemed to be drenched in the miraculous fluid he'd dubbed 'liquid gold.'

"Sara and Marc, I can't even begin to tell you how sorry I am that you had to go through this. But you all must agree we have to call the authorities. We can't sit here as if none of this happened." Julie picked up her purse, rummaging for her phone.

"Mullins will be prosecuted, I promise you, but it doesn't change the fact that we need to get you all into the hospital. If only for your own safety."

"It's not that simple, Julie." Marc said.

"Dr. Richards, please. I'd like to ask you to take a moment to hear me out." Stephen told her then about his dreams, about Jillian's dreams and how they were related to the miracles.

"Mr. Jacobs, surely you can't ask me to let you walk out the door with Jillian before the authorities are called? We are sitting here with a criminal, quite probably insane, who only moments ago, attempted to murder that girl's parents and kidnap her."

"There was no attempt. He succeeded. Murder, Dr. Richards. Dr. Macomb was without a pulse for longer than thirty minutes. His chest was blown wide open." Stephen gestured toward the blood that had pooled in the middle of the floor.

"He should have died from the large amount of blood he lost, yet he began to heal in a matter of minutes. Another miracle."

"As far as your story, well, I just can't process all that right now. It's true, these things are not able to be explained easily, but how do you propose to keep Jillian safe if you take her away? She wasn't even safe in her own home." Julie kept looking for her phone.

"I could ask you the same question." Stephen held out his arms to encompass the scene before them.

Marc hesitated before he spoke, unsure of how to proceed. Things were tumultuous enough. He did not want to offend their family doctor.

"Julie, how can we be sure the Government won't use what we have learned about Jillian's pregnancy to further their own self-interest? I am frightened to even consider the possibilities. I have to agree with Mullins and I'm loathe to agree with anything that bastard said. In retrospect though, I think he might be right. Who knows where this will lead." Marc was still trying to grasp what they had been through.

"I appreciate the trauma you have all experienced, and for that reason alone, I want you admitted. Jillian needs to be examined. Sara, you have a horrible looking wound on your temple. Mr. Jacobs, your head is bruised and swollen where you banged it when you fell, and you could very well have suffered a concussion. So could Mullins, from the look of that frying pan," Julie said.

Julie knew the family's emotions were on overdrive, but she had to get them to agree to come to the hospital with her. She shuddered to think of what almost happened at their house this morning. And right under the nose of the CIA. Well, the Government could deal with Mullins however they saw fit, because her concerns lay solely with this family.

Stephen faced Marc and Julie.

"Please, Marc. I'm begging. You must give me permission now to leave with Jillian. I understand your concerns, I really do. I promise to guard her and the child with my life. It is a grave responsibility, but this prophecy has been written by a power so much greater than us. We are committed to obey the will of God. I am not some random zealot standing on a street corner. Your own daughter will attest to that."

Stephen struggled with his desire to take Jillian without permission, but he knew it would be futile unless her parents agreed. They would be fugitives regardless, this much he knew.

"Stephen, stop! I need time to process this." Marc turned his head, refusing to meet Stephen's eyes. Although very confused, part of him knew there had to be truth to what Stephen said and he was terrified of that truth. He feared he would lose Jillian forever, no matter what he decided. His role as her sole protector was in jeopardy and he was unsure how to behave. "I just need time to think this through."

"Marc, there is no more time. If we don't act before she is imprisoned in that hospital, I don't know what will happen. We may never be able to get her out," Stephen said.

"Please, Mr. Jacobs, don't be melodramatic. She will not be in prison, nor held against her will." Julie stopped searching for her phone, realizing with a jolt that she must have left it in the car.

"Marc, please. Remember Jillian and the child. They are the ones who will lose in this." Stephen continued to beg relentlessly. He knew his chances were growing slim…his window of opportunity to save them was closing quickly.

"Stephen, you back off now. Marc has been through enough. We all have." Aunt Susie came in with the coffee tray and set it down on the sofa table with a clatter. "You aren't running off with our Jillian. It's just not right."

"Susie is right, Marc. Regardless of what has happened, we really don't know that much about him." Sara lifted the water once again to Marc's lips.

"It's nothing against you, Stephen, but you surely must understand how apprehensive we feel, in light of these circumstances. And we owe you our lives. You saved us this morning. We will never be able to repay you for that. Ever," she said.

"Stephen…," Marc began.

"Marc, you said if God sent a sign, you would reconsider. What more can you ask of him than your total recovery from death. Like Lazarus, you have literally risen from the grave. And we were all witness."

"Maybe I wasn't dead, Stephen. I have no memory of what happened after the gun went off."

"What of the wound, then? Even if you weren't dead, how do you explain the healing of the wound? You are making your decision out of fear, Marc."

Marc struggled to stand, but Sara pushed him back into the chair.

"*Fear?* Hell, yes, I'm afraid. How could I not be? No, Stephen. *No.* She is not leaving our sight and that is final. I am not letting you, or anyone else, take my daughter away. How do we really know the miracles have anything to do with God? Or Jillian?"

The helplessness Marc had felt this morning loomed large in his mind, his voice rising with each word until he was almost screaming in rage. He turned to Dr. Richards.

"Julie, let the driver know we'll be out to the car shortly. We are almost ready."

Julie rose to walk toward the door, thankful they were finally coming to their senses, but hesitated when she heard Jillian descending the stairs. The teenager was wearing a hooded sweatshirt and dragging her backpack behind her. It thumped heavily as she walked slowly down the steps.

Julie was immediately reminded of how dangerous this situation could have been for Jillian. She wanted to check her little patient from head to toe before they left the house. As Jillian reached the living room, she smiled at her parents. Standing in the doorway, she calmly removed the hood of her sweatshirt, revealing the soft white skin of her freshly shorn head.

With a collective gasp of shock, the adults looked at the smiling teen and tried to make sense of what she had done.

"Hi, honey. Are you okay?" Julie asked, reaching for her medical bag. "How are you feeling?"

"I'm not going with you to the hospital, Dr. Richards. Arianna has given me a sign. I am to leave with Stephen and this will help us blend into the crowd." Jillian ran her hand over her scalp and pulled the hood up before she entered the room, taking great care to avoid Mullins.

"Daddy, I know you are afraid for me, but this is God's will." Jillian knelt before her parents, reaching up to touch her mother's cheek.

"Mommy, you were so brave today, and I could feel how much love you have for me. But I must go with Stephen. He is telling the truth. He is my protector and will help me do this thing. We must cherish this life I carry. It has nothing to do with us and, at the same time, everything to do with us." Jillian went to Stephen and reached for his hand.

"*Jillian Grace, you get over here this instant!* You are talking nonsense, and look what you've done to your beautiful hair. I can't believe this." Sara started weeping again, lowering her face to her hands. "What has happened to our family?"

"Daddy, you asked for a sign. I think I can help you." Jillian let go of Stephen.

She walked over to her Aunt Susie, and taking both of her hands, looked into her eyes for a long moment before she spoke.

"Auntie, even now as we stand here, you bear a daughter. She will follow my son and write his story, and it will be called the new gospel. I will see you all at the gate of the New World, I promise. For whoever believes in the Lord, will be with him in eternity."

"Jillian Grace, that is not even funny. Do you realize how cruel you are being to your Aunt Susie, after all she has been through with us?" Marc stared at his daughter in disbelief. He could only imagine the pain and suffering Susie and Tommy had endured for so many years, trying unsuccessfully to conceive a child. And now in her fifties, those days behind her, it was unconscionable that his daughter could be so malicious and cruel to this woman they all loved.

"Now, Marc, you wait just a minute. I don't think she's trying to be mean," Susie touched Jillian's cheek. "I think she's still in shock. Dr. Richards, please. Go ahead now, and get the car ready." Susie held onto her niece, kissing her forehead.

"Now, I want you to listen to your old auntie. Your hair will grow back, but we need to get you settled and check up on this baby of yours. Mom and Dad really need to see a doctor, too. Just look at them…they're a mess. They won't go unless you do, so why don't we just get our stuff together and leave like we planned?" Susie let Jillian go and bent to pick up the backpack she left on the floor when she came into the room. "We can talk about all this other stuff after everyone gets checked over."

Stephen moved then, shaken when he remembered that long ago, the Blessed Mother's cousin Elizabeth was found to be with child in her old age. She had given birth to John the Baptist. Stephen moved closer to Susie.

"Wait, Dr. Richards. I know this sounds farfetched. But, Marc and Sara, if what Jillian is saying is true, and Aunt Susie is with child, would you consider that a concrete sign from God? Would you let her come with me then?"

"Stephen, can't you just..." Sara started to speak, but Stephen held up his hand.

"Please, Sara. Would you? If what Jillian says is true, would you believe and let us leave?"

"If Aunt Susie is *not* with child, Stephen, will you promise to stop? Will you just leave us to our family and go home, taking your talk of dreams and prophecy with you?" Sara replied.

"Yes. I will. I give you my word." Stephen turned to Dr. Richards.

"Is there a way to verify this here and now? Do you have the necessary tools in your bag?"

"Oh, dear Lord. This is ludicrous. Jillian, do you still have the pregnancy tests I sent home with you to monitor your HCG production?" Julie grabbed her medical bag and carried it over to the sofa.

"Yes, I'll go up to my room and get them." Jillian turned and ran up the steps, taking them two at a time.

"Aunt Susie, are you willing? I brought the Doppler to check the heartbeat on Jillian's baby, but I think we can put this to rest quickly if you just take the test." Dr. Richards said.

"Susie, you do not have to do this. I am so sorry." Marc looked at his sister-in-law, loving her like never before, when she reached for the test that Jillian held out to her.

"I might be fifty-five, but I remember very well how these work. Tommy and I should have bought stock in these things quite a few years ago, when we were trying to have a baby of our own. I'll do this, but do you two promise you will just forget all this nonsense when this test comes up negative? Do you promise?" Aunt Susie looked from Stephen to Jillian, and noticed they were holding tightly to each other's hand.

"We promise with all our hearts." Jillian answered for both of them.

Aunt Susie turned without a word and walked down the hallway, closing the door to the powder room behind her. Sara stayed next to Marc on the armchair, afraid to move lest she lose him again. Julie Richards looked at her watch, trying to decide how much longer Mullins would remain sedated. She noticed that she had been in the house now for at least forty-five minutes. She had to call the hospital soon or Barton would send in the artillery.

It seemed like forever, but they finally heard the door open in the hallway. Aunt Susie walked back into the room with the little white stick resting on her open palm. She walked over to Jillian and Stephen and embraced them, falling to her knees at their feet.

"Praise to God and believe in this New World they keep talking about. These children *are* surely blessed."

Sara jumped up from her seat next to Marc and rushed over to her sister, helping her rise from her knees.

"Susie, what on earth are you saying?" Sara asked.

Dr. Richards took the test strip from Susie's outstretched hand. In the middle of the result window was one word. Pregnant.

No one spoke as Dr. Richards led Susie to the sofa and helped her lay down, pushing aside her robe and placing the Doppler on her soft belly. The room was quiet except for muffled tears and the soft whoosh-whoosh of her baby's heartbeat. It filled the silent room like a prayer.

Chapter Eighty Six

Cami sat on the edge of the small sofa in Father Andrews study and watched as Stephen's colleague, Arshad Ahmed, walked over to the window for the third time in twenty minutes.

"Alright already, Arshad, have a seat." They'll be here as soon as they get here."

"Are you sure Stephen said this morning? It's already ten thirty and I have a meeting with the other fellows at two o'clock this afternoon. I can't be late. This is the first opportunity we've had to meet as a group since the so-called miracles started." He sulked, but walked over and sat across from Stephen's sister, sighing heavily.

"You won't be late. Anyway, you will be able to talk to Dr. Macomb yourself on the ride back to the hospital. From there it's just a hop, skip and jump to the campus on foot. You'll have it made once you get through the barricades." Cami picked up a magazine from the table and flipped through the pages.

She thought back to yesterday and Stephen's phone call to her. He hadn't given her many details, only that she was to meet with Arshad and walk to the church with him, timing it so they could be there early in the morning. If everything worked according to plan, they would be riding back to the hospital with the Macomb's in Stephen and Jillian's place.

Father Andrews had been waiting for them as they approached the back door this morning at eight o'clock.

"Good morning, Arshad. It is good to see you again, and you must be Camellia. Come in, come in. Stephen has shared so much about your family, I feel I know you. Arshad, I must thank you for escorting Cami to the church. Stephen was quite worried about her being out on these streets by herself in this climate of unrest. He was quite upset that he was detained and unable to meet her."

"Stephen is a good man. He would undoubtedly do the same for me if my sister were in a strange town. I have enjoyed knowing him and look forward to learning more of him as the school year progresses. *If* the year progresses, I should add. I am interested to hear your thoughts on these miracles, Father. I understand the Bishop is investigating on behalf of the Church."

"I will come to the campus next week and we will have a forum on that very subject. Now come in and have something to eat. Mrs. Murray has prepared cinnamon rolls and you must enjoy them. Our own little bit of heaven." Father Andrews walked them into the kitchen, taking the bag Cami quietly handed to him.

"Arshad, if you will excuse us for a few moments, I must speak to Miss Jacobs privately. Help yourself to more coffee and please, take your food into the study where you will be more comfortable. You can set up your laptop and work while you have breakfast. As soon as Dr. Macomb arrives, you will be taken directly back to the University. I know you have an important meeting to attend this afternoon." Father Andrews put his hand on Cami's back and guiding her to his office, closed the door.

He turned and looked at this little bit of a girl and was impressed with her fearlessness. She was so like her brother in her earnestness and conviction. He could see the determination burning in her eyes. He made the sign of the cross on her forehead and walked with her to the window.

"Stephen said that all you have to do is ride back with the Macomb's as far as the hospital. You are to get out of the car, just before they reach the last barricade, and go your separate ways. There is a slight curve at that point and the car will have to yield. You should be able to exit without the car behind you even realizing that you've gone. The CIA is not expecting anything out of the ordinary at this point, anyway. That should allow Stephen and the girl enough time to make it to your truck, unobserved. Four people come into the church, four people leave. That's all anyone needs to know."

"What of Arshad?" Cami asked.

"Stephen believes Arshad won't even realize he has been part of anything unusual until well after they have escaped, if ever. I will calm him down, should the time come when that becomes necessary. And Arshad will want to please Dr. Macomb. Believe me, the less known by everyone the better."

"I am so frightened, Father Andrews. My brother is heading into dangerous territory. The Government will not take the disappearance of the girl lightly. What if someone breaks their silence?" Cami's voice caught, as tears pooled and threatened to spill.

"When Stephen first came to me, child, I doubted his dreams. I questioned his sanity, if you must know the truth. So much has happened since that first meeting that simply cannot be explained away. We must believe this is God's plan. The truth is, we were never meant to know the hour or the day of the Lord's return. We can try to guess based on the book of Revelation. But St. John interpreted visions of events that were to take place thousands of years beyond his time. He described images of things he had never seen before. That in itself is amazing. That we are such an intimate part of these happenings humbles me. I pray that I may have courage should the time come for me to defend my own faith, and the life of the little virgin."

"My brother is a good man, Father Andrews. He will protect her and the child with his life."

"God will watch over them, Camellia. Never forget that. We should get back to our guest, child. I trust the keys to the truck and anything else you have left for your brother is in this bag?"

"Yes, Father. Everything is there. Cash, too. Tell him I love him. Please, tell him I love him."

She had been waiting patiently in the study with Stephen's associate since Father Andrews escorted her back. Arshad continued to work on his laptop, but was clearly becoming increasingly worried about returning to the campus in time for his meeting. Cami put the magazine back on the table and met Arshad's steady gaze.

"They'll be here soon, I promise."

At last, Father Andrews poked his head into the study, delivering the message that Arshad had been anxiously waiting to hear.

"Come along now, my children. The car is ready. We'll walk through the courtyard and around to meet the car in front of the church."

Arshad almost jumped from the chair, he was so on edge, and Camellia felt her heart in her throat as she realized she would not be this close to her brother again for a very long time. The tears that threatened to spill earlier, finally found a silent path down her cheeks.

Chapter Eighty Seven

As the Hummer snaked through the streets of Nashville toward the Cathedral, the four occupants sitting in the back did not speak. The interior of the car had been designed to carry officers and dignitaries, and for that reason, was configured in such a way as to ensure the privacy of confidential conversations in the passenger compartment. A thick bullet proof glass partitioned the driver's seat from the rear, and two bench seats in the back of the SUV faced each other, with a small table between, much like a booth in a restaurant. Many plans had been strategized and decisions finalized at that very table. But this group was silent, each lost in their own thoughts.

Stephen and Jillian sat in the first seat, backs to the driver, and Marc and Sara sat together on the opposite side of the table. Each couple held tight to their partner's hand, and no one dared speak of what was going to take place in a few short minutes.

Sara could not bring herself to look at Jillian. She didn't trust herself to speak. She looked out the window, watching people carry out their daily routine, as if her own heart was not breaking at the thought of letting her precious child go away from her. Marc, on the other hand, could not take his eyes from Jillian's face, at last willing to accept his daughter's role in the miracle that was unfolding before his eyes. That she was so calm and accepting, filled him with pride and love. He looked at the man sitting beside his little girl and finally believed, with every cell of his being, that Stephen had indeed been commissioned by the Almighty to carry out this prophecy. He was overcome and remorseful that it had taken him so long to see the truth.

Stephen held tight to Jillian's hand and Jillian to his. She sat with her eyes closed, her hood pulled tightly around her newly bald head. As he looked out the window, Stephen recognized at once how smart she had been. Scores of young men and women walked along the side of the road in search of a cure, a miracle of their own, their loss of hair a testament to the therapies undergone to fight the diseases that had racked their frail bodies. The two of them would blend in seamlessly, disappearing easily into the crowd.

One final turn and the Cathedral rose before them in its resplendent glory, majestic against the morning sky. Marc and Sara straightened in their seats, their grip on each other's hand tightening, offering a lifeline to one another. Sara's resolve was rapidly crumbling and she had to force herself not to throw her arms around her daughter and dig in her heels, begging her not to leave. It seemed the decision was no longer hers to make.

The driver slowed to a stop in front of the Cathedral, believing that they wished to be blessed by their pastor before they went back to the hospital. Marc reached across Sara and opened the door himself, motioning the driver to stay seated, to afford them privacy. He noticed that the Government car following them had remained a respectable distance behind, and Marc prayed the agent would be preoccupied and pay little attention to the departing occupants. The less anyone saw of Jillian and Stephen, the better. He hopped to the pavement and reached up for Sara's hand, as Stephen grabbed the heavy backpacks and turned for Jillian.

Marc looked into the Hummer.

"Wait here until I motion for you. Shall we…" He helped his wife out of the car.

Marc and Sara hurried toward the heavy wooden doors of the church and opened them quickly, as the National Guard held the surging crowd behind the barricades. People strained to see who was being allowed to breach the inner sanctum of the Cathedral, when normally the schedule allowing such visits was strictly adhered to. They threw prayer cards and rosaries, begging the couple to take them inside and place them before the altar. Marc and Sara kept their eyes straight ahead, not trusting themselves to look into the crowd. Marc held the doors open just enough to allow passage, motioning the young couple to follow suit.

Seeing that the way was clear, Jillian and Stephen hurried from the Hummer and into the Cathedral, following her parents into the vestibule. A bright shaft of sunlight was extinguished as the massive doors closed behind them, leaving them bathed in the subdued tranquil atmosphere of the church, the peaceful sound of water trickling into the baptismal font in the background.

As their eyes slowly adjusted to the interior of the dimly lit Cathedral, Father Andrews hurried forward, pausing only to lock the doors behind them. Taking Marc and Sara's hands in his, he nodded greetings to them and then turned to embrace Stephen.

"I have been worried about you, my son. I see you have at last found the way to follow the dictate of your dreams."

"It seems the messengers are relentless in their quest for the child and his mother," Stephen answered.

Father Andrews quickly blessed the group, then led them out of the vestibule and into the open sanctuary, his robes flowing behind him. He stopped only to genuflect in front of the altar then turned, bowing in front of Jillian.

"You are truly the blessed one, chosen by the Lord. I humbly ask you to remember me when the time comes for us to meet again."

"Okay, Father, you're freaking me out now," Jillian said.

They smiled at her youthfulness, no admonitions forthcoming from her parents. Jillian believed with all her being that everything Arianna told her was true, but she felt no different herself. To be called blessed seemed a sacrilege to her, when she felt so much like she always had. Besides, she really didn't have anything to do with what happened to her.

"I know I have a special job to do, but I'm just me, no bowing required," she said to the priest.

"Blessed you are my child, and the babe you carry. I pray I shall see you again in the New World." Father Andrews kissed her hand, then gathered the group around him.

"I will leave you to say your goodbyes privately. I'm sorry. This pains me, but you must be brief. I will gather your sister, Stephen, and a very impatient Arshad. You have only five minutes. Marc and Sara, we shall meet you at the car. God be with you all."

Jillian took off her sweatshirt and handed it to Father Andrews. He turned quickly and left the room, leaving them alone to offer comfort to each other. Jillian turned to her parents and smiled, trying to be brave. Marc reached for her, hugging her tightly, surprised at the intensity of the emotions threatening to overcome him.

"Daddy, I'm scared," she whispered to him, starting to cry then, knowing she would never see her parents like this again.

"Shhh, my sweet love. Don't cry, little one. Would you stay with us if I begged you not to leave? Would you come with us to the hospital? It's not too late to change your mind, Bean." Marc held her chin in his hand, looking deep into her eyes, but she shook her head.

Sara embraced them both, running her hands across Jillian's smooth head, her resolve collapsing then, great wrenching sobs of anguish, too deep for words.

"I don't know how to live with this, my baby girl," Sara said.

"Jill, it's time." Stephen stepped in, gently separated them, his own grief and worry a tight ache in his throat. He turned to Marc and Sara and bowed his head.

"I commit to you here and now, my deep love for your daughter and the child she carries. I know we will meet again in the New World. As it has been written."

"Oh, brother." Jillian rolled her eyes at Stephen, trying to smile through her tears. "I will see you both again, I promise."

Jillian reluctantly backed away from her parents and crossed the aisle to stand beside Stephen. As they came together at the altar in the vast Cathedral, Stephen pulled her small form tight to his chest, where she could feel his strong heartbeat against her cheek. They watched together as her parents walked away, each step echoing loudly on the marble floor, a breach against the profound silence of the Cathedral's canopy. When they reached the vestibule, her father turned once more to look at them, standing small and united at the front of the church. He nodded to them, and holding his bereft wife close to his side, they slipped through the open door and disappeared from view.

Mommy. Daddy! Jillian longed to run after them, ached to scream for them, but in truth she made no sound at all.

Stephen bent and kissed her forehead, then led her to the confessional where he found Cami's bag, left for him by Father Andrews. Stephen picked it up and adjusted both their backpacks as he opened the secret panel and they disappeared into the dark, making their way slowly down the steps that led to the catacombs.

The afternoon sun was breaking through the stained glass of the vast empty Cathedral, sending its rainbow prisms to shine on the statuary that lined the sanctuary's stately walls. There was no one to see the lone tear that fell from the statue of the Madonna, a bed of candles blazing at her cold marble feet. No one to see the tear fall from her eye and extinguish a candle, sending black waxy smoke spiraling up and away, melding into the rich incense of the air, as if it had never been there at all.

Chapter Eighty Eight

The ambulance pulled out of the driveway with Mullins stowed safely in back, handcuffed to the gurney. Julie Richards went back to the Macomb's living room. She had only been seated for a moment when she and Aunt Susie heard the squeal of tires, followed immediately by the screech of brakes, as a car swerved into the driveway and skidded to a stop just beyond the pathway to the front door. They heard the car door slam and Julie looked up at Susie.

"The cavalry has arrived. This isn't going to be pretty, so hold on to your bonnet."

"I imagine I've seen worse already today," Susie answered.

Daniel Barker shoved his way past the police officer and slammed the front door as he barged into the room and confronted Julie.

"What the hell happened here?"

"Whoa there, calm down, Sherlock. It seems Dr. Mullins paid an uninvited visit to the Macomb's this morning, trying to kidnap Jillian and intent on doing harm if need be, to carry out his threat. Marc and Sara are on their way back to the hospital as we speak."

"With a small detour, as I understand it." Barker was furious and didn't try to disguise it. This case was imploding on his watch. He tried to pinpoint the exact moment things had gotten so out of control.

"Why was Mullins here, and why would he take the girl when she was about to be admitted to his hospital? Did he say anything about that? I know he was pissed about sharing his research with Dr. Sabot and the guys from the Government lab, but why risk his career, and certainly imprisonment on a federal offense?"

"Dr. Mullins obviously thought he could get away with this. His research was important to him, the proverbial brass ring, and he saw it as a way of attaining fame and fortune. And power. Perhaps he thought he would lose control if all his patients were at your beck and call."

"Maybe, but I'm not buying that. There is something else going on here and as soon as that bastard comes to, I'll get to the bottom of it." Finally calming down long enough to notice Susie sitting on the edge of the sofa, Barker paused for the first time.

"Ma'am, were you here during the entire episode?" Barker looked around the room, noticing that the blood from Marc's body had created a stain where it had soaked into the rug.

"Yes, sir, I was here for a lot of it. I already told the police officer what happened as far as I could. I came in after everything had already started. I bopped him one, I did." Susie pointed to the pan laying on the floor, already bagged for evidence.

"Listen, Daniel, can I talk to you privately for a minute?" Julie kissed Susie on the cheek, whispering as she did, "You relax. Everything will be fine, I promise."

Julie walked out to the front yard, Daniel close behind. She noticed the crime scene tape that surrounded the yard, and watched as the technicians finished taking pictures of the fence behind the garage. Sensing that Barker had stopped behind her, she whirled around to face him.

"That woman is exhausted and probably saved everyone's life this morning, so take it easy on her."

"Take it easy? Do you have any idea what is happening down at headquarters? You had the audacity to allow these people do a little sightseeing on their way to the hospital?" Barker took out a pack of cigarettes and lit one, inhaling deeply. He turned around abruptly, standing face to face with Julie Richards.

Taking a deep breath, Julie tried to compose herself before attempting to answer him in a civil manner.

"One, I don't really care what is happening down at headquarters, and maybe you shouldn't either. Maybe you should have been a little more worried about what was happening under the nose of one of your own agents. Two, these people deserve some comfort right now, wherever they can get it. If they need to visit their own parish priest before we throw them into seclusion, they have a right to that much, at the very least. I take it they are not under arrest? And three, everyone will cooperate with you, but don't come bullying your way in here like this is an episode of CSI, and expect us to jump when you say jump. With the exception of one lunatic, who is now on his way to the hospital in your custody, we all want the same thing." Julie prayed the thudding of her heart would not give away her participation in the latest events of the morning.

Barker threw the cigarette on the grass and stamped the smoldering butt with the heel of his shoe.

"Listen, the truth is, we screwed up and I owe the Macomb's an apology. Mullins was operating under the radar. We never expected this, never expected danger to come at them from the inside. We'll question everyone, carefully and considerately, and we'll get to the bottom of the whole thing. We won't resort to torture, I promise. Truce?" Barker held out his hand and Julie took it, fighting a sudden wave of nausea as she reminded herself of the new role she had just taken on. Accomplice.

"I'm going to go talk to the officers who arrived first on the scene, and then I'm going back to the hospital command post. I think they've just about wrapped up the investigation here, and as soon as the photographers are finished, the aunt can do whatever she wants to in there. I want to be at the hospital when Mullins comes to." Barker wrote something on the back of his business card and handed it to Julie. "My cell. Call me when you get back to the hospital."

Julie took the card and turned back to the house without a word.

"So, did you give him a piece of your mind?" Susie stood in the dining room doorway, the phone to her ear.

"Sort of. You better sit down and rest for awhile. All of the excitement can't have been very good for you this morning."

"Are you kidding me? I couldn't rest now if I tried. I have Tommy on the phone, or at least I'm trying to reach him. I'm going to have him come here to stay with me. I'm not sure what, when or where everything is going to happen, but I know he's going to want us to be together. I think I'll wait until I have him here to tell him the news." Susie patted her tummy under her robe. When he answered the phone, she motioned goodbye and walked into the kitchen.

Julie went to the sofa and gathered the strewn contents of her medical bag. As she picked up the Doppler and folded it back into the case, she saw the pregnancy test poking out from between the cushions on the couch. Holding it to her heart, she sank to the edge of the sofa and let herself cry.

As a physician, she had never questioned the power of God nor his ability to perform miracles. She saw it every day in her practice. Even the patients who didn't survive, who died and moved on, were a part of the natural cycle of the earth and the life God created for us here. She'd witnessed so much in her practice that had astonished her and filled her with respect for the Creator. She never understood how anyone could doubt his existence. The complexity of the human body alone was enough to astound. What she had witnessed here this morning had changed her forever.

Julie straightened, wiping her eyes, exhausted but relieved to finally find release for the morning's emotions. She regained her composure as she closed her bag and walked toward the kitchen to say goodbye to Susie. Julie had sworn that she would tell no one of her pregnancy, lest the Government decide that she, too, must be hospitalized for observation. Susie and Tommy deserved this time alone, to savor the miraculous answer to their many years of prayers. Strangely enough, Julie knew that this pregnancy would be a normal healthy one, and the precautions she would normally take for a high risk pregnancy due to advanced maternal age, would not be necessary here. When Tommy arrived, she would spirit them both to her office under cover of darkness, to ultrasound the fetus for them, to determine the gestational age and to make it more real. She somehow knew that Jillian was right…it would be a baby girl.

Susie met her in the hallway, a smile softening her face and reaching her eyes with its magic.

"Tommy is coming. I had to fill him in on what happened here this morning, in case we make the news tonight, but he promised to keep it under wraps. He should be here sometime tomorrow. It's hard to believe I've been here less than a week and look how our lives have changed."

"I'm happy for you, Susie. You were very brave today, you know. I see where your niece gets her strength. I'm not sure I would have been able to act so selflessly."

"Yes, you would, honey. If it was helping the people you love, you wouldn't even think twice about it. Look what you are doing for our family right now." Susie pulled her robe tight around her. "I think I am going to go up and shower when you've gone, and maybe try to take a nap."

"The CIA said they are keeping two agents and a car here to watch the house until further notice. This time, they'll be patrolling constantly. I'll be glad when Tommy gets here and you aren't alone. Are you sure you'll be okay?" Julie stepped over the stain on the rug, shivering.

"I'll be fine. I need some time to meditate, anyway. I have some serious praying to do."

"Okay. I'm going to get one of those guys to help me roll up this rug before I go, and we'll put it in the garage. I think I got most of the glass cleaned up with the vacuum, but don't walk barefoot in here, just to be sure."

Julie returned with an agent trailing close behind her, and together they carried the bloodstained carpet out the front door. She hugged Susie and made her promise to get some rest, waiting on the porch until she heard the deadbolt slide firmly into place. She was on her way to the police car for a ride back to the hospital, when an agent ran up to the Captain in charge of the crime scene.

Julie's phone rang in her purse. She had managed to snatch it from the Hummer, before the Macomb's left. She rummaged blindly until she held the phone in her hand. It was Daniel Barker.

"Where are you?" he growled into the phone.

Julie answered him, her eyes never leaving the agent, who was urgently relaying a message to the Captain.

"I am getting into the police car as we speak and heading back to the hospital. What's wrong?"

"I'll tell you what's wrong. The Macomb's just arrived at the hospital and guess what? No Jillian. We seem to have a run-away on our hands."

"Oh, my God! I'm on my way."

"And that's not all. We found Mullins' car on the next block with some very interesting evidence in the back seat. It looks like Mullins was planning to keep the girl sequestered in a rental house he recently acquired. At least for the short term. He hired some illegals to stand guard and they have been singing like canaries. It looks like he also made some connections with someone in the Middle East about a serum he was developing."

"I can't believe it. Thank God, you have him in custody."

"Yeah, and from what we have been able to piece together so far, Jillian Macomb is more intricately involved in the miracles that we ever could have imagined. In fact, according to Mullins, she may well be the source. We will do whatever it takes to find that girl, Dr. Richards."

Julie closed her phone and dropped it into her purse, while the police officer reached out and opened her door. As she bent to enter the squad car, she smiled and offered a silent prayer of thanks. They made it out.

The door closed behind her and she leaned her head back on the seat. Were they any better than Mullins and his selfish quest for power...all of them hoping to prosper through the innocence of a child?

She couldn't help noticing the perseverance in the faces of the hopeful who lined the side of the road as they drove slowly by. On this late summer afternoon, how amazing it was to realize that in our quest for faith, we are all so much alike, the healthy and the infirm, the troubled and the free. All of us are moving purposefully toward our ultimate destinations and believing in something just beyond our reach...beyond our sight. Hope.

Chapter Eighty Nine

Phillip! Phillip, where are you?" Bishop Tomlin bellowed, slamming the kitchen door to the rectory and throwing his briefcase on the table.

Father Andrews heard him from the study and crossed himself quickly, before he rose and made his way into the kitchen to meet his unruly guest.

"What is it, Charles, for goodness sake. You'll wake the dead with all your bluster."

"Never mind all that. Did you see the Macomb girl this afternoon? I understand the family paid you a visit on their way to the hospital." Bishop Tomlin ripped off a paper towel and wiped the sweat from his forehead, at the same time loosening the collar of his cassock.

"For heaven's sake, Charles, let me get you something cold to drink before you pass out." Father Andrews opened the refrigerator and handed the Bishop a bottle of water.

"Answer me, Phillip. I am not in the mood for word games with you. Did you see them this afternoon? The CIA is going to be here shortly to quiz you, so you better think about everything that transpired. I cannot believe the child is missing." Tomlin swiped the cold bottle across his brow and looked expectantly at the priest.

"I am shocked, Charles. You say she is missing? I only saw them for a short time, to offer a blessing if you will, before they entered the hospital.

What happened?" Father Andrews was trying hard to remain calm. The CIA. *This could get tricky.*

"Evidently, somewhere between here and the hospital, the girl and a young man disappeared from the vehicle without a trace, and the parents are not talking." Bishop Tomlin leaned against the counter.

"Well, Charles, surely there can be no problem if the girl and her parents agreed to this. It sounds as if they are only trying to protect her if they won't talk about her whereabouts. She is not in trouble, I take it?" Fr. Andrew's heart was hammering in his chest. *Calm down, Phillip, old boy. This is only the beginning of your walk through the fire. God will guide you.*

"That is the least of it. An attempt was made on the life of Dr. and Mrs. Macomb this morning and the girl was almost kidnapped. So you see, Phillip, the authorities won't rest until they have her. They think that she is the first miracle. They call her the second Madonna. The second Virgin. And it turns out that the child she carries is the cause of the miracles. Make no mistake, Phillip. They will move heaven and earth to get her back." Bishop Tomlin eyed the old priest closely.

"Well, the family was understandably upset this morning, but that's to be expected with everything that has been going on lately. Not to mention that they must now face a return to the hospital. I'm sure they will lead the CIA right to her, as soon as they feel certain their child will be safe. They made no mention to me of a disturbance this morning, although Mrs. Macomb did have a nasty bruise on her temple. I never thought to question her about it because they were in such a hurry."

"You have no idea, Phillip, how they managed to arrive at the hospital without their daughter?" Bishop Tomlin pressed.

"I'm sure if I knew where the girl was, I would tell you. What have you discovered during your investigation of the miracles, Charles?" Father Andrews asked, perspiration forming on his brow.

"We need the girl, Phillip. I believe she holds the key. From everything I have been able to gather, she is both the beginning and the end of the phenomena. I think we may be witness to something greater than anything we will ever see again in the lifetime of this world. I truly believe this is authentic, Phillip. And I intend to be there, front and center, with the proof. So, if you happen to *remember* anything of importance, it would be in your best interest to deliver the information to me firsthand. I will be waiting." Bishop Tomlin turned and stalked out of the kitchen, slamming the door to his room.

Father Andrews made his way back to the sanctuary and knelt in the pew closest to the altar. He reached into his robes and withdrew the document, taking care to unroll it cautiously, knowing in his heart that this would be part of the new covenant, and he was charged as custodian of these holy words. He read the words again, committing them to memory, then ran his fingers across the signatures at the bottom of the page. He knew that the eyes of civil law did not matter here, but in the eyes of God, the fulfillment of a prophecy had just taken place.

He rolled the parchment carefully and knelt before the statue of the Madonna, who cradled the infant Jesus in her arms. He lit the candle at her feet, offering a prayer of hope for the continued protection of the new family. Rising to his feet, he placed the parchment in a gold cylinder and carefully reached around the back of the Lady and Child, sliding the slender tube into the small hollowed crevice behind her, so that it fell gently into the niche in the catacombs below.

He had not moved an inch, when a great shock of sunlight blazed through the stained glass window. Shimmering crystals of pure color danced around the marble statue, capturing him in a spectrum of magnificent light. He bowed his head, sure of Our Lady's blessing, and more certain than ever that this was the way of the Lord.

He closed his eyes and let himself reflect on the morning. The soft light of the candles had illuminated the stone walls of the catacombs beneath the Cathedral, as Stephen and Jillian bent to offer their names to the parchment, a single tear falling to the paper she held in her hand. He could still hear the whisper of their hushed vows as they knelt before him for one final blessing, before they ran through the tunnel and disappeared from his sight.

When they had gone, he rolled the parchment securely, the importance of this afternoon burned into his memory for all eternity.

The Holy Marriage of

Stephen Daniel Jacobs and Jillian Grace Macomb

Blessed

Before the Eyes of God the Almighty

On this First Day of July in the Holy Year of Our Lord

Two Thousand and Eighteen

The Promise of a New and Eternal Covenant

Is Realized

The Beginning of the New World

Paradise.

It is written.

Chapter Ninety
December 2018

J illian, move away from the window." Stephen quickly crossed the room.

Gently reaching in front of her, he lowered the shades and pulled the curtains back in place, careful to keep the least bit of light from escaping into the night beyond the windows. He turned to face her and looked into her eyes for a long silent moment, then returned to the task at hand. He knew she could hear him rummaging through their belongings, her apprehension slowly seeping into his own soul.

Out the corner of his eye, he watched as she pulled the sweater tight around her swollen frame, as if shielding herself against an invisible enemy. With an increased sense of urgency, the consequences of leaving the safety of their shelter filled him with dread. They had been hiding for almost five months, and the thought of exposing her to danger again, forcing her to abandon the security she clung to so readily in this place, weighed heavily on him. He remembered the menacing sound of the helicopters searching for them as they escaped, and the relief he felt when they finally slipped into these woods.

"No one could possibly have a clue about this cabin. I can't see three feet in front of the door, it's so overgrown. Do you really think we could be discovered after so many months, if they haven't stumbled on us so far? I don't want to leave now, anyway. I've gotten used to it here," Jillian said.

Stephen dropped the bag he was packing. He did not trust himself to look at her.

"Jillian Grace, I know you are afraid," he said quietly.

"Where would we go, Stephen? And what about junior, here? It's almost time for the baby. I can feel it," she said. "Do you really want to go traipsing through the woods with a baby tied to your back?"

He heard the shallowness of her breath, knew very well by now the sound of panic building in her voice. Without a doubt, until these last few days, they had both pushed away thoughts of the inevitable delivery of the baby.

Stephen put his hand in the air as if he could somehow physically block her words.

"Jillian, stop. Try to stay calm. Who knows what tomorrow will bring, little one? We must stay the course and wait."

"I know all that. I just want you to come over and sit with me. Tell me it will be okay."

"I will, in just a little while. You know the time is approaching when we will have to leave this place. The dreams are starting again. More vivid, more clear. We have to go back."

"Go back! Are you crazy, mister?" Jillian ran to him then, grabbing his wrist and forcing him to look at her.

"Stephen, look at me! Have you lost your mind? They might still be looking for us, and if they are, what will happen if we go back? What happens if we aren't so lucky this time? Would we be walking right back into the same mess we ran away from? I need my mom." Jillian started to cry.

He pulled her gently to him, the power of his love for her a crushing weight in his chest. His role as protector filled him with anxious worry like nothing he'd felt before, and he didn't know how he could ever prepare her for the imminent struggle they faced in the days ahead. He had never meant to fall in love with her, his wife. He knew that just as with everything else that had happened, it was beyond his control.

"I thought we would be able to stay here for a while after the birth, but..." he said, leaving the unspoken words hanging in the air between them.

"Do you have any idea where we will go, Stephen? What if they've taken my parents away? How will we keep Benjamin safe?" asked Jillian.

"Gabriel will lead us, Jillian. Benjamin is the Lord's child. We have to trust."

"Stephen, you know I trust you. I do trust you, but I'm afraid for him. I don't know much about taking care of a baby. And leaving here on top of that? How can we promise to keep him safe when they are still looking for him?" Jillian clutched Stephen's hand tightly, the wind outside the cabin steadily growing stronger.

"I need you to go now and do whatever you need to do, so you are as comfortable as you can be for the next few hours. I just want to get things ready, so when the time comes we can move quickly."

"You know I'm not trying to be difficult here, but really, Stephen," Jillian cupped her hands beneath her belly. "Comfortable?" she said, attempting to smile. "Comfortable? Really?"

The reality of the return trip through the dark woods which had once promised them safety and life, now filled them both with a sense of impending doom. Jillian looked back at him with sadness, tears threatening to fall again.

Their universe had grown smaller than the head of a pin in this forest. Stephen listened as the winter wind grew fierce, jolting him back to the present.

"I think there's a storm brewing, Jillian. I don't like the sound of that wind. I think we may be in for a blizzard." Glancing quickly at her belly, he was almost overcome with the huge responsibility that had been thrust upon him.

"Listen, Jill. This is all part of the plan. I believe that. I have faith in that and so should you."

He felt the tension of the storm mounting, and his nerves were stretched past the breaking point. It took every ounce of effort he possessed to remain outwardly calm for her sake. He had been so careful not to share the entire dream with her, giving her only bits and pieces so as not to frighten her more than she already was.

The growing turmoil in the world following their disappearance had been well documented in the newspapers he was able to get his hands on when he dared to venture out alone, under cover of darkness. The world they had known when they left had changed drastically, world power struggling against world power, in rapidly escalating unrest.

Gabriel had come to him with the final vision, leaving Stephen shaken to the core. He had always wanted to believe that the birth of this child would lead them to the end of their journey, but Gabriel made it clear that it was only beginning.

Stephen kissed her forehead and walked her over to the rocker, tucking the quilt around her legs and pulling a stool under her feet.

"I'll be finished in a few minutes, Jill. Why don't you try to read for awhile?"

Jillian took the book he offered and opened it, pretending to read. He didn't realize she watched him as he worked, his familiar movements a fascinating comfort to her. After a while she dozed, warmth from the small fire lulling her to sleep. The heavens opened and a blizzard raged outside the little cabin…hail, sleet and snow slamming against its sturdy walls. Thunder and lightning pierced the sky, as the freakish storm grew more fierce and dangerous by the second.

She drifted in and out of her dreams, until the bright light that was Arianna came and gently lifted her hand.

"Arianna, I thought you had forgotten about me," Jillian said.

"I will never leave you, my child. I have always been here, waiting with you."

"Stephen says we have to leave soon, and I'm afraid. What will happen to us, Arianna? What about the baby?"

"You will follow the star path, Jillian, and trust Stephen. The gates of the New World will open for you, and when the time comes, you will enter the Garden as a family. Rejoice, sweet Jillian. Your time has come. The angels of the Lord are coming to greet the child. They will help you find your way."

Arianna's essence grew dim and Jillian knew she was leaving.

"Arianna, wait! I want to ask you something before you go," Jillian cried out.

Once again, Arianna's face filled her dream.

"What is it, my sweet child?"

"I love him, Arianna. I want to be with him as my husband. Is that wrong?" Jillian whispered.

"In the eyes of the Lord, from the moment you accepted his protection you have been one with him, Jillian. When you reach the Garden, your union shall be fulfilled, the prophecies complete. Now you must try to rest. There is much to be done." Arianna disappeared, slowly fading from her dreams.

The storm continued to rage outside the cabin walls, growing in intensity. Stephen pulled aside the curtain and tried to see, but the snow obliterated everything in its path, swirling and drifting, threatening to imprison them. He hung the kettle on the fireplace, looking over his shoulder at Jillian, sleeping peacefully in the chair.

He could feel air seeping through the planks that made up the walls, while outside the little cabin the wind howled, threatening and cold. A clap of thunder exploded, shaking the foundation of their nest.

"*Stephen!*" Jillian screamed, bringing Stephen running to her side.

"I'm here, Jill, I'm here. It was only the thunder, honey. It's okay." He tried to comfort her, talking quietly, soothingly.

"No, Stephen, it's something more. It's time. It's time for the baby. Stephen, I'm scared."

He knelt before her, and studied her face as she struggled not to cry out.

"Are you in much pain?"

"I think my water broke, Stephen, and I have cramps. My back is hurting, aching."

"Okay. Let's get you into the bedroom so you can lie down. We have to change your clothes Jillian, so you don't get cold," Stephen said.

He helped her to the pallet and tried to make her as comfortable as he could.

* * *

Hours later, he lay beside her, his hands stiff from rubbing the small of her back as he tried desperately to ease her obvious discomfort. He was only vaguely aware of the storm. He could hear the howling wind and pellets of ice as they hit the wall of the cabin, but he was much less concerned with what happened outside, than with the impending birth of the baby.

"Stephen, it hurts. Please…I can't do this, Stephen. I want my mom." Jillian thrashed on the pallet, pushing him away.

He felt her belly tense with each contraction, and knew they were getting stronger and closer together. He held a cup of water to her lips, and tried to keep a cool cloth pressed against her forehead.

"Stephen, I have to throw up." He held the basin under her chin, much like he had on the night they arrived.

"Jill, you are doing great. You are doing fine, my love."

"I have to push now. I'm so scared, Stephen. *It hurts.* It burns. *I can't do this.*" Jillian raised herself onto her elbows, and Stephen quickly pushed pillows behind her back to support her as she strained to push.

"Jillian, I am going to see if I can feel his head, honey. Let me check you."

"Ooohhh! Stephen. I can feel him coming. *Mommy! I can't do this. Help me.*" Jillian was sobbing in pain and terror.

The wind intensified, the thunder was now one long crescendo of terrifying sound. The winter lightning, a phenomenon in its own right, seemed to hang suspended in the night sky, growing brighter and stronger, filling the tiny cabin with its light. The night sky was filled with a cascading waterfall of bright stars, originating from one larger star above, the brightest of them all.

The whole world seemed to stand still then, all eyes rose to the heavens to behold this most wondrous sight.

"Stephen, what's happening? Why is the light here?" Jillian said, grimacing through her pain.

"Can you see them, Stephen? Look, there in the corner. Can you see them, too?" Jillian strained to comprehend the vision before her, pain racking her tiny frame. A man and woman stood together silently, keeping vigil with a smile. She recognized Arianna and Gabriel standing with them, and knew instinctively that they were good.

Stephen raised his eyes then, and saw them, too, his throat closing with the wonder of the vision and the emotions that passed through him at that moment. Was it really the most Holy Mary and Joseph standing there, watching over this most blessed birth? The covenant that had begun with their Son, was being born again in flesh for all, the promise of eternity.

The wind grew still, giving way to the sound of angels. Jillian could hear them…their singing filled the air with love.

"*Stephen! Now!*" She raised herself then, and pushed as one with the force of nature, intent now on delivering her son into his Father's world.

Stephen lifted his head and looked into her eyes, both of them overcome, as the child spilled from her body to fill his outstretched hands.

At that precise moment, the storm and the glorious sounds of the angels faded, giving way to a complete and profound silence. The peaceful stillness reached far and wide, touching every corner of the earth.

As light from the stars filled the skies above the cabin with a heavenly glow, Stephen bowed his head… thankful for all that had led them here, to this moment in time.

He raised the tiny child toward the heavens and the baby boy drew a hearty breath, filling the peaceful silence that had fallen upon the earth with his first cry.

Epilogue

B eginning on the 'night of many stars,' as that night had come to be called, they arrived one by one, from near and far, and Father Andrews took them in, asking no questions as they told him of their dreams. They came from all walks of life and every known religious persuasion, and as he came to know through his own dreams, this was the way of the Lord our God. There was no one true form of worship. Only one true God, who was to be praised above all others with love and trust, and with faith as strong as a child's pure hope.

They gathered now, to wait for the child Benjamin to come home. Father Andrews knew by then, that the end of the world was near. He opened the door to the catacombs, and led each of the faithful down the stone steps as soon as they arrived, stopping only long enough to offer blessings and help to those who were in need.

He nodded as he passed Sara and Marc, who were keeping vigil in a grotto with Stephen's mother and the rest of his family, who had arrived only this morning. They waited in prayer for their children to come home. Johnny Boone and his mother were helping people get settled. They ministered to anyone who needed comfort and aid, no complaints from anyone now, as the dreams foretold clearly for them, the promise that was soon to unfold.

In the months that followed the disappearance of the girl and her miracle baby, the final apocalyptic war of the world had begun.

Disease and famine plagued the land in record time. Volcanoes erupted, floods washed over the earth and the fury of the wind could be felt throughout every nation. Many of God's faithful, as well as the followers of the Beast, suffered cruel and hard and untimely deaths. All Governments operated as police states now, enforcing strict curfews and stern and unforgiving punishments. Only by the grace of God had the catacombs remained a safe haven for God's chosen few.

Julie Richards had come to see him soon after Susie secretly gave birth to the baby girl they named Hannah. Father Andrews offered them shelter the moment he heard the child had been born. For these last months, all newborns were taken from their parents and put through rigorous testing, not reunited with their families, until it was proven beyond all doubt that they were not the miracle baby. Some of the more fragile infants did not survive the rigors of such testing. Those in charge considered this to be a necessary risk.

Hannah was born four weeks before the 'night of many stars,' and she was a strong, beautiful child who filled her doting parent's eyes with joy. Father Andrews was finally able to convince Julie Richards to believe in the power of her own dreams, and so she stayed with them, attending to the needs of the many people waiting patiently with her.

Bishop Tomlin had decided to move into Bradford University Hospital to be close to the 'pulse' as he called it, that he might reap whatever rewards his research into the miracles brought forth. Perhaps a promotion to Cardinal would be forthcoming. Father Andrews waited for him to come back to the Cathedral, but he never returned. He prayed that his bishop would be one of the chosen.

The last evening of the year 2018 began like most nights these last few weeks. There were more than four thousand people keeping vigil with him now, hidden in the catacombs below the great Cathedral. The sheer numbers did not frighten him as they might have in the past. Perhaps another miracle, they were plagued with neither hunger nor thirst and were blessedly strong and unafraid.

*   *   *

This evening, Father Andrews sat in the front pew of the sanctuary for a quiet moment of personal reflection and prayer. He rose slowly, and walked down the aisle to the front door of the Cathedral, to be sure it was locked for the night. As he turned the deadbolt firmly into place, he heard a soft knock coming from the back door of the sacristy which led to the courtyard. He felt the flesh on the back of his neck prickle. Shaken, he hurried to the door, fearful the authorities had finally discovered their hiding place.

"Who is there at this late hour?" He did not open the heavy wooden door, but called out instead.

"Father, we have come home." Stephen answered simply, as the baby stirred in Jillian's arms.

Phillip Andrews quickly opened the door and pulled the little family into the safe confines of the sacristy, hugging them all in a tearful embrace.

"Praise be to God, you are finally home."

He led them quickly to the baptismal font, and offering a prayer of gratitude, poured the holy water over the tiny head of the new prince.

*   *   *

The soldier had been making rounds in the darkness behind the Cathedral when he saw them enter the gate to the courtyard. He pulled the radio from his pocket and made one call. He smiled as he put it back into his jacket, sure he would be commended, and moved down the street to the front of the Cathedral to wait for the authorities to arrive.

*   *   *

Reunited with their families at last, Stephen and Jillian joined them in the grotto of the catacombs. The miracle that was Benjamin gave proof to the word of God and the promise of the Kingdom of Heaven. The chamber beneath the Cathedral was filled with much rejoicing and praise, as word of his arrival spread through the tunnels. The chosen ones gazed with awe upon the newborn and their hearts were filled with renewed hope. The promise of Paradise would soon be fulfilled.

*   *   *

Outside the Cathedral they gathered, five hundred strong. The militia, emboldened by the cover of the dark night, waited with restless fervor as they watched their captain apply the explosive putty to the lock on the Cathedral door, then slowly back away, awaiting the order to set the charge. An undercurrent of excitement permeated the air, in anticipation that at last the miracle child would be apprehended and once more within the control of the new Government. Those who had chosen to harbor the child and his mother would pay the ultimate price for their disregard of the revolution.

*   *   *

Stephen pulled Jillian into his arms as she held the baby, the new family shielding the catacombs behind them with an armor of love, as the sound of the first explosion above them ripped through the quiet tunnels beneath the Cathedral. He held her chin in his hand and lowered his lips to hers, their first kiss and a testament to the Covenant he knew would soon be delivered to them.

*   *   *

One man sat alone behind a desk, silent and trembling as he contemplated the enormity of the action he was about to take. His finger poised over the red button, he knew what he had to do. If the source of the miraculous healings could not belong to his country, then no one must live to possess the power. That acquisition would predicate complete control of the world. He sold his soul to Satan for one moment of glory and had nothing left to barter. He closed his eyes and thought of the lake and his sweet unsuspecting family who waited for him there. He raised his finger and moved it one inch closer to his final act of power.

*   *   *

Those gathered within the catacombs grew silent, as mayhem and destruction were carried out above them. Soldiers desecrated the holy space of the Cathedral, the one place on earth that stood strong and constant as a final testament to peace and God's love. It would only be a matter of seconds until the troops found their way into the space below. Jillian kissed her baby's head and pulled him close to her breast, as she and Stephen stood together, defiantly waiting for them to come. Looking at each other, their gaze never wavered as they heard the door to the staircase ripped from its hinges.

*   *   *

The man wept as he depressed the plunger, realizing only then, that this moment had been inevitable from the start. God had given man the power to choose. We have always had the power to choose. Everything he cherished had been lost long ago, and in less than the space of a single breath he was vaporized into nothingness.

*   *   *

The thousands gathered below the Cathedral felt the shock of the sudden shift. They heard the howling of a nuclear wind, the terrified screams of the militia above them lasting only seconds, before their agonized voices were silenced forever. They felt the force of the powerful waves ripple beneath their feet, as the great mountains of the earth plunged into the oceans. The wondrous planet Earth cracked and broke, heaving the burden of its sudden weight into oblivion, its gravity dissipated, leaving nothing but heavy black emptiness in its place. The rush of the ocean's water echoed loudly as it spiraled into space, only vapor and ash left to rise from whatever small fragments had yet to succumb to the total annihilation. The mouth of the great black void sucked the evil from its own chaotic ending, then closed, forever sealed, uniting the wicked tormented spirits, who were doomed to remain forever within its dark and mighty jaws.

*   *   *

Silence fell upon the catacombs. Stephen was the first to move and he raised his eyes slowly, watching in awe, as pure light poured down the stairway where the door to the catacombs once stood. The souls of the faithful rose triumphantly from death, like stars, their soft radiant light joining endless throngs of angels, as they formed a new path of brilliance and purity for them to follow to their Father's throne. He and Jillian looked at each other with wonder as she pressed her newborn Son close to her. Joining hands, they moved forward, leading the faithful into the light together.

"I am the Alpha and the Omega,

the beginning and the end,

the first and the last.

Blessed *are* they that do his commandments,

that they may have right to the tree of life,

and may enter in through the gates into the city."

Revelation 22:13-14

Acknowledgements

Writing this novel, by necessity, was a solitary endeavor, but also one that I never could have carried out alone. For the unwavering support of my family and friends, I am eternally grateful.

To Lloyd Jaeger, my husband ~ you never doubted that I could do it. Not once. You believed in me even when I found it hard to believe in myself. You are my champion and I love you.

To Stephanie Buhalis, my daughter ~ the feedback and encouragement you gave me after you read those raw early drafts is what kept me moving forward. "Now go write your book" is how you ended every phone conversation with me ~ My daughter, my sweet friend.

To Derek Crawford, my son ~ and Erica Crawford, his wife ~ your love and enthusiasm for this project helped me go the distance. And GNO, always a much needed diversion.

To Matt Jaeger, my son ~ webmaster extraordinaire and go-to person for all things technological, you have saved me from panic on many occasions, and I am grateful to know you are always there when I need you. Kiss on the head. Bump. I am so proud of you.

To Kevin Jaeger, my son ~ "Mom, this is epic" was the highest praise coming from my college bound teenager, after he read the manuscript from cover to cover in one day. That meant so much to me. Kiss on the head. Smile. You are the best.

To Judy Brenner Watson, my sister ~ I was so nervous putting that manuscript in the mail for the first time. The highest compliment "I forgot my sister was the author" meant more to me than you will ever know.

To my amazing early readers ~ George Buhalis, Melanie Buhalis, Carmie Tocco Buhalis, Sherry Verstraete (I love you, sissy), Mary Verstraete Lachowicz, Lynn Debano Sandvig, Beth Mann Debano and Patty Doyle Debano. Whether you read the manuscript, or gave me feedback on the jacket copy, your input was valuable and I hereby apologize for stalking and hovering over your shoulders while you read, as I waited breathlessly for your responses!

And most especially ~ To my incredibly talented editor. My sister, friend and self-professed 'comma queen' Kathy Debano. Word by word, line by line, paragraph by paragraph, and page by page, you understood me and what I was trying to say. I will forever thank God that this was the right time for both of us.